CAPTAIN

All That Glitters

Captain

Shalaena Medford

Copyright ©2023 by Shalaena Medford
Cover Art © 2023 B.R. Soule
Map © 2022 by Malaena Medford
Book Design by Shalaena Medford

All rights reserved. In accordance with the U.S. Copyright Act of 1976, the scanning, uploading, and electronic sharing of any part of this book without permission of the publisher is unlawful piracy and theft of the author's intellectual property. This book or any portion thereof may not be reproduced or used in any manner whatsoever without the express written permission of the publisher except for the use of brief quotations in a book review.
Thank you for your support of the author's rights

Printed in the United States of America

Title Font: Zapfino
Body Font: Palatino Linotype

First Edition: June 2023

ISBN 978-1-0880-3344-9 (IngramSpark hardcover)
ISBN 978-1-0881-4985-0 (IngramSpark paperback)

Acknowledgements

First and foremost, I would like to thank my cover artist B.R. Soule for yet another amazing cover! Your work always makes me smile.

Thank you to the beta readers who came in clutch for me. Malaena, for your hilarious comments, and being an insufferable brat about phrasing and accuracy. L. Lindberg for helping me see problems I never would have thought were problems, and explaining it in a way I could understand, and for sassing Song in your comments—she needs it. Thank you both for being nit-picky and not afraid to hurt my feelings—which you did, but I got over it just fine, and this book is all the better for it. Vee Aurelius, you didn't get too far, but I'm not upset, seeing as a hurricane came along and displaced you, then destroyed your car. You tried, but nature said no.

I especially want to thank you, the reader who has (presumably) read book one and loved it enough to return for more. I hope you enjoy seeing where Song goes!

Northern Lands

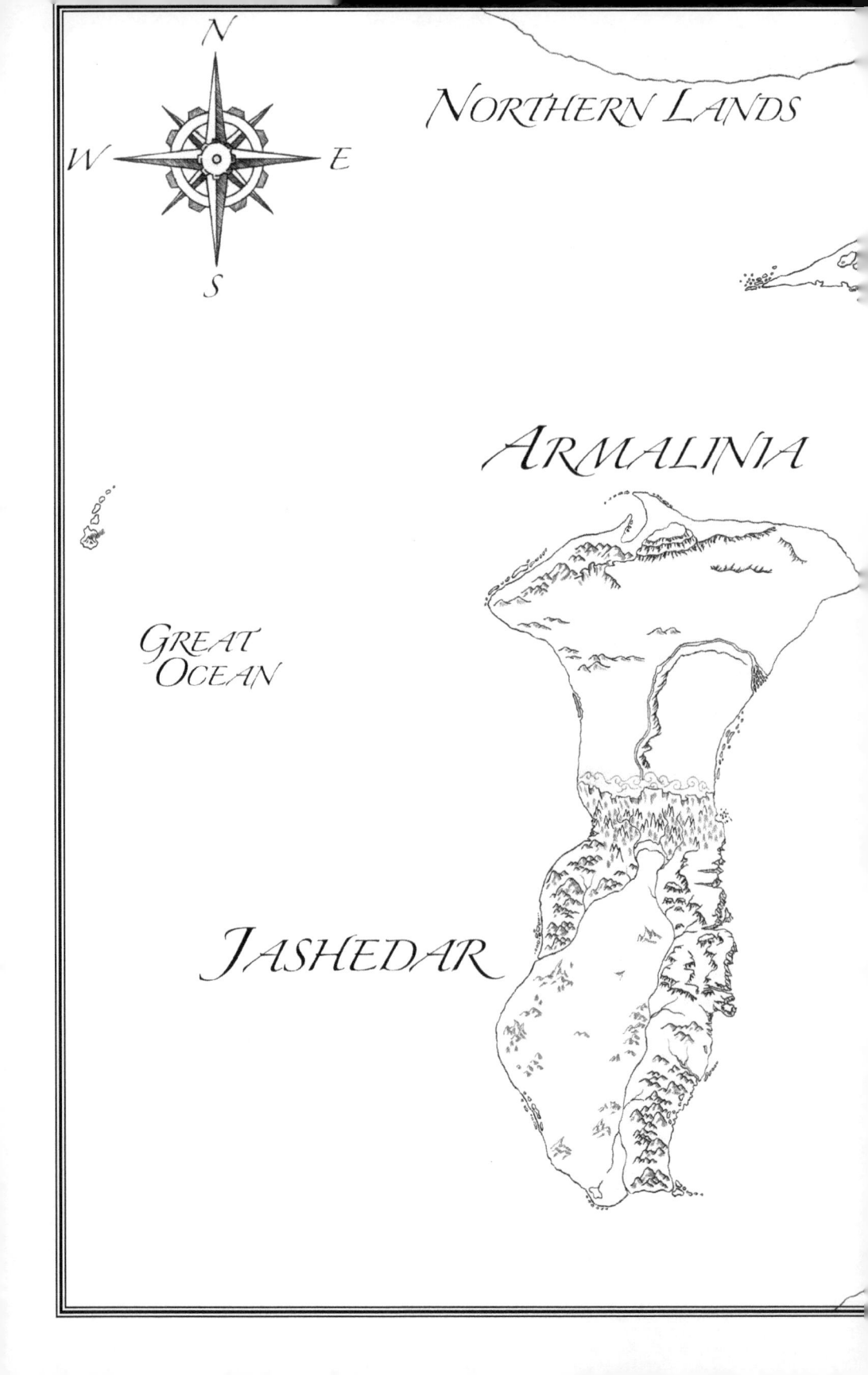

Armalinia

Great Ocean

Jashedar

Andalise

Pishing

Telbhaniich-Zardi

Great Ocean

Kerriwen

Aibhànocht

Telbhaniich-Zardi

Chavise-Kambhor

Aibhànocht

Thìse
Abhain-aimh

Jashedar

Screaming Cliffs

Blind Woods   Talegrove

★ Tamminpring

◆ Shorton

Winterlands

Shoalpek ◆

Armalinia

- Djorri Cove
- Brr'shtull River
- Pajisr
- Screaming Cliffs

Pishing

Duchamp Family Banner

Mercy In Death

"A smile better suits a hero..."

~Haurchefant Greystone

One

The wind whistled through the pirate city atop the cliff, making the dreary night that much more chilly. A discarded newspaper tumbled along the empty cobblestone streets of Talegrove's half-moon city center. It caught on a gas streetlamp and quivered, as though dancing to the music emanating from a nearby tavern. The page waved as a flag, displaying a sketch of a hooded figure beneath a bold and daunting headline:

Massacre in the Northern Skies
Caleb Song Responsible

After another quick flutter, the paper slipped away from the lamppost and skittered along the ground before plunging over the side of the cliff and into the thick fog surrounding the Impasse Mountains.

Glass shattered within a tavern. The music came to an abrupt halt. The light drifting over the cobblestones blinked off and on as shadows raced across the yellow-tinted windows. Men shouted, and a woman screamed as a table thundered to the floor. The musician's lute gave a staccato whine once, twice, then one final time as the strings snapped with a sharp *twang*. Fists met skin. A chair splintered and cracked, followed by a grunt as something heavy thudded to the floor.

"Out! Out with ye!" the innkeeper's gruff voice boomed over the din.

The door of the tavern slammed open, releasing the sounds of the brawl into the placid night. The burly innkeeper stood framed by the light, his shadow stretching out across the cobblestones. A narrow figure in a black coat with a raised hood squirmed in his grasp.

"I'll take the lot of you!" the figure shouted with a voice too high for a man, but too low for a woman. Their fists flailed in the air like a threat—those still inside stared with disinterest at the prospect of also being thrown out.

The innkeeper tossed the figure into the street. "And don't ye dare come back, Song."

"They started it!" she shouted.

"Ye heard me, boy. Git on with ye!"

Song turned away and spat the blood from her mouth, then wiped the thin red trickle from her nose. A slender figure with long auburn hair slipped out past the innkeeper as he shut the door. The blue eyes watched her sway against the chill of the night.

"They didn't start it, Song." His voice, as usual, remained quiet and patient.

Her upper lip curled, but she refused to look at him. "Oh, bugger off, *Whispers*." She turned away and strode to the fountain in the middle of the city center. The water dribbling from each of the three ornate tiers into the huge stone basin enticed her, but also made her think about finding a chamber pot or a dark corner in a dingy alley.

Leslie's jaw clenched, but he otherwise didn't react to the nickname as he followed close behind. He set a steadying hand on her back as she bent to vomit beside the round basin. When the contents of her stomach had finished spilling onto the cobblestones, Song spun and slapped his hand away.

"Don't you dare touch me!" she growled.

"Song, I didn't—"

"Yes, you did!" She dropped to sit on the stone ledge and reached a hand into the collecting water. She rinsed her mouth, ignoring the man beside her as he folded his arms and kept his gaze on the side of her hood.

"If he'd just let that bullet hit me…" His voice trailed off, as though waiting for her to refuse the suggestion. Instead, the bumping of a shop's sign blowing in the wind punctuated the otherwise tense silence.

Song spat a mouthful of water onto the cobblestones at his feet. "He should've. The blood of a Krell should not have been shed for a…a…" She swallowed back the bile creeping up her throat.

"A slave?"

She shook her head as the nausea subsided. "I was going to say a nobody…but now that you mention it."

"I'm a *free man*," he hissed.

"You're the one who said it." She splashed a handful of water at him. "Now bugger off and leave me to my mourning."

"He was my captain, same as yours—"

"He was more than a captain to me! He was the father I should've had!" She lurched at him, pounding her fists against his chest. "And you! You killed him! It's all your fault!"

"And what if the bullet had been meant for you?" Leslie wrapped his hands around her wrists to stop their assault on him.

"It wasn't!"

"How do you know? How do you know Dash didn't die protecting you?" He shook her by the arms. An angry fire she'd never seen before burned in his eyes. "No, of course he didn't, right? Because that would make his precious Song responsible for his death."

"It wasn't my fault!" Tears rolled to her chin.

He jerked her arms again, yanking her closer to look into his eyes. "It's not my fault, either."

Song broke into angry sobs. "Yes, it is," she squeaked.

He released her and she fell to the ground, a hand over her mouth to muffle her crying.

Leslie stood over her for several minutes before he spoke again. "It's time you retire for the night."

"I said bugger off." Song sniffed and wiped her eyes and nose on her sleeve. She looked up at him, but he gave no hint of moving. She shoved on his leg. "Bugger off! Why won't you leave me alone?"

She wasn't referring only to that night, but every night since they'd docked in Talegrove after Dashaelan's funeral. Leslie hadn't left her side, remaining sober as she drank herself into a plastered fury and fought any and all who dared look her way. She hated every minute he was near her. Hated the beautiful blue eyes keeping watch and reminding her of how Dashaelan's ice-blue gaze once did the same. But now he was gone, and she didn't want anyone, least of all Leslie, stepping in to take over the job.

She took a steadying breath. "I think it's time to turn in. But not because you told me to." She pushed to her feet, elbowing Leslie away as he tried to help. She wobbled on her ankles back toward the inn.

"Giln kicked you out." Leslie took her arm to steer her away.

She rammed her elbow into his ribs to escape his grasp. "My things are in there."

"I'll get them for you." He pulled her back, and she glared at him. "He'll keep tossing you out."

Song growled. "Fine." She ripped from his grasp again and wobbled toward another inn.

"You can't go in there."

"Like spit, I can't!"

"Marjori had you tossed out two nights ago."

Song stopped and stared at the cobblestones underfoot. "Don't know why I get thrown out when smelly pirates keep getting into it with me. Just defending myself."

"You're starting the fights."

"Shouldn't be looking at me. Do they know who I am? They want the reward for rescuing—"

Leslie pressed a palm over her lips. "Shh!" His eyes scanned the area, then met hers. "They're looking at you because you're wanted for blowing a skyship out of the air using only your words. They're looking at Caleb Song. No one else."

She ripped his hand from her mouth. "Dash would never let them stare at me." She pushed out of his reach. After a few steps, she realized she had nowhere to go. Song sniffed, trying to disguise it as one of indifference rather than the forewarning of tears. "Fetch my things, then."

"Will you wait here for me?"

She looked away from him, squaring her jaw in defiance.

He sighed. "Don't wander too far."

"Stop bossing me. You're not my father."

Leslie shook his head. "Neither was Dash."

He brushed past her shoulder. Song clenched her jaw and spun on him. With a furious shout, she threw herself against his back, knocking him to the ground. Before she could jam his face into the cobblestones, he rolled over and grabbed her hands. She fell sideways and shoved her knee into his gut. She ripped free from his grasp and sent her fists into his face, neck, and torso. Leslie grabbed her wrists and rolled on top of her, shoving her forearms against her chest and leaning his weight down on them.

"You get off me right now," she said.

"No."

"Unhand me!"

"Not until you listen to me!" His voice rose and the angry fire lit his eyes again, stunning her into silence. "I am not going to walk away from you, Song. I didn't kill Dash, and I most certainly don't want to replace him. Don't compare me to him, and don't you *ever* compare either of us to your father."

"Then stop ordering me around," she growled through her teeth.

"I'm not ordering you. You saw what the whiskey did to me, you know my demons. I am begging you, Song, please, stay here where I can find you."

"You think my own demons will carry me to the edge of the mountain?"

His grip on her softened. "Or into the woods to never be seen again. Please, Song, stay here."

"Don't worry, Whispers, I'm not pathetic enough to find the landing at the bottom of the cliff."

Leslie released her and moved to let her up, sitting back on his heels. "I miss you, Song."

She shook her head in disbelief. "I'm right here."

"No, you're not. I don't know who it is I'm looking at right now, but it isn't the Song I know. It isn't the Song Dash loved."

She slapped him across the cheek. "You stop saying his name."

He said nothing for a minute, his jaw working past his emotions, then looked at her. "I'll fetch your things."

She waited until he was closed back inside the inn before she stumbled across the round city center toward a dark alley, tears blinding her behind a blur of anger and sorrow. She tripped over a bin, knocking the contents across the alley before she crashed into the foul-smelling pile of papers and old food. The scent turned her stomach, and she vomited again. Song crawled a short way away from the puddle of stomach acid and whiskey before giving up and curling into a ball, surrounded by the trash.

"Oh look," she said to no one, "Tsingsei is in the rubbish pile. How appropriate." She didn't bother to wipe the tears rolling across the bridge of her nose and seeping into her hair. She closed her eyes and let the silent tears fall until the whiskey dragged her out of consciousness.

Two

Sunlight trickled over Song's face, burning through her eyelids and irritating her into wakefulness. The coarse sheets itched against her skin, the lumps in the mattress jammed into bruises she must've acquired the night before. Floral notes tickled her nose—or was it her clean and brushed hair doing the tickling? The grime and odors from days without bathing had been scrubbed from the exposed skin of her limbs and face.

Song's battered trunk of belongings sat at the foot of the bed; her coat—washed and oiled—hung on the wall by the door. When she'd had her fill of staring, she stood to strip. Still half awake, she poured water from the pitcher into the basin on the dresser. She wetted the rag and cringed at the high-pitched little tinkles of water droplets stabbing into her ears. After applying the soap, she washed all the areas someone—undoubtedly Leslie—hadn't gotten to without stripping her. She wanted to be angry about any doting he did, but the small bath, while respecting her body, gave her some form of comfort—which annoyed her. After rinsing, she dressed, and pulled on her coat. The leather had retained some smell of refuse and whiskey, but only when she pressed her nose to it.

With a sigh, she opened the door a crack to peek into the hallway. As he had been every morning since they'd made berth in Talegrove, Leslie sat in a chair just outside, his legs stretched out before him, crossed at the ankles, arms folded. But this time he was asleep, his chin resting on his chest. Song pulled the door closed as quietly as she could and tip-toed around him. In the tavern below, she leaned her elbows on the countertop and peered at the bottles the barmaid was too busy to watch. She snagged a whiskey and turned to leave with it tucked under the open front of her coat.

"That's an expensive whiskey you've got there, laddie."

Song turned to purse embarrassed lips at the innkeeper. He was a tall, muscular man with a sharp jaw and kind eyes.

"The expensive ones are the only ones worth drinking." She reached into her purse and dropped ten quoine onto the counter.

"It's a twenty quoine bottle." He stared her down as her temper rose in her sobriety. "I don't want to kick you out, Song, but I can't allow anyone room to take advantage of my kindness. Don't make me toss you out for mourning."

Song dropped another fifteen quoine onto the counter. "I can't promise I'll behave."

"And I can't promise to be patient with you." He scooped the quoine into his fist and sighed at her. "I'm gonna miss that Jinjur something fierce. Ain't right for him to be gone."

Song's throat tightened, and tears stung her eyelids. "Thank you. Now if you'll excuse me."

She left before he could say another word. Song took a hefty swig of whiskey, then directed her gaze to the cobblestones and began walking. Soon enough, she found herself standing on the edge of the Blind Woods, staring down the dark, foggy path that had claimed so many lives.

"I wouldn't go in there if I were you."

Song jumped and growled, but didn't cast her gaze down at the meter-and-a-quarter-tall Keeper of Talegrove standing beside her. "If I wanted a little gnome at my elbow telling me what I shouldn't do, I'd... Well, I don't want one. And I never will. Bugger off, you creeping little man."

Shadow smiled. "Are you done?"

"You're too small to make noise when you walk." She put the bottle to her lips, but pulled it away before taking a drink. "And it's not right for someone to go creeping about like you do."

"Anything else you'd like to tell me?"

"Yes." She thought, took a drink, and pursed her lips. "No."

"So you're quite finished?"

"Quite."

"There are easier ways to spend time with the dead than becoming one of them."

She made an incredulous face at him. "Are you saying I could talk to spirits?"

Shadow laughed. "Nothing quite so fantastic. Come." He led her just inside the forest and to the right of the road, where the trees opened wide to a clearing filled with stone monuments. "The marble forest. Well, they're not all marble, but it has a nice ring to it, don't you think? I like to come here sometimes, to remind myself of my own mortality."

But Song wasn't listening to him. She was entranced by the largest monument, a tall granite block with the statue of a woman sitting on one hip and holding a strange flower Song had never seen. It had a nebula of petals circling into an intricate bloom, and long, wide leaves with sharp tips along the outer edge.

"Ahh, I see you've been caught by Lady Fiyora." Shadow smiled and led her to the monument.

"Who?"

He motioned at the name etched into the base. "Lady Fiyora Duchamp. No one knew she even existed until she died."

Song touched the cool stone hand. "What was she like?"

"I'm afraid I never met her. I didn't come to Talegrove until after her death. Though, I was here for the placement of this rather exquisite statue."

"Who put it here?"

Shadow thought. "A man with no friends, I imagine. May have been her husband, but I can't be sure."

"Husband?"

"*Beloved wife and friend.* It says it right there."

Song shook her head. "But she looks so young."

Shadow cleared his throat and sighed. "I asked the man how old she was."

"And?"

"She was your age." He looked around the cemetery, then back at Song. "I must be getting back to town. Care to join me?"

"No. I think I'll stay with Lady Fiyora for a while." She tore her gaze away from the statue's face to look down at him. "Perhaps I'll find a way to talk to the dead."

Shadow laughed. "With all I've seen from you, I wouldn't doubt it, dear Song. I wouldn't doubt it at all. Let me know if you make contact, hmm?"

Her lips contorted into a rueful smile. "Of course."

Once Shadow had gone, Song let the hazy memories of spectres in the back of her mind drift forward again, like a shipwreck returning to shore. She stared at the statue's face and took a pull from the bottle in her grasp as a tear trickled down her cheek. After a while, she circled the monument and stopped to stare at a bronze placard set into the backside of the base.

Sorry it took so long, brother.

Leslie found her there hours later. She'd managed to climb up onto the base to curl up against the hip of the statue and tucked herself into the bend of the knees. She ignored him for a long time. He kept his distance and remained silent. Song met his gaze.

"I found Lady Duchamp." She pointed down at the name, but Leslie didn't look. "Quite beautiful, isn't she?"

His eyes remained fixed on Song.

She took a thoughtful drink. "How did you find me?"

Leslie waited a long time before replying so quietly she strained to hear. "Small town."

"Hmm." She turned over to look up at the sky.

He cleared his throat. "You shouldn't climb up—" He stopped as Song laughed.

"Ladies do not climb trees!" she said in her best imitation of the Pishing accent.

"What?"

Song giggled. "Can I tell you a secret?" She turned a cheshire grin on Leslie, who had kept his eyes trained on her as though refusing to let himself look anywhere else. She dropped her voice to a whisper. "I'm a lady, too!" Song took a triumphant drink as a celebration of what she thought was a fantastic imitation of the accent, though to sober ears, it was not.

"What are you talking about?" Leslie's voice was so quiet, so confused, that her laughing stopped.

Tears rolled down her cheeks. "She died alone," she whispered. "I know she did."

Leslie squared his jaw. "Song, get down from there."

"She died alone!" she shouted. "She shouldn't have died alone!"

"Get. Down." The words growled through Leslie's teeth.

"Shadow said nobody knew she existed. You lived with them. Did you know?"

"I said—"

"No! Answer the bloody question!"

Leslie took a deep breath and held it. "She was taken from her crib as a newborn. No one knew what happened to her."

Song tipped the bottle up, but nothing came to her lips. She dropped it to the grass below as her chin wrinkled. "I'm so sorry," she wailed. "I never should've let go."

"Come down from there. Please."

"I should've held on tighter," she cried into her palms.

"Song." Leslie set a hand on her leg as he cast a pleading expression up to her. When she leaned forward in mournful acquiescence, he pulled her down by the waist to set her feet on the ground.

"I was too young. I couldn't hold on tight enough."

He pushed her hood back and smoothed her hair. "It's not your fault," he whispered, as though he both understood what she was talking about, and also had no idea.

Song frowned, her bottom lip quivering as she looked up into his eyes. She found within them only kindness, rather than the impatient anger she'd expected.

But then she remembered how Dashaelan had looked at him. The fear in her beloved captain's eyes as he watched this man go below deck. The desperation with which he begged her to lock him in the cage. She'd never gotten her answer as to why. Why had Dashaelan lost all trust in Leslie after all the time they'd spent in an amicable agreement over Song? Why had it been imperative he be locked away?

Song didn't like the ideas that presented themselves as answers to her burning questions. Things about Leslie that made him worse than William, the man who'd tried to force himself on her at knifepoint only to have his fingers broken before Dashaelan threw him overboard to be drowned by her *kijæm*. Those thoughts brought back the nagging urge to remove him from the crew she didn't even want to captain. Every time she sobered, she had the idea. And every time she drank, she wanted to cry and maybe hit him a few times but not tell him why, so he could be as confused as she felt.

She pushed away from Leslie to study him better. He was still the gentle man that had been kind and patient with her every day. She saw only her friend and her partner. That is what confused her the most—so much so that she had to get away. She pushed past him to run out of the cemetery and back to the inn. Song locked herself in her room. She needed to be alone to mourn those who rested in the marble forest and at the bottom of the ocean.

Three

*D*ays passed as they had before: more liquor and more crying. And all the while Leslie stayed by her side to catch her when she fell, or offer water when she vomited. He wouldn't make a sound as she elbowed him away from her. Her only reprieve from his constant attention were the rare mornings when she woke before him and sneaked away to be alone. Many times, she returned to the cemetery to talk to Lady Fiyora. She spoke of silly things, and confided in the stone like a best mate. Every so often she'd look at the little smile on the lips of the statue's face and another distant memory would hit her and she'd drink it away.

    She wasn't even sure if they were actual memories, or if maybe her mind was imagining the statue as a real person. Olive green eyes, caramel-colored hair, and the warmest smile anyone had ever given Song—it felt like a memory, and yet felt like a dream. Was she dreaming up a different reality in which that beautiful now-stone face read bedtime stories to her? Was it her imagination that she'd comforted the woman when she found her crying in a cupboard under the stairs? In all the memories or hallucinations—whichever it was, Song couldn't be sure—Fiyora looked to be the same age, or maybe a year or two younger than the statue did now. Not knowing what was real or even what to do with it, Song kept it to herself, tucking it away in her heart to never see the light of day.

She spent nights in the tavern, drinking until she couldn't remember anything in the morning. One such night, the barmaid had enthralled her. Her hair was a dull blonde and, though her features were hard and flustered, there was something about her which reminded Song of the faceless farm girl from what felt like an entire lifetime ago.

"What is your name?" she asked, holding the woman's skirt so she couldn't leave.

Her eyes shifted to Song's left, where Leslie sat across the table, watching the scene unfold. "I'm Joyce," she answered.

"You are lovely, Joyce. Perhaps you could warm my bed tonight?"

"Song," Leslie's voice urged across the table, distracting her long enough for Joyce to free her skirts and shuffle away.

She growled in frustration. "She was pretty."

He presented her with an exasperated look. "That's the same barmaid you've made passes at for three days."

Song narrowed her eyes across the room. "Blimey, three days? She just gets prettier, doesn't she?"

"You need to stop this." An unfamiliar emotion barbed his voice, though he tried to hide it. He averted his gaze from hers and scanned the room.

She stared into the glass of whiskey nestled in her palms. "Such a lovely girl. I knew this girl once. Her father owned a farm. Saved my life, she did. Prettiest thing I'd ever woken to. Under the dirt and in a nice dress, she could pass for a lady in Garda. But no, she was confined to a farm in the middle of nowhere, fishing dead bodies and one Gould from the ocean." A short scoff of a laugh snorted through her nose.

"I think it's time to retire," Leslie said.

The abruptness of his suggestion caught Song off guard. She smacked her lips at him, hoping it conveyed her displeasure at the rude interruption. She stared at the table, trying to remember what she'd been saying so she could finish her story. But it wasn't written in the wood and was lost to her. "I suppose," she said with an exasperated sigh.

Song stood, and the room spun around her. Leslie rushed to wrap one of her arms over his shoulders and set his other at her waist. She wanted to bat him away—she wasn't the one who needed support; it was the room that was spinning!—but at the moment it seemed too much effort. He guided her up the stairs, then let her walk the rest of the way to her room alone. She pushed her hands against the wall, muttering for it to stop moving, then entered her room and leaned against the door, staring at the bareness of it.

This is what her life had been reduced to. A small room with an uncomfortable bed to lie on when Leslie dictated it was time for her to stop drinking. But he wasn't the boss of her. He was just another crew member Dashaelan had left without a captain. It was too much. She pulled the leather cord out of her shirt and stared at the key in her palm.

"Damn you, Dash." She slipped it back into her shirt.

Shouts came from the other side of the door, and she pressed her ear to the wood. A man was arguing with someone— probably Leslie, since she couldn't hear anything said by the second individual.

"I weren't meanin' no harm! Just like a word, is all!" His voice was frantic in a familiar way, but the pitch didn't fit into the picture her drunken mind tried to paint.

The sudden thump of a fist on flesh came through the door, followed by a quick scuffle.

"All right! All right! Just tell Song—" Raucous laughter from the tavern below cut off the rest of the man's sentence.

Song ripped the door open to find Leslie approaching.

"Something wrong?" he asked.

"Who was that?"

He sighed. "Bounty hunter, I presume. Or a writer for the post. Either way, I've sent him off."

"Maybe I wanted to talk to him. I'll go down there right now and give him a story the entire world would read."

"And what story is that?"

"The story of how Tsingsei Gou—"

Leslie pressed his palm to her mouth and forced her back into her room. He pushed her against the door and looked into her eyes. "Is that really what you want? To be found out and carted back home to pay for what you've done, and bring even more shame to your parents?"

He released her lips, and she licked them, the salt of his palm settling on the tip of her tongue. "I think I'd like another drink." She spun to open the door.

Leslie slammed it back shut and wrapped an arm around her waist to pull her away.

"Unhand me!" She shoved him, but only caused herself to move.

The room turned on its side. Leslie's arms enveloped her, setting the room right-side-up again. He held her so close that she could feel his heart pounding in his chest pressed against hers. Every breath he took moved her in rhythm to him.

"Why won't you leave me alone?" she whispered.

The world stopped as she looked up at him. But then he kissed her. She hadn't seen the desperation in his eyes until it was too late, and now he was kissing her with such passion that Song forgot everything. Her mind numbed over for a moment before deciding it did not approve. She shoved him away and slapped him across the cheek.

"Don't you *ever* kiss me," she hissed.

She strode away from him, crossing to lie in the bed, but hesitated. She wasn't tired. Song wanted, more than anything, to forget. Everything. She wanted her mind to quiet; wanted to go back to the beginning before everything had unraveled at the seams and her life had lain her bare and battered. Song wanted Dashaelan to be alive again. And she wanted... She wasn't sure anymore. Perhaps to be normal? Perhaps not. Maybe she *could* be fixed. How could she know if it was possible if she didn't try?

She spun to look at Leslie. His soft features were, indeed, attractive to her on some level. Enough so that it burned inside her, louder than the anger she'd been nursing. She rushed at him and leapt into his arms. She planted desperate kisses to his lips. Her fingers wove through his hair, softer than hers and delicate to touch. He pressed his palm between her shoulder blades, bringing her closer to him before pulling back again to stare at her.

"I thought you said never to kiss you," he said.

"You're not kissing me." She pressed her lips to his once more. "I'm kissing you."

"Why?" he muttered into her lips.

"Would you rather I stop?"

She met his gaze, and for the longest second thought he might let her go. For some imperceivable reason, that terrified her. She was safe, cocooned in his arms, surrounded by his warmth. He returned her kisses and she could taste his passion on his tongue. Song worked to remove her coat, letting it slide from one arm, then the other, landing abandoned on the floor.

She lowered herself from him to pull at his shirt. He gripped the lower hem, holding it fast against her tugging.

She growled. "Take it off."

He shook his head.

Song stooped to grab the dagger hidden within his right boot. "Take it off or I cut it off." She set the blade against the hem of his shirt, biting her lower lip and raising her eyebrows, daring him to call her bluff.

But he didn't. He met her gaze, ignoring her threat. She ripped the knife upward through the beige linen, each thread groaning in protest. When the blade reached Leslie's navel, his hands set around hers. He pulled the shirt over his head and threw it in a heap far away from where she could damage it further. She dropped the dagger to the floor. Once she was unarmed, Leslie pulled her shirt up, tossing it to lie with his. He lifted her back into his arms and pressed her against the wall. The uneven plaster bit into her shoulder blades. The chill of it seeped through her thin under-shirt and into her skin. She ran her palms along his back, drifting over rough, raised scars which criss-crossed over his otherwise smooth skin. A small part of her wanted to stop and ask him about them, but she ignored it.

Without warning, he pulled away from her and set her feet back on the floor. "Why are you doing this, Song?"

"Why not?" She pressed herself into him again.

"Stop. You don't want to do this." He pushed back on her shoulders.

She stopped fighting against his resistance, holding back the anger at being told what she did or didn't want to do. How would he know what she wanted? "What do you mean?"

He paused, testing his words. "I'm not your type." His eyes searched hers, hoping that was enough.

It wasn't.

"And right now you're drunk, which just makes this an even bigger mistake."

"I'll deal with that in the morning," she said. She wrapped her hands behind his neck and pulled him into another kiss, hoping the objections were through.

But he pulled away again. "Song, this isn't you."

She didn't want to cry in front of him, not the ugly sobbing kind, like what bubbled from her angry and broken heart. "Well, what if I don't want to be me right now!" She shoved him away from her and spun to lean against the wall, hiding her face in her elbow. "Maybe I want to be normal for one bloody night!" she shouted, and punched the wall. Her fist ached and her knuckles welcomed the cool sting of torn flesh meeting the air. She gained control of at least her facial expressions and turned around to plead with him. "Maybe that's how to fix all of this." She threw her hands wide, gesturing at nothing and everything.

He didn't seem to understand. "Fix what?"

Frustration sent her voice to a growl. "Everything! If I were normal, then none of this would've happened. I would still be the brat nobody even likes...and Dash would still be alive."

Understanding washed over his face and he stared at his feet.

"So please, Leslie…cure me." She pressed herself into him again.

He wrapped his arms around her shoulders and kissed her forehead. "There is nothing to be cured. I understand your frustration, but this isn't the answer. This is just something to regret." A note of contrition barbed his tone.

"Who's to say I'll even remember come morning?"

He smirked against the side of her head where he'd pressed his cheek into her hair. "Which makes it all the more wrong."

"But—"

He set his finger against her lips and moved the two of them to the bed, never letting her stray from his embrace as they lay down. Song set her head on his shoulder and stared at the swirling texture of the wall.

"If in the morning you remember any of this…and you still want it…then who am I to deny an order from my captain?"

Song hated that word. It wasn't hers; it was Dashaelan's. "I'm not your captain."

"According to that key around your neck, you are."

"I'd be a terrible captain," she admitted. She pulled the key up to dangle in front of her eyes, then let it drop into the small space between them.

Leslie squeezed her shoulders as a small comfort. "Dash didn't think so."

She wanted to object. To say Dashaelan didn't know what he was talking about. She wanted to scream at the world for taking him away from her so that now she couldn't ask him if that's really what he wanted. Instead, she let new tears run across the bridge of her nose and spread themselves in the crease between her cheek and Leslie's shoulder.

She ran her fingertips along the smooth skin of Leslie's sternum. *A man's chest should not be so smooth*, she thought. But that's what confused her so. Was she attracted to him because of the more feminine qualities he possessed? Or was there something about him which set Song's desire burning for just a taste of a man's love…? *His* love?

Leslie took her hand, massaging her palm with his thumb. Her eyes grew heavy and she let his soft breathing lull her to sleep.

Four

In the morning, Song blinked in confusion at the man beside her. Hazy memories, which did not fit together in any sort of sense, stumbled through her mind. He stared up at the ceiling, his lips pressed into a hard line of determination.

"Dare I ask what is going on?" she asked, sitting up and wrapping her forearms over her chest.

"You tried to seduce me," he said.

She studied him, then laughed. "Brilliant. Toothy put you up to this?"

"No one put me up to anything. You wanted me to cure you. You blamed all of your misfortune on your love of women."

She contemplated this as she studied his serious expression. "And did you cure me?"

"I refused. But if you still want me to try…"

She sighed, thinking. She knew nothing of intimacy. Her mother had refused an education in the area, claiming it was Song's future husband's job. Fear of what it could mean physically and emotionally balled into her chest, stretching her lungs until she struggled to breathe. More than anything, she feared that if she let Leslie show her what it meant, she would discover emotions for him, which she didn't want. Love would ruin everything. And what if he did cure her? What if she came out of the encounter with eyes only for him? Everything would change. She wasn't ready for that.

Instead of admitting her terror, she said, "Should've done it while I was drunk. I'm not sure I could ever make love to a man sober."

Leslie smirked, but there was a sadness in it which Song could not ignore. She deflated, fighting the urge to lie back beside him to comfort him. Instead, she stood to dress as he sat on the edge of the bed.

"Why me, Song? Even in your inebriated state, you had to have some reason."

She turned to smile at him. "You're pretty."

"I'm *pretty*? How can you say such a thing? I'm rugged and handsome!"

"You're clean shaven with soft features. I dare say if you had the right equipment, I would keep you as my lover." She gave him a sly wink and Leslie huffed, unsure whether to accept the compliment or take it as an insult. Her smile dimmed. "Actually, I think it might be because we're partners. Mutual respect. Trust."

Song's mood hardened as her sobered mind replayed the day she'd lost the only father figure she'd ever wanted. Without the buffer of drink softening her, the nagging to remove Leslie from the crew resurfaced. She couldn't keep dancing around it. She either had to learn to forgive him for caring too much about her, or she had to cut him off. Being sober and grumpy, though, her mind returned to what it believed was the most logical choice for dealing with him.

"I don't think Dash trusted you, though. Not in the end… I want you off the Bounty."

He didn't try masking his shock at such an admission. "Why?"

"He asked me to lock you up." She captured his gaze with her own. "That's why I took you to the cell, Leslie. Not to kill you, but to lock you in it."

He thought about it. "If he didn't trust me, then why did he save me?" His voice was low, as though admitting such a claim any louder might bring the roof down over his head. "That bullet was meant for me, Song," he continued when she said nothing.

Her throat clenched. "Why would he ask me to lock you up if he was ready to sacrifice himself for you?"

"I don't know."

"Regardless, I don't know if I can trust you anymore. Not until I find out the truth. I want you off the Bounty."

"We have a contract," Leslie reminded her.

"Then end it."

"No. I will stay aboard, at your side, until the debt has been satisfied."

She folded her arms over her chest and set her jaw. "And when might that be?"

He released a long, thoughtful breath, then stood and turned his back to her to retrieve his shirt from the corner. Song's palms itched with some distant memory of feeling haphazard lines climbing up his back like a distorted ladder. They were scars, thick and angry, torn across his skin and doubling over on each other. When Leslie turned to face her, she kept her eyes locked onto his torso. He hung his head and sighed at the floor.

"The debt will be satisfied when it's satisfied, Song." He pulled his shirt over his head.

She swept her gaze up to his. "What are those scars from?"

"I think you know the answer to that question."

She let out a frustrated breath and stared at the floor. "You may stay on until—"

"Save it," he snapped. "I don't need your pity." He strode past her.

"I thought you wanted—"

He spun and advanced on her until her back pressed into the wall and his chest was a breath away from pushing against hers. His eyes searched deep within hers for a long, silent moment in which she feared he may kiss her. Instead, his brow lowered when he found the pity for him shivering in her heart.

"Damn what I wanted. And damn you, Song." With that, he left the room, slamming the door behind him.

Song's ears rang, and her head pounded in the aftermath. She sank to the floor, her eyes remaining fixated on the door. She willed him to return and insist on staying aboard the Stars' Bounty, but she had a feeling he wouldn't.

After a long while, she pulled herself from the floor to finish dressing, then stopped in the tavern below for a cup of hot tea. She sat in painful silence beside Sunshine as he pretended to ignore her. She feared he would try to talk about her being captain. It wasn't something she was prepared for. It was never something she'd wanted. The Stars' Bounty had always been Dashaelan's, and in her mind, it always would be.

"I wasn't ready," she said to her teacup.

"Lesson one," Sunshine intoned.

Song scoffed. "I will never be ready."

"He said the same thing, you know." Sunshine chewed slowly on his eggs, staring off into some distant memory. "Dash never wanted to be captain, but old Garmont…he saw something in him that I suspect Dash saw in you."

"What's that?"

Sunshine gave her an emphatic shrug. "Hell if I know. I don't see nothin' in nobody."

Song hooked her lips in a wry smile. "That's a bloody lie if I ever heard one." She studied the side of his face as he busied himself with his plate of food. "You're a learned man, Sunshine. Why turn pirate?"

"You're a learned woman," he countered.

She didn't reply for a long while. "I can't do this," she admitted on a whisper.

"Whispers would smack your mouth to hear that word," he said. "Ain't no can't in that boy."

"I told Leslie to leave the crew."

"Why would you go and do a thing like that?"

"Dash ordered me to lock Leslie up before the Glory intercepted us. Something had him on edge. Terrified, even. Dash couldn't trust him, so I don't see how I can." She sipped her tea, burning the tip of her tongue.

Sunshine turned to look at her. "You've got it completely backward, Song. Go tell Whispers—"

"It's too late. He won't come back."

"Song, he's—"

"I don't want to talk about him. Change the subject, or keep your mouth closed."

Sunshine sucked in a long breath. He held it as though unsure about continuing. "Is that an order from my captain?"

She sneered at her tea. "It's a demand from a friend."

"It's a mistake—"

She stabbed his butter knife into the table and turned to purse her lips at him. "Stop talking about it."

"You're so good at givin' orders already. May as well go make yourself at home in the captain's cabin. Who knows…may find somethin' interestin' in there." Sunshine wiped his mouth and stood.

"Like what?"

"Beats me, don't it?" With that, he left.

She glared at the unfinished meal, then tossed the knife onto the plate with a scoff. As curious as she was, her anger screamed at her to remain defiant. The thought of entering Dashaelan's cabin without him, or claiming it as her own, agreed with the fury in her heart. And so her mind answered Sunshine's suggestion with a resounding 'no.' She didn't want to go into Dashaelan's empty cabin, knowing that once she had, it would make his death that much more undeniable. She growled and shoved away from the table, leaving the rest of her tea abandoned as she dropped a quoine on the tabletop and left the inn.

Shadow fell into step beside her, saying nothing for a long time. "Are we staying out of trouble today?"

She stopped, digesting the words and finding the hidden meaning behind them. "My crew is adamant of my sobriety."

"But are you?" He gave her his patient smile.

"Why haven't you banished me from Talegrove, Shadow?"

"Dashaelan Krell was a good man with many friends and even more enemies. We all grieve in our own ways, Song. As unacceptable as your behavior has been, I know it is only because you've lost a very dear friend. I can't deny you your mourning, but I can ask that the wanton violence and over-intoxication stops today."

They stood in silence, observing each other.

"It stops today, Shadow."

"Ah, good. Joyce will be thrilled beyond belief." He turned to leave.

"Who is Joyce?"

Shadow chuckled but continued away to the other side of the city center.

Five

As the Stars' Bounty drifted away from the port, Song stared at the shrinking figure of Bruce. Leslie was nowhere to be seen and had avoided her for the days prior to their departure. In the pit of her stomach, she knew that if he'd seen them off, she'd have let him back onto the crew. She raised her hand in farewell to the huge man. His arm raised in return before the fog swallowed him.

"Three new crew members, two we came with stayed behind," Sunshine said beside her.

"What?" she asked.

"Force of habit. I always count the men before launch, so Dash could focus on other things."

She gazed around at the men on deck, all eyeing her. The key burned against her skin, reminding her why this crew now looked to her.

"Where to?" Maps asked.

Song glanced at him, then out into the consuming fog. "I… don't know." She turned her sights to everyone else. "I don't know," she said in response to all the questions she knew they had.

They nodded or turned their heads down to look at the deck. Without the buffer of intoxication, the truth of it all crashed in on her. She ran below deck as her chin set to quivering.

Song spent the night in her old hammock. In the morning, she strained to hear Leslie's footsteps. As her mind fully woke, it reminded her she'd kicked him off the crew. A new hopelessness washed over her and she rolled over to cry into the pillow. She felt as though she'd lost everything. A few crew members came down to check on her, but she ignored them for the most part. It wasn't until sunset that Sunshine came in, gripping his mug of tea. His eyes narrowed down at her.

"A captain that cries all day is as good as a captain that drinks all day," he muttered.

"Oh, bugger off, old man." She wiped her nose on a sleeve and turned to look at him. "I shouldn't be captain."

"But you are. So maybe you should act it."

"I don't want it!" she screamed. "I never wanted to be captain!"

"Dash wanted it. Now stop bein' a useless brat and get out there and honor him."

Song's eyes widened on him. "I beg your pardon?"

"I will drag you out on deck by your hair, if I have to." He punched her in the shoulder. "Come on. Don't make me doubt Dash's judgment more than you've already done."

"What?"

"Dash never would've kicked Whispers off this ship."

"Why not?"

"You told me not to talk about it."

Song scoffed and rolled her eyes. "Now you're just being petulant."

"Petulance begets petulance. Now, get out of that hammock and maybe come learn a thing or two." Sunshine's black eyes captured hers for a minute in torturous silence.

She pursed her lips and nodded. "Fine. I'll...try, I suppose."

"Tryin' is all I'm askin' for."

She leaned back and sighed at the ceiling. "Just give me a moment."

He nodded and left her to dress. She took her time and arrived on deck as the sky darkened to twilight. A new crewman approached and removed a grey flatcap, which he wrung in his hands.

"I know your face," she said.

"Please…sir…I-I was part of the crew that… On the Glory…" His hands shook harder. "I won't never disrespect ye. I weren't the one that shot yer cap'n, nor that who squealed, but I-I'd like to make up for it. Sir."

She pursed her lips in a thin line. When she'd blown the other ship out of the sky, a handful of the other crew had still been aboard the Stars' Bounty. Her crew had locked them in the holding cell, then released them in Talegrove. At least one had gone to the presses to share a tale which raised the price on her head. She'd never thought one of them would be bold enough to try crewing on the Stars' Bounty. Ponce gave a small, wicked smile as he watched. She took down her hood.

"Song is fine. And you are?"

"Oswold," he said, brown eyes rounded in shock.

"Dash liked to idly threaten to throw new members overboard if they didn't pull their weight," she said with a small laugh. "So…I guess I…" She cleared her throat. "Let's just assume I made the same threat."

"I won't let ye down, Cap'n."

She pointed at him with a limp, distracted finger, her eyes far away. "Don't… Don't call me that."

His gaze shot across the deck at the various onlookers. "Aye, eh…Song."

She nodded once. "As you were."

She stared at the wood of Dashaelan's cabin door for several minutes. The eyes of the crewmen on deck burned into the back of her head. She untucked the key from her shirt and stared at it. Such a little thing, and yet it held implications of suffocating proportions. It was a burden, weighing her down, burning its imprint into her palm. It slid into the small hole just over the handle; she turned it and the lock clicked open. After a long time to catch her breath, Song gripped the handle and opened the door.

It was strange being in there now. The chamber felt abandoned and lonely. Her eyes swept the room, taking in every detail she'd overlooked the many times she had been in there before. Now it seemed so different, even though it was as Dashaelan had left it: the liquor cabinet on the far side away from the door; hammock tucked around the corner from where she stood; Dashaelan's trunk secured in front of the long, thin closet holding his coats. A glass and a bottle of his favorite whiskey sat open on the table in the middle of the room. His favorite chair—worn from him sitting in it over the years, though they were all identical—stood away from the others, as though he'd shoved out of it in a hurry. She didn't want a single detail to ever change, but knew that eventually it must.

Then she saw it—a large, heavy parchment poster which had fluttered into a corner beside the cushioned bay bench and now lay abandoned. It was the parchment Sunshine had taken to Dashaelan right before the fight. Picking it up, she scanned the front; it was a wanted poster. For a moment, she thought her heart had stopped as her breathing hitched in her throat. Song reread the information framing the all-too-familiar face. She folded the poster and shoved it into a pouch at her hip, then ran out to ascend the steps.

"Come about! Maps, come about!"

"Cap— Er, Song?" Maps cocked an eyebrow over the wire frame of his spectacles.

"We have to go back to Talegrove. Immediately." She pushed him aside and turned the ship around as fast as she could without putting it in danger.

"What's in Talegrove?" he asked, already charting their return.

"A liar."

When the Stars' Bounty had once again docked in Talegrove the next morning, Song leapt from the bow and ran to the first inn. A peacekeeper threw her out before she could say a single word.

"That was a short trip," Shadow said at her elbow.

"False start. Where is Leslie?" She turned to eye the small man, her brow furrowed. "What?"

He had a funny sort of smirk on his face. "You're just a very curious thing, dear Song."

"Thank you? Leslie, please."

He stared at her, all patience in direct contrast with her own impatience. "Leslie was the—"

"The bloody Jinjur!" she all but shouted.

He chuckled. "I know who Leslie is. He left, actually."

Her anger quieted for a second before accepting this information as kindling to blaze hotter. "He *what?*"

"Left."

"I heard that part, I'm just… Gods damn it all, where did he go?"

Shadow shrugged. "Hopped on a ship a few hours after you left port."

"Who said he could join another crew?" she bellowed.

His eyelids slid down in a slow blink as the smile remained on his lips. "You did…when you kicked him off yours."

She balled a fist and growled. "You know what?" Instead of finishing her thought, she spun on her heel and stomped away.

"The big one is still here," he called after her.

Song stopped and turned. "He left Bruce?"

"No."

"But you just said—"

"Bruce stayed of his own accord. Tried to keep Leslie here, too." Shadow's mouth curved up in his patient smile.

"Well, where is he?"

"I didn't hear a please."

She growled again. "Please take me to Bruce."

"Song," the gruff voice said behind her.

She jolted and spun, eyes wide. "How do you walk so bloody quiet?" She shook her head as he shrugged. "Why did you stay?"

"You'd be back." Bruce grinned and shifted the weight of his duffel bag in his fists. "I knew."

"Are you coming with me?" she asked.

"Yes. You will find Leslie." With that, he turned and headed for the skyship docks.

Shadow watched him in silence. "He is also a curious thing." Then he smiled up at her. "Apology accepted. Go track down your man before he gets too far. I believe it was Captain Perily's sailer. Two-masted schooner; green sails. Careful with that one, he's jumpy."

"Did you catch any talk of where they're headed?"

"Southeast, I think. Aibhànocht. Bundle up, it's worse than the far southern reaches of Jashedar there."

Song cocked her head. She'd never been to Aibhànocht—Dashaelan hated the snow and had always done his best to avoid the far southern and northern ends of the world. "Thank you, Shadow. I'll bring you a nice trinket next time."

"Oh, a bribe. I like bribes. Be well, Song."

With that, she was off, back to the Stars' Bounty. She hollered for them to get going, then jumped over the railing and onto the deck as they pushed off. She relayed the information to Maps, then ducked below to find Bruce. They smiled at each other as he secured his things by his massive hammock.

"Hello, Song."

"Hello, Bruce. How did you know I'd return?"

He thought about it. "Leslie."

She cocked her head. "What about him?"

"Friends fight, but are still friends."

"What if I only came back so I could beat him bloody?"

His brow furrowed, and she withdrew the wanted poster, then held it out to him. "Leslie." Bruce nodded. "This angers you?"

"He *lied*. To all of us."

"Didn't lie. You lied. Leslie never lied."

She scoffed and folded the poster back up, then shoved it into her pouch. "He lied. Now...help in the cargo holds. Pinch was saying they need organizing."

Bruce nodded. "Your anger glitters bright." He grinned as she gawped up at him. He patted the top of her head and left.

"What does that even bloody mean?" she muttered. Song returned to the main deck and took her place at the helm. "I swear," she said to Maps, "Bruce says some strange things."

"That he does. You know, he likes you. Says your glitter is pretty."

She lowered her hood and blinked, her head caught in a slow shake. "My *glitter*? What glitter?"

"Perhaps he means your *kijæm*," Toothy said from the top of the steps on her left. "It's sparkly."

She blinked and said a soft command. A ball of shimmering, twinkling *kijæm* built itself over her palm, like smoke blowing into a bottle. What could it mean that he always spoke about how she glittered, and that it was more intense when she was angry? Everyone knew what she had done, how her *kijæm* had lain as a shimmering blanket across men and skyship, burning both in her fury. Perhaps that's what the man had meant.

"Do you know what it is, anyway?" Toothy asked. He prodded the sphere, and it shifted around his finger, then returned to swirling in the tight ball once he'd retracted it.

"No," she said. "It doesn't seem to stop moving, does it?" With a few words, she sent it away. The strange cloud dissipated as though blown by the breeze.

"Too bad he's simple," Maps said, "could ask what he means."

Song looked at the navigator but made no reply. She didn't think Bruce was simple. He knew too much, but his words were simple, if not a struggle for him to say.

As the day wore on, Song wandered to the bow to stare out at the ocean stretching below them as they flew low enough to spot the schooner. After a while there, she climbed up on the railing, then hopped to the bowsprit and sat, leaning her back against the railing. She rested one boot on the wood and let the other dangle over the side as the cold air pinched her cheeks—it would only get worse as they continued southeast.

"I am glad we are going to get Whispers," Thumbs said. "He is my friend."

"I'm not sure a single person aboard wouldn't say that about him," she said.

"He is nice," he agreed. "Sunshine would never admit if they were friends."

"Sunshine wouldn't admit he was *my* friend if you paid him."

Thumbs laughed and leaned forward, resting his elbows on the railing. They said nothing for a long time.

"I would like to purchase some supplies in Aibhànocht. Dash never stopped there, so I never got to try the herbs fresh. And they have this creature—a *rebhìdh*—that has great amounts of fat and so the meat is sweet. It is best fresh, of course."

Song smirked. "Was the *rebhìdh* part of your original plan, or are you just trying to make me hungry?"

"If you want Song to do something, you give her food or the promise of food." He delivered a devilish grin.

"What can I say? I'm a woman of simple desires."

"You're a woman of the same desires as the rest of us," Sunshine said behind her. "Food, treasure, and women. In no particular order."

Song laughed. "If I have food, give me treasure. If I have treasure, give me food—"

"And more treasure," Thumbs said, grinning.

"A woman in either situation is perfect."

The three talked of other countries and cuisine for most of the day. Song wanted to try dishes from everywhere, and have Thumbs learn to make all her favorites. A few other crew members joined over the hours, and the conversation shifted around and around different subjects, until they all drew quiet for an unknown reason.

> "I left my home for adventure's call
> It carried me 'way on an ocean squall..."

Behind them, Ponce sang to the beat as he scrubbed a stain on the deck. Five voices joined his to finish out the verse.

*"I found my home away from shore
And I won't go back no more."*

The entire crew on deck, and many below, lent their voices to the chorus.

*Give us ale and give us plunder
Give us quoine and precious stone
Fly the black and shine your dagger
As we sail to the unknown*

*I found myself up in the skies
Sun at my back, mark in my eyes
My true love lies with quoine and jewels
Oh, me lover, don't be cruel*

*I'm a man of simple pleasures
And I know I'm not alone
I've a heart that longs to wander
For adventure is my home
Give us ale and give us plunder
Give us quoine and precious stone
Fly the black and shine your dagger
As we sail to the unknown*

By the time the song had finished, every man on the skyship had joined. Song grinned at the horizon. Soon, someone started another song, and then another. They sang songs of pillage and riches, of beautiful women and licentious ways. When the sun had set and most were retiring, Sunshine returned to get her away from the bow. It took him convincing her she wouldn't miss the sailor overnight with the lead it had on them. Even so, he would wake her.

She lay in the hammock in the captain's cabin—the first time she'd done so since becoming captain. Her thoughts kept her awake long into the night. When she did sleep, nightmares plagued her mind. As furious as she was with Leslie, the dream in which she lost him forever made her snap upright, covered in sweat. The resulting nausea and tightly wound nerves writhing within her prevented her from falling asleep again.

Six

Song had barely slept in days due to nightmares and the gnawing fear that she'd lost Leslie for good. She hadn't realized until he'd been absent that he was her best friend in the world, now that Dashaelan was gone. She still strained to hear his soft footsteps in the mornings, before her mind woke enough to remind her he was no longer aboard.

The sun had just started to peek over the horizon. The grey clouds hung thick over the ship, threatening to drop snow on them at any moment. She was too tired to do anything but sit on the steps, leaning against the railing as she nursed a mug of strong tea. Bells stood at the bow, keeping watch below for the ship. By Maps's estimations, they would reach Aibhànocht by nightfall. Either Perily's ship had already arrived in the country, or they'd passed the schooner sometime in the night.

"Ship!" Bells shouted.

Song rushed to the bow and peered through her telescope. "Dark sails. I've no idea the color, though."

"Not white. Either you're right or you're wrong."

She presented him with an unimpressed expression. "As though there's a third option."

"Third option is dead." He laughed.

"Right, then." She ducked below deck and blew her whistle. "We got dark sails, lads! Get your lazy hides outta bed!" She caught Ponce and a man nicknamed Bishop—though she'd heard it was his previous occupation—and pointed to the grappling ballista at the front of the ship. "Aim for something you know you won't miss. Wait for my signal." She then strode to Sunshine. "Slow our speed and circle over, lowering altitude. I'll jump off once overhead. Tilt the Bounty's nose for a grapple of the sailer's stern. When they give the affirmative, full reverse on the prop, right?"

"Aye, Song." Sunshine nodded to the two as they emerged and signaled to him they were ready.

As they flew overhead, she leapt over, slowing her descent with *kijæm* until she landed at the center of the deck. Shouts of surprise rippled across the deck, accompanied by swords unsheathing. She released a tired, heavy sigh, but didn't move. A deckhand disappeared into the captain's cabin.

"All right, gents, we can do this the easy way or the really easy way," she said. "Let's start with a question. Whose ship is this?"

A tired man exited the captain's cabin with the deckhand. "Mine."

"Oh, hello Captain *Mine*." Her weariness had sent a roughness into her voice and erased the little patience she usually possessed.

"Captain Perily. How did you get onto my ship?"

"I fell," Song said. "*Et'noo-æb ehth lahn-gis.*"

"What did you say?"

"I was just signaling to my crew that this is the right ship." She didn't turn as men shouted and the captain's eyes widened over her shoulder. "May want to brace yourself." She gripped a rung of the capstan, holding tight as the ship lurched.

"Are you *really* trying to pirate a pirate?" he demanded.

"*Slai's ehth lerf.*" The sails above her lit from her *kijæm* as it worked to lower the gaffs, neatly folding the sails against the booms on the masts. "Not unless you start something you and your men cannot finish." A sword unsheathed just behind her right shoulder. "Like that." Song turned and sighed at the man. "Look, mate, I'm bloody tired. Sheath your weapon." When he didn't respond, she said a command and every sword on deck ripped from the men's grasps—some after a spirited struggle—or out of their scabbards, then flew up in a bright blue flurry to embed themselves in the mainmast.

"What do you want?" Perily demanded.

"You've something of mine aboard your ship."

He folded his arms. "I don't recall stealing from you, boy. Who are you?"

"Song?" The voice was so quiet she almost didn't hear him over the water slapping against the hull. "What are you doing here?"

"Leslie!" she said with an enthusiasm so tainted by her lethargy that it came across as sarcasm. "Get your things, then."

"Wait, this is Caleb Song?" Perily asked. "You're just—"

"A boy, yes, I know. Don't interrupt. It's *rude*."

"You presume to—"

Leslie set his hand on the man's shoulder. "Don't. You won't win that fight."

"Or any fight. I am tired and in absolutely no mood to fight anyone. But if you make me blow up your ship because you can't hold your tongue for two seconds—"

"Song, stop idly threatening everyone."

She went to him, her teeth clenched together. "You, especially, had better keep your mouth shut. You think this is a rescue mission? That I'm here because I realized the folly in my ways?" She scoffed. "I just want you aboard *my* ship, so it's harder for you to escape when I cut out your lying tongue. Now, get your things."

An expression of confusion and injury crossed his features. "I don't know what I lied about—"

"*Get*…your things."

He swallowed, then nodded. "Aye, Captain."

"*Oh!* Don't you bloody call me that, you Jinjur sod!"

"Don't call me a Jinjur."

"Stop being argumentative!"

"Stop being a brat."

She balled her fists. "Get your things *now* or you're leaving all of it behind, damn you."

He pressed his lips together at her, then spun on his heel and disappeared below deck. After a few words, her tea stein came flying down. She took a sip and cringed.

"Damn. It's gone cold." She leaned back against the capstan, nestling between two rungs. "Sorry about all this, Perily. Really, I am." Song looked back to the Stars' Bounty as it hovered, the propeller still and the crew watching over the railing. "Once I've got my man, I'll let you on your way. Pirate's honor."

He gave her a dubious look. "That's really all you wanted?"

She nodded, gulping down tea as fast as she could.

"He must be some crewman."

She smiled and gave a humorless laugh. "He is. But really, I don't think you want that particular man anywhere near your crew. You'll thank me when you see the posters."

"How'd you know what ship I was on?" Leslie asked.

"Shadow, of course. Soft spot for me, you know." She sent his trunk up with a few words.

"Oi! Watch where you're flingin' things!" Toothy shouted.

Song waved to him over her head and flung the empty mug up next, so it sailed right past his head; Toothy yelped and ducked. "Next time we meet may not be so pleasant, Captain Perily. Until then, I wish you successful plunders."

He eyed her, still suspicious. "And you…Captain Song."

"Don't *bloody* call me that. Goodbye."

She wrapped her arms under Leslie's. His eyes widened in shock as he realized what was about to happen. His objections went ignored as she gave the command. Her *kijæm* lifted them from the deck of the schooner, and Leslie gripped her tighter until their feet set on the deck of the Stars' Bounty. Her blue mist flitted about as she ordered it to aid their disengagement from the sailer. The swords fell to the deck; the grappling hooks released from the sailer's stern; the ropes coiled themselves on the skyship's deck.

Once finished, she squared her jaw at Leslie. "Get in Dash—*my* cabin. Do you want *tea?*" she asked, as though just saying it angered her.

"Um, sure?" Leslie eyed the others before heading into the captain's cabin as she disappeared below. When Song entered and set a mug on the table for him, he eyed it, one eyebrow raised in suspicion.

"I didn't spit in it. Though, I should have," she said.

"I expected yelling and for you to be cutting out my tongue. Not for us to be sitting down for tea," he said.

"I'm too tired just yet." She took off her coat and pulled her hair out of the haphazard plait, then ruffled it. It circled her face as a dark mess, half wavy from the braid.

"You…look terrible."

Song smacked her lips at him. "Thanks."

"What's wrong?"

She took a drink and set the mug down so hard a bit of tea splashed out onto the table. "You."

"You're the one who kicked me off the ship," he said.

"Yes. And had I known what I do now, I would've waited until I could scream at you and then throw you into the ocean."

"Are you just going to dance around the actual issue while threatening me? If so, I'd rather go be useful on deck." Leslie stood and strode to the door. As he opened it, her mug crashed against the wood. Hot tea splashed outward around him.

"*Shut that bloody door!*" Song thundered, standing so fast her chair fell backward. "You're not going anywhere, you *liar!* You absolute *coward!*"

He slammed the door and clenched his jaw. "Liar? Coward? Any others you'd like to add?"

"Heartless *bastard!*"

"Little rich coming from you."

"Shut your damned liar's mouth!" She pulled the wanted poster from her pouch and hurled it toward him, but it caught on the air and fluttered pathetically to her feet. She scraped it back up and strode over—trying to open it but failing—then jammed it against his chest, still folded. "Now, tell me what the hell that is!"

He didn't move or open the parchment, just blinked at her.

"Well?"

"I'm sorry, I thought I was shutting my liar's mouth."

"*Don't you get smart with me!*" She grabbed his mug and threw it against the door behind him.

Leslie rolled his eyes and unfolded the poster. After a quick glance, he scoffed and lowered it. "I *told* you this would happen. That Roman would put a bounty on my head."

"Yes, well, I bet you hoped he wouldn't use *your real bloody name!*" She tossed her fallen chair at the wall, but it didn't make it all the way there before tipping to another side and coming to a sad, premature stop.

"He did, it's right…" He stared where he'd jammed his finger into the paper. "Why is Leslie…listed as an alias?"

"Because it's not your name!" she shouted.

"Yes, it is," he said, looking over the rest.

"No, it's not!"

"Song—"

"Why can't you just admit it?"

"Song, I—"

"Is that what you were really doing here?"

"That's not—"

"Stop lying!"

"I'm not lying," he said a bit louder.

"Say it out loud so I can see your face when you—"

"My name is Leslie!" he shouted, making her jolt in shock.

"No, it bloody isn't! You're—"

"*I am not Wesley Krell!*" he thundered, matching her volume. He crumbled up the poster and threw it.

"Don't yell at me!"

"Then shut your bloody mouth! Gods damn you!" When he shouted, he couldn't maintain the soft Andalisian accent, and so dropped into the harsher one of Pishing.

"Then stop lying!"

"I'm not lying!"

"Why would you hide it, then?"

"I didn't hide anything! My name is Leslie!"

"What's your surname, then?"

He opened his mouth to respond, but stopped as though no one had ever asked before. "I don't have one," he said, falling back into the fake accent as his voice softened to its usual near-whisper. "But it sure isn't Krell."

"I don't believe you! Is that why you joined Dash's crew? Of any you could've gone to, you chose Dashaelan *Krell?*"

"*If* that was my name, and I knew it, then I would've steered clear of this damned ship! Or better yet, come to make him pay!"

"Why?"

"Because *my father sold me!*" he shouted.

Song stepped back, eyes wide as though he'd splashed her with freezing water. "What?"

"That bastard sold me to Lord Duchamp, Song. He never visited, never wrote. My father sold me and never looked back. The captain you loved—we *all* loved—could never be so heartless."

"Then how do you explain this poster?"

"I can't."

"Then—"

"Don't, Song. Don't place Dash in that position, because you won't like the man my father was. If you loved him, you won't try to tell me he's the man I've hated my entire life."

Song scoffed. "Leslie, what if you—"

"I said *stop.*" He clenched his jaw and fixed a scowl on her. "Don't dishonor his memory. He was a good man, but thankfully, he wasn't my father."

Song released a long breath and shuffled to the bay bench as her weariness caught up past the tea. Leslie hesitated, then joined her. They didn't talk for several minutes as he studied her face, and she stared at the toppled chair and the crumpled poster beside it.

"We all loved Dash," he said after a while. "Even the ones he forgot our names, or threatened. Or didn't seem to like. You know, at first, I thought any wrong move would get me tossed overboard. One word from Song and Dash would get rid of me."

She released a soft laugh. "He actually liked you. Perhaps a little too much when it came to me."

"How so?"

"He was talking like I should marry you or something! Then again, I think he was trying to tell me he wanted me to be captain when he retired. I misunderstood and thought he was hinting I should also retire and settle down with a man. So, I probably interpreted that all wrong, too."

Leslie chuckled on a soft breath. "I sure hope so. I don't want to marry you, Song."

"Well, I'm glad that's settled. Wait...what's wrong with me that you wouldn't?" She furrowed her brow and leaned away to look at him.

Leslie narrowed his eyes at her. "Really?"

"Yes, really!"

He pinched the bridge of his nose. "Song, you're insulted that a *man* wouldn't want to marry you? Do you want to marry a man?"

"I don't want to marry anyone. Too many pretty girls to ruin... eventually." A pink heat crept into her cheeks.

"Then why are you offended?"

"Because I figured there was more to it than *you* not being *my* type."

He smirked. "I don't want to get married, either."

"Looking to ruin some pretty ladies?"

"I'd wager I've ruined more ladies than you have."

Her eyes narrowed. "If your count is higher than zero, you'd be correct." Song's lips crooked sideways. "If either of us had a mind to marry, I still wouldn't marry you."

"How long is the list of reasons why not?"

"It circles the globe. Twice."

"Only twice?" He chuckled. "And what's on it?"

Her face scrunched in a mischievous smile. "Every single thing you've done to abuse, torture, and torment me. You're too tall—"

"You're barely shorter than me."

"What are you, a couple hands shy of two meters?"

"Give or take."

"In any case, you talk too softly, walk too softly, *and*...you don't let me get away with any nonsense."

Leslie chuckled. "I wouldn't marry *you* because *you're* too tall. You're mean and impatient, short-tempered and over-dramatic. Also, you're a spoiled brat. But the biggest reason is probably your father."

She laughed through her nose. "My father is actually a kind man. Too busy for me, but still kind. You should see my collection of porcelain dolls he's bribed me with since I was little."

"You have a collection of *dolls?* You?"

Song nudged her shoulder against him. "I didn't want them. The first was plenty. I've several that selling just one could pay the men a month's wages. Paid those prices just to aggravate him."

He blinked at her. "Why dolls?"

She smiled. "It started with one when I was four. Tattered second-hand thing he'd bought from a girl on the street. I'd loved it so much that I suppose he thought it was the proper way to make up for lost time."

They stayed quiet for a minute, then Leslie took a breath. "What sort of house did you grow up in?"

"A mansion."

"No, I mean...what does it look like?"

"Large redbrick with golden-yellow brick accents. Twenty rooms, three floors, large ballroom with vaulted glass ceiling and glass-panel walls, music room, library, staff quarters, elaborate garden with an obligatory hedge maze, private stables..." She slowed as he gave her a look. "And a...matching tall brick wall to keep out the riffraff. It's the largest house in the Eastern District... possibly the entire country."

He blinked again. "And it's in Garda?"

"Yes?"

Leslie stared at her for another minute, a smile tugging at his lips. Then he rested his chin on his fists. "Duchamp Hall is ten rooms. I lived inside until I got older. Even then, Caius offered me all the opportunities afforded to Roman."

"And you didn't ever say no?"

He chuckled. "When your choices are hard labor or a nobleman's education, you don't turn down the latter."

"Fair point." Song yawned, hooked her arm in his, and leaned against his shoulder again, her eyes closed. "Bloody nightmares while you were gone, you know."

"What of?"

"Dash's death. Sometimes it was losing you in his place. Or both of you at once."

Leslie untangled their arms and urged her to lie out on the bay bench, which she didn't resist. "No wonder you look like the worse end of a horse."

She snorted a laugh, though her eyes remained closed. "No. That's just my face… I kept waking up early, expecting to hear your footsteps coming to toss me from my hammock."

"I've trained you well."

"You've *traumatized* me well." She grinned and looked at him. "Care to join me? For old time's sake?"

One of his eyebrows raised. "Old times?"

"Last time we were less far south than this, and it was colder. We spent an embarrassing number of days practically cuddling." She giggled. "And again when you got yourself so sick you couldn't leave my bed. Where did you wander off to that night, anyway?"

He didn't say anything for a minute. "If I lie with you, can you live without an answer to that?"

She pouted. "No. But I don't have a choice, so—" Song shifted to allow him room.

Leslie took the blanket from her hammock and spread it over her, then lay beside her underneath it. "Sorry I yelled at you."

"Are you kidding? It was kind of impressive. Besides, I'm not sorry for yelling at you." She turned her head to smirk at him, then leaned her cheek on his shoulder.

He hesitated a moment, then said, "Thank you for coming back for me. Feels like…coming home."

"You are home. Don't ever…leave…" Her breathing slowed, and she fell asleep right there against him.

Seven

*L*eslie had pulled up a chair beside the bay bench, which is where Song found him when she woke. He had a book in his hands and had dressed in warm clothes. She leaned up on one elbow, closing her eyes as her head throbbed. On the pillow, where her face had rested, sat a bloody rag. She squinted at it, then at the man beside her. Her peripheral vision blurred, causing her eyes to strain. However, everything in the center of her sight stood out in sharp definition. She could make out the woodgrain of the wall across the room. Song closed her eyes and shook her head, trying to clear her vision and perhaps the fullness pressing at her temples. She opened them and focused again on the bloodstained cloth.

"Oh. I thought I was just exhausted…" she said in a near whisper. "Didn't even do much."

Leslie leaned toward her, his gaze sweeping over her features. "Perhaps using *kijæm* at all in such a tired state is dangerous. How do you feel?"

"Hung over."

"When you're ready, we can join the men in Thìse."

"Where is Thìse?"

"Western coast of Aibhànocht," he said. "You'll want thick clothing. Luckily it's not winter."

She furrowed her brow at the multiple blankets tucked around her. "Why do people live in these bloody frigid places?"

Leslie shrugged. "Sometimes it's a matter of wherever they ended up after leaving their original country. Other times it could be that they like the cold."

"The latter proves insanity." Song released a long, audible sigh. "I don't have warm clothes."

"I had Sunshine and Thumbs bring a few things for you."

"Splendid... I'm starving. How long was I out?"

"Almost two days. How many eilfass can you eat?" He retrieved an outfit from the table as she sat up.

"Three."

"Only three?" He chuckled. "Let me heat some water so you can wash up."

She nodded and stretched. "Thank you."

He returned a short while later with the water, then left her alone. Once she'd cleaned all traces of blood from her face, she pulled on the new clothes, put up her hood and met him on deck. They walked together, making slow progress as she wobbled and he remained close to catch her should she stumble. She grumbled to herself as they followed a path worn through the snow. The inn they entered was warm and filled with laughter and loud music. They joined their comrades at a table, where Thumbs huddled in the corner, keeping his head down.

She smiled at him. "You teach a few cooks how it's done, yet?"

His dark eyes flicked to her, then to the other patrons. "They do not like me here."

"What?"

Pinch made a face beside him. "Easy to forget that Aibhànocht and Kerriwen don't get along."

"Why not?" she asked.

"Wars a century ago. No one is willing to forgive the other, even after the truce. Stubborn bastards on both sides."

"How do you know?"

"I'm from Abhain-aimh, farther inland."

She saw the resemblance, now that he'd pointed it out. He was naturally paler than the rest of the crew, save Leslie—though both burned to a deep red when left out too long in the sun. Pinch had white-blond hair and grey eyes, like many of the folk in the tavern. A few strayed from that light hair and eyes, with black hair and dark or blue eyes. There seemed to be no in-between.

"Bet you didn't think I was a 'Nochtie, ey?" Pinch said.

Leslie smirked. "I guessed as much. I'd put quoine on Sunshine also being from these parts."

Now that she thought about it, the two men did have similar accents, though Song had never known what it was, and Sunshine's was faint in comparison. It had heavier r's and more of a wide-mouthed pronunciation to it.

"What parts are you from?" Pinch asked.

He directed a soft, almost sad smile at the table. "Everywhere. And nowhere."

Pinch nodded with feigned interest, then pulled a thick paper from inside his coat. "That's an interesting way of saying Pishing, now, ain't it?"

Leslie snatched the page, unfolding it enough to verify it as the wanted poster for him before ripping it in half.

"Right, right. Not Pishing, then? Last name isn't Krell, neither?"

He closed his eyes as though begging for patience, so he didn't see the eyes of all their nearby comrades shift toward him.

"He's just Leslie," Song said.

The others' eyes flicked between the two.

"Well? Get back to yourselves. And somebody, for the love of whatever they worship down here, bring me an ale and some food."

"Your kind," Pinch said.

"What?"

"They revere *you*. Gifted."

She froze, staring at him. "That's preposterous."

He chuckled. "Nope. If you were born here, they would've taken you to their monastery, trained you, then sent you out as a priestess. Call you the *aibhridh*. Here to spread the gospel."

She made a face. "Whose gospel?"

"No idea. You'll have to ask someone who paid attention in *thiùrin*. I could never be bothered."

Song pursed her lips. "Then, as your captain *and* priestess of your deity, I demand you get me a drink and some hot food." She snatched a roll from his plate when he stood, laughing as she tore a piece off. After one bite, she stared at it. "This tastes fishy."

"That'd be the fish, captain!" Pinch laughed as he strode away.

Song pursed her lips after him.

"Thank you," Leslie murmured.

She smiled and bumped her shoulder against his. "It's what friends are for, right?" But she frowned once he looked away. She could honor his choice to claim the poster false, but she didn't have to accept it herself. In fact, she found her gaze lingering a bit longer on his features, trying to spot some Dashaelan in them.

Once the barmaid set food in front of them, Song shoveled it into her mouth faster than she could chew it, while Leslie gave the meal his full attention. Afterward, she went upstairs—not without help—to bathe and find her room. A fire crackled in the small corner stove, the large bed nearby warm from it.

"Which room is yours?" she asked Leslie as she removed her shoes and coat.

"Why?"

"So I can bother you when I get bored, of course." She grinned, and he chuckled.

"I don't have one. This was the last vacancy."

"Then what were you planning on doing?"

Leslie shrugged. "Chair outside your door? Worked for weeks."

Song sat on the edge of the bed and leaned back. "Well, this bed is rather sizable… If you promise to stay on the other side of it, you're welcome to sleep here."

He paused to think, then nodded. "Thank you."

A long breath escaped her lips. "I'm too weary to do anything; it's too cold to go anywhere; and I'm wide bloody awake after sleeping for days." She flopped back to stare at the ceiling.

He didn't say anything for a while as he leaned against the wall, arms folded. "Do you know what I did in Tarn?"

Her eyes shifted from side to side as she thought. "I don't believe I do, no. Was it indecorous?" She gave him a sly wink.

"Ignoble at best. I ran a backroom card table. The Western District has strict gambling rules. So, my table was illegal."

"Scandalous," she said with a snort. "Not an honorable profession for the most honorable man I know."

He gave a rueful chuckle. "You'd be surprised how wrong you are to call me that."

"Forgive me if I refuse to imagine you as anything but." Her brow furrowed. "How did you end up with such a place, though?"

"At first I was a player, then the dealer passed it onto me."

"Ah... Anyway, why are we talking about Tarn?"

"Would you like for me to teach you how to play cards? You don't have to leave the room, and we can make false bets."

She scoffed. "I know how to play. I've played with the men before."

"You've never played with me, though."

Song grinned. "True. Seems about time we did. Real bets are fine. Find us some cards, then?"

He smiled and pushed away from the wall. "As you wish."

A long time passed with Leslie gone. Song wrapped herself in a blanket and crossed the room to sit in a chair beside the heating stove. When the knock came and Leslie entered, he'd not only acquired a deck of cards, but also betting chips made from painted bone discs, and five crew members: Ponce, Toothy, Bells, Bishop, and Oswold.

"You really never played a hand with Whispers?" Ponce asked.

"To be fair, she's missed out on a lot of fun the men have," Toothy said. "And last time she played cards, Dash took everything she had!"

She furrowed her brow, and the others grew solemn. "He actually gave it all back," she said, breaking the long silence. "Is that why you never invited me to play again? Because I'm bad at it?"

"You're just always so busy, is all," Ponce said.

"You don't sleep in the barracks, and keep busy with training," Bells said.

"Could've asked me if I wanted to join," Song muttered.

The men sat in a circle on the floor, and she slid from her chair to join them. She found herself knee to knee with Ponce on one side and Bells on the other. The latter gave her a look as Leslie shuffled the deck with practiced dexterity and speed. Toothy handed everyone an even amount of chips. Cards came flitting across the floorboards to slide to a stop before each player.

"No peeking," Bells said as he lifted his, cupping his hands around his cards.

"I wasn't going to." She stuck her tongue out at him.

While they played, she kept quiet as the men talked. Song made sure to listen, though. As much as she wanted to deny it, she was the captain now, and all these men's lives were in her hands. She had to make an effort to get to know them better. At the very least, know their names and where they were from.

Bishop, a former priest from Jashedar, was on a mission of self-discovery after his church had burned down. What brought him onto a pirate ship, though? A holy man having a crisis of identity should not have led him to such an extreme. Song had no interest in his past profession, but others listened and Leslie engaged him with questions just to learn something new.

Oswold was a merchant from the Winterlands in southern Jashedar, who'd lost everything after a series of poor investments. He'd lost his shop and his savings. Soon after, his wife had left with their children. He was, at best, a man with ambition. At worst, he was a man with nothing to lose. Oswold eyed her sideways every so often, a look on his face equal parts fear and awe.

"Keep staring at me, and I might think you fancy me, Oswold," she said, a wry smile on her lips as she studied her new hand.

He cleared his throat. "Sorry."

"Don't apologize, just tell me why you keep doing it."

The others stared at him, as though his answer held a special relevance to them, too.

"I've never been so close to a Magic before. And what ye did…"

She set her cards face down on the floor and leaned back on her palms. "What I did?"

"Never heard of a power so great."

She chuckled. "Read some books. I'm sure you'll find something. Now stop staring at me like a side-show. I'm a person, not some god-touched what-do-you-call-it."

"The *ai*—"

"I wasn't asking, Leslie," she grouched.

Hours passed as they talked and laughed. It set her at ease, getting to know these men better. She realized then that she barely even knew Ponce and Toothy. Her inner circle had been so small over the years that she'd failed to pay attention to anyone more than surface level.

Those two were southern Andalisian, from Anarchaia, and had been friends from a young age. As Toothy put it, 'It was best mates at first arse-kicking.' Somehow, the two had bonded over a tussle in the streets. Toothy was forthcoming about his own poor upbringing, but Ponce remained tight-lipped about his life before piracy. Song thought he'd always held himself with that rigid posture which had been trained into her and other aristocrats from birth, but she didn't want to make assumptions.

A knock sounded at the door, and after being granted permission, Pinch opened it. He scanned the faces of those on the floor. "Oh, so there really is an unseemly gathering in here."

Song pressed her lips together and threw a poker chip at his chest. "Are you here to join us?"

"No, no. Was just checking. And wanted to let you know I handled the Thumbs situation."

"Oh?"

"Just needed a vouch, is all. He'll probably be in the kitchen with Bhìra all night—or in her bed." He gave a wicked grin.

"Lucky dog. Anywhat— G'night." Pinch closed the door.

"He'd better not forget he promised me food," Song grumbled.

A few rounds later, after going all-in and losing everything, Ponce sat up and stretched his hands over his head. "About time I turn in. Night gents—and Song."

Once he'd left, Toothy snorted a laugh. "He could at least *pretend* a bit better."

The others laughed, but Song kept quiet, feeling like she was on the outside of an inside joke, and too afraid to ask for details. As though the sudden reminder of the time hit everyone at once, the game ended and the others filed out to return to their rooms. She stood as the last of them left, leaving Leslie to pick up the bone chips and cards. A ratty coat lay stretched across her bed. She lifted it and turned it this way and that. It was Ponce's, she was sure of it. She tucked it over her arm and wandered down the hall. He grunted behind the door as she neared.

"*Kawl-nuh!*" The lock clicked, and she opened the door, a hand out as though wielding her *kijæm*.

As fast as she'd opened the door, she swung it closed, locked it once more, and cringed at the wood. She returned to her room to find Leslie comfortable in the bed, a book in his hands. He observed her in silence.

"Thought you were returning that to Ponce."

She pinched the bridge of her nose. "He's...busy."

"Oh."

"With...Pinch..."

"Oh..."

Someone pounded on the door behind her and she jumped, gripping the man's coat to her as she spun. She opened the door on Ponce, who pushed into the room, his stern gaze fixed on her.

"What did you see?" he demanded.

She pursed her lips. "I saw only your business."

"Keep your mouth shut," he growled.

"It's the worst kept secret on the ship," Leslie intoned.

Ponce stared daggers at him and ripped his coat from Song's grasp. "Would hate for other secrets to get out." He gave them each a long look, then stalked from the room.

"What's he mean 'other secrets'?" She pulled her boots and coat off, then padded across the cold floorboards.

"Probably something about me being in your bed." He gave her a wry smile and shrugged.

"Does everyone really know about those two?" she asked as she situated herself beneath the puffy brown comforter and furs.

Leslie laughed and closed his book. "Anyone who doesn't is either as oblivious as you, or they're willfully ignorant. Pinch and Ponce are the only ones who call each other by their real names. If you send one to the cargo hold, the other vanishes as well. They think they're keeping it secret, but the rest of the men just don't care enough to take that away from them."

"What are their real names?" she asked.

"Ponce is Henry. Pinch is Nebhàr."

"I understand why they hide," she whispered after a long silence. "They shouldn't have to. We're bloody pirates. What do we care what societies think?"

"Does that mean you'll bring a woman aboard for yourself?"

She scrunched her face at him. "No. I'm not there just yet. But perhaps those two are?"

"Perhaps."

"Would it be so crazy to let them have this? Openly?"

He released a long breath and put his hands behind his head. "Could always give them the option. What do you know of Armalinia?"

She shrugged. "Desert country. Expensive exports. Mother said they're hedonistic."

He chuckled. "Aren't we all? In Armalinia, love is not restricted. Nor are they so strict of societal norms our countries observe. You walking around in trousers wouldn't faze them in the slightest. Men wearing skirts is just as normal. Polygamy is commonplace."

"Why?"

"Why what?"

"Why is Armalinia so lenient with things like that?"

"Tell me something, in what way does who you're attracted to affect your country's politics?"

She chewed on her bottom lip and shook her head.

"In what way does how many wives you choose to take effect Andalise's economy?"

She shook her head again.

"How does the person you spend your life with affect your parents?"

"Besides their shame?"

"A shame ingrained in them by your society. But that does not affect them beyond their mood. Armalinia saw it that way long ago and removed all those restrictions. What you do in private as an individual does not affect their economy, their government, their laws. Why restrict things with so little impact on the country as a whole?"

Song nibbled at her bottom lip as she thought. "So…we treat the Bounty like Armalinia. No rules over things that don't matter in the grand scheme of things."

"Sounds like a great idea to me."

They stayed quiet for several minutes before her lips twisted up into a smirk. "Any crew members catch your eye?"

He laughed and shook his head. "I have very high standards."

"And no one meets them? Not even one? Not even *Toothy*?"

He cringed. "He's a lovely chap, really. But the whole missing all of his teeth is where I'm afraid I must draw the line. You're free to have him."

She scrunched her nose. "Oh, no, I couldn't possibly. He's all yours."

Leslie chuckled up at the ceiling and closed his eyes. "Good night, Song."

"Goodnight, Leslie. Sweet dreams…of Toothy, but with teeth. Could you imagine?"

"Go to sleep, Song."

"Thumbs, then."

He said nothing, then raised one corner of his lips. "Thumbs it is."

She giggled and lowered the wick on her lamp.

Eight

Song woke late in the morning to a knocking at her door. The other side of the bed had been made, and the room was empty. She sniffed and squinted at the door.

"Bugger off!"

"Song, a word, please," Pinch said from the other side.

A blush at her memory of catching the two in bed together stabbed at her cheekbones. She climbed out of the bed and wrapped the blanket around herself, then opened the door for him. He entered, holding a white cloth bundle tied together with an expensive ribbon.

"I'm sorry," she blurted, "about last night." She closed the door behind him.

He set the bundle on the bed and stared down at it. "Henry assured me you won't tell anyone on account of he knows a secret of yours."

"Blackmail only works if the secret is not, in fact, a rumor. Are you here to try bribery instead?"

He chuckled. "No, this has nothing to do with that. Sunshine and I got to talking, and we thought it might do you some good to speak with the *Thoràn Bhàlemorai*." When she gave him a blank stare, he chuckled. "The voice of our God. She's here in Thìse."

"When you say the voice…"

"Think of her as a high priestess, but more politically powerful. She has more authority than a king."

"And this?" Song fiddled with the cloth bundle.

"She sent them this morning after praying over our request for you to meet her. You must wear this. You can wear your own boots, but you'll have to take them off in the temple."

"Why should I speak with this woman?"

Pinch raised one shoulder. "She might have answers to all your questions about *kijæm*. Couldn't hurt to talk to someone who actually knows about it, right? Might learn a thing or two?"

She thought over everything and smiled. "Thank you. Much better than blackmail."

Song ate a light breakfast, then bathed and dressed in the bright blue gown the same color as the glittering within her *kijæm*. It was long and soft, with flowing sleeves and a wide collar that left her shoulders bare. The dress was too large in the bust, but tied in the front, so she could pull it as tight as it could go. She shoved her feet into her boots, then wrapped the white cloak around herself. White furs draped over the shoulders adding more warmth than her coat would have. Pinch leaned against the doorway to scrutinize her. He'd bathed and donned black trousers and shirt, with a black cloak with grey furs on his shoulders.

"Damn. You're sure you only like women?"

She blushed. "What if Ponce heard you saying that?"

"He'd laugh and buy me a night with a woman who looks like you."

"That's..."

"Flattering?"

"Appalling. Don't ever say it again."

He chuckled. "Wouldn't be able to find one, anyway. Perhaps a boy..."

"You're not helping your case." She threw her hairbrush at him.

Sunshine pushed the door open. He'd dressed in all black with the same sort of cloak as Pinch. He looked her over and gave a small nod. "Suits you."

"This doesn't make me an ivory, right?"

Pinch and Sunshine chuckled as she closed the door.

"*Aibhridh*," Sunshine said. "No, you'd have to go through the entire process. You're still something reverent, but not initiated."

She made a face as he led her down the stairs. "You do know this all sounds like utter rubbish, right?"

"Don't say that to the *Thoràn Bhàlemorai*," Pinch said. "Or anyone else, for that matter. Blasphemy, even of yourself, can get you stoned."

Song swallowed away a nervous knot as they entered the main room of the tavern. Local men and women stood upon seeing her. They averted their gazes, then dropped to one knee. Those of her crew who sat at the tables stared between the Nochties and Song, bewildered but also charmed in their own right over seeing her in the gown.

"I hate this," she hissed at Sunshine beside her. "Anyone could recognize me."

But the citizens all kept their eyes on the floor, as though it was forbidden to look upon her.

Pinch reached behind and dropped the hood over her head. "Let's not keep her waiting."

They exited the building to a still, cold outside. The sky was clear and small mounds of snow dotted over the land and the humble cottages and huts. Citizens of the village stopped and knelt as she passed. They reached a large building that seemed to have been stamped into the side of an obsidian cliff. The polished black stone shone in the sunlight. The building had a decorative entryway book-ended by three columns on each side as though to hold up the curved arch at the top. Patterns of vines with thorns—which she recognized as painful frostthorn—wound around the columns in a display of artistic mastery.

The three entered and removed their cloaks and boots, handing them to a man in black, who set them on an ornate shelf. Sunshine and Pinch sat on one bench to clean their feet. Song sat on the opposite bench as the man in black cleaned hers. She gritted her teeth, toes squirming over the tickle.

After that, she followed them into the chapel across the warm black stone floor where a woman with black hair wearing a silver robe stood on a half-step platform with a raised altar behind her. Rectangular carpets, each with two flat square pillows, sprawled from what served as a center aisle, peppering the floor in neat rows. Sconces and candelabra lit the room, reflecting from the polished black stone walls to create a dark illumination that Song felt in the pit of her stomach as both mystical and foreboding.

Women flanked the woman in silver on either side, dressed in white with shimmering blue accents. One woman in grey tilted her head and smiled as she studied Song with her black eyes. It was a look which felt familiar to Song. One that stared straight into her heart as though nothing could be hidden from that gaze.

"Bright. Thick," she said.

Song swallowed and hesitated. "What?"

"Your Gift," the woman in silver said. "Myrmhin can see it." She turned her attention to the woman beside her. "Can you tell me anything else?"

She shook her head. "They don't speak."

"Curious." The woman in silver descended from the raised stage and approached Song. Her brows pushed together as she set her soft fingertips beneath Song's chin. "They always talk to her…"

"What do you mean?" Song asked.

The woman smiled, her blue eyes crinkling at the corners. "There are those who can communicate with the Gift, but cannot use it. We call them *thànbhridh*. Myrmhin is one. Her mother was the previous *Thoràn Bhàlemorai*."

"I have so many questions…"

"I know. Come."

"We'll wait here," Sunshine said as he and Pinch sat on soft mats.

"But—"

"Men aren't allowed," the woman said. She turned and strode away so fluidly, she might have been floating beneath her gown. She didn't look back to make sure Song followed, just trusted that she would.

"Why not?" Song followed her into a room darker than a moonless night.

"Men with the Gift are dangerous. More often than not, they must be extinguished from this world. If not, they become obsessed with their own power."

"And women do not?"

The woman gave no reply. Song clenched her teeth, already feeling at odds with whatever the women might share.

Johanna, her handmaid in Garda, had always said corruption knew no gender. She'd been talking of money and social standing, but Song imagined it applied to anything. Her mother had been the example, the way she treated others as though they were required to bend the world to her will. Johanna had tried from early in Song's life to keep her humbled. It had worked to a point, but now, thinking back over her former life, she recognized the behavior. She'd been a brat. And one day she might've become another Annie Gould. The thought made her cringe to herself before she forced the expression away.

The door shut behind them, snuffing out the little light from the chapel. The women's breathing echoed off the stone walls.

"Show us your light, child."

"Oh." Song hesitated, then gave the command, "*Tyl.*"

A swirling shimmer came to life over Song's head, twisting and wrapping around itself, casting just enough light for her to see the *Thoràn Bhàlemorai*, and Myrmhin. The former looked unimpressed, but the latter seemed frustrated.

"All of it," Myrmhin said.

The way she spoke, the way she acted, reminded Song of Bruce. Like she was grasping at longer sentences, but could never catch them, and so said what little she could.

"What do you mean?" Song asked.

The woman pointed at the slithering mass. "Small."

"You're holding back," the woman in silver said. "Or your Gift is. What we're looking at is only a fraction of what she sees surrounding you."

"*Moor eth liff. Meth d'nylb.*"

The mist swirled and glittered before expanding to encompass them, pressing out around them to the walls and ceiling. It wound around the *Thoràn Bhàlemorai*, sparkling and blinking in rapid bursts. Her skin and dress seemed to glow before tendrils of the shifting mist rose from around her to mingle with the rest. The women stared at her, eyes wide. Myrmhin dropped to her knees and threw herself forward on the floor.

"Did I do something wrong?" Song blurted.

"*Bhàlemorai Ciarbha,*" the woman mumbled into the black stone at her nose.

The *Thoràn Bhàlemorai's* demeanor changed from calm, mystical authority to terse impatience as she stared between Song and the woman prostrate on the ground. "She's not even one of us. Get up!"

The woman stood and stared at Song with tears sparkling in her eyes. "She is!"

"What?" Song demanded.

"You took Àbhril's Gift. Your Gift speaks. You steal Gifts."

The Touched slaver on the Garda's Pride surged into her mind. "No. His betrayed him and left."

"No," she hissed, her grin manic. "You took it. Your Gift is of the first. Ancient. Rare." She stared in wonder at the slithering mist filled with glimmering lights, as though listening to a chorus.

Song quivered. "*Shiugnit-skei.*" The light blinked out, leaving the three in a consuming darkness. "I should go."

She backed away, but as though Myrmhin could see her, she reached out and wrapped her hand around Song's wrist. "No. Àbhril, please! *Bhàlemorai Ciarbha!*"

"An outsider wouldn't be His chosen," Àbhril hissed. She whispered, and her own *kijæm* illuminated the room. Compared to the light Song had created, it was dull and unimpressive.

Song ripped free of Myrmhin's grasp and strode for the door. Àbhril spoke low and her *kijæm* slithered around to block her path. Song set her hand to it and it flexed against her palm. The light glowed brighter at the pressure, then pushed back, refusing to let her pass. She turned around to meet the woman's gaze.

"Do you dream of *Au Caesaries?*" Àbhril asked.

"I don't know what that is," Song said.

"Do you get nosebleeds after using your Gift?"

Song swallowed and knew she couldn't lie after that hesitation. "Just once."

Àbhril released a sigh of relief. "See? You're mistaken," she said to the woman beside her.

Myrmhin stared at Song longer, then curled her white-blonde hair behind her ear. She nodded and stared at her feet. "Sorry, Àbhril. I won't make mistakes again." Her eyes slid over to study Song again, and somehow she knew the woman was lying to appease the *Thoràn Bhàlemorai*.

"What do the nosebleeds mean?" Song asked.

Àbhril motioned for her to follow through a door on the other side of the small room. "*Tùairise*. Melding. *Zechnif*—what you know as *kijæm*—will bond with a wielder over time. This causes headaches and nosebleeds. Most *aibhridh* pull back their use to not exacerbate the problem."

As she spoke, she led Song through a hallway with walls that glistened. The air was hot and humid, choking her with hints of sulphur. Mixed with the sulphur smell were flower oils, heavy in an attempt to cover up the worst of it. They emerged into a tall chamber, illuminated by the sun overhead, shining through a frosted glass dome. It reflected from mirrors on the polished black stone walls, bouncing around to light the chamber better than a lantern might.

In the middle of the room sat a large, shallow pool, steaming and gently swirling. A trickling waterfall fed the pool, and it emptied out on the other side in a winding narrow ditch carved into the floor that twisted through columns like an exploring snake, before disappearing down a small, dark tunnel. At that moment, the pool sat empty, but the seats within the basin and around the edges left Song assuming the women might bathe together there.

On the other side of the pool, Àbhril stopped in front of a statue. It had been carved directly from the stone floor, and so was immovable; a permanent feature within the holy hall. The statue towered over them, the man's face smiling. He had features of a people she wasn't familiar with, and a style of dress which she'd never encountered. He wore something like an unbuttoned suit jacket that was long, reaching to his knees, with deep, buttoned pockets. A rectangular medal had been fastened to the lapel, and around his neck sat a thick ribbon with a rectangle medallion hanging lengthwise on the end.

"Who is this?"

"Behold the face of our God. *Bhàlemorai*. You aren't one of us, but as one of the worthy, He is your God, too."

Song bit down on her comment, remembering what Pinch had said. *Don't tell me who my god is.* Instead, she said, "Why is your god a man?"

Àbhril blinked and quirked her eyebrow up. "What?"

"Why is your god a man if you don't believe men should hold the *kijæm*? You kill them, and yet you worship one."

The woman's nostrils flared. "He is not a man, He is God."

"You said that. But why not a goddess?"

"We didn't choose Him. He chose us."

Song moved her head in a sort of single nod. "Right." She stared at the man a little longer, counting the ways it didn't add up. Rather than pressing the issue, she spun in a slow circle to take in the room's entirety again. "What happens to someone who doesn't reduce their *kijæm* use?"

"Few have ever pushed themselves too far, but it has been done. The symptoms worsen, they lose consciousness. One was recorded to have bled from the ears. Then the dreams started.

One collapsed one day and never woke up, trapped in a slumber, which killed her slowly. Others have died from blood loss, or… other unfortunate events."

"That's a good argument against extensive use." She licked her lips and gazed around the room. "Do you have a…book? With all these stories and warnings, so I might study it."

"We have our scriptures that all within Aibhànocht study and pray over."

Song nodded, but chewed on the inside of her lip.

Àbhril smiled. "But the one you want is only for those initiated as an *aibhridh*."

"Let me guess, you don't want me initiated."

Myrmhin stepped closer to the woman. "My dream."

Àbhril nodded at her, then studied Song. "Show her."

The women led Song through a door, closing it behind them. They stood in a hallway protected from the dampness of the hot spring stream. The dry air welcomed her like a soft hug, and she sucked in a deep, grateful breath. Within this long hallway were a multitude of doors, all shut tight as though hiding secrets. At the end, on the left, Myrmhin opened the door to a small room with expensive furnishings. She strode to a drawing table at the back and shuffled through the papers across the top. As she did this, Song stared at the drawings peppering the walls.

"Here." Myrmhin held up a large page.

Song jolted at the detailed sketch of herself in her coat, the hood raised. Beside that one were sketches of her from the shoulders up at different angles.

"She saw you in a dream before you arrived," Àbhril said.

"When my crew decided to come here."

"We took it as a sign that you would be a new initiate."

Song took several deep breaths as she thought. She wanted to get her hands on the book, which told of those who'd melded too far, but she did not want to pledge herself to a god she didn't believe in.

"I wouldn't have to live here, would I?"

"You would. For at least one year, before we'd allow you out in the world, trained, to be a missionary."

Song nodded, already prepared to high-tail it out of the temple at the first hint of a hostage situation. "I'll think about it. Can I at least see this book you speak of?"

"Leabhir ain Tùairise." She smiled. "You may look on it, but not read it. Not sure you'd understand it, anyway."

She led Song out into the hallway again and into the first room to the right of the door leading out to the main chamber. Inside was a humble library. A single wall of shelves housed scrolls and books of varying ages. Several tables lined another wall, and on one sat an ancient scroll beside a loose page half filled out. Song guessed someone to be in the middle of transferring the contents from the scroll onto papers, which would later be bound together in a book.

In the middle of this small library stood a pedestal with light falling over it from above. On it sat a closed book with a tooled leather cover. It had swirling patterns which reminded her of the *kijæm* and how it flowed through the air like a streak of mist. The letters on the front didn't match what the woman had said. There was a bh where the woman had pronounced a v. Tentatively, she reached up to run her fingertips over the letters, feeling the tome. She had expected to feel some sort of mystical wonder, or excitement. Instead, her heart burned with greed and a hunger which could only be sated by the knowledge contained within those pages.

"We expect an answer by tomorrow," Àbhril said.

An idea formed in Song's mind, and she pursed her lips. "This is a thick tome. How many pages is it?"

"Eight hundred and seventy-four individual pages are there. We expect more to be added over time, of course. Come. It is nearly midday prayer. You may observe, if you wish."

Song followed the woman back to the humid main chamber. "Perhaps another time. I'm famished and a friend promised me a *rebhìdh.*"

Àbhril nodded, lips quirking at Song's botched pronunciation. "Try it with roast winter pears and a sprig of *abhainrùs*. You'll never taste anything like it, I promise."

They entered the main chapel, where Sunshine and Pinch still knelt in silence. Song said nothing to the men as they shoved into their boots, donned their cloaks, and left. When they'd reached a good distance away, Pinch cocked an eyebrow down at her.

"You're rather quiet."

"Indeed," she said.

"Did you learn anything?" Sunshine asked.

"I did. Forgive me for not sharing with you."

"Damn," Pinch said, "I'd thought surely you would fill us in on the secret goings-on back there."

Song gave him a reserved smile, but said nothing. She knew all too well that Àbhril could be spying on her to see if she would, in fact, tell the men about the inner chambers. She wouldn't put it past the woman, given her clear distrust. Not to mention, it was something Song would do.

She spent hours mulling things over, making a plan in her head. When dinnertime came, she stared at Leslie as she pulled on her boots.

"Do you know how to read this country's language?" Song asked as she buckled her coat.

"I do."

"Fluently?"

"What are you up to, Song?"

"Yes or no?"

"Yes. But Sunshine and Pinch—"

"Do you think they're serving the fishy rolls again tonight?" With that she left the room, not waiting for him to tug on his boots and join her. She couldn't say her plan out loud and risk Àbhril spying on her at that moment.

A few minutes later, Leslie slid onto the bench beside her. "Are you going to tell me—"

"Do you remember that thing about cups in cupboards?"

His brows pushed together, and he nodded, seeming to recall the lesson he'd given her about farseeing. "Yes. But—"

"Oh, they do have the rolls!" She lurched away from him to snatch two from a large plate as the barmaid set it down. Once back in her spot, she shoved one into Leslie's mouth.

The man eyed her as he chewed on a bite, his nose wrinkled in a faint disgusted manner, which she was too preoccupied to question. Whatever thoughts lingered behind those blue eyes, he seemed to have taken her hint to keep it to himself.

She stayed in the tavern late into the night, the only people left being herself and Sunshine. She stared across at him. He ignored it for some time before meeting her gaze.

"Problem?" he asked.

"Those priestesses have answers no one else does."

"Answers to what questions?"

"Ones about *kijæm*. It's a secret they guard close."

He thought about this and nodded. "Sounds right. Will they share it with you?"

"Yes. With a caveat. I have to join them and stay here for a year. Then *maybe* they'll let me read a book which I can't even understand the language of."

"A gift and a slap in the face," he muttered. "Have you made a decision, then?"

Song emptied her stein and dropped some quoine on the table to pay for both of their drinks. She stood and studied him. "Dawn."

"I'll spread the word."

Nine

Her crew didn't question the early departure. Even Pinch kept his mouth closed, though he gave Song several long looks as he helped load crates of supplies. A figure in a grey cloak with white fur at the shoulders, the hood raised, rushed to the dock. Workers averted their gazes, and a few who were able to, knelt. The woman strode to Song and leaned close.

"Private talk?" Myrmhin hissed.

Song blinked, then pulled her into the captain's cabin. "Well, this is suspicious at best."

"Àbhril is a fool."

"Why?" She leaned back against the table, arms folded together.

"She doesn't see."

"See what?"

"You." Myrmhin pushed Song's hood down, her black eyes bouncing to stare at Song's blue ones. "I see you."

"I'm not staying. And it has nothing to do with Àbhril. I don't believe in your god, and I refuse to be held prisoner to learn about my Gift."

She shook her head. "Don't stay. Take me."

Song blinked and stood up straight. "What?"

"Take me."

"Are you in danger? Do you hate your life here?"

"No. I'm safe."

"But...?" She growled when the woman stared at the wood of the table, her eyes scanning side to side. "Myrmhin, you can't come with me. I'm a privateer, love. What we do is dangerous."

Myrmhin giggled. "Pirate, Song."

Song jolted. "What?"

"I know you."

She swallowed, unsure how to feel about a complete stranger knowing her secrets. "I'm not taking you with me."

Myrmhin leaned close, setting her palm to Song's chest as she batted her eyelashes. For one agonizing minute, neither moved. Song contemplated taking the woman away from her home and the temple she belonged to. It didn't even give her pause that an entire country's Touched women could pursue to steal back their *thànbhridh*.

A wry smile cracked Song's mouth open. "Are you seducing me?"

Myrmhin smirked. "Trying."

"And if I say no?"

"I try harder." She leaned closer, her lips a whisper from Song's.

"Why?" she asked, tempted in equal parts to back away, but also to lean forward and claim the offered kiss. Instead, she remained unmoving.

"Because you have my faith."

"Elaborate."

"You will find it. *Au Caesaries*."

Song leaned back and sat against the table, putting an arm's length between them. "Oh, dear, sweet Myrmhin. No. I won't find your paradise. I won't find the home of your god or whatever else you think. You claim to know me? Then you should know I'm not interested in gods. I'm interested in quoine and plunder and pleasure."

"I can pleasure."

Song bit her lip at the shiver that ran down her spine and knotted in expectant desire in her core. Instead of acting on it, she pinched Myrmhin's chin and wiggled it. "A pirate crew is no place for someone like you—"

"I am not weak!"

"I just meant—"

"I am not simple!"

"I know. You're probably the smartest woman in the temple. And none of those fools even knows it. They underestimate you, and that is their folly."

Then Myrmhin pressed forward and kissed Song—who raised her eyebrows, but didn't protest. The woman was skilled, though used more tongue than Song found comfortable. Song again contemplated taking the woman—until she remembered her plan, which hinged on her being at the temple. After a minute, she pulled away and looked into Myrmhin's eyes.

Her mouth crooked sideways in a grin. "I have always wanted to be seduced before… But you need to stay here, Myrmhin. If I find this *Au Caesaries* place, I'll come back for you."

"Promise."

"On my honor."

Myrmhin studied her, teeth clenched together as she thought. "You still do not believe."

"No."

"It's real. It is a place on this plane. Other *Ciarbha* have seen. It is always the same."

Song took a contemplative breath, ready to wave away the religious nonsense. Curiosity, though, made her ask, "And what do they claim to see?"

"Smoke. Sunrise. They hear music." She hummed, and the tune made the hairs along Song's arms stand on end. "Do you know it?"

"No," Song lied. "All right, Myrmhin, it's about time I shove off before Àbhril comes and forces me to join your ranks. I'm sorry, but I've no interest in joining you, or being your Chosen."

"*Bhàlemorai* doesn't care your interest. He chose you, you do not choose Him." She reached into her cloak and withdrew a parchment scroll. Myrmhin chewed on her bottom lip, then pressed the scroll to Song's chest. "You will find it. My faith is yours, Song *Bhàlemorai Ciarbha.*"

"And if I don't?"

"Then you die like the others." With that, the woman lifted her hood and exited the cabin.

Sunshine leaned into the doorway. "Everything all right?"

Song released a long breath. "I think so. Are we ready to depart?"

He shook his head. "Can't seem to track Thumbs down."

With a groan, Song trudged off the ship and back to the inn. Once there, a barmaid directed her to a house not far. She knocked and waited. Then knocked again. She pounded on the door. A moment later, a woman opened it just far enough to look out. She was wrapped in a blanket and probably nothing else, based on the noises Song had been trying to pretend weren't coming from the house she stood before.

"*Dàmhghit? Ciunas ì feisìr lobh cabhreat?*" the woman asked, her tone clipped and frustrated.

Song delivered a smile, albeit pained, and more grimace than anything. "I'm looking for Thumbs."

"Who?"

"A Kerri man. Bald—"

"Oh! Lev! *Tà*, he's here. I, um…" She glanced over her shoulder.

Song hoped her blush didn't show as she let out a long breath of steam. "Tell him he's got thirty minutes, and then we leave port with or without him."

"Oh. Right, then."

"Enjoy."

The woman shut and locked the door. The lewd noises resumed as Song strode away. She couldn't help but laugh and also grimace. She returned to the skyship and passed on the half hour warning, then returned to her cabin to spend the time unbothered.

As they prepared to leave port at the allotted time, Thumbs came running across the boardwalk and jumped onto the ship. He stared up at her as he caught his breath. "You were not really going to leave me behind, were you?"

"I didn't want to rob you of the chance to remain in that woman's bed for the rest of your life," Song said from the helm.

He laughed. "It would take more than that to make me leave this ship, Song. Besides, I made you a promise!" He lifted a sack from his shoulder. "Fresh *rebhìdh* stew for lunch." He went below, whistling.

Sunshine stood at her side. "Did you really think he would have stayed behind?"

Song laughed. "If I thought he'd stay, I would have left port instead of giving him time to finish with the cook."

"You're too kind."

"I'd do the same for you."

Sunshine scoffed. "Can't romance someone in two days. I won't need your kindness."

They stood in silence as Song bit back her questions. Grumpy old Sunshine preferring to romance someone? She didn't know whether to laugh or tell him it was adorable.

"Cargo is secure and every man we came with is on board. No new crew members, either. We're ready to depart at your order."

"Let's go about it, then."

They left port, and Song watched as the obsidian mountain faded until the white winter clouds consumed it. When they'd gone a considerable distance, she gave the helm to Maps and went below to find Leslie. She stopped to stare at Thumb's dark skin on the back of his bald head. He had a small, dead critter in his hands, which he slit open at the belly, then ripped the skin straight off in one swift, practiced motion.

"That's disgusting," she said.

He smiled and set it on a pile of skinned critters, then grabbed another. "It should be worth it."

"The inn cook didn't know your name when I asked for Thumbs."

He chuckled. "She did not want to call me by Thumbs."

"Called you Lev?"

He grinned wider up at her. "We have known each other for

how many years? And you still cannot just come out and ask my full name."

She gave her boots a sheepish grin. "What's your real name, Thumbs?"

"Levariijoriikinush Tun'Karalailiio."

Her eyes widened at her feet. Then she blinked at him. "Beautiful. I've already forgotten it."

He released a loud, happy belly-laugh. "I expect as much from those outside Kerriwen. Easier to just start with Thumbs and keep it there."

Song laughed and shook her head, then leaned forward and gave him a small one-armed hug. "Glad you didn't stay behind. Otherwise I'd starve to death."

"Cannot have that."

Afterward, she entered the crew's quarters to find Leslie with Bruce, sitting in the corner and having a typical one-sided conversation over Bruce's sketch pad. She had so many questions for the huge man—mainly why would he choose to stay aboard when he was so against the violence of piracy? Did he stay for Leslie? As his black eyes snapped up to settle on her like she was a beacon, she wondered if maybe he was drawn to her, as Myrmhin was. Or maybe he didn't have a reason, and it was vain of her to think either of them had that much interest in her.

Then again, Myrmhin's words from the day before drifted into her mind. *Your Gift is of the first. Ancient. Rare.* Of all the questions she should have asked the woman before she left, that one would haunt her the most.

"New drawings?" Song asked, trying to smile as the thought of Myrmhin dragged her back into the unease from before.

"Yes," Bruce said. Instead of showing her, he closed his book. "We're finished." He motioned for Leslie to go to her.

"I take it you needed to talk to me?" Leslie asked.

"Yes. In my cabin, please?"

He followed her up and waited in a patient silence as she

paced, thinking and unsure how to phrase what she needed to say. Leslie poked at the scroll on the table.

"No, I don't know what it is. I've got something more important on my mind," she said.

"And you asked for me because?"

"I needed an expert."

Leslie gave her a coy smile. "You'll have to narrow it down a bit."

"Your humility is truly a thing of legend," she said with a scoff and a smile. "This is something you should be...uniquely qualified to help with."

"What's that?" Leslie took a seat and leaned back, eyeing her.

She let out a breath. "The Song of Freedom."

He pressed his lips together as they sat in a long silence. "Why do you ask about that?"

Song poured herself a drink, then sat across from him, lifting her boots onto the table as she leaned back. "Did you know it's why I'm called Song?"

His brow furrowed. "I did not..."

"Altain said my name is noise. Sing and say, so he called me Song, for the Song of Freedom. Which is why I find it so strange that a priestess of Aibhànocht would hum it and not know the name, nor its importance to another country's people."

The crease between his brows pressed deeper. "Explain everything."

Song recounted the conversation with Myrmhin to him. He listened, a finger over his lips as he cradled his chin in thought.

"I thought if I knew more about the origin of the song, I could find some sort of meaning within it."

"The lyrics have changed over the centuries," he said, his gaze far off. "I don't know the original words, but I wonder..."

She motioned for him to continue.

"People have always said it's a *guide*, not a *hope*. I wonder if it's a physical guide, rather than a spiritual guide, as I grew up knowing."

"A place on the horizon where the sun rises," Song said. "That is the single-most vague direction I've ever heard."

Leslie took a breath and raised his shoulders. "I'm sorry I can't be of more help. It's a song the more devout followers of the god of slaves sing."

Song raised an eyebrow at him. "And you are not a devout follower?"

He shook his head, but didn't elaborate.

"And we can't exactly go wandering into Pishing to ask," she grumbled.

"We could try Telbhaniich-Zardi. The merchants there have a way of obtaining information, if you're willing to pay a handsome fee."

Song's eyebrow rose high over the other. The merchant country was something of mixed repute, depending on who was asked. Someone in her father's position would spit on the very foundations the island country was built on.

Pirates, on the other hand, sang its praises. It was a neutral territory, where every country could safely sell goods from their land. It had its own laws, which were upheld to the extreme—thieves lost a hand as a warning and their life at a second offense. There were no third chances. However, they refused to uphold laws from other countries, or even aid in the capture of a wanted person—which her father had ranted about on more than one occasion.

"Why can't they just bloody arrest him and send him here?" he shouted one evening, furious over a pirate evading capture yet again by hunkering down in Telbhaniich-Zardi. "Their neutrality ensures that villains go free!"

Mrs. Gould shushed him. "You're supposed to leave your work at the office, darling."

Song chewed on the inside of her bottom lip. "I'd love to go there. See what it's really about."

Leslie gave her a one-sided smile. "You've visited almost every country at this point."

She smiled and thought about her travels. "Maybe we can finish my list this year?"

Worry furrowed his brow. "That poster Pinch had..."

"Probably held onto it for a good while just to spring it on you."

"No. He found it in Thìse."

Song straightened, dropping the legs of her chair to the floor. "That far from Pishing? That fast?"

"From the northern curve of Andalise, to the frigid south in Aibhànocht... I wouldn't be surprised if Roman sent the posters to every city of every country." His eyes met hers. "Sooner or later, someone who isn't our crew mates will find one of those when I'm nearby."

"And?"

"And I can't avoid it forever."

"Anyone who wants you will have to go through me first. I'm not afraid to kill anyone who so much as looks in your direction."

"You can't kill the entire world." He chuckled.

"In reality, I only have to kill one man."

Leslie's jaw tightened as he clenched his teeth. He gave her a bitter smile, but said nothing.

"You don't object?"

"I would enjoy nothing more than helping you in that endeavor, actually. But killing a nobleman... That's how you gain the highest bounty in the world."

She licked her lips and nodded, eyes narrowed. "I'm sorry, are you talking me into it or out of it?"

He laughed. "Would you like me to go tell Maps our next destination?"

"While you're at it, make it known you're *officially* my first mate, and they'd best obey your orders as though they were mine."

"Even after you kicked me out?"

She scoffed. "You were gone for a week. Doesn't count."

As Leslie left the cabin, she picked up the scroll and fidgeted with it. Her fingers pinched the ribbon holding it closed for a second, before she decided she couldn't concentrate on anything but Leslie's bounty at that moment. She set the scroll in her trunk to look at later, then returned to her chair.

Song stared out at the propeller blurring across the windows. She had to think of some way to get him out of the predicament she'd put him in in the first place. If he'd never used Roman Duchamp's name to get her into the ball as a distraction, then the posters for him never would have gone up. She had to fix this mess, but had to come up with a perfect solution that erased the bounty, ensured his safety, and it had to be a plan he didn't morally object to.

Leslie was right, she couldn't kill the entire world. But no matter how hard he might warn her against it, a large part of her had already started thinking up ways to kill a lord of Pishing. What other choice did she have?

Ten

$\mathcal{D}$ays passed in which the Stars' Bounty traveled north. The only other vessel they'd crossed paths with had been a passenger skyship. Song didn't exit her cabin to give the order to intercept. The other vessel had adjusted course away from the golden zeppelin in anticipation of a chase, which never happened. Song's crew had knocked at the cabin door several times over the hours, but she never responded.

It was sunset by the time anyone dared enter the captain's cabin without knocking. Leslie stood in the doorway, a few concerned crew members looking over his shoulder into the room. Once his eyes settled on Song—hunched over a mess of items, bawling into her hands—he closed the door on the others. He leaned back, but said nothing, as though waiting for her to invite him into her grief.

"I keep expecting him to open the door and yell at me for rifling through his things," she admitted on a jerking sob.

"How much have you had to drink?" he asked, his eyes settling on the whiskey bottle beside her.

"I'm not *drunk*, I'm *sad*." She wiped her face with a handkerchief and settled her reddened gaze on him. "Will you help me?"

"With?"

"Going through his things."

Leslie shifted in discomfort. "I'm not sure it'd be appropriate."

"Leslie, he was your—"

"I'd rather you didn't perpetuate that rumor."

She ground her teeth together until her jaw ached. "Fine. But he *was* your captain."

He sighed. "Song—"

"Please. I can't do it alone."

He stared down at her, his eyes scanning across her tear-streaked face. He let out a long breath and closed his eyes. "All right. Fine. For you, though. Not for him."

Though it broke her heart, she accepted the tentative, almost rueful help. Leslie found a space nearby and sat surrounded by the various items. She settled her gaze on him again, saying nothing for a minute.

"What am I helping with?" he asked.

"I don't know what some of it is. I don't know what is worth keeping or…what you might want."

"I want none of it."

She raised one shoulder and avoided his gaze. "Maybe you'll change your mind for the right item."

He released another, more weary breath and shook his head, but said nothing. Instead, he picked up a book and scanned the cover before leafing through it.

Song studied him in silence as he ignored her. "I kind of see it now."

"Hmm?"

"In the eyes. Yours are bluer, though."

His brow lowered into a soft scowl.

"And there. You scowl similar…"

"Please…stop. For all we know, it's not even true."

"The poster—"

"A poster is not proof. Please stop bringing it up."

She took in a mouthful of whiskey and fought to swallow it past the lump in her throat. "Sorry."

They fell into another silence as she looked over the trinkets she'd had in front of her for hours. Leslie closed the book and gazed around at the mess.

"Which pile is to keep?"

Song scanned over everything. "I hadn't made piles just yet. Do you want it?"

"No. I just can't stand the thought of throwing out a book." He set the item in a new place away from the bulk of the mess. Leslie opened another and closed it again, then held it out for her. "You can decide what to do with this."

She opened it to discover dated, handwritten entries. It was one of Dashaelan's personal journals.

"A man as famous as him…it would be a shame to toss out his story." She set it over the other book.

"Perhaps it might teach you a thing or two about being a captain," he said.

Song let out a long, thoughtful breath as her gaze swept over Leslie's features again. "It's a strange coincidence."

He said nothing, but slid his eyes from the contents of the book in his palms to look at her.

"That of all the skyships, you ended up on this one."

He set the book aside and focused on the first of many figurines she'd pulled down from shelves along the wall. "Not really. It was about money, as you know. William's first idea had been to find Tsingsei Gould for the reward. More than enough to pay his debt to me." His gaze settled on her again as a smirk tempted the corner of his lips. "Funny how that turned out."

Song lifted the key from within her shirt and settled it in her palm as she stared at it. "Leslie—"

"No."

"You don't know what I was going to say."

"You're staring at his key and you insist on reminding me of what that damned poster claims. You're trying to pass it off to me."

"A Krell should be captain."

He set another figurine with the first in a collection, away from the stack of books. "I'm more Duchamp than I am Krell—*if* the poster is even true."

"Why are you so against the very idea of Dash being your father?" she asked in a whisper. "Because you claim he sold you?"

He stared at his empty palms and shook his head. "Can we get this over with and please stop talking about my possible relation to him?"

She nodded and opened another journal. A folded page, yellow with age, had been tucked into the front cover. A single faded word was scrawled across the back: *Wesley*. She gave the man beside her a sidelong look, closed the journal, and added it to the stack to keep.

Dashaelan had many journals, filled with rough penmanship and misspelled words. But they were his history, and he seemed to have kept detailed entries near daily, covering things he learned, things he'd done, and what was on his mind. The few times Song had glanced through them before setting them aside, she'd seen 'Wesley' on almost every page. That is, until the newest journal, cover still in good condition and pages crisp white. Her name peppered the pages. She would figure out the order of the journals later and read through another time, she resolved. Song wanted to know his story, and perhaps share it with the world.

She stared at Leslie as he studied a statue of a woman with four arms—two pressed together at her chest and two holding the sun over her head. He caught her looking at him and turned it to show Song.

"Gemesthie."

She blinked at the statue, then looked back at him. "You can have anything, you know."

"I don't want it," he said, his lips pursed as he set the statue in the chest of things to get rid of. "Any of it. Especially not the idol of a Pishing god."

Her eyes drifted to the book containing the letter. She said nothing, and they continued sorting. Song did her best not to bring up the possible relation anymore. In her mind, it had to be true. Why would the high lord of Ebrinar send out the bounty on the wrong name? And not just any name, one attached to an infamous pirate. A name no one even knew lived on, because Dashaelan had been selective of who he shared his family with.

The mess dwindled down as the two worked through it in silence. They sat nearer to each other, looking over papers to determine the use of them, when Leslie addressed the tension still lingering in the room.

"He was a good man. I'm sorry."

Her lips pulled into a small smile. "He wasn't without his faults, though. None of us are."

He plucked a necklace from inside a little box: a small bronze medallion on a leather cord. He turned it in his fingers, then slipped it over her head.

"What's this?"

"Vruuna. Goddess of family." He showed her the one side with a woman sitting cross-legged and holding a bundled infant, then flipped it to the other containing a feline with feathered wings. "Kirol, god of protection." He smiled and dropped it into her shirt collar, where it clanged against the key.

Her lips twisted at him. "I thought you weren't the gods-worshiping sort."

He shrugged. "I'm not. Not even Byruumie, god of the slaves. To be honest, if they did exist, and I met them, I'd spit in their eyes."

"You hate the gods more than men?" She picked up another journal and flipped through it.

"Can't hate what you don't believe in," Leslie replied.

"What proof do you have that they don't exist?" she asked.

He stared evenly at her. "Unanswered prayers. Slavery. Famine. Roman's continued existence… My list is long. What proof do you have that they do exist?"

She blinked at him and shrugged her shoulders. "I never followed in the Pishing gods. But I don't believe in there being no gods at all."

"The God of Aibhànocht?"

She made a face. "Definitely not."

"Why?"

"Because, can you imagine some god looking at *me*, of all people, and deciding, 'yes, I want this brat to have my power'?"

Leslie chuckled. "No offense, but you wouldn't be my first choice."

"Choose a prince! Not some idiot on a skyship with no plan." Song huffed.

"If it's not god-given, then where did it come from?"

"A head injury," she said, scanning over a faded wanted poster of Dashaelan.

The young man drawn onto the parchment looked far more like Leslie, with just the five o'clock shadow at his jaw instead of his full beard. Song said nothing to Leslie, but set it aside to nail to the wall beside her own, later. It amused her to discover he, too, kept posters of himself as some form of pirate pride.

Partway through organizing his stack of research and plans regarding Duke Carey Barton, she snapped upright, straightening her back with an excited gasp. "Leslie! I know how to honor him."

"Hmm?"

"Dash. His greatest desire in life, besides reuniting with his son, of course, was the Jewel of Castildi!"

Leslie slid to her side to read from the book in her fingers. "I saw the Jewel once. I stole a glimpse when serving Caius tea while he…enjoyed its presence." He made a face.

"Yes, it's something the rich and powerful are wont to do—stare at something they'll never own. My parents paid a fortune just to have it in the house for a day. I wasn't allowed to go into the room. Too young." She stuck out her tongue and wrinkled her nose as though making the face at her mother and father.

"I think Caius was secretly treating me, to be honest. I wasn't the one who served him tea daily."

She smiled. "He wanted you to see it. Was it beautiful?"

"It was astounding." He ran his fingers down the lines of Dashaelan's writing, then turned the page to read on.

"Barton's course takes him from Kerriwen to Armalinia this month," Song remembered aloud.

"Did Dash ever come up with a plan?"

"Actually, I did. He didn't like it." She laughed.

"What was it?"

"Barton has a weakness for the presence of ladies. It's been reported that he's rescued women from pirate vessels on more than one occasion."

His brow lowered at her. "And what do you think happened to those women once he rescued them?"

She pursed her lips, not wanting to say it aloud as though it would jinx her. "That was never reported."

"He paid them off. One of his men came to play cards at my table while the Jewel was in Tarn for some wealthy function. Rarely were the women…enthusiastic. But he compensated with quoine and threatened them all to keep quiet about how he made them repay his kindness for rescuing them."

She wrinkled her nose at him and smiled. "Then I suppose you'll have to rescue me before he takes his payment. If you *really* think I'm that helpless."

"Song, I don't want you to—"

"First you get mad that I'm not giving orders, and then when I do, you object?" She snapped the book closed and stacked it with the things she planned on keeping for herself. "Are you sure you shouldn't be captain? You're really good at trying to boss me around."

"Oh, was that an order?"

"Yes. And we're doing it with or without you."

Leslie made a face at her and stood as they sorted the last item. "So, are we still heading to Telbhaniich-Zardi?"

"Yes. Just to wait."

"I would like to go over your plan again and again. This has to go off without a hitch. I don't want anything happening to you."

Song delivered a coy smile. "My hero. You forget who of us has *kijæm* at her beck and call."

As he left, Sunshine's words replayed in her mind. *Whispers would lay waste to every man in sight if anything happened to you.*

Memories played of Leslie's desperate kisses. It wasn't the first time the memories resurfaced, but as she'd done before, she shoved it down as though doing so would erase the event. She wondered if he thought about it—and *what* he thought, for that matter. Thus far, he didn't seem to be letting it occupy his mind. She hoped it would stay that way.

Eleven

Song sat at the front of the ship, enjoying her meal and the conversation with Leslie, Toothy, Ponce, and Pinch. Toothy had been telling a story about his younger sister trying to romance Ponce, which had Song choking on her food to keep back her laughter. Pinch leaned over to whisper something in Leslie's ear. She grew quiet as the atmosphere changed around them. Leslie glared at the other man.

"Oh, come on. Just a hint?" Pinch said.

Song blinked, and in that time Leslie had grabbed Pinch by the collar. He stood, dragging the other man with him, then hit his fist against the side of Pinch's face with all his weight behind it. Pinch fell to the deck. Leslie bent to grab his collar and hit him again.

"Woah! What on—!" Song shouted, letting her meal clatter to her feet as she stood.

But Ponce was faster, leaping onto Leslie's back, his arm around Leslie's throat as he tried to drag him backward. Leslie lurched forward, throwing Ponce over his shoulder, where he landed on Pinch. Toothy came at him next, but Song shoved him to the side with an elbow in his ribs. She gripped the back of Leslie's shirt. He spun on her and she ducked under his fist, which lost momentum as he realized who he'd swung at. She punched into his gut before standing and sending another to his jaw. He threw his hands up in surrender and backed away, taking short, controlled breaths.

She pursed her lips, her eyes flashing a warning. "In my cabin, now," she growled. "All four of you!" she shouted when only Leslie made to follow the order.

She stormed in after them, shoving Pinch into a chair—the other two took the hint and sat. Leslie made himself comfortable on the bay bench, his glare never straying from Pinch.

"I'm going to give you all one chance to tell me what the *hell* is going on before I show you what it's like on the other side of my interrogations."

None said anything for a long time.

Leslie shook his head. "Better tell her, Pinch."

"You are *not* immune." She jabbed a finger in the air at him.

Leslie pursed his lips indignantly at being grouped with the others. When no one said anything, she took the dagger from the sheath at Toothy's waist and grabbed Ponce's right wrist, slamming his palm down on the table. She separated his pinky from the others and held the knife over it.

"Start talking." She directed her glare at Pinch.

"You'd better tell her fast," Leslie said.

"All right!" Ponce shouted, catching her off guard. "There's a pool—a bet of sorts…"

"What sort?" Song demanded, pressing the knife to his skin.

"Small or bound," he sputtered. She pushed against his knuckle and he shouted, "*Small or bound!* I'm not lying!"

After a quick inspection of Ponce's unmarred skin, she straightened and shoved the dagger into Toothy's hands. "Sharpen your dagger, it's rubbish."

"Aye." He slid the dagger back where it belonged, keeping his gaze on the floor as though eye contact might anger her more.

"Now, small or bound what?" she demanded.

All four men shifted uncomfortably.

"Are we children now? Come on!"

"You… Your…" Toothy motioned at Song with his forehead, but avoided raising his eyes to her.

"My what?" She crossed her arms over her chest, and it occurred to her. "My *breasts*?"

None of them would look at her then.

"Are you all in on this?" She looked at Leslie.

His palms pressed into the air before him. "I am not a part of it, nor do I want to be."

"Then what was that fiasco out there?"

He chewed on his answer, a grimace on his face, as though it tasted bitter in his mouth. "He was asking me to confirm one or the other so they could split the pot."

"Why you?"

Pinch shrugged. "Well, you know. You two are like…"

"Like what?" She narrowed her eyes, daring him to answer.

"Nothin', I just thought he might know, is all."

Song paced the room, her eyes meeting Leslie's for a second, before she swept her gaze over the other three. She couldn't start tearing her crew apart. No, she had to be diplomatic about it. Instill in the men that their captain's body was not a subject for bets. "How much is your pot worth?"

"Just over a thousand quoine," Ponce said.

She raised her eyebrows. "I didn't realize you felt so passionately about my breasts."

Leslie tried to hide his amused smirk, but she caught it and shot him a warning glare.

"That is a rather large pot to go unsolved. Leslie."

He stood, attentive to her orders.

"Gather the men on deck. All of them. Wake the night crew and get Bones out of the crow's nest."

He nodded and strode past her to carry out her command.

She turned her attention to Toothy. "I expected more from you." Then she pursed her lips at Ponce and Pinch. "Gather your pot and bring it to me on deck. You're all dismissed."

Once alone, she strode to the liquor cabinet and poured a small amount of whiskey into a glass. "I can see why you drank so much, old man." She raised the glass as a toast to Dashaelan, then swallowed it in one gulp and went out to the deck.

The word must have spread as to why the men were called to order, as they stared at their feet in embarrassment. She stood on the lowest step leading to the raised helm and leaned on the banister, sweeping her gaze over them. Ponce came forward with a jangling pouch. She extended her hand and accepted the offering.

"It has come to my attention," she began, "that certain aspects of my anatomy are a popular conversational topic among you." She shook the purse and tutted. "Over a thousand quoine bet on something none of you have the business even thinking about, let alone discussing. Dashaelan would be ashamed."

The ones who'd crewed with him hung their heads.

"First, I'd like to know which of you didn't bet."

Sunshine, rumpled with dark circles shadowing his eyes, snorted from where he leaned against the railing. "Didn't even ask me. Probably knew I'd slit their throats at the suggestion."

"Pretty much," Ponce admitted.

"Who else?" Song asked.

Pinch motioned at the sack. "There's a list inside."

"How convenient," she said, unamused. She read down the list. The names of those who'd refused had been crossed out. It gladdened her to see whose allegiance extended beyond the bare minimum and into their honor, but the shortness of that list wounded her. "Four?" she asked. "Only four of you have some sort of moral conscience?"

"This is a pirate ship," a new swabby argued. "Morals got no place here."

She turned her glower on him. Sunshine threw his fist into the swabby's jaw, knocking him to the deck. After a moment, he said, "I just saved your life."

No one challenged that fact as Song pursed her lips and crumpled the list in her palm. "Leslie," she said, keeping her voice calm, "inform the crew what my breasts are."

He stood motionless as all eyes turned to him. He caught the look in her eyes and knew his answer. "Your own business."

"Thank you."

"What about the quoine?" Ponce asked.

"I'm sure I can find something to do with it." She wrapped the strap over her wrist. "If I ever hear of bets made on my body again, I will drop all of you into the ocean and get myself another crew." She strode to hold open the door of her cabin. "Leslie, Sunshine, Thumbs, Doctor. With me, now. The rest of you scurvy blighters best get back to your posts."

She waited as the four men entered her cabin, then locked the door behind them. Sunshine helped himself to a glass of rum as Leslie returned to the bay bench and the other two sat at the table.

"What was the bet now?" Sunshine asked, leaning back in his chair to put his boots on the table.

"Whether I bind my breasts or they're just small. Never occurred to any of them that nonexistent was an option."

"I told them no," Thumbs insisted. "That is not right to talk about a lady or your captain in such a way. Dash would be furious."

"Doctor, what about you?" Song asked.

He gave an apathetic shrug. "I knew the answer and didn't think it was fair to have such an advantage."

Sunshine snorted into his rum, and Thumbs pretended to cough. Song smirked and tossed the purse onto the table.

"Little over a thousand split five ways is how much?"

Sunshine pretended to count on his fingers for a moment before grabbing the sack. "Paycheck bonus." He upended the purse and let the quoine collect in a small pile.

"I have no need—"

"It's yours, Doctor," Song interrupted his objection. "Take it or it'll just sit collecting dust."

"Split it between you four," he objected again.

"I ain't havin' nothin' to do with your cut," Sunshine growled as he set to work separating the quoine into five piles.

"The rest of the crew will not be pleased to hear you've done this," Leslie warned, lowering himself into the chair beside Song.

"I know nothing of what happened to their quoine," Thumbs said, already counting each quoine up the side of one stack. "Maybe Song threw it in the ocean. But this here?" He dragged an unfinished stack to his chest in a loving hug; some rolled away, back into the original pile. "This here is mine."

Sunshine scoffed in exasperation, shooting him a dirty look. "I wasn't done countin' that." He scooped the quoine out of Thumbs's hands. "It can be yours in a moment."

"While you figure all that out, I'm going to go back on deck and make sure there isn't a mutiny afoot." Song stood and exited alone to find the deck being cleaned and everyone minding their business, not a word spoken among them.

The new swabby was coiling ropes beside the mast, his jaw already darkening from Sunshine's fist. They'd picked him up in Talegrove, but she'd yet to even speak to him, let alone learn his name. He was a wide man, sturdy, albeit short. His hair was black and curly; wide amber eyes that tilted up at the outer corners; bronze skin somewhere between the dark brown, almost black of Thumbs, and the copper tan of Bruce. She'd never seen someone with features like his.

She sauntered over, watching him as he pretended not to notice. It wasn't until she stood right in front of him that he straightened to an untrained attention.

"What's your name?" she asked.

"I don't think you want to hear it." He chuckled.

"No nickname yet?"

"Not yet, miss— Cap— Song."

She smiled and released a breathy chuckle. "Tell me, are you any good at tying knots?"

"Yes."

"Are you the best at it?"

His eyes shifted to the others on deck, who all stopped to stare in curiosity, but none of them had any answers for him. "I, um, no. Probably not."

"Show me your sheet knot."

He blinked at her, then stooped and lifted a rope. He twisted the end up into a perfect sheet knot.

"Stopper."

He untied the sheet knot and did that one next.

"Single shackle."

This knot took him a bit longer, as he wasn't familiar with it.

"Pile hitch," she said when he'd accomplished the previous one. "Sit, use your ankle," she said when he looked around for something to secure it to. Song pointed at the railing.

Terror in his eyes, he walked over, leaned against the railing, and tied the knot. He breathed a sigh of relief when she nodded and tapped her lips with her index finger.

"Running bowline," she said.

He paused in untying the rope. "I don't know that one."

"That's an odd one not to know. It's quite commonly used."

"I was gettin' to it." He released a nervous chuckle.

"Let me teach you." She held out her hand, and he laid the rope in her palm. Song knelt and wrapped it around one of his ankles, then twisted it into the proper knot. "The bowline is one of the best knots. Do you want to know why?"

"Sure?"

She tightened it around his ankle and straightened. "Because it's strong enough to hold through almost anything. Like this." Then she shoved on his chest, launching him over the railing. She struggled, but managed to hold the rope tight and wrap it around a nearby hitch before it got away from her and sent the man into a free-fall. Song leaned forward on the railing, staring down at the man screaming as he dangled upside-down beside the hull.

As much of the crew that could fit crowded out along the railing to watch.

"Song, stop this!" Leslie growled at her shoulder.

"No," she said in a bored tone. She called down, "How's that knot holding up? Good and tight, I hope."

"Y-yes, Song!" he shouted.

"Have you learned from this?"

"Yes, Song!"

"What did you learn?"

"Morals do got a place on your ship, Captain Song."

She smiled at Leslie. "See? I can be a good teacher, too!" She hooked her finger up through the air. *"Puh mih'h ngir'b."*

The rope glowed blue and slithered up over the railing and onto the deck. Her *kijæm* deposited the man atop the neat coil.

Song knelt and untied the rope, then held out her hand to help him stand. "Next time, there won't be a rope attached to your ankle. Do you understand?"

He nodded, still shaking.

"That goes for everyone who forgets Dashaelan's code!" she shouted. "We're pirates, not *animals!* Pirates can have honor. Pirates can be gentlemen. Forget it again, and you all end up hanging over the side of this ship. Understood?" Song clasped her hands at the small of her back, smiling as everyone made sounds of agreement. She turned back to the man. "Now, go sit and calm down with a cup of rum. Then get back up here and work on your knots…Knots." She grinned and winked at him. "Have Toothy show you some of his special ones." She patted his shoulder and sauntered back to her cabin with all the calm in the world.

―――

The sky had gone dark outside. Song sat at the table, feet on the top as she leaned back in her chair. She'd since pondered how harsh she'd been on the crew, but had concluded that she'd been just harsh enough. If she'd gone too soft, they might have pushed boundaries again to test her. A knock echoed into the room, and she let out a long sigh.

"Come." She opened one eye to watch Ponce enter her quarters and stare at her, his lips pursed together. "Yes?"

"Word in private, please?"

She motioned at a chair across from her and stood to pour him a drink. He closed the door and took a seat. They sat in silence, sipping their rum. Ponce spun the glass in place on the table, then took another drink. He had a twitchy air about him, as though jittery from a thousand thoughts, all fighting to break free at once.

"If this is about your quoine—"

"It ain't about the quoine," he said. After a long pause, where he seemed to be collecting himself, he looked her in the eyes. "You and I have a great deal in common."

"Do we, now? Like what?"

"My love of men cost me a better life than this, Song." He let out a deep sigh and closed his eyes. "My full name…is Henry Xavier Barton the Third of Anarchaia, South District, Andalise."

She stared at him with wide eyes, unable to even blink. "As in…"

"Aye. Duke Carey Barton is my older half-brother."

Neither said anything as Song processed the implications, and Ponce steeled himself to continue.

"He's the one that outed me to our father when I was sixteen."

"Why is he a duke? Andalise has no royals."

He shook his head with a bitter chuckle. "A chosen title. Pompous cad."

"I imagine you're telling me this because you heard something?" she said.

"A few men were wondering what your plans are for what we do next. Sunshine said you might pick up the Barton heist where Dash left off."

"It is one of my ideas, yes."

He finished his rum and motioned for permission to get a refill. Song nodded. Once he'd sat again, the bottle now between them, his confidence grew.

"Is that why you fled your comfortable life? Were you outed?" he asked.

"No, but I feared I would be. That, and I was being forced to choose a suitor."

"I didn't flee. I was disowned. Stayed with Toothy for a while. Then Carey went off with the Jewel. Our grandfather left that to *me*. So, I started asking around to join crews with an interest in it, not telling anyone who I am. Just go by Ponce, cause that's what Toothy called me."

"That's why you joined Dash's crew."

Ponce nodded. "I know how much it meant to Dash, so I was going to let him keep it. I just don't want Carey to have it."

"Will you claim the Jewel now that Dash is gone?"

He shrugged. "I don't know. I just want to make Carey suffer, and I want him to know it was me that did it."

Song's mouth twisted in a devious smirk. "Why let him *know* when you can look him in the eyes as *you* make him suffer?"

"You're better at that than I am."

She lifted a shoulder. "Just think of something that will hurt him more than anything. Not physically. The Jewel is one thing, but you need to think more personally. What would break him?"

"I don't know."

"Think on it. I'll bring you in on our planning. I assume you know his weaknesses and can give us the advantage of knowledge."

"He's a womanizer."

"Everyone knows *that*. That's part of the plan." She finished her drink. "Get your supper. And don't worry, your secret is safe with me. No one will know of Henry Xavier Barton the Third."

"Thank you."

"Not like I want to even say that name again. It's a bloody mouthful." She gave him a wicked smile as he went to the door.

He stopped and stared at her longer, a half smile toying with his lips.

"What?"

"It's just…funny, is all."

"What is?"

He released a soft chuckle. "You really don't remember, do you?" Ponce leaned against the wall, arms folded, as he waited for something to occur to her.

"Remember what?"

"We've met before, you and I. You were ten, I was fourteen. Our parents wanted to see how we got along."

Song furrowed her brow. "It must've been awful, and I blocked it from my memories."

"It was a summer in the country with your cousins. You kicked me in the shin and wanted to climb trees the whole time."

She snorted a laugh as a vague memory returned to her. "And you sat below reading poetry out loud like some sad sod. I thought you were my cousin! Why did our parents…" Her smile fell. "Oh."

"Unify two of the most powerful families in Andalise. Inspired idea, which I was completely against, for obvious reasons. Now, come to find out, it would've been a great cover for the both of us."

She swallowed some rum, leaving the glass just under her nose to smell the contents. "If you hadn't been disowned, we'd be married right now."

"Tsingsei Barton."

She made a face at the name, then took another long drink.

His lips fluctuated between a smile and a frown. "You're welcome, I suppose. Nebhàr makes everything worth it."

"At least we're not living a lie and hating it." She smiled. "You may go."

He nodded and left. Song leaned back in her chair and let out a long breath. She'd become a secret-keeper to the crew. Not that it was terrible, but it felt like such a burden at times—to be expected to hold on to information and never let it go. Then again, they all knew who she was under the hood. It seemed an even trade-off.

Twelve

Cannons boomed across the distance. Beneath her feet, wood splintered and shattered. The bite of the gunpowder smoke crept into her nostrils and throat as she opened her mouth.

"*Fire!*"

Crew members relayed the command down below deck and the cannons underfoot thundered, tearing into the hull of the other skyship. Dead men on the other deck twitched at the motion. Leslie's black-and-silver-bladed sword stretched to the throat of the merchant vessel's captain. The man dropped his own sword and lifted his hands in the air. Word traveled across the ships and down to the cannoneers of each.

Her own men trickled up to swing across and help bind the other crew as the opposite cannoneers filed onto the deck, hands at the backs of their heads.

Sunshine patted her on the shoulder. "Bounty took some damage, but damn fine job. Dash would be proud."

Song frowned, but followed him to the other ship. "Hello, gentlemen," she said, striding down the row. "This won't take long, and then all of you can be on your way, uninjured. Well, no more injured than you are now."

"You're that cabin boy," a man said. "Song."

"My reputation precedes me!"

"That's *Captain* Song, now," Sunshine said.

She pursed her lips at him, but let the title affix itself to her name in the minds of the merchant crew. "I'll ask you what I ask everyone. Do you know of Captain Darian's crew?"

"We're merchants. We don't know pirates, except to steer clear," the captain said.

She withdrew her revolver and held it to his forehead. "I doubt that's all you know."

A figure dashed across the deck toward her. Song's arm swung through the air, her shock squeezing back the trigger before aiming. The young boy dropped to the deck. Song's heart thundered, her eyes wide. What had she just done?

The captain shouted, but remained on his knees as Sunshine pressed down on his shoulders to keep him from attacking Song. After a long silence, the boy lifted his head to wail and cup his ear, where her bullet had torn a circle through the cartilage.

I missed…? I never miss.

Relief flooded her, though she steeled herself against showing it. She holstered her firearm and strode to him, lifting him by the front of his shirt. He couldn't have been much older than ten.

Song crouched to his eye level. "What is a boy your age doing on a merchant ship?"

The boy cried harder out of fear.

"I'm all he's got," the captain said, no longer fighting against Sunshine. "Please, don't hurt him."

"Unfortunately, I have to," she said. She lifted the boy and asked her *kijæm* to carry her across to the Stars' Bounty. She dragged him into her cabin, ignoring as he wailed in her ear. "You can stop crying now. I'm not going to harm you. What's your name?"

"Djiard," he said over the spit dribbling from his lips as he continued to sob.

"Djiard. Where are you from?"

"I want my papa." His accent, like the captain's, was heavy Armalinian.

Song had always thought the accent sounded like a person speaking with a marble on their tongue—small mouthed to keep the object behind their lips. Both the father and child had that copper skin like Bruce and hair so dark it was nearly black.

She fished one of Dashaelan's odd stuffed animals from the chest of things she'd decided to get rid of. Part of her assumed they were toys intended for Leslie, which had never reached their destination, and so he'd kept them. She set the toy in the wailing boy's arms and grabbed her bottle of whiskey.

"Hold tight to that critter."

His arms tightened around the feline as she forced his head down and doused his ear in liquor. The boy shrieked in pain as she gripped him tight and held him down.

"It's only going to get worse." She whispered for her *kijæm* to burn the wound closed. Once the mist dispersed and his screaming stopped, she brushed his long bangs to the side. "You ever wanted to be a pirate? I could use a cabin boy."

Djiard shook his head. "No. I want my father."

She let out a long breath. "Me, too, lad." She fished a candy stick from the cup she'd recently discovered hidden in the back of the liquor cupboard. She'd never known Dashaelan had a sweet tooth, but apparently it was another well kept secret of his. "Here you go, Djiard."

He stared at her with tear-filled eyes. "Papa said pirates are mean."

"I am mean. Shot your ear, didn't I?" Song stared at him as he shoved the end of the candy into his mouth. "Have you ever met a pirate before?"

He shook his head.

"Stay in this room and don't touch anything. If you follow that order, you can keep the toy. Can you do that?"

He nodded.

She patted him on the head as a hiccup shook his chest. Song left her cabin and crossed to the other ship.

"What did you do to my son!" the merchant captain bellowed.

"You swear you know nothing of Darian?"

"Why would I know anything about Darian?"

Song shrugged. "People hear rumors. Have you heard any?"

"No." He glowered, eyes misty with fury.

She smiled at him. "Oh, don't give me that look. Your son is fine. For now. So long as you tell the truth."

He took a deep breath. "Alton!"

A man on his knees halfway down the ship leaned forward. "Aye, captain?"

"You crewed with Darian. Right?"

His long, greasy black hair hung down into his eyes. Song froze, staring hard at him. Was this the boy she'd sought for years now? The name was so close, and for a long, curious moment, she figured the captain's accent may have played a trick on her ears. When she approached, though, brown irises stared up at her, rather than the green she couldn't remember the shade of. It had been so long, and she'd seen so many faces, that her first true friend had been reduced to 'a boy with black hair and green eyes'. She didn't have time to dwell on the hollow pit in her stomach as she studied this man on his knees before her.

"Say your name again?" she said.

"Alton."

She pinched her lips together. "Right. Did you know an Alt*ai*n on Darian's crew?"

Alton shook his head. "Doesn't ring a bell." His accent was that of Jashedar's—harder r's than Andalise, but softer than Pishing—solidifying the disappointed lump in her gut.

She squared her jaw and sucked in a deep breath. "Captain, a trade. Djiard for Alton."

Alton's brow furrowed. "No!"

"Done!" the captain barked.

"Lovely!" Song pulled the man up by the arm and used her *kijæm* to carry both of them across. She steered him into the weapons hold, where the single cell stood in the far corner. They'd never used it for anything but spare cargo—save for the men from the Glory after she'd blown it out of the sky. She locked him in and smiled through the bars. "We're going to be friends, you and I."

He spat at her, and it hit her coat. "Might as well throw me overboard now. Filthy pirate bastard."

Song fished out her handkerchief to wipe the saliva from the black leather. "Welcome aboard." She turned to find Pinch and Bells patching the holes from cannon fire—she would have to ask about injuries later. "Pinch, tell him some of your dirty jokes. Make sure he feels well at home."

"You want me to feel at home? Let me out!"

"But you look so cozy!" Bells said to him.

Song returned above deck, winding through men returning with cargo. Once they'd finished looting the other ship, she returned to her cabin to find Djiard up on his toes, trying to get into the liquor cabinet.

"Thought I said not to touch anything," she said.

Djiard dropped and scurried back to the chair.

"I like sweets, too." She fished another candy stick out and handed it to him. "You sure you don't want to be a cabin boy?"

He nodded, his lips too occupied with the candy to respond.

"All right." She studied his injury. If past wounds were anything to go by, it would heal well. "Sorry about your ear. Let's go, then."

He took her hand and walked with her out to the deck. She carried him over to the other ship and set him down in front of his father. The boy stared up at her and held out the toy. Instead of taking it back, she sneered at the captain.

"Not to tell you your business, but maybe a career change that doesn't endanger your *young* child is in order. Children need good parents. Otherwise, they end up like me." She smirked down at the captain.

Song walked away, and the boy cuddled the stuffed feline to his chest. Once the last of her men had cleared the deck of the merchant vessel, she retreated to the Stars' Bounty. As they flew away, she sent the command for the binds to untie and let the men carry on.

"Nice haul," Toothy said beside her. "Got the manifest here."

"What do I do with this?" she asked, staring over the list of items the other ship had carried.

"Dash always had someone double check and cross things off the list that we hadn't taken. Then when we sell things, you can keep track of the incoming quoine."

She pursed her lips at the paper, then at him. "Oh."

"He always sent Pinch and Ponce to do it. Ponce is good with numbers. Pinch…"

"Would follow anyway, so they can fool around." She let out a long breath and took the page. "I'll get them started. Thank you."

"I'll be in the crow's nest."

"Do you ever get sick of it? Being alone up there."

Toothy shrugged. "Sometimes. We all have our place, though."

Song went below, stopping in to ensure Thumbs knew to make food for an extra mouth. Then she found Ponce and Pinch with Bells, patching another hole. She called Bishop over to take Pinch's place, then led the couple to the cargo hold.

"I'm told you two like to…handle the cargo manifest," she said.

"Dash let us work in a pair, yes," Pinch said.

Song held out the papers and let out a long breath. "Because everyone knows what you do when you're alone together. I'm literally the last person to find out." Her eyes bounced between the two as they pursed their lips in uncertainty. "Look… Why don't you two just…stop hiding it? Hmm? Lead by example."

"Who are we leading?" Ponce asked.

"Me. How can I ever accept myself if the others like me also hide it?"

Pinch gave Ponce a devilish smile. "I'm game for it."

She gave them both a long look. "From now on, the Bounty is a place where we can all be ourselves. Openly. I think Dash would've liked that."

"What if I liked wearing dresses?" Ponce challenged.

"Do you?"

"No."

She gave him a wry smile. "That's a shame. You'd be quite fetching in one of those Aibhànocht priestess dresses."

Pinch laughed. "He would, wouldn't he?"

Ponce made a face at both of them.

"If a man wanted to wear a dress, he could. I wear dresses sometimes. I wear trousers all the time. Seems hypocritical for me to deny others. Anyway…keep the noise to a respectful level." Song left the cargo hold, closing the door behind her.

That afternoon, Song scrubbed her hair and slipped on the Aibhànocht dress. She swiped a layer of blue shadow across her eyelids, but no more makeup than that. The men stayed clear of the weapons hold, save for Leslie and Sunshine, who refused to let her go in alone, dressed as a woman. She carried a tray with a bowl of Thumbs's stew and a stein of orange water. Leslie unlocked the cell to let her set the tray on the floor just inside. Once he'd locked it again, she untied Alton's wrists.

"Eat," she said, pushing up the higher, feminine tone reserved for her mother, and now when she played dress-up as her former self.

"Who are you?" Alton asked.

"A friend."

"A spy for Captain Song."

She smiled. "Guilty as charged."

He sniffed the stew.

"It's safe. Nothing in it but the cook's delicious ingredients. He would go on strike if we were to put anything into his cooking."

As she'd hoped would happen, Alton relaxed around a woman. He took her at her word about the food, shoveling some into his mouth.

"Are you here to feed me before Song tortures me?" Alton asked.

She giggled into her fingertips. "No, of course not. But I am here to talk."

"About?"

"Song just wants to know about Darian."

He took a deep breath and stared into the stein. "And if I don't want to talk about him?"

She shrugged. "That's fine, I suppose. We can talk about something else."

"Something like what I'd like to do to you if you open the cage?"

Leslie's fist tightened on the hilt of his sword.

"I'd be respectful!" Alton said. "An absolute gentleman. I would respect you over and over."

She forced a shy laugh. "Oh. Please, you're making me blush."

"Just say the word and open the door. You and me—"

"Time's up," Leslie growled, his glare focused on him, before his gaze settled on her.

"Next time, leave the guard dogs above deck."

Song let out a long breath and lowered her head in acquiescence to Leslie. "I'm not sure the guard dogs will ever leave me alone with you again after that…offer."

He reached through the bars to grab her wrist. Leslie and Sunshine both drew their swords and strode forward, but did not attack as she warned them away with a look.

"What's your name, dearie?" Alton asked.

She paused, contemplating giving him a false name. "Tsingsei Gould. Goodnight, Alton."

He released her and stared with wide, bewildered eyes in her wake.

Sunshine and Leslie followed her into her cabin.

"Why'd you give him your real name?" the former asked.

"Diplomacy," Leslie suggested, his eyes narrowed. "You really think you can get useful information out of this man?"

"I do," she said, arms raised as she twisted her hair into a plait. "He might know how Darian thinks. It'll give us an advantage."

"And you're not torturin' it out of him?" Sunshine asked.

"Trying something new. If he doesn't give me what I want, *then* I'll torture him." She laughed as they gave her similar perturbed expressions. "Leave, so I may change."

They left her alone, and she donned her usual clothing. She sat back in a chair, her feet on the table. Alton's lewd suggestions replayed in her mind for hours until it forced her to her feet to pace. As determined as she'd tried to be to not let it bother her, it only tightened the furious knot in her stomach. This ship was her home, and she wasn't going to let some man make her feel uncomfortable and unsafe with his perverse idea of a joke. It wasn't funny, not to her, and not to any woman she'd ever known. Tsingsei Gould, the gentlewoman schooled in smiling and shrugging off men being vulgar, couldn't say anything. It would be unseemly and unladylike. And it would allow him to think he could continue the behavior.

Captain Song, on the other hand, could say and do whatever she pleased. What she wanted to do was to cause him endless suffering for his verbal violation. But she couldn't just yet, and so she thought of another, less bloody torture. She lifted her hood and strode to the cell.

"*Pu mi-h yt.*"

Blue twisted around his wrists and yanked him upward. The rope she'd left on the floor earlier knotted around his wrists, then attached to the top of the cage, stretching him out.

Alton's eyes locked onto her. "What's this about?"

She took a slow, threatening step toward him. "Keep your licentious thoughts away from Miss Gould, or I will separate you from your manhood. Do you understand?"

"I was just flirting! She liked it!"

"Do you understand?"

"Right, fine. She's your woman, then?"

Song turned on her heel and strode from the room.

"Are you going to untie me? 'Ey! *'Ey!*"

She ascended the stairs and stopped where Thumbs and Bells scrubbed the day's dishes. "Alton gets hardtack until I change my mind."

"Did he not like the meal?" Thumbs asked.

"He liked it. That's why he gets none."

"Aye Cap— Song."

She patted his shoulder and crossed the crew's quarters to where Bruce and Leslie spoke together. "Leslie."

"Song?"

"I feel like hitting something."

He twisted one side of his lips in a wry smile. "I'll be on deck shortly."

She waited at the bow, her sword and utility belt on the step up, her coat draped over the railing. When Leslie emerged, she gave him a moment to remove his sword belt before striking out at him. He raised his arm up to knock her blow away from his chest, then spun to kick her in the stomach. They fought back and forth for a few minutes before he grabbed her fist and held tight.

"Why are you so angry?"

"Because I hate not being able to stand up for myself as Tsingsei." She struck with her other fist.

"You can."

"I really can't. What would people say if Tsingsei Gould had a mean right hook? Ladies aren't allowed to stand up for themselves. We're expected to smile and bite our tongues to keep the men comfortable. But damn it, this is my bloody home! I should feel safe here!"

"You're safe," he assured. "We won't let—"

"I don't need men to protect me from other men!"

Leslie flinched as she hit his shoulder hard with her fist. "I agree. You can take care of yourself. I was more speaking about strength in numbers. We've got your back, but only if you need us."

She paused, then gave him a single thankful nod.

They resumed fighting, and Leslie pursed his lips. "What else has you so angry, Song?"

"Everything. It's all wrong! Dash is gone, Altain is still missing, and now I've got some bloke locked in the cage simply because he *might* know something useful!"

"So let him out."

"I can't."

"Why not?"

She growled. "Because what if he knows something useful?"

"Why don't you just give up on your friend?" Leslie said as he struck her ribs.

"Would you say the same if it were you I sought?"

He chuckled. "No, of course I wouldn't."

Song kicked his knee sideways and followed with a punch, which sent him to his other knee. "Then why say it?"

He stood and jabbed at her. "To make you more determined. Everyone knows the way to get—*urgh!*" He doubled over after her toe struck his navel too hard. "The way to get you to do something is either food, or tell you not to."

She thought about this, eyelids lowered in annoyance, then returned to sparring. She continued to vent her frustrations about Alton and Altain, being captain, and even about the wanted posters bearing Leslie's likeness and how they might handle it. Leslie, however, stopped replying after a while, as sweat stuck his hair to his face and caused his shirt to cling to his skin. She assessed his state and in a near-failed maneuver, tripped him to the deck.

"Are you suddenly out of shape?" she asked with a laugh.

Leslie, still catching his breath, looked up at her, then took her offered hand up. "We've been at this for hours and you've been talking non-stop the whole time. How are you not even a little worn out?"

Song blinked at him, then stared around at the sunset painting the deck. "I...outlasted *you?*"

"First time for everything," he said with a chuckle.

"But...I'm not tired. I could keep going for another hour. More!"

Leslie shook his head. "I can't, so we're either done for the day, or you can find another partner."

She turned her eyes to the few men watching, including the three newest crew members. All three jolted and stepped back, as though refusing to even be considered. Song released a long breath and retrieved her coat and belt.

"Maybe you're losing your touch," she said. "It's been a while since we've sparred."

He smiled at the teasing. "Oh, yes, it must be me. Getting too old."

She scoffed as he descended the stairs. "What a load of bollocks."

Song stood outside the cage in her dress, her hair down and face made up. Alton's lips pressed so tight a ring of white rimmed them. It was a stark contrast to the dark circles around his eyes. He shifted on his feet, moving his weight from one to the other.

"You look terrible," she said.

"Thank you. I feel terrible, too. Song is a right arse, he is."

She smiled. "I think Song is going rather lenient on you."

"This is lenient?"

"It is. Though I'm sure you're used to the cruelty of someone like Captain Darian?"

Alton scoffed.

"What is Darian like? I've heard rumors, but one can never be too sure what's true and what isn't." Song sat on a stool, resting her hands in her lap.

"Is your captain like the rumors?" he asked.

"We're not talking about my captain. We're talking about Darian."

"Not interested."

She released a long, patient sigh. "Why not?"

"I'm only alive because I knew Darian. The second I give it up, I'm as good as dead." Alton spit his contempt onto the floor.

Song nodded to the men at the doorway. Leslie entered the cage to untie the man as Sunshine went up to the galley. Once his hands were free, Alton fought against Leslie. He managed to wrap his hand around the hilt of the Pishing blade. Leslie wrapped his own hand over the one on his sword, then rammed his shoulder into Alton's chest to pin him against the wall behind him. With a single punch to the jaw, Leslie sent the man to the floor, then strode from the cage.

Song watched all this from her seat outside. She hid her vicarious pride at Leslie's expert handling of the situation. She couldn't help staring whenever he fought, hoping to one day match his expertise. Perhaps that was the strange feeling which had confused her before. She'd mistaken admiration for adoration and had almost made a fool of herself in Talegrove.

Sunshine returned and set a tray beside her stool. On it were two steins—one with black tea and one with water—a bowl of porridge, and a sad round cake of hardtack. Song plucked a rehydrated berry from the porridge and bit it between her front teeth.

"Are you done misbehaving?" she asked.

Alton pursed his lips, his eyes fixed on the steaming bowl. "I could've taken him if I'd been rested."

She smirked. "No, you couldn't."

He scoffed down his nose at her, then stared at the food again. "So. Darian?"

"Give us a bite, and maybe I'll talk, yeah?"

She let out a long, deflating breath and retrieved the hardtack and water. Song stepped to the cage and lowered to set the items on the floor just inside, her eyes trapping his in an endless stare. Then she returned to her stool, sat, and lifted the porridge into her hands to swirl the spoon through the sticky mess.

"You know, I'm starting to wonder if you're a liar." She took a bite, her eyes locked on his.

Alton stared at the flavorless wafer in his fingers, his shoulders sagging. "I'm not a liar. And I'm not interested in playing your games, little girl."

"Captain Song likes games," she said. "And if you won't play along, then… Well, I can't make the threats. Not fair to the captain, is it?"

When he said nothing, but gnawed at the hardtack, she stood and took slow, calculated steps to the cage.

"I'm giving you the choice of being honest and open before Song loses patience."

"Least he could've done was send a *pretty* face to tempt me."

She forced a slow smile onto her lips, biting back the urge to grab him and slam his face against the bars. "I see." With that, she took the tray and left.

Leslie and Sunshine followed behind her.

Song didn't return below for the rest of the day. Sunshine delivered the man's hardtack and water instead, but didn't say a word to him. She gave the order for the crew to stay out of the weapons hold, though if they had to go in, they weren't to look the man in the eyes, let alone say anything to him. It had been Leslie's idea. Wait until the man begged to speak to her, just for someone to talk to. She wasn't sure how long it would go on before the man cracked. But as the two-year mark of her separation from Altain neared, she decided she could be as patient as necessary.

Thirteen

*S*ong snorted awake at the gentle shaking. She rubbed her eyes and gave Leslie a bewildered stare. "Since when don't you dump me out of my hammock?"

He gave her a wry smile. "I'm not waking you to train. We're nearing Telbhaniich-Zardi, and I thought you might like the view from overhead."

Her brow furrowed. "It's just another country, isn't it?"

Leslie chuckled.

"What?"

"You should come see for yourself."

She made a face at him. "Get me some tea, then."

He left her to dress. She didn't bother to braid her hair. She took a seat on the stairs beside the helm, where Leslie joined her with two mugs of tea. The sun hadn't yet begun to rise as the blanket of night still covered the world. Somehow, it felt more peaceful than it had any right to be. Song leaned her head on Leslie's shoulder and settled against his warm side.

"The wind is cold," she murmured the excuse for the question he hadn't asked.

In response, he reached back to yank her hood over her head, then settled his arm just behind her, resting against her back. She made a face he couldn't see in the depths of her hood.

"Excuse me," she said, but neither moved to correct the hood nor their posture. Nor did they say anything after, as the silence of the night urged them to be quiet.

Other crew members came onto the deck as they woke each other. Pinch put his arm around Ponce, but the latter still seemed like he was trying to hide the depth of their relationship. Song smiled. It wasn't quite where she'd hoped the openness would be with those two, but it was a start.

"Lights!" Hairy shouted from the bow.

"Take us lower," Leslie said to Sunshine at the helm. He stood and led Song to the bow by her elbow.

The skyship descended as they neared what appeared to be the sunrise, spreading its golden light over the land. Song lowered her goggles and extended the lenses. Her mouth dropped open at the sight.

A massive city stretched across the horizon. Rather than sunlight, the brightness was that of thousands of candles, lanterns, gas lamps—she couldn't be sure what each was, just that it was countless flickering yellow flames. They lined street after street in stretches and checkerboard patterns. They filled crossroads and walking paths through parks, illuminated the sides of stagecoaches and carriages.

A bright light passed through the air, blinding her before it continued along. It was at the top of a tower that twirled two bright beams around and around—a lighthouse. But it wasn't alone, as several more stood over the land as leviathans in the dark, warning skyships of the tall buildings and the roadway of aerial piers stacked upon each other and forming a city of their own above the bright city below.

Song stared farther through the distance, straining to make out where it all ended. "How big is this city?"

"Ah, yes," Knots said behind her. "Chavìse-Kàmbhor. Trading capital of the world. This city stretches from coast to coast."

"That's massive," Ponce said from the other side of the bow.

Song stared out at the bright city. "Why are the names so…"

He laughed. "Don't you know anything besides knots?" He winked at her and leaned on the railing. "We're a little bit of everything here, and so is our language. You hear the Nochtie in it, and the Kerri tongue-twisters."

She blinked at him in stunned silence. "I was wondering about your accent."

"Mine's a very light one, mind you."

"What do you even call someone from here?"

"Zardjiian."

"And are your personal names just as confusing?"

"Well…my name is Kariidjen Farr-Iqilaì. Shortname is Farr." He trilled the r at the end of his shortname in a manner Song had never heard before.

Song gaped, her mind blank of any retort—smart or otherwise.

Knots chuckled. "I warned you that you didn't want to know my name."

The Stars' Bounty crept over the city in silence as the crew took in the sights, smells, and sounds all wafting up to them from below. Sunshine steered around hot air balloons and miniature skyships. Merchants leaned out at them with various items they were trying to peddle to the newcomers.

"Fresh baked bread! First batch of the morning. Still warm." The man held out a paper-wrapped bundle.

On the other side, a woman held up a steaming teapot. "Interest you in a hot cuppa?"

Another man leaned on the long handle of a scrubbing brush. "Scrub your zeppelin for you? Shine it proper, like!"

Song marveled at the accents. The r's in the middle of words were heavy, like those of Pishing; r's at the end of a word were soft, like Andalise. They spoke with wide mouths like Aibhànocht; a's had more of an 'eye' sound, i's had an eh sound, e's were long ee sounds, and the o's were puckered and heavy. It took her several seconds of processing their words to understand what they'd said, and by that time they were almost behind the Stars' Bounty.

Sunshine wove through the vessels in the skies with expert ease, then slid into an opening along the lower dock between a battered corvette—its belly shallow and body long—and a small sloop no more than one third the size of the Stars' Bounty.

"Right," Song said, loud enough to catch everyone's attention. "We can't leave Alton alone on board. We'll need to take it in shifts."

She retrieved a paper and made a list, then posted it to her cabin door. Sunshine promised to be the one to feed the man his hardtack. By the time they made it to the lift in the nearest of the four towers, the dull sunrise had set the horizon ablaze. Song stared at the elevator as her men packed inside. Toothy motioned for her to join, but her feet wouldn't move.

"Are there stairs?" she asked.

"No," Knots said. "Well, maybe at another tower." He motioned at the other towers sprouting up from the city, all a considerable distance from one another, and a long walk from where they'd docked.

She clenched her jaw, nodded, and stepped back. "Oh, bollocks, I left something on the Bounty." With that, she turned and strode away before one of them dragged her into the cage.

"What did you forget?" Leslie asked at her elbow, eyeing the knapsack on her shoulder.

"Bloody nothing. I'm not getting into the damned lift."

"Why not?"

"Because... You know what? It's none of your bloody business, now is it?"

"You're afraid of lifts?" he said.

"And you're afraid of being burned. What of it?"

He chuckled and shook his head. "Nothing. Just...how do you plan to get down?"

She took a deep, challenging breath, squared her shoulders as she stared him down, and strode to the edge of the skywalk. *"Mawtawb ehth oot em kait."* She took the last step off into empty air and plummeted down before a swirling mist rushed to catch her. It slowed her descent and set her feet on the cobblestones just meters from the lift door. She ignored the gaping figures peppered through the early morning streets, their eyes trained on her. Some didn't even hide their pointing fingers.

When the lift stopped with a hiss and a *thunk*, the lift-master opened the gate to let the men exit. Toothy stopped and narrowed his eyes at her.

"What took you so long?" she asked.

"Cheating bastard."

"It's not cheating, it's getting creative." She grinned as he passed.

"You coming?" Ponce asked.

"No, I'll wait for Leslie. Enjoy yourselves, gents."

When Leslie emerged from the cage with more of her crew, he gave her a wry smile. "You just have to make an entrance, don't you?"

She laughed. "It wasn't an entrance, it was getting down."

"Could've found the stairs." He stared at the side of her hood as they walked. "You just like jumping off things, I think."

"It is rather exhilarating."

They continued in silence, both taking in the sights. Song stopped at a message board which stood in the middle of the street, as though it had sprouted from the cobblestones. The two searched for their respective posters in order to remove and destroy them. Not a single wanted poster of any sort was displayed, just advertisements and general announcements. Leslie circled around the other side, then returned with a similar puzzled expression.

"Looking for something?" Knots asked as he, Bishop, and Bells also stopped.

"A few somethings," she said. "Posters for me and Leslie."

He cocked an eyebrow at Leslie. "What are you wanted for?"

Leslie clenched his jaw, brow lowered. "Impersonating a Pishing lord and…"

"And?"

He couldn't help the sneer that curled his upper lip. "…Runaway slave."

Knots barked a laugh. "You won't find any posters for runaway slaves here. You can buy anything in Telbhaniich-Zardi, except a slave. What about you, Song?"

"Two posters for me," she said.

"And?"

"I like to collect my own posters. Wanted to see if my bounty has gone up."

He shook his head and chuckled. "No pirate posters here, unless you break Zardjiian law. We're a right pain in the rest of the world's arse." He said it with a hint of pride and a satisfied grin.

"The other is the reward poster for Tsingsei Gould."

His brow furrowed. "What do you want with hers?"

Her own eyes narrowed. "Really?"

Bells laughed and slapped the back of his head and leaned close to mutter, "Her name ain't really Song, ya dolt."

"Well, excuse me if I've never seen Tsingsei Gould before!" Knots batted Bells away from him.

"Perhaps people are forgetting," Leslie said.

"One can only hope. If you see one, burn it." She directed the last bit to all of them. "Right, then. Let's find an inn with beds available, shall we?"

By the time Song found a room for herself, after the others took them before she could, her feet ached from the kilometers of walking. She and Leslie took the last two rooms of a more posh hotel, where the hostess stared down her nose at their smell, but rented the rooms out all the same. With a passive aggressive mention of the bathing room's location, she left Song at her door, then guided Leslie to his own on the upper floor.

After leaving her belongings in the room, she sought out the bath and locked herself inside. Like most inns across the world, this one had a water heater in the corner. Song ran herself a hot bath, splashing in some fragrant soap that bubbled in a sudsy mountain under the faucets. Once stripped, she settled into the steaming water, groaning as it loosened the knots in her muscles. She brushed her hair, then held her breath and sank below the surface to let the water tangle through her tresses. Song took her sweet time soaking and washing every part of herself again and again to scrub away the smell and filth of skyship life.

Once she'd finished and dressed, she rubbed some of the expensive oils on her coat to cover the smell of her sweat that would never fully come out of the leather. When she exited, she found Leslie leaning against the wall.

"All yours."

"Could you possibly take any longer?" he asked with a chuckle.

"There's hot water," she said. "And oils and bubbles. You're going to take forever, too."

"Good hygiene does take time," he said, then closed and locked the door.

Song stopped at the front desk to obtain directions to the nearest cleaner. She memorized them for later, when she could drop her duffel of dirty clothes and have them washed while she conducted her business during the day. Few places they stayed had such a place, but the larger cities usually did. Annie Gould would have scoffed at the mere notion. She never trusted cleaner workers to not ruin or steal one of her expensive gowns.

With all that taken care of, she returned to her room, took off her coat and boots, and sprawled across the large bed, her face buried in the floral scent of the comforter.

"Song?" Leslie called from the other side of the door, then pounded on it.

Her head snapped up, and she took a deep, groggy breath. She ambled to the door, stretching and groaning, then unlocked and opened it.

"Oh, you just fell asleep," he said, taking in her rumpled state.

"Someone woke me at an unreasonable hour this morning. Also, the bed is like lying on a cloud. Come feel it."

He closed the door and followed, chuckling, then dropped backward across the bed. "Oh. I...don't ever want to stay at another seedy inn again."

"Right?"

"No wonder you fell asleep."

"What did you think happened?"

Leslie gestured vaguely. "Maybe someone saw you. Or you left and were wandering alone out in the city."

"This city is far too big for me to even tempt the idea of wandering off alone in it."

"Shall we go get lost together, or just sleep?"

Song rolled over to stare at the purple satin canopy over the bed. When she remained silent, Leslie lifted his head to look at her.

"Song?"

"I'm thinking about it. I mean, it's rather tempting."

He chuckled. "Decide before I fall asleep."

She released a long breath. "I'm hungry. Stomach wins. Let's go."

When they exited the hotel, the sun was out, though the sky was dark. Song glanced up, expecting to see clouds covering the sun. Instead, she had to stop and look again, eyes wide at the sight overhead. Skyships of all sizes and types crowded the airspace over the city. They moved at a crawl, winding around each other in an ever-moving mass. How none of them collided remained a mystery to her.

After dropping off their clothing at the cleaner, they went in search of food. The only meaty options on the merchant island seemed to be fish, though there were a select few other choices, like poultry or other small animals. After a heated debate between Leslie and Song, they found a restaurant which served the seafood raw. It intrigued Song, but Leslie held back a sneer as a plate of it passed their small table near the door.

"You look like you've just gotten a whiff of the latrine," she said.

Leslie made a face. "Have I ever told you how much I hate the smell of the ocean?"

She blinked at him. "No? What's that got to do with your sour face?"

"I hate the smell of fish, too."

"Then how do you eat it?"

"I don't."

Song narrowed her eyes. "You ate the fishy rolls in Thìse."

"Because I had no other choice for bread. That was the only fish I've consumed since I was your age."

"Did you at least enjoy it?"

"I contemplated ordering an ale to combat the taste," he said. "And I despise ale."

Song chuckled. "Will you at least *try* some with me?"

His brow lowered, but he didn't say anything either way as someone came to set their orders in front of them. Song gave his poultry meal a critical eye, then stared at her various fishes.

"Trade you a bite for a bite of yours?" she asked.

Leslie pressed his lips together. "I don't want any of yours."

"Oh, but please?"

He didn't budge.

"Just one teeny nibble?"

Leslie lowered his brow at her as she cut a strange circle of grain and fish in half and used a spoon to hold it out to him.

"Please? I don't want to try it alone." Song grinned. "I'll buy you an expensive book."

With a grumble and a glare, he took the offered spoon and sneered down at the mass. Song picked up her own half and together they deposited the food into their mouths. She paused in her chewing to stare at Leslie, who let it sit in his closed mouth without moving. Then he bit down once and gagged. He took a napkin, and—being as discreet as possible—spat it into the cloth, then wiped his tongue. He flinched with another threatened gag, then took her drink and swallowed a few gulps, swishing between his teeth with the second. By the time he'd finished with all that, Song had chewed the squishy fish and firm grain surrounded by an odd papery texture and swallowed, deciding she might have a new favorite food.

"What are you drinking?" Leslie asked, face pinched as he stared at the little cup.

She shrugged. "I never heard of it, so I wanted to try." Song took the cup and sipped it, then frowned. "Oh. It's liquor." Her eyes met his.

"I'll be fine."

"Are you sure? I won't find you on the sky docks later tonight?"

"It was just a little. I can hold that much." He gave her a sideways smile. "Stop worrying about me. I might get the wrong ideas."

"Wouldn't want that."

They ate in silence—besides the minstrels in the corner—Leslie glancing at her every so often, and Song playing with drunken memories of the night she'd tried to seduce him. What had he said the next day? That she'd had to have some reason for it. Perhaps she did. But she'd be damned before she'd ever voice what she thought it might be. She didn't know what love was or how it felt, and there was *something* there for Leslie above anyone else. But how could she know what it was if it was so different from anything she'd ever felt before?

After eating, the two wandered for the rest of the day—seeing the sights and heading nowhere in particular. After dinner, Song's feet ached from the wandering. Ponce and Pinch appeared at Song's sides, separating her from Leslie.

"Come with us, Captain," Pinch said.

"Why?"

"Special surprise."

She made a face. "I don't like special surprises."

Leslie chuckled. "I'm going to return to the hotel. Enjoy your…" He motioned for a word, which eluded him.

"It'll be a good time!" Ponce insisted.

"I'm positive it will be anything but," she growled. Song waved to Leslie and let the two cart her off down a side street.

Fourteen

Song swallowed and took steadying breaths to calm her thundering heart. Her eyes darted around the room. Everyone stared back at her.

"Well?" Pinch said.

She pursed her lips at him.

"Any one you like. On us," Ponce said.

She swallowed again.

"I have heard of you," one woman said. She took a few slow steps. "You are the infamous Song? Cabin boy, no?"

"Captain, now," Ponce said.

The women smiled or tittered, a few seeming more interested. The one who approached reached down to unlace her bodice and let it fall, exposing her breasts. She took Song's hand, removed the glove, and set her palm on one of the soft mounds. Song could've gotten lost in that feeling. Lost in the woman biting into her bottom lip as she stared with dark brown eyes through her eyelashes into Song's hood.

"I like dangerous men," she said.

Men.

The word stuck in Song's mind like a pinprick. She lifted her hand away from the soft skin, plucked her glove from the woman's confused grasp, and turned for the door.

"Song?" Pinch asked.

"Not tonight," she said as she spun around to back out. "Sorry, I promised…things."

"Liar," Ponce said.

"True." And then she was out the door and down the steps before anyone could drag her back inside.

Song tried not to rush back to the hotel, but felt like the entire world was watching her cowardly retreat from the brothel. The hostess didn't acknowledge her as she strode past. When Song got into her room, she closed the door and leaned against it, eyes pinched closed and lips pursed so tight they hurt.

Absolute bloody coward.

She reached to unbuckle the first of the three on her coat, then froze. Her eyes widened at the lewd noises coming from the room above her. Heat flooded her face. She spun around and strode back into the hallway, locked the door, and escaped out into the streets of the city.

"Where are you even bloody going?" she muttered to herself.

With a scoff, she strode forward to a street she hadn't yet been down. After a bit of wandering, she happened across a book shop. Two spiraling columns of books decorated either side of the door. The shelves were so full that books stood in piles in between. The man inside seemed all too eager for her patronage as he came forward, wringing his hands together in an awkward, nervous way—albeit friendly.

"Mhàlèriicom tei—"

Song held up her hand to stop him. "Do you speak Common tongue?"

He gave a nervous chuckle. "Right, sorry. I should start with that, ya. Not many outsiders stop in for books."

She smiled, hoping it would soothe him into relaxing his raised shoulders and fidgeting hands, but it didn't.

"Looking for anything in particular?"

Song shook her head and looked around. "I owe a friend something expensive. He'll read anything, I think."

"How expensive?" He led her down an aisle to the back, where a door sat between two filled floor-to-ceiling shelves.

"How expensive can a book get?"

He gave her a sly smile, then opened the door and spoke with a woman in Zardjiian. She exited the room, stopped to give Song a small curtsey, then shuffled to the front of the shop. He motioned for her to follow into the back room and to what looked like a prison cell. Along the back wall, far from reachable past the bars, was a wall of shelves.

"These are the expensive ones. Some are forbidden in certain countries."

She lifted one corner of her lips. "Got anything that would incur the wrath of Pishing?"

He squinted at the spines in the distance. "Wait here, please." He unlocked the cell door and strode in to hover his finger over spines as he scanned the tomes. "I know it's here somewhere. This won't be a cheap tome, mind you."

"What is it?"

"Centuries ago, when the armies of Jashedar conquered Jinjran, the people made these books to remember their history. The conquering king ordered all copies seized and burned. *Ah!*" He grabbed the book in question—a thick tome near as tall as the shelf it occupied—and strode back, running his fingers over the cover as though memorizing the debossment of the words in the black leather. "Precious few remain in the world, and fewer translated to Common from Jin, like this one. If you're caught with a copy in Pishing, you will be executed and the copy burned. Is that rare and forbidden enough for you?" He turned it to show her the title.

Jinjran Before the Usurpation
~
A Remembered History of the Jinjur Peoples

Song grinned and eyed the tome covetously. "How much for a book like that?"

"One thousand quoine."

She flinched. "That's far more than I expected. I could rent a small ship for that price."

His smile fell. "Oh. I do have a—"

Song took his arm as he turned to go back to the shelves. "I said it's more than I expected, not more than I would pay."

He smiled and nodded, then exited the cell, clinging to the rare tome as he locked the door behind himself. As he led her back through the aisles at the front of the store, she paused.

"Do you…"

He raised his eyebrows, encouraging her to continue.

"Do you sell…brown paper novels?" She felt embarrassed for even asking, but couldn't deny being curious as to why her mother had bought them here and there.

"We do." He led her down another aisle.

His nonchalant demeanor set her a little more at ease as he helped find a novel that suited her tastes. The man remained patient and kept any comments to himself as she sputtered and blushed. He muttered something in Zardjiian, but she caught the word Andalise in his complaint.

As she counted out the quoine, he re-counted it, and the woman wrapped both tomes in brown paper and twine, then slipped them into a canvas bag. Song hated parting with so much in one place, and for only two books. She hoped it would be worth it, and that Leslie would find the forbidden knowledge as intriguing as she. No one had to know she'd bought a dirty book. If nothing else, she hoped she learned something she could use. Eventually. When she didn't panic and run away like a pathetic sod. After obtaining directions from him to a nearby stationer's shop, she left, thanking the man until his smile turned to one of embarrassment over her repeated adulations.

At the stationer's shop, the woman gathered what Song requested into a stiff paper box. Five sheafs of two hundred sheets of paper; five ink pots—three black, one blue, and one red; binding supplies; and one rectangle of leather to tie around it with two long leather ribbons. She paid, gritting her teeth at the near empty purse in her hip pouch.

She made her way back to the hotel in the lamp-lit darkness, box in her hands and canvas bag under her arm, taking her time to enjoy the night—giving whoever was screaming over her room enough time to go hoarse, or leave. She had no idea how much time someone even needed.

Back at her room, a woman bustled past as she slid the key in. One glance told her this glistening woman with smeared makeup, hastily fixing her mousy brown hair, was the source of the noise. The woman strode closer until Song could smell sweat and floral perfume. Rather than say anything as the woman glanced at her, she shoved into her room and shut the door.

Song slid the box of supplies onto the small side table. She set the canvas bag containing the wrapped books on the floor beside it. It was late. The sun had been set for a long time, and many were turning in for the night.

Is it late enough?

She removed her coat and boots, double checked the lock on her door, and unpacked the items from the box. She set the paper in an enormous stack and uncorked the first of the ink bottles. Then she sat cross-legged, hands on her knees, and closed her eyes.

"*Zy sniwerm oorth.*"

It took a moment, but her sight slowly came to within Myrmhin's chamber. Her vision roamed about the room and found drawings of herself. As Song thought about it, two pale hands reached out and picked up the pages. The hands moved to the corner, opened the heater, and dropped the pages inside as she whispered the command.

Then she walked out into the dark hallway, somehow able to see despite the sconces being extinguished. A flickering caught her attention. On the ceiling, she found a constantly moving mass, like the *kijæm* mist. It glittered in the darkness as faint sparkles, winking like a blanket of stars in the night sky. It was everywhere. Creeping and swirling along the floor, climbing up the walls, even darting to and fro in front of her. She reached out one pale hand, which didn't belong to her, and the little lights flitted over to settle on her fingers like a butterfly. She walked to the room with the huge sacred tome and opened it.

"Ngeth'erveh epawk."

Song opened one eye, keeping track of both locations in each. The sparkling mist reached into the inkpot and came out as a black string. The mist swirled across the page left to right, then right to left, from the top to the bottom, filling it out with an exact copy of the page within the temple. Once it completed, she turned the paper to its clean side. Simultaneously, the pale hand in the vision of her left eye turned the page inside the book. The *kijæm* worked to copy that, then the next. She remained like this for so long she lost track of time.

When the ink pot dried, she uncorked the next, and the mist reached into the fresh one. After a long while, her head felt heavy, but she'd not finished. Song pushed herself to keep going.

Just a little more.

Something tickled down her lips. Her vision blurred. Still, she copied the text. If she could finish the whole thing in one night, then she wouldn't have to take the risk again later.

Song's vision spotted. Her shoulders sagged. Her head weighed down, and the room spun. She wiped at the trickling over her mouth and discovered a river of blood that painted her hand. Something dripped from her ears. She brushed it with her clean hand to discover her fingers were now bloody. She'd overdone it. Song cursed under her breath. She teetered as she tried to stand, but crashed to the floor.

Fifteen

Song drifted in and out of consciousness, barely able to recognize anything. A word here, a touch there. She had no concept of time. She didn't dream. Once or twice, she genuinely wondered if she'd died.

When she managed to force her eyes open, she had a sliver's worth of sight. On her left, sitting in a chair but hunched over the bed, head down and one arm sprawled outward, was Leslie. He was fast asleep, a tuft of auburn hair dancing in the breath from his nose. To her right at the little table sat Sunshine, playing a card game with Doctor.

Her head refused to move, as though weighed down. Her lips twitched to speak, but didn't open, and so her question of 'what happened?' came out as a soft *mmm*.

Doctor stood and walked to her in his calm way, though Sunshine made it over first as he lurched up and crossed the room in two long strides. After a pause of contemplation, he backhanded Song hard across the cheek. Her head jerked left to point at Leslie. Her eyes widened just a little as she fought to turn her head back to the previous position to stare at him.

Doctor nudged Sunshine out of the way with his patient hand and straightened her head. He set his palm on her forehead and two fingers against her wrist. "How are you feeling?"

Rather than respond with words, she scrunched her face and gave a weak, soft pout through her nose.

To the other side, Leslie stood, the motions having roused him. He stared down at her with black circles around his eyes and something she never imagined on his jaw—several days' worth of unkempt stubble. The roots of his hair clung to each other, telling of days collecting the oils from his scalp. She'd never seen him so disheveled, and almost didn't believe that she was seeing it now.

No one said anything for several minutes as Doctor looked her over, testing her vision and pressing a sore spot at her temple. Leslie had sat back down to stare at the comforter, his arms crossed and jaw clenched. Sunshine still stood over her, looking ready to hit her again the moment Doctor moved out of his way. Doctor helped her sip a little water, and by the time all the fussing had finished, she was ready to go back to sleep. She couldn't focus on Sunshine as he muttered something that entered her ears and distorted to incomprehensible babble. Her eyes crossed and vision blurred. And then she fell back under.

Please. Someone. Anyone. I don't know where I am.

The man's voice repeated in Song's mind, though she remained wrapped in the depths of an ending slumber.

Son of a bitch, it worked… Oh, God, what have I done?

Song's eyes slit open to search for the voice; perhaps she could then get context as to who 'Abitch' was, and what their son had to do with anything.

Someone, please. I just want to go home.

Leslie's mouth was closed, his jaw clenched tight. Doctor and Sunshine were gone. As her mind woke, she realized she didn't recognize the voice playing in her dream.

Tyr er'w oowe, ahrek. Kait'sim a saw sith.

Now that she was more awake than asleep, she realized she'd been dreaming in *kijæm*. The man's voice in her head…had been speaking *kijæm*. She wanted to take some time to contemplate this. Perhaps she could find a Touched in the city. Surely there had to be at least one who knew something. But when Leslie's eyes landed on hers, they locked her in place, and her mind abandoned the planned mission to focus on just how bedraggled the man was.

"You look terrible," she said.

Song sat up as he chewed on whatever he wanted to say. She blinked at how rested and energized she felt—as though she hadn't recently bled a frightening amount from her nose and ears.

"How long was I out?"

Leslie bit his anger between his teeth. "Over a week." He didn't bother to fake the Andalisian accent.

"Oh..." She pushed the covers aside and swung her legs out. Someone had stripped her, and dressed her in clean underthings. She decided not to ask who.

Leslie glared under his lowered brows. She could almost hear the grinding of his teeth as he held something back.

"Just bloody say it," she said.

He stood and balled his fists at his sides. "I found you in a pool of blood."

"I'm fine, aren't I?"

"Fine? *Fine?* Song, I found you in the afternoon, wearing the same clothes from the day before. When did you do it?"

"I don't know. After dark? Sometime after the loud woman left." She pushed to her feet, her eyes scanning every surface with feverish urgency. "Where is my book?"

"*Your* book? That is the holy book of Aibhànocht! That is not *yours!*"

She growled, a sneer forming on her lips. "That is *my* holy book of Aibhànocht. You saw what I did to get it! What did you do with it?"

"It's hidden. Why did you do this, Song?"

"For answers, obviously! I deserve these answers. I deserve to know what melding is and how I can avoid it killing me." Song strode forward into his space. "Give my book back."

"No."

"Give it back!"

"No!"

Anger flared within her. A phrase popped into her mind, and she said it without thinking or knowing what it meant. What happened next did so all at once. Leslie's anger shifted to shock and fear. Through her eyes, he also shifted from a man to some sort of bright object in shades of red, orange, yellow, and green, framed by a purple wall behind him. His heartbeat sounded in her ears—loud, as though her head were within his ribcage. The pounding raced faster as his fear took over.

Leslie lurched backward, away from her. "What did you do?"

His whisper was so desperate, so frightened, that her mood shifted away from the volatile anger.

"*Taivitkæ'ed*," she spoke the command that came to her tongue. Her vision snapped back to normal, and his heartbeat stopped thundering in her mind. "What do you mean? I didn't do anything, I just copied the book. Most of it. I need to finish."

Leslie shook his head as though caught in a daydream. "You can't. You can't keep doing this, Song."

"Why not?"

"You're losing yourself."

"What are you on about?" she demanded.

"Your eyes just now…were red. Bright red. Glowing like a light. Just like your *kijæm* when you burned those men alive."

She took a few tentative steps toward him as he shied away from her. "I'm not going to hurt you. I could never hurt *you*."

He frowned. "What is happening to you, Song?"

She reached for him, taking his hand when he held it out for her. "I don't know. That's why I need that book. And I need you to translate it for me. I need your help."

After a hesitant silence, he nodded. "All right. My Nochtie is rusty, though. Pinch would probably be willing to help."

"Where is the book? I need to finish it."

Leslie released a long sigh, then strode to her bed and knelt to reach beneath the sham. "How much do you have left?"

Song turned the stack of papers over to find the page number. "Twenty, give or take. Damn. I was so close. I didn't want to have to go back."

"What's wrong with going back?"

She clenched her jaw and looked at him through her eyelashes. "I'm using a woman in the temple. If I see through someone, like Bruce or her, then it's easier to focus on what I'm trying to see."

"A conduit."

"Yes. I don't want to put her in danger…but I need the entire book. Damn."

Leslie hung his head in defeat. "I'll…watch over you as you do it. I know it's just a few pages, but I'd rather you do these things with someone present to make sure you're all right."

"All right. I suppose that is a fair argument."

"And after that, I think it's time you limit your use… Or stop it altogether."

Song jolted like he'd struck her. Her mouth gaped open. "What? Why?"

"Because you almost *died!*"

Song scoffed and waved a dismissive hand at him over her shoulder as she searched for her clothes. "I was fine!"

"You wouldn't be, if Sunshine's blood wasn't in your veins right now."

She froze and turned to him. "His what? How?"

"A transfusion—which on its own could've killed you."

"Why didn't it?"

"Something about compatibility. I don't know, I'm not a doctor, and I wasn't paying attention. The Zardjiian doctor tested several of the crew. We all wanted to help. Sunshine was the safest bet, according to him." Leslie ran his fingers through his greasy hair and lowered into the chair he'd spent days sitting in. "Until you have all the answers, you need to stop using *kijæm*. It *will* kill you if you don't."

With a bitter release of breath, she sank into the nearest chair and buried her face in her hands. She didn't want the tears to come to her eyes, but they did. So she hid them from him.

"You can be Song without the *kijæm*," he said so softly she almost missed it.

"But it's part of me, Leslie. Whether I want it or not, it's branded on my very being."

"If I could remove my own brand, I would. We're stuck with our marks. But I do well pretending mine isn't there. I'm sure you can do the same. You must remember how to be a regular person." He moved across the room to kneel in front of her. Without a word, Leslie leaned forward to wrap her in a soft embrace.

"I don't know if I can do it," she whispered.

"Your crew will help however you need."

"I don't know if I can fully let go."

He took a deep breath and shook his head. "A little at a time. No big things. Deal?"

"Deal. Just small things when necessary."

"I'll be beside you for all of it."

"Promise?"

"I promise."

Song glared at the clock on the end table for what felt like the hundredth time. When she turned back to Leslie, his gaze had caught on her. After a while of staring, he returned his attention to the page in the holy book.

"Pinch and Ponce took me to a brothel," she said, breaking the long silence.

Leslie chuckled. "That's where they carted you off to?"

She nodded. "I left, though."

"Why?"

Song narrowed her eyes. "I would think you'd be proud of me."

Leslie leaned back and gave her a soft smile. "Because of how I feel about it?" He chuckled as she nodded again. "If you're going to pay for a woman, this country is one of the better ones to do it in. The women are treated well. I still would rather not. But you could do so with a clear conscience."

She made a face as her cheeks heated over the conversation. "Do you just…go without entirely?"

"No. I'm sure you don't care for details beyond that."

"It's like you know me."

They laughed as she crossed the room to glare at the little clock, as though the rude expression could speed up time. Song paced as Leslie returned to reading.

"Anything new?" she asked.

"I told you, my Nochtie is rusty. The beginning of this is an old dialect. A native would be able to read this better than I can."

She didn't move as she chewed on this. "I'll go find Pinch."

Song left before he could object. She strode through the streets, trying to remember which inn Pinch and Ponce had found a room at. The expressions leveled at her never grew old—at least, those from non-natives. The Zardjiian people didn't care one way or the other, and she suspected it was due to the lack of posters. Sure, some knew the name Caleb Song, but most couldn't have put that name on the hooded figure striding down the road. People of a lighter complexion, though, stopped to gape.

It was just outside the inn where she realized someone was following her. A sword unsheathed. Song spun, brandishing her saber and blocking the weapon.

"Bold of you to attack in public view of everyone," she said to the man.

His light eyes met hers. "Big bounty on your head, lad." His accent was that of western Andalise, reminiscent to Stitch, the seamstress with the dropped h's and stuttered t's.

"Is it? How much has it grown to?"

"You threatened a senator, they say. Thirty thousand, just for that."

She tilted her head. "Do you know if everyone pools into the bounty, or do you just get the one from the country you take my head to?"

His brow furrowed. "What?"

"Would you get thirty thousand if you take me to Andalise, or would you get that *plus* what I'm worth in other countries? I hear Jashedar is cross with me."

"You sure talk a lot. How do you convince your own crew not to turn you in?"

"Because I'm charming, of course." She smiled and unsheathed her eilfass tusk dagger. Song pressed forward against the man's sword and held her dagger to his throat. "Go ahead and take my head to Senator Gould and—"

A whistle blew as two constables rushed up to them. The two broke apart.

Song sheathed her weapons and held up her hands. "Sorry officer. He was trying to take my head. I was just defending myself."

"Do you know who this is?" the man growled, jerking a thumb at her.

The constable shouted in Zardjiian to a shoe shine the next block over. The man shouted something back.

"You are under arrest for harassment and assault. Put your hands behind your back."

The constables separated the man from Song. After they'd cuffed his hands behind his back, the second constable turned to her.

"You can come to the station to press charges, sir."

Song blinked, dumbfounded. "You really don't care who I am?"

The constable shook his head—more like he didn't believe her surprise—then handed her a card with a precinct address on it. She pocketed the card and continued inside the inn, a giddy grin on her face. Pinch and Ponce were, thankfully, in the tavern below the inn.

Ponce looked her up and down. "Why are you grinning like an idiot?"

"Did you return to the brothel?" Pinch asked.

"I did not," she said. "But a man seeking my head for the bounty was just arrested, and I was set free. How bloody beautiful is that?"

They stared at her, then laughed.

"I may need to look at living here full time." She sat at the edge of the table and stole a half eaten bread roll from Pinch's plate. "I need you."

"Why, Captain, I thought you'd never ask." He winked as Ponce chuckled into his stein.

"Not like that, you louse. Can you read Nochtie?"

"What makes you think I can't?"

She shrugged. "I don't know your upbringing."

He shook his head, blue gaze locking onto Ponce's brown eyes. "Aibhànocht gives all children the same education, no matter their status. Unlike Andalise. You know Henry taught Baird to read?"

Song narrowed her eyes. "Who the hell is Baird?"

"Toothy," Ponce said. "It's so much easier when you stick to one name."

Song waved the subject away. "Anyway, I need you to read something."

"What is this something?"

She leaned closer. "The holy book of Aibhànocht that the priestesses don't want you menfolk to know about." She pushed away from the table and strode out the door, knowing they'd be right behind her.

The two caught up with her a block away and fell into step on either side of her. Pinch dropped his arm across her shoulder and leaned down to speak.

"Dare I ask how you obtained said book? Is it authentic?"

"It is not authentic, just a replica," she said. "I copied it."

"When?" Ponce asked.

"Last week."

The men exchanged a look. "Is that what nearly killed you? Copying a book?"

"It was more the distance which did me in."

They inundated her with question after question as they walked, and she had to assure them she wasn't pulling their legs. When Song entered her room, she paused to observe Leslie glowering at the book, the page finally having been turned as a sign of his woeful progress. Upon seeing Pinch, he stood.

"Have at it. I only understand half of it, and I'm sure some of them are names."

Pinch sat, his brow furrowed as he turned it back to the first page. "Bugger me…"

"Told you," Song said.

"What do you want to know from it?"

She raised a shoulder. "I don't know what's in it. Anything important pertaining to the nature and uses of *kijæm*, what is melding, and how do I avoid dying like all the others?"

"If all the others have died, how do you expect to find out how to avoid it?" Ponce asked.

Song thought, then met his gaze. "Tell me how *they* died and I'll avoid what they did."

"I'll need a pen, some paper, ink, and a drink," Pinch said.

Ponce moved the other chair to Pinch's left side and scooted in close until the other man draped his arm across his shoulders as he read. Song retrieved the items requested, and he set them up on his right, pen in hand, as he prepared to take notes.

She looked at the clock. "It's late enough, I think." Her eyes met Leslie's.

He pursed his lips, but nodded. She set herself on the floor with several sheets of paper and all three colors of ink uncorked. She closed her eyes, woke in Myrmhin's chamber, and guided the woman out into the glittering hallway. The woman's fingers worked to turn the book to the back and find where Song had left off.

"*Sehjaip ng'esim ehth epawk.*"

She opened one eye, like before, and kept her eyes trained on her work. In her peripherals, though, the three men gaped in astonishment as the page filled out. She turned it over, and the next page did as well. After a while of staring, Pinch returned to translating, and Leslie stared at her rather than the *kijæm*.

"Myrmhin!" a woman snapped. It seemed to come from behind Song, but she knew it came from behind the woman whose eye she saw through.

Song ignored the voice. "Just a little longer," she hissed, and turned the page.

A minute passed. Then her vision spun in her left eye as someone jerked Myrmhin around. Àbhril's face filled her sight.

"What have you done?" Àbhril growled.

A blade unsheathed. Song and Myrmhin raised their hands over their faces. They cried out as one. Àbhril brought the dagger down into their shared left eye.

"*Noesh'tkehnok ehth kairb!*" Song shouted as she crashed to her back.

The *kijæm* stopped flitting across the paper and flickered out like extinguished candles. Leslie leaned forward on his knees, arm reaching out for her. The other two stood, locked in a paralysis of uncertainty. No one said anything as Song panted up at the ceiling from behind her crossed arms.

"What happened?" Leslie asked.

"She caught me," Song whispered.

"And?"

She swallowed and sat up, then shook her head. Her gaze met Leslie's and his shoulders sagged as he guessed what had happened. Song was glad for this. She didn't want to say out loud the fear that she'd gotten Myrmhin killed. The woman had been her lone advocate and had trusted her. And Song had likely killed her.

Sixteen

The police precinct stood alone on a city block, a jail tucked into the shadows behind it. Song waited with her breakfast—a hot tea and a buttered flaky pastry so delicious she thought she could die happy now that she'd had it. Her pot of tea had grown cold by the time the door to the precinct opened and her target strode out, searching for the person who'd paid his bail. But she had tucked herself around a corner across the street. She gulped down the last of her tea. She set the cup on the little outdoor café table behind her, set the quoine in a neat stack beside it, and sauntered across the road to follow as the man turned down a side street.

He tried to be covert about looking over his shoulder and spotting her, but it was what she'd hoped for. She wanted him to think he could lure her into a dead end or a disgusting back alley. And she would follow him. But she was the one doing the luring.

He turned left down an alley, and she grinned at the predictability of men like him. When she rounded the corner, his blade slid to her throat from behind.

"Did you pay my bail just to follow me?"

"I did."

"Why?"

"I like to send messages," she said.

His free hand wrapped over her hood and yanked it down. "What the—"

Song drew her sword to bat his away and spin on him. "Shouldn't have done that."

"Wait, I know your face…"

"I'm warning you to forget it."

He squinted and tilted his head. "You look an awful lot like that Gould girl…"

"Well, I wasn't planning on killing you, but you just had to go and recognize me."

"You're worth more than I imagined." He took a step forward, and she took one back.

"You really think you'd get both? What do you think would happen? My father would bury you for even daring to imply I'm Caleb Song. And then all I have to do is tell him you put your hands on me, and you'd rot in jail…if he didn't have you hanged for it."

The hinges of his jaw tensed as he thought it over.

"There is no way you take me in and win."

"All right, I won't say nothing."

Song grinned and released a low chuckle. "No. No, it's too late. I can't take you at your word."

He raised his sword, feinted a lunge at her, then spun on the ball of his foot and sprinted away.

She released a long sigh. "*Kært.*"

Her vision shifted into the strange black, purple and teal world, but she saw him clear as day as he ran around the corner. His heart thundered in her ears. Even if she'd lost sight of him, the sound gave away his position. Song pulled up her hood and strode after him.

"So it is sport you've chosen."

He glanced over his shoulder at her, then looked again. His heart raced faster as he stumbled over his feet. He sped toward the main street as she maintained her pace and whistled a soft tune half a block behind him.

"I won't tell a soul! I promise!" he shouted, turning to walk backward. "Will you have mercy, then?"

"I don't believe you. I can't let you go with what you know."

He turned and sprinted into the busy main street.

"Deh'h si'h oot lot'sip si'h awr'd."

Crimson swirls converged on him, wrapping around his hand and forcing him to draw his revolver. Constables rushed from the precinct, blowing their whistles. The entire world stopped around him as he held the gun to his temple.

"Captain—"

"Ryf."

"—Song is—"

Blam!

Molten yellow spewed from the side of his head like a volcano, before he crumpled to the ground to be swallowed by the chaotic wave of yellow-orange as people converged on him or ran away screaming.

"Taivitkæ'ed." Song's vision returned to normal. She turned to stroll through another back alley.

———

Song had a busy day as she collected her clothing from the cleaners, donned her only dress, and found Leslie in his room so he might accompany her to find dressmakers. The tailors from various places measured her to refit styles she'd liked.

That night, a few choice men joined her in her hotel room. Sunshine stared Ponce up and down, arms folded. The latter didn't break eye contact.

"Should've said something sooner, you dumb sod," Sunshine said on a scoff.

Song stretched out on the bed, making herself comfortable against a stack of pillows. "Well, he's said something now. So, he's here."

Leslie had taken up a spot against one of the posts at the foot of the bed, his legs out in front of him as he, too, made himself comfortable on Song's bed. "May as well get started."

Sunshine stood and opened the satchel he'd brought from the Stars' Bounty. He spread the map and journals out on the table for Ponce to look over. "Barton—Carey—moves like clockwork. Always has. He's a creature of habit."

"Always was, yes," Ponce said.

"What sort of information can you give us that we don't know?" Song asked.

"Why don't you go over everything for the two new members of this?" Leslie said.

Sunshine took a deep breath. "All right. Carey Barton follows the same path every year. In a few days' time, he'll be skirting around Telbhaniich-Zardi. He never stops here. Too big of a risk because of airspace congestion and local apathy toward foreign laws and affairs. Dash had the idea to intercept him just past the country, a place where he won't be too suspicious of other craft nearby, but far enough that other ships wouldn't happen upon us."

"He wasn't sure how to get onto the ship," Song said. "I told him it's me. I'll get on board as a damsel in distress."

Leslie clenched his jaw. "I don't like that idea."

"Neither did he."

"The problem we never could solve was getting the rest of us onto it," Sunshine said.

Ponce found a clean paper and drew across the page. Song watched with interest as his left hand traced out the shape of a vessel.

"I can almost guarantee he's still using the family ship."

"And?" Song asked.

"Dash doesn't have a blueprint of it." Ponce finished the sketch as she hopped from the bed to look over his shoulder. "It's a fortress on the outside. But once you're inside, if you know where to go, you can disable it with ease." He drew an area near the back of the skyship. "Found it when I was ten or so. Accidentally left us stranded off the coast."

"I can cripple it, and the rest of you can board," Song said.

"The cannons would tear us to shreds before we were close enough to swing across," Sunshine said.

"Is there a way to…get under the ship?" Leslie asked.

The other three stared at him.

"It's something I've heard of being done before. While those on deck were distracted, a handful of men crossed from the belly of one ship to the other using a rope."

"How?" Song asked.

"I don't know. I didn't ask for details."

She wetted her lips and thought. "All right. I can send a rope across—"

Leslie clenched his jaw. "Song."

"That won't kill me. I won't even break a sweat with something that small."

He pursed his lips, but didn't continue.

"Three men will cross and figure out a way to take the cannons out of the equation. Make as little noise as possible."

"There might still be doors connected to the rooms. The cannons are on decks two and four," Ponce said.

"Right, so barricade the doors, or take the fuses."

"We should douse the lights on the Bounty and follow close behind," Sunshine said. "New moon coming up. Hopefully the timing lines up for us."

Song nodded. "All right. Let's plan this to the letter tonight. Tomorrow we buy supplies and head out to find the perfect spot for ambush."

Suicide or Murder?
Suspicious Death in Chavīse-Kāmbhor

Song stared at the headline on the paper Sunshine held up to read. She bit into her jelly-filled pastry and turned away to meet Leslie's gaze.

"What?" she demanded.

"What did you do?" Leslie asked.

"Nothing!"

"A man shot himself in the head in public," Sunshine said behind the paper.

"See? Nothing to do with it."

"His last words were 'Captain Song is'."

"Coincidence."

"Witnesses say his hand and revolver were glowing red."

Song used her thumb to wipe away a spot of apple jelly from her cheek, then stuck it into her mouth. "Could've been anything."

Leslie's brow lowered, and he fixed a disappointed stare on her that was so intense she averted her gaze. "Song, it wasn't self defense, was it?"

"The article says he was running in panic," Sunshine said.

She gave a small shrug, a frown tugging down the corners of her lips as guilt weighed down on her like an anchor.

"I thought we taught you better than to kill in cold blood," Leslie said.

Her gaze flicked to him long enough to confirm his expression hadn't changed. He hadn't needed to verbally chastise her. All he had to do was give her that look, and she wanted to crawl into a hole to hide from the shame he stirred up in her heart.

"Why did you murder a man in broad daylight?" Leslie asked.

She swallowed her mouthful and released a long, drawn-out sigh. "All right, *fine*. He ripped my hood down and recognized me. I didn't trust him to not tell everyone. And look! I was right. His last words prove it. And *technically*, I didn't kill him."

"You used your *kijæm* to make him do it."

"Yes."

"Then yes, Song, *you* did," Leslie said.

"All right, fine, I did. But don't tell Bruce. He'll be so upset and will remind me that the glitters don't like it."

Leslie folded his arms. "If they don't like it, maybe you should stop."

Song scoffed. "If they didn't like it, then why do they do it?"

"What are 'they'?" Sunshine muttered.

"I will let you know the moment I find out."

The three set out to find vendors around the city who could deliver to the dock by sundown. They'd decided night would be the best time to leave, as the skies were congested during the day. It took them hours, sometimes walking, often waiting in a line, and on occasion catching a horse-drawn carriage.

By the time Song checked out of her hotel room, it was dusk, and the sun was setting. She gripped her duffel in one hand, her knapsack over her shoulder. She found the sky harbor station and approached a man with documents clipped to a board.

"Are you the harbormaster?" she asked.

"I am. I imagine you're asking about your cargo?"

"Yes. The Stars' Bounty. Has it all arrived?"

He eyed what little he could see under her hood. "Captain Song, eh? Smaller than I expected." He scanned over the manifest on his board. "Ah, yes. That pallet right there is the last of it." He motioned at a wooden surface attached to ropes.

"Thank you." She tossed him a quoine and strode over to sit on a barrel. She gave the dock hand on the corner a smirk.

He shook his head as though wanting to object, and motioned for someone above to start the ascent. The pallet raised a little at a time, stopping as the steam motor hissed below. She couldn't tell how the system worked, as it used pulleys and chains hidden within the metal beams above them. When they arrived at that beam, they stopped and the man reached up to do something Song couldn't see. Without warning, the pallet slid on a slight incline toward the long pier where the Stars' Bounty remained roped to the dock. She laughed as a thrill shot through her. The man enabled a braking system that slowed the pallet before it came to a stop against a beam. He pulled a lever and the entire platform lowered to settle on the dock.

"You have the funnest job in the world, sir," she said, then gave him several quoine and hopped off as her men came forward to unload the supplies.

"Another fancy entrance," Leslie said.

She scoffed. "I was making sure our cargo made it safely."

"I'm sure you were."

She made a face and strode past him.

Once they'd gotten out of the mild sunset traffic, Song took Maps into their meeting, so he could look over the Barton course logs and form his own plan. Dashaelan had always been a captain who wanted total control, but Song liked that she could trust certain crew members with specific duties. She also fancied herself intelligent enough to know Maps was far more qualified to that task than she was.

The next day, as they hovered over the ocean, she called the crew on deck.

"I wanted to do something for Dash. Something to honor him." She raised one shoulder in a morose shrug. "I figured completing one of his greatest desires would be sufficient. And so, as some of you no doubt have heard, we're stealing the Jewel of Castildi."

The announcement received murmurs and whistles of astonished approval.

"Within the next few days, Barton and his crew will pass near here. Every man will be on the lookout. Then his men will rescue a poor distressed maiden from Captain Song." She chuckled as some men laughed. "Ponce, Toothy, and Leslie will cross to the ship from underneath while I've got them distracted. I'll disable the prop, they will disable the cannons, and you lot will board and disable the crew. I'd prefer minimal death, but if it's between you and them, make sure it's them. Who is with me on this?"

Every fist raised, accompanied by shouts.

"The ayes have it! Sharpen the swords and clean the cannons, gents. I want everything to go perfectly. Dismissed!" Song waited, one eyebrow raised, as the men dispersed, but Knots came closer. "Yes?"

"Alton asked to speak to Miss Gould this morning when I gave him the hardtack."

She blinked. "That was hours ago."

He gave her a sly smile. "So it was."

"You forced me to wait *hours* to speak with a man I'm trying to get answers from?"

His smile wavered. "Oh. Right, I'm—"

She laughed. "So gullible. Work on that. I would've made him wait, anyway."

"Any chance I can convince you to let me be one of the three to board?"

Song shook her head. "I chose those three for a reason. Prove yourself useful and you, too, will get worthy assignments. Until then, stay in line and do as you're told. Excuse me while I go fetch Miss Gould."

He chuckled. "Aye, Captain."

Once dressed and made up, Song descended to the weapons hold to sit in front of the cage. Leslie and Bruce watched over her this time. Alton stared at Bruce with a wary eye.

"I hear you wanted to speak with me?" she said.

"Your captain plays a dirty game."

"Oh, I'm just here to listen to you complain about Song? Have a good day." She stood, but he reached through the bars, waving for her to stay.

Alton was weak, skinny, with dark circles around his eyes—almost hidden behind his filth. "Please. Feed me something besides hardtack, and I'll tell you everything I know about Darian. I don't know what use it might be to you, but I'll tell you, anyway."

Song looked at Leslie. "It's about lunch. Have Thumbs prepare extra for our prisoner."

Leslie nodded and strode up to relay the message.

She set her sights back on Alton. "Start talking."

He released a long breath. "Deals a deal. All right. Forget everything you know about Darian. All the rumors. He's nothing like that. He's not cruel or uncaring."

"Great swordsman?"

"Well, he was that before, yes. Slashed open his palm, though. Deep. Didn't heal right. He can't hold a sword in his right hand anymore. He drops them. Learned to fight left-handed, but he's rubbish, so he doesn't do any of the fighting."

"What's he like if he's not cruel?"

"What's Captain Song like?"

Song smacked her lips. "Fair, I'd say. Caring. Kind."

"Dangerous," Bruce said from the corner as Leslie returned with a tray of food. "Loyal."

"Yes, those are true as well."

Song smiled as she accepted the tray. Alton moved to the back of the cage, his hands in the air as Leslie unlocked the door. She set the tray on the floor and backed away. Alton dove for the bowl the moment the door closed. He shoved a huge bite into his mouth, opening his lips to suck in air to cool the scalding food.

"Song has a loyalty to this crew," she continued after a minute. "A loyalty to that boy you claim you don't know."

"What did you say he looked like?" he asked after forcing the hot food down with a grimace.

"Black hair. Green eyes. His name is Altain."

Alton laughed. "Do you realize how many people you just described?"

"Surely you heard the name?"

"How many pirates use their real names? Does this crew call you Miss Gould?"

She pursed her lips. "They do not."

Alton said nothing as he shoveled food into his mouth, his eyes scanning between the three. "Does Song's loyalty apply to new crew members as well?"

She sauntered to the cage, an eyebrow raised with interest. "Why do you ask?"

"I really don't like jail cells."

"You got out of piracy and joined a merchant crew."

"Straight and narrow for my woman, yeah."

"And yet…"

"Merchant crew don't make enough to get her out of a hovel. She found a man who could. Piracy pays better, and a single man can do as he wishes."

Song folded her arms, a little smirk playing at her lips. "What could you possibly offer that Song doesn't already have?"

Alton took a deep breath and met her gaze. "I can tell you about his new skyship."

"What about it?"

"They call her the Harpy's Claw. She's a nightmare. And if you're not ready…everyone on this ship will die."

Seventeen

*I*n the early evening, Song called her crew to another meeting on deck. This time, she held up a paper she'd worked on for hours with the help of Sunshine and Leslie.

"Gents, I know Dash never did this, but I think it's time this crew had a written code of conduct. Any who break it will face imprisonment, banishment from this crew, or death." She unrolled the scroll and read off the rules.

1. Your loyalty is to Song and this crew. Our secrets are your secrets.
    Price: Your tongue.
2. All looted goods belong to the captain until sold. Special requests may be made.
3. Conduct yourself honorably.
4. Do not harm women or children unless they are a threat.
5. All crew members are expressly forbidden from raping any man, woman, or child, so long as they fly with Song.
    Price: Your life.

"Why do some list the punishment specifically?" Thumbs asked.

"Because I don't want anyone to question what they will get for breaking these rules. I'll allow negotiations based on severity. But I assure you, if the world finds out who I am under my hood, and it was a member of my crew who told...I *will* cut out your tongue and use my father's influence to erase the claim." She rested on one hip and looked over the men. "The same goes for sharing any secret which is not yours to share. As for the rape, that is non-negotiable. I don't care if it's on a ship we board or in a city we berth in, do it and it costs your life. The only variable will be how much you suffer, and for how long, before you're put down."

Leslie held up a paper where he'd written every man's name in his elegant penmanship beside a line. "Come and sign this. Any man who doesn't will be taken back to Telbhaniich-Zardi after the Barton mission, but will not share in the spoils." He strode to the helm and set it on the map table with a pen and inkpot.

The men formed a line going up one set of stairs and back down the other. Song smiled as every man signed in the best way they could—whether or not they could write. Once finished, the men returned to looking out for the Midnight Wonder—Barton's skyship. Song raised her hood and took the page of rules and the one of signatures downstairs. Alton scrambled to his feet when she walked in. She strode right up to the bars.

"Do you want out of this cage?" she asked.

"I do."

"I have terms."

"Naturally."

She read off the rules, then held up the page of crew names. "The rest of my crew have signed this, all agreeing to my terms."

"And you?"

"I signed it, too. Every living soul I care about is on this page... except one. If you want to be on it, you'll help me get that one."

Alton nodded once. "You have my word."

"Right, well, words mean nothing. We've an important heist coming up. Prove your loyalty to me."

Alton nodded.

"I'll send Leslie down with a bucket and clean clothes so you can wash up." With that, she left and relayed the message. Song nailed the code of conduct to the wall beside her cabin door, then joined the men on deck with spyglasses to their eyes. She lowered her goggles and extended them to see as far as they would allow.

Nearly an hour later, Ponce laughed a little way down from her. "Oy, Hardtack, you clean up nicely."

"My name is—"

"Don't care," Ponce said, then turned back around to stare out at the darkening horizon.

Song laughed and dragged her goggles back to her hairline. "First thing you should learn on this ship: you don't get to choose what anyone calls you. And the more you protest, the more they'll call you that."

"Just ask Whispers," Pinch said.

"Who's Whispers?" Alton asked.

Song motioned beside him. "Leslie. I call him by his name, though. As for me, everyone calls me Song…" She lowered her hood. "*Not* Miss Gould."

His eyes rounded. "W-wait, you're—"

"And don't you go spreading that if you wish to keep your tongue."

He stared around, as though looking for anyone as baffled as he was. She motioned for him to follow her into her cabin. Leslie joined, shutting the door behind them. She poured a small bit of rum into a glass and set it in front of Alton.

"All right, then. Darian's ship. Tell me about it." She poured herself some whiskey and sat across from him as Leslie stood by the door, arms crossed.

Alton jerked a thumb over his shoulder. "Does he always just stand there like that?"

"Only when I'm keeping an eye on someone," Leslie said.

"Oh, that's why they call you Whispers." He sipped his rum, then fidgeted with the glass. "I suppose it's good to have a man like you around for her safety." He motioned with his glass at Song.

"She can take care of herself."

She smiled. "Aw, thank you Leslie." She pointed between Alton's eyes. "He only says that because he's the one who trained me. Trust me when I say I can give almost as good as he does."

"What you lack in brute strength," Leslie said, "you make up for in stamina."

Alton held up a hand. "Look, all due respect, but I don't want to get caught between this sexual tension you've got going—"

"He's not my type—"

"I'm not judging—"

"I like women."

"Oh…"

Song rolled her eyes. "All right. Where were we?"

"He was supposed to be describing Darian's new ship," Leslie said.

She motioned at Alton. "Proceed."

"Right, well, it's a big girl about the size of this one. He runs a skeleton crew, though, to keep weight down," Alton said.

"Why?"

"There's a mechanism in the belly of her. Ain't seen it used, yet—"

The door burst open and Bells leaned in. "Midnight Wonder on the horizon. Heading west."

"You're sure?" Song lurched to her feet and abandoned her whiskey.

"Blue ship, silver zeppelin. Ponce said it's been the same his whole life."

"Right. Everyone out, I need to change. Bells, tell Maps to follow at a distance. Everyone else, go below to the quarters. Douse all lights but those on deck. One low lantern below. I'll meet you there."

The men left her. Once changed into a new dress, Song doused the lights in her chamber. No light shone in through the bay windows on the moonless night.

"*Krahd ehth ni es.*"

The world shone in a monochrome version of itself, tinged by a faint blue. Able to see clearly enough to not ram her knee into the table, she strode outside. As she descended the stairs, she unbraided her hair and ran her fingers through it to untangle the gentle waves. The men murmured as she entered the quarters. All eyes settled on her.

"What?"

"Your eyes are glowing," Pinch said.

"Blue this time," Leslie said.

"*This* time?" Toothy demanded.

"What did you do?"

She made a face at him. "Seeing in the dark so I don't break a toe—or my neck going down those stairs."

Someone raised the wick on the lantern, and Song flinched at the sudden brightness. Her vision returned to normal without her having said anything.

"It's not right," Hairy said, his gaze sweeping over her. "You're too clean."

She looked down at herself. "I agree." Without another word, she gripped the dress at the bodice and pulled until the seams popped.

"Need some help?" Sunshine asked.

"Please."

She stood still and waited as he tore and cut the dress in various areas. Pinch left and returned with a cup of black powder. She rubbed it over her face and arms as he pressed some into the skirt of her dress. They knotted her hair into a tatty mess.

Maps appeared in the doorway, breathless and excited. "We're close enough. Bells confirmed, it's the Midnight Wonder." He scurried back up the stairs to return to the helm.

"Hit me," she said.

Sunshine patted her cheek.

"Hard. Leave a mark." She looked to the back of the room where Leslie prepared with Ponce and Toothy. "Leslie, hit me."

"No."

"Oh, but please."

"He would not hit you if you spat in his eye." Thumbs laughed.

An idea rushed into her mind and she decided to act on it. "Or feed him some of your slop."

Thumbs sobered. "What did you say?"

"You heard me. Your food tastes like refuse."

"You are just saying that to make me mad." And it was working.

"I would rather eat sea scum than another bowl of your wretched mash."

Thumbs's fist clenched. "Take that back."

"The only reason we keep your clumsy hide on board is pity. We just say it's your food because none of us wants to cook."

He pursed his lips at her.

"Shouldn't you be in the kitchen right now? Vomiting out another pot of stew?"

Before anyone could stop him, Thumbs strode to Song and sent his fist into her mouth. Her teeth bit into the flesh at the back of her lips, her head jerked backward, and she grabbed the wall behind her to keep her balance.

"Bloody hell, I had no idea you could hit that hard. Am I bleeding?" She set her fingers to her lips, but nothing came away.

"I am so sorry!" Thumbs reached out toward her.

"Hit me again," she said. "Right here." She pointed at her cheekbone.

"I cannot," he whined.

Song smirked. "Your porridge is like frogs' eyes—"

His knuckles careened into her cheekbone and she fell to her knees.

She pushed to her feet with his help. "Your aim is surprisingly accurate. Don't stop."

"But—"

"Hit me or swim home, swabby," she growled.

Thumbs took her by the shoulders, steadying her before striking a few more times. When he finished, he shook his hand out and took her chin in his fingertips.

"I am sorry."

"How do I look?"

"Battered."

She smiled. "Have some stew cooking when I get back, right?" She patted his shoulder and kissed his cheek.

"Extra mushrooms."

"Time to get scared," Sunshine said.

Hairy removed his shirt and gripped the dulled dagger in his fist. He delivered a wicked smile her way. Song took a deep breath...and laughed.

"I'm sorry," she gasped. "I'm sorry I just..."

"He's gonna attack you and you're laughin'?" Sunshine demanded.

Song nodded, trying to catch her breath through her laughter. "It's *Hairy!*"

"Song, he's goin' to kill you!"

She laughed harder. "He couldn't hurt me if he tried!"

Leslie strode closer, staring down his nose at her. "Close your eyes."

She did as he said, though couldn't stop the small giggles shaking her.

"You're a long way from home, Miss Gould," he said in his native accent, the r's curling hard around his tongue, heavy o's, and all his vowels sounding wrong. "Keep your eyes closed," he warned when she lifted one lid to look at him. "Look at her," he said to the others. "Who wouldn't want to take the virtue of Miss Tsingsei Gould herself?" One of his hands wrapped under her jaw as though presenting her face to the room.

Her heart pounded at the unfamiliar accent with his voice, the darkness, and his repeated use of her name.

"Pretty girl like you surrounded by pirates? You should be terrified."

Fingers caressed along her collarbone. She flinched. The cold steel of a dagger dragged over the knife scar on her neck and she squeaked in shock. Her hands trembled and she balled them into fists at her sides.

"Such pretty skin," Hairy said in a manner that sent shivers of revulsion up her spine.

They pulled her from the wall, a hand over her eyes. They left her standing alone as they circled around to touch her one at a time. Some tugged her hair, another smelled it, another walked his fingers up her shoulder to her neck. They laughed as she squeaked each time. As they did this, they said her name, called it, sang it, whispered it.

"Tsiiingsei!"

"Tsingsei Gooould!"

"Miss Gould!"

Her heart pounded in her ears as she remembered the cruel game her cousins in the country had played on her. They were all much older and thought it would be funny to blindfold her and play a game much like this—only neither was truly a game, but rather minor tortures meant to terrify her.

Her feet shuffled backward a little at a time.

"Oh, no you don't," Leslie said. Then he grabbed her wrist, spun her around, and pinned her against the wall, her cheek smashed to the wood by his palm on the other side of her head. "Who's first?"

She shuddered and screamed. In the back of her mind, she knew they were only trying to scare her. Yet also dancing with that truth was the fear that somewhere deep inside them, this is how they viewed her, this is what they thought. Any day, any moment, they'd be done listening to a mere girl, done being honorable to her, and they'd turn on her in this manner.

It wasn't unheard of for a woman to be taken advantage of by a pirate crew—even to the point of death—and yet somehow her mind had let her fall into a sure security that she was always safe with Dashaelan's crew.

Her eyes tore open, and she shoved with all her might against Leslie's strength, then took off running for the stairs, screaming. Behind her, the men jeered and shouted and laughed, only fueling the feeling strangling her heart. She scrambled forward as Hairy reached out to grab her skirts. She turned to kick him away, then raced up the stairs and out into the cold night.

There it was, the Midnight Wonder, shimmering with its lanterns in the darkness like a beacon for her salvation. Before she fell victim to her own panic, she managed a quick command to her *kijæm* that once in range it drag the prepared rope from a cannon door to secure it some place safe on the other vessel.

"Help me!" she screamed, running to the railing and hanging over the side as though she could stretch the distance. "Help me, please!"

Hairy wrapped his arms from behind her, pressing his palm over her mouth. The sweat of his hand stung against her splitting lip. He threw her to the deck, and she screamed as he climbed over her. He rolled away from her as a man stormed up behind and hit the back of Hairy's head with the butt of a revolver. This man wore a fine officer's uniform. Another man dressed the same swung onto the deck.

"Please," she sobbed as he helped her to her feet. "Help me."

"You're safe now," he said, cocking his revolver and aiming it at Hairy.

Song gasped and threw herself against him as he fired, causing his bullet to enter the wood of the deck. "Thank you!" she shouted.

He growled and tried to shake free of her. The rest of the Stars' Bounty's crew raced up the stairs. Song pressed herself harder into the man so he collided with the other.

"They'll kill us all!" she shouted. "Please! Before Captain Song hears you!"

Panic entered the man's eyes. "This is Song's ship?"

"Yes!"

He spun her into the other man, who wrapped an arm around her waist to pull her to him as he whistled for a return rope.

They swung to the other ship, Song glancing down as the last man shinnied across the rope spanning from the Stars' Bounty to the Midnight Wonder. When her feet landed on deck, she collapsed to her knees. Sobs wracked her chest as she buried her face in her palms and screamed until she hadn't the energy to be scared anymore.

Eighteen

Word had spread across the deck as Song quieted. The men murmured amongst themselves that the notorious Song had worked his way up in the world to captain. It filled her with a strange pride to hear them speak of her with that fearful edge to their words. But she had to remember that for the time being, she was just an abused and frightened lady.

A new man came on deck. His hair was light brown with streaks of white, and time had engraved his age upon his face. She saw right away the resemblance to Ponce in his kind brown eyes.

"What's the meaning of all this?" he demanded.

The others stood at attention. "There was a lady," one said.

"Oh." His interest was palpable. "I see."

"Rescued her from Captain Song, sir."

"He's a captain now? How dreadful that must have been." He set a hand on Song's back and crouched to look at her. "What's your name, dear?"

"Annie," she blurted her mother's name.

"Annie, how would you like to get out of that tattered dress and join me in my cabin?" He gave her a handsome, inviting smile.

"I'd like that very much, sir," she replied.

To her shock, he didn't lead her to the captain's cabin, but rather took her below into a lavish room two decks down. She guessed herself to be between the two cannon decks. Ponce hadn't told her about this, so she supposed it was a new feature for security reasons. She thought over the layout sketches. From her position, it would not be easy to get to the propeller mechanism. She would have to do it by *kijæm*.

Carey gave her a fine gown and let her change behind a divider made of dark wooden panels. He left the room as she washed in a bucket and changed into the dress, which fit loose at the bust and short at the skirt's hem. As she did this, she closed one eye and whispered command after command, sending her *kijæm* searching through the ship. There wasn't a real crew's quarters, just hammocks strung up where there was room, or men cozied up to a wall or crate. On the second cannon deck, she found her three tying up gagged men who'd been sleeping against cannons.

"I'm up one deck," she whispered as Leslie stared straight at her from one of the hundreds of angles she viewed from.

He blinked in bewilderment, then his eyes angled overhead. He nodded, and her sight continued up through a crack in the floor, past herself. Her open eye watched the mist swirl up in a long, slithering string from the floor to the ceiling. Her sight paused in the second cannon room, where she ordered the tendrils of mist to gag and bind those men, then shut and lock the sliding metal blast door. At the end of this room, she spotted part of the perpetual motion mechanism this ship's propeller relied on.

Every ship was different, based on when and where they'd been built. This ship happened to be older than she was, and relied on an outdated system easy to tamper with—though she was no expert, that's just the way Ponce had put it. One tiny switch near the back, easily forgotten and easier to overlook, and the bars pumping up and down slowed to a halt.

By the time she'd finished all this, she had washed, brushed her hair, and secured the dress around herself. It was a mahogany gown with an artificial bustle made by pulling up and layering swaths of fabric from the skirt around her hips to her backside.

When she walked around the side of the separator, she found Carey setting places at a small table.

"I thought you might be hungry," he said.

"Oh, I couldn't impose—"

"Please." He took her hand and guided her to a chair, then kissed the top of her hand as she sat. "I insist."

"And I respectfully decline. I am more tired than hungry."

"Right," he said, his tone light and almost careless, though his features flashed their annoyance. "How silly of me." He sat opposite her and smiled. "I'm Duke Carey Barton. I'm sure you've heard of me."

"Once or twice," she said, forcing a shy smile.

After an awkward minute of silence, he stood and approached her one slow step at a time, running the side of his thumb along his lower lip as he stared lower than her face. He took her hand and urged her to stand. Barton ran a hand along her waist and breathed out a lustful sigh.

"This doesn't quite fit you, does it?"

She hadn't been prepared for how uncomfortable this part would make her, but she clenched her jaw and played along. "It fits well enough. Better than nothing."

"Are you sure about that?" His gaze lingered at the deflated bodice where more ample breasts would fit.

A pale face over Carey's shoulder caught her attention as Leslie stared in at her from an unshuttered window. Leslie scowled at the man, then ducked below the sill.

"Such a skinny thing," he muttered. "How in the world did you fight off pirates?"

Song smirked and gripped his hand as he reached for the row of buttons down the front. "I didn't." She squeezed his hand, twisting his fingers, then hopped backward, unsheathing his sword as she went. She pointed the blade at him and unlocked the window, pulling one pane in as Leslie pushed the other.

He clambered inside, drew his sword on Carey, and pulled a satchel from his shoulders, which Song took. She returned behind the divider to dress in her pirate garb as Leslie tied the man to a chair.

"Who are you people?" Carey demanded.

"Don't you remember what ship your men took me from?" She strode around, satchel over a shoulder as she buckled her utility belt.

"You…" His eyes widened at her, then he turned to Leslie. "You're…Captain Song! But…he's supposed to be only a boy!"

"Oi," Song growled, "over here." She wiggled her fingers in a little wave and gave him a cheerful grin. She retrieved his sword from the table and pointed it at his throat. "That's right, let that sink in a bit."

The absolute insult which overtook Barton's features when he realized he'd been had from the beginning by Captain Song herself sent a thrill through her. Shadow's words echoed in her mind and she knew that this man's insult at being duped by a woman would ensure he told the tale of a mighty man captaining the Stars' Bounty.

"You little harlot!"

Leslie hit him with the hilt of his sword. "That's my captain you're talking about. You mind your tongue. That there is a lady."

"Oh, you flatter me." She winked at Leslie and set about searching for the Jewel of Castildi. After she'd torn apart most of the room in her wake, she growled and went to where Carey gritted his teeth in the chair. "Where's the Jewel?" she asked, as sweet as her frustration would allow.

He glared at her.

"We can do this the easy way, or I can start removing precious body parts." She wiggled the tip of the blade against the wooden chair between his legs.

"It's not here," he scoffed.

Song tutted. "I don't believe the duke is playing nice, Leslie. Take his pinkie."

Leslie pursed his lips at her, his brow lowered. "You're not torturing him."

She scoffed. "I wasn't *going* to, no. Dash was adamant that it doesn't work. But Barton didn't know that, now did he?"

"Sorry."

A gentle knock sounded at the door, and Song opened it.

"Bounty is here," Ponce said.

"You, in." She dragged the man into the room by his shirt, then pointed at Leslie. "Go help on deck."

As Leslie passed her, he said, "Just…don't torture him. You're better than that."

"I said I wasn't going to," she hissed.

Leslie left, and Song turned to smile at Carey as she pulled her hair into a hasty braid. But his eyes were on Ponce.

"Henry?" he asked, unsure.

"Bet you didn't think I'd grow to be the more handsome of us," Ponce said.

"You turned *pirate?* If our father knew—"

"He still wouldn't care about me. That's why you outed me, isn't it? So you could have all of it to yourself."

Carey growled in his throat, but said nothing.

"So, where were we?" Song asked. "The Jewel. Where is it?" When he didn't respond, she sighed and withdrew her dagger, then crouched behind him and grabbed his left pinkie finger. "Where is it?"

"I'd rather die."

"That can be arranged."

"But then you won't find it."

Song laughed low. "You really think I won't tear your ship apart plank by plank?"

He said nothing.

"I will ask one more time where it is."

"Suck my knob, pirate scum."

Song set her sharp blade to his skin and pressed down. She took her sweet time cutting through the flesh at his knuckle. He screamed the whole time, and she didn't even threaten to silence him. She stabbed the tip of her knife between the bones and twisted until the finger came loose with a crack of sinew and connective tissue. She grimaced at it and stood to circle around him.

"Sorry about that. Never severed a finger before." She set the appendage on his thigh, as though presenting him with a gift.

"Careful. Don't want him to bleed out," Ponce said.

"Oh, right. *Dnoo'w ehth zy'ertawk.*"

Mist formed around his finger and turned orange, then settled on his skin with a sharp sizzle. The stench seared into her nostrils—a stomach-churning scent she would never forget, and never grow used to. Sickly and sweet, unlike any other meat being cooked.

When the burning finished, and his screams subsided, she smiled again. "So? The jewel?"

"You said you weren't going to torture it out of me," Carey said

She laughed and crouched to lift his finger from the floor and set it back onto his thigh. "I'm not torturing it out of you! I'm punishing you for annoying me. Now, where is the Jewel?"

"Take off that shirt and try your hand at seduction. You might be better at it." He spat on her cheek.

Song whipped a cloth napkin off the table and wiped her cheek. "I see."

She strode around and cut off his ring finger after pocketing the ring from it. As that finger's wound burned, she removed all of his rings, shoving them into her pouch. She circled back around and flung the finger into his face.

"Consider that your warning that I am not amused."

"Just give it up and we'll leave you be," Ponce said.

Carey sneered at them. He slouched in his seat, panting and covered in a shimmering layer of sweat. He released a long, defeated sigh and closed his eyes. "Fine. It's in the powder barrel."

"Which one?"

"Under the side table in the corner."

Song found the barrel in question and dragged it forward, popping the lid off to let the contents spill out onto the floor. She sifted her fingers through the silty substance until she found a silk pouch buried within. She tore it open. Her eyes sparkled and her hand shook with excitement to be holding the one thing Dashaelan had wanted more than anything in the world, besides his son.

Ponce strode to her and took the Jewel of Castildi. After barely a glance, he threw it on the floor and crushed it with his heel. It shattered into thousands of pieces and dust like crushed glass. "Where's the real one, you halfwit?"

Carey glared at him.

Someone knocked on the door, and Song leaned to it. "Who is it?"

"Pinch."

She unbarred the door and cracked it open. Once she confirmed he was alone, she let him in. Pinch's face scrunched in disgust.

"Sorry," she said, "I burned him a little."

"Whispers asked me to make sure you're not torturing him."

Song's mouth dropped open. "I'm hurt that he wouldn't trust me! Ponce, have I tortured him?"

Ponce shook his head. "No, not that I've seen."

"Eh…" Pinch stared at the fingers on the floor.

"They just came off! I swear! Poor man falls apart under pressure."

He barked a laugh. "If Henry says you ain't torturing his brother…you ain't torturing his brother." He winked at her and turned to scrutinize the man tied to the chair. "Lucky me, I got the good-looking Barton. I've got some choice words for you." He cracked the knuckles of one hand as he took a step closer to the tied man.

Ponce held out a hand to stop Pinch, then asked again, "Where is the real one? Tell us and I promise you won't lose another finger and my beloved won't batter you unrecognizable."

Carey sneered.

"It's my bloody birthright!" Ponce shouted, causing all of them to jump. "If you ever cared about me as a brother, you'll let me at least have this!"

"The maiden's hand," he muttered. "Now, untie me."

"No," Song said. "First, I check that it's authentic. Then we'll see." She shrugged into her coat and buckled it as she ascended the stairs. Once on the main deck, her hood already raised, she glanced around. "Casualties?"

"Ten injured on their crew," Leslie said. "Five injured on ours. They're back on the Bounty with Doctor. Surprise was on our side."

"That it was. Dash's plan was near perfect." She smiled at him and strode forward.

The bound men stared up at her, unable to see the face within her hood. She'd half a mind to show herself to them in a twisted craving for satisfaction, knowing how shamed they'd feel for having willingly brought Captain Song aboard their vessel.

"Leslie, I know I promised you I would cut back on *kijæm*, but… *S'dnæh snehdaim ehth em ngerb.*"

Blue swirls twirled around her and surged toward the figurehead of the ship. However, her *kijæm* collided against a barrier before it reached the woman under the bowsprit. Her mist pressed upon the shifting blue wall as it refused passage from any angle.

"He's got his own Touched."

"I'll get it—"

Song barred Leslie's advance with her arm. "If you go anywhere near the figurehead, it will attack you."

"Is there anything you can do about it?"

"Yes. But you won't like it."

He clenched his jaw. "Don't overexert yourself."

"*T'chuht ehth em ngerb.*"

She waited. Several minutes passed before a man floated into view, suspended by his feet. Spectacles threatened to fall from their precarious perch on his forehead. His long blond hair stood on end, quivering with his movements. He flailed, but couldn't escape.

"Hello there. You must've been hiding well."

He grunted in irritation.

"Drop your wards around the figurehead and I'll let you go."

"I would rather die," he spat.

"And I would rather grant you a life of weakness. How does that sound?" She stood over him, tilting her head to see his upside-down face better.

"What do you mean?" he asked after a minute of fruitless struggling.

"Why, your *kijæm*, of course."

He scoffed. "I'd like to see you try."

"Would you, now?" Song grinned, and it seemed to unsettle him. "*Kijæm si'h eryw'kah.*" She didn't know if the phrase would work, since the only times she'd stolen someone's *kijæm* had been accidental.

Her blue mist spread across the deck like a blanket. Once every inch was covered, it turned red all at once. Swirls of blue seeped from the wood of the ship and from the man. The brightness rose as it spiraled and danced in red and blue and purple. Everyone on deck had to shield their eyes against the dizzying light display. Then, a little at a time, the blue spirals flickered out and were swallowed by the red. It streamed from the man's open mouth and nostrils, dragging blood with it, until everything belonged to her. The winding tendrils dropped the man, shifted to blue, and fluttered away.

"What's it like?" she asked as he whimpered. "Losing your power like that."

"It's like you tore off my arm," he sputtered. "I'm no longer whole. Of all the cruel tortures…" His voice faded as he stared at his shaking hands, as though he'd lost the will to even speak.

"Beautiful," she whispered. Song stood and returned to the bow. "*Z'dnæh znehdaim ehth em ngerb.*"

Long snakes of mist wrapped around the figurehead's wrists like ropes. They spun around faster and faster, wood shavings flying out in arcs around them. The hands detached and floated over to set into Song's palms. The severed wood was sanded smooth in a tight spiral that swirled all the way to the center in a hypnotic whorl.

"How are you feeling?" Leslie asked.

"Fine."

"So far."

"Yes. I'll hurry with the rest." She rushed below and knocked at the door, not blinking at the screams coming from the other side.

Pinch opened the door and delivered a wicked smile. "He's nearly finished."

"I've got the maiden's hands."

"Is that Song?" Ponce called. "I could use your Gift."

Pinch opened the door wider. "Don't look," he said to her.

"At what—*ah, bollocks*. I'm scarred for life." She squeezed her eyes closed behind her raised forearm, blocking the view of Carey screaming pained obscenities at his brother from a pool of blood, his trousers on the floor and his genitals out. Her only saving grace was the amount of blood obscuring his groin from clear view. "Nineteen years, I survived without that sight. Why is there so much blood?"

"Carey's a gelding, now, that's why," Ponce said with a laugh. "Can you patch him up?"

"I suppose." She hissed the words as Ponce cleaned his hands in the bucket of water she'd used earlier.

He accepted the hands from Song and set about prying at cracks with his dagger. The palm of the right hand popped open and a long, jagged stone in a roughly cut triangle clattered to the table.

"Hello, beautiful," he said, holding it up to stare at it lit from behind. "This is it. Genuine article. Pure rojed have these bits of yellow, like a lightning web. Difficult to fake. This one's pattern is all too familiar to me. He could never fool me." Ponce smiled, his eyes lit with a joy she'd never seen before. He'd been reunited with his birthright. His family legacy.

"May I?"

He set the stone in her palm. It was heavier than she'd anticipated. It was long and sharp like a dagger, reaching from the base of her palm to the center of her middle finger. The stone had a chilling blood red color to it; a haphazard web of yellow-golden color streaked through like lightning. Ponce took it back and wrapped it in one of the silk napkins, then secured it within her hip pouch.

By the time they'd finished, Carey had stopped screaming. The acrid scent of his burning flesh stifled them all. Song had the urge to be sick over it, but swallowed her bile away and resisted turning around.

"Well, then, brother," Ponce said, "I sure hope you successfully planted seed in some woman, or it looks as though the Barton name will end with you."

Carey said nothing.

"Doesn't feel so good, does it? Having your family jewels taken from you by force. Your legacy gone. Do you think Father will disown you over this?" He chuckled. "Or maybe they'd accept me back, as I am now the only Barton son who can produce heirs."

"Can't produce with another man," Carey said, though his tone betrayed how hopeless he was despite his bold words.

"I'm only *interested* in men. Doesn't mean I wouldn't step outside my comfort zone just to spite you. After all, I did just handle your stones."

"Are we done here?" Song asked after a stifled gag.

"I do believe we are." Ponce took Pinch's hand and threaded his fingers through the other man's. "I got what I came here for."

The three left and ascended the stairs. Leslie made a face at the smell clinging to them. Song's crew returned to the Stars' Bounty. She used her *kijæm* to open the blast doors in the cannon rooms, then fix the propeller. She stood over the former Touched as he stared at his hands.

"Why?" he whispered at the deck.

"Should've done what I asked. You can untie the rest of your crew. Or you can chase your misery over the side of the ship and leave these men to die. The choice is yours."

"How...did you do it?"

Song raised one apathetic shoulder. "I don't know."

She returned to her ship and stood beside Maps at the helm as the propeller started and he steered them away. The man didn't move for a minute before standing and going to untie the first of many.

Nineteen

*L*anterns illuminated the deck of the Stars' Bounty. Crates of expensive liquors sat open. Men played instruments as others danced around—some dragging Song from the steps to twirl her a few times.

"To Song!" Bells shouted, raising a bottle over his head.

"To Dash!" she shouted, raising her own in reply.

The men cheered, and the laughter seeped into her core.

"Can we see it again?" Hairy asked Ponce.

He withdrew the napkin from his pocket, then held the stone aloft.

"How much is that worth?" Bells asked.

"Millions," Ponce said.

Murmurs rippled through the men.

"We're not selling it," Song barked. "This heist was not about money. This was about honoring Dash and returning the stone to its rightful owner."

"As its rightful owner," Ponce turned to Song, "I present you this gift, Captain Song. A rare jewel for a rare woman."

"What? No, it's yours," she said past the blush heating her ears and cheeks.

"Yes. Mine to give to anyone I want. We couldn't have done it without you, Song. Besides, if I keep it, it'll sit in a chest. It belongs around the neck of a lovely woman."

"Should we find a lovely woman for it, then?"

The men laughed around them, though stayed sedate, staring between the two with shared anticipation.

"To me, you're the most handsome woman I've seen. And we all know I prefer handsome over pretty."

She made a face. "You made it weird."

"Take the bloody gem, Song." Ponce shoved his hands closer to her.

She let out a long breath as silence captured the deck. Song took the Jewel of Castildi from his palms and wrapped a fist around the wide, rounded end, then held it up in the air. Everyone cheered and drank toasts. Song took the gem into her cabin and locked it inside her trunk. When she returned to the party, Pinch dropped his forearm onto her shoulders and leaned closer to murmur to her.

"Thank you for doing that. It's all Henry has wanted in life since I met him."

"Of course," she said. Song sat beside Leslie at the bow step. "I told you I'd be fine."

"I knew you would be. Doesn't make me worry less." He stared at the recorder in his fists. "Did you tell your *kijæm* to do that thing...?"

"What thing?"

"When you told me where you were, your *kijæm* formed into a sort of copy of your face. And it spoke using your voice, albeit distorted. Like ten of you speaking through a metal pipe. It was... unsettling. But also breathtaking."

She furrowed her brow, but also smirked. "Breathtaking? Oh, you flatter me."

He chuckled. "You know what I mean."

She sucked in a deep breath and shook her head. "I didn't tell it to do any of that. I just said where I was and hoped somehow you heard it."

"Oh, so it wasn't you winking at me, either?"

Song shoved her shoulder against him. "*No.* I had one eye open so I could see what I was doing while also viewing through the *kijæm.*"

Leslie leaned back with a sly smile. "I'd rather pretend it was a wink."

She laughed and leaned back in a similar manner. They sat in a long, happy silence, watching the men celebrate. She breathed deep and released a sigh of contentment. "What should we do now?"

"Barton was likely headed for the *Gauv kha Djita.*"

"The what?"

"It's an annual festival in Armalinia. Crowds from across the world go to Pajisr. No quoine, just trades."

"What do you trade?" she asked.

"Anything. They particularly like things from other countries. It's a celebration of culture and allies."

Song rested her cheek on her shoulder. "Sounds like a grand party."

"It is. Lasts two weeks."

"How do they feel about pirates?"

Leslie chuckled. "Not friendly, but not hostile during the *Gauv kha Djita.* Mind the laws of the land and they'll ignore you." He gave her a crooked smile. "Though they also won't stop someone from kidnapping a pirate with a large bounty on her head."

"Then it's a good thing I've got dresses to wear. Would they protect a poor, innocent runaway?"

"Tsingsei Gould is harmless, so yes, they would protect you."

"Good. I would hate to have to kill people to escape and blur the line between Tsingsei and Song." She squinted at the celebrating men.

Everyone was all smiles. Even Sunshine didn't look half as grumpy as usual. Ponce and Pinch were nowhere to be found. Alton was smiling and nursing a drink from a wooden cup as he listened to Bells and Toothy tell him a story which had their hands flapping about to emphasize their points.

"How did Alton do?"

Leslie stared at where her eyes were trained. "Good. Didn't question orders or go off on his own."

"Does he belong on this ship?"

Leslie motioned to Bruce, who had set himself up as a grinning wallflower beside her door the whole night. The large man made his way through the crew members, grunting apologies as he passed. He lowered down beside Song and smiled.

"Happy night."

She smiled. "Indeed, it is. How was your night on the Bounty?"

"I saw," he said. He spread his hands palm-down in front of him. "His glitters became your glitters."

Song chewed on her bottom lip as she thought about it. "Do you know how it happens?"

"The glitters talk."

"To each other?" Leslie asked.

Bruce nodded.

"So *kijæm*…isn't one thing?" Song urged. "It's many?"

"Yes."

After a moment of silence, Leslie said, "Bruce, what do you make of Alton?"

Bruce scrutinized the man in question. "Coward. Saves self."

"Should I kick him off the crew?" Song asked.

"No. He fears you. He will obey."

She nodded and breathed deep the humid night air, glad to have the scent of burning flesh cleaned from herself. "We'll see if he returns to the crew after the festival. If he does, he can sign the contract."

Song stood and whistled for the men to quiet down. All eyes turned to her.

"I know we just had a few relaxing weeks in Telbhaniich-Zardi, but what do you lot say to a huge party in Armalinia to celebrate the Jewel of Castildi?"

Roars of approving cheers filled the air.

She raised her drink to point the mouth of it at Maps. "Chart a course to Pajisr, my good man!"

"Ay, Captain!"

Song squinted at the light streaming in from her bay windows. She didn't remember getting into her hammock, but seeing her boots set neatly below her gave away that she had not done it herself. She rolled out of the swaying fabric and fell to the floor on her back, her tailbone having taken the fall for her. Song grimaced and wondered if she actually had to get out of bed, or if maybe she could remain there for the rest of her life—or at least until the hangover abated.

Her door opened, and she watched battered boots come in and circle around the table. Leslie stood over her, one eyebrow raised. Song met his upside-down stare with a scrunched expression and a soft whimper.

"You look as good as the rest of the crew."

"Worth it," she groaned. She closed her eyes and crossed her forearms over her face. "How long is the flight to Armalinia?"

"About three days to Pajisr from here. Give or take."

She took in a deep breath, then let it out in a long, drawn-out grumble. "All right."

"Would you like help off the floor?"

"No, no, I can manage."

He waited a minute as she didn't even attempt to move, before saying, "Are you sure?"

"Eventually."

Leslie chuckled and left the room.

Song didn't move for a long time—hours, she thought. When she dragged herself up off the floor, she did so with as much groaning as possible. After finding her goggles and sliding them over her eyes to block as much light from her peripheries as possible, she adjusted the sight to neutral. After that, she dragged her coat up over her shoulders, not bothering with any buckles. Song crawled on hands and knees to the door, half wanting to give up ten minutes ago, and half determined to get a mug of hot tea.

"You know what this reminds me of?" Leslie said over her as she crawled out.

Song turned her head to squint at where he stood on the steps.

"That first time your *kijæm* took a real toll on you. In Talegrove."

She paused to contemplate this. "Feels about like that. But also with a hangover." Song crawled to the stairs and sat curled up at the bottom. "Will you get me a tea?" she whimpered.

"You didn't say please."

"Bloody…now. Damn you."

Leslie flicked her hood up as he passed, casting her head in darkness.

"Thank you," she pouted.

He returned a few minutes later and crouched to wrap her hands around the mug before letting go of it. He fished a handkerchief from his pocket and rubbed just under her nose.

"Did I have a nosebleed?" she asked.

Leslie let out a long breath, then gave up scrubbing at the dried blood. "You did."

"I went as easy as I could."

"I know."

Her eyes focused on his through the lenses. "You think I should stop entirely."

"At least until Pinch has translated more of that book. Perhaps if we knew what killed the other Gifted…"

Song wrapped her hand through his and smiled. "I'll stop. Just for you."

"Are you sure?"

"I can't bother you if I'm dead, now, can I? Call me selfish, but I enjoy living. Still so much I need to do and see."

Leslie released her hand and sat beside her on the step. "Such as?"

"Bed a beautiful woman." Song's lips twisted into a wicked smile against the mug.

"And after that?"

"What do you mean?"

"You completed Dash and Ponce's life goals. What is yours?"

She thought about this, but the only word that came to her mind was power. She wanted more of it. Song wanted to be the most powerful Touched in all of history. She wanted travelers of both air and sea to fear crossing her path, knowing they were no match. Instead of saying this to him, knowing how he would feel about such a desire, she thought over the map of the world.

"I can't focus on me until you're safe from Roman," she said. "But…you know that bit on the map at the top?"

"Yes?"

"It doesn't have a name. Every map I've ever seen, it has no name."

Leslie nodded. "And every map draws it differently."

"Why do you think that is?"

"Because no one has ever actually stayed long enough to bother," Maps said from the helm. "Cartographer friend of mine said it's too bloody cold. No point going farther than the coast. We know it's there, but not what it looks like or what's there."

"Once we've dealt with Roman," Song said, "we'll go there. And we'll bloody name it ourselves." She looked over her shoulder at the man at the helm. "And you can be the man who draws it. Everyone in the world will know the name… What's your bloody name?"

"Sherwin Valtrisse."

Song barked a laugh, then grimaced at the noise. "I like that name. Sounds like a count or a duke."

Leslie smiled beside her. "I like that idea. Better than what I expected you to say."

"What did you expect me to say?"

"Something ambitious that would get you killed."

She chuckled and sipped her tea. "Who said investigating the north land isn't that very thing?"

"There's another place we could go," Maps said. "The Great Ocean."

"From the western coast of Armalinia to the eastern coast of Pishing," Leslie said. "They say it's three times as wide as this ocean we're over."

Song scoffed. "People have gone there before."

"But how do we know there really is nothing?" Maps asked. "Easy to miss something in that much nothing."

"We're pirates, not discoverers."

He laughed. "Who said we can't be both?"

As the days passed, the spirits of the crew remained high, though they didn't drink as hard as that first night. They flew in near constant music—sometimes shouting for silence when Pinch would try to teach Ponce how to play his concertina. Knots took it upon himself to teach Song how to throw knives. Her aim was spot on, but the knives would bounce off the mainmast as her throws would make them hit on the length or the pommel. Leslie agreed to teach her to fight with his sword, sparring with her as he wielded her saber in an unsure manner.

"That's the only sword I've ever handled in my life," Leslie complained in an attempt to shut up the laughter over his extreme caution.

It didn't work. The men laughed every time he slashed as though the saber had two sharp edges. Song teased him as well—it was fair game, since he was good at just about everything. Eventually, he traded places with Sunshine. When Sunshine grew too exhausted, Toothy stepped in. By the time she started to feel tired, she'd trained with five different men and had almost mastered wielding the Pishing blade.

They reached the eastern shore of Armalinia at sunset after days of flying. The only other time Song had been to this country had happened in her sleep so long ago, and so far above ground, that she never got a good look at the land. She hopped over the railing and onto the bowsprit to stare in wonder.

The first sight she locked onto as she sat was a frothing shoal at a river mouth. The river water navigated around small islands and boulders to meet the crashing ocean waves in a grand, splashing display. Beyond the clear blue water of the river bordered by vibrant green, was a golden sandy color stretching as far as the eye could see in a flat, almost featureless expanse of desert. To the left, though, was a low cliff plateau stretching far away into the grey distance she knew must be the Screaming Cliffs hidden behind its thick curtain of fog. Her goggles couldn't magnify the distant structures to the right, so she used a spyglass. Treacherous formations loomed over the desert dunes, their layers displayed as red and white rainbows.

"Such an inhospitable landscape," Song said to herself.

"Home," Bruce said behind her.

She jumped, not having known he'd joined her. "You're Armalinian?"

"Yes."

"You speak like someone from Jashedar."

He chuckled. "Yes." He sat and used a thigh to steady his sketchbook.

Song offered him the spyglass. He looked through it to draw the distant formations better. She sat and leaned back, looking at his drawing through the bars.

"You're very good."

"Speak bad, draw good," he said.

She observed him for a silent minute as she thought on his words. They were so simple, and yet she understood the much deeper meaning. "You learned to draw so you could communicate with people better?"

"Yes."

"You know, if you learned to fight—"

"No. I like peace."

"And yet you stay on this ship."

He smiled, but didn't look up. "Leslie is family. You are family."

"You're our family, too."

He finished his sketch and wrote something at the bottom.

"Can I see?"

Bruce passed the sketchbook to her.

"Is this the title?"

He nodded.

Song wondered at the words. She flipped through his other drawings—other landscapes, parts of the ship, and various crew members. All had titles at the bottom. It wouldn't have been anything to blink at, except that they were not in Common tongue. At first she thought it might have been Armalinian, but the symbols were foreign to her, and looked nothing like any she'd seen before. On one page, she found a full paragraph of his thoughts. They were clear and fully formed. All in this language which she didn't recognize, and yet understood. Then it hit her. She twisted her neck around to stare dumbfounded at the man.

"*Kijæm ni tyr ooe,*" she said.

"*Jahoog'ngail ertho eneh nath dnætserd'nuh oot er'eze rahf sti.*"

Song jolted and spun the rest of her body around to face him, eyes wide. "You just spoke a full sentence in *kijæm.*" She leaned around to see past him. "Leslie!"

The man looked up from where he and Maps conversed, the former at the helm, while the latter pointed to various areas on a map pinned to the table. Maps took the helm and Leslie strode to the bow.

"Is something wrong?"

"Bruce speaks *kijæm.* Did you know that?"

Leslie looked at the man.

"Fluently... A full sentence, Leslie."

He crouched beside his friend, his hands clasped. "Are you Gifted?"

"No," Bruce said.

"He's like Myrmhin in Aibhànocht. Connected to it, but can't use it." Her stomach knotted at the thought of Myrmhin, but she ignored it. She met Leslie's gaze—the blue of his eyes darker in the sunset glow of the sandy country. "We need to get on that translation."

"After *Gauv kha Djita*," Leslie said. "Would be unfair to all involved to force us missing it."

"Fine. After." Song handed the book to Bruce and turned around. She leaned back against the bars of the railing, extending one leg out along the bowsprit and dangling the other off the side, and sighed out at the hot desert. One way or another, she decided, she would know all the secrets of *kijæm*, and the secrets of those who wielded it.

Twenty

Wesley

Song took a drink of her diluted rum, relishing the hint of orange from the water. She stared at the letter on the table, contemplating breaking the blue wax seal on the other side. It had paralyzed her like this for an hour, uncertainty staying her hands.

He's never going to bloody read it. What would it hurt?

She wiped her lips on the back of her hand and leaned forward to lift the letter with the caution of someone handling a delicate butterfly. Her eilfass tusk dagger's blade slid under the seal, opening the letter without breaking the star stamped into the wax. With a deep breath, she unfolded it. When it didn't crumble in her hands, she released the sigh held in her throat.

My dear son, Wesley,

I'm writing this letter in the hopes of one day reuniting, though some days I fear it will never happen. You probably think I forgot about you or didn't love you, but that's not true. I think about you every day, and I love you more than all the treasure in all the world. I beg you to read this and try to understand.

Your mother died giving birth to you, as I told you when you were little. But you may not remember that. After I lost her, it grew harder to pay the taxes on our farm. I fell so far behind that I knew Lord Duchamp would take the farm from us. I was ready for this, and had made plans to stay with a friend. But Duchamp didn't take the farm. He took something far more precious to me. He took you. I argued with him, but I couldn't persuade him. I tried to visit you several times, but Lady Duchamp thought it would be too painful and confusing for you, so I stopped.

I worked hard to pay off the debt and get you back. Out of desperation, I resorted to piracy. I only hope you can forgive me for it. I tried to remain a good man I hope you could look up to, but history will decide if I did. You were eleven when I'd made enough quoine to pay my debt and buy your freedom. But when I tried, Lord Duchamp had raised the price due to your value as a worker. They couldn't find you so we could visit, and so I left heartbroken but determined to make up the difference.

You were sixteen the next time I visited. I don't know where you were that day, but no one could find you, and again, the price of your freedom had gone up. I feared no sum would satisfy Lord Duchamp.

I saved all the money I could, even borrowed from Thersial, my closest friend whom I hope you can get to know one day. Together, we'd collected more than enough. I hadn't seen you in fifteen years, and I hoped you wouldn't hate me, though I know you'd have forgotten me by then. I wanted to arrive for your nineteenth birthday, but bad weather delayed me by a week. That's not important. When I arrived, Lord Duchamp had died of some illness, and his son had taken his place. He told me you'd fled Carliolace the night his father died.

I'd missed you by three days.

And now I fear I will die before I ever find you again. But if by some miracle this letter makes it to you, know that I love you. I tried my damnedest, but in the end, I failed you. If you're reading this and I'm still alive, then perhaps you might forgive me, and we can go from there.

I love you, son.

Your father,
Dashaelan Krell

Underneath in a different handwriting was a quick:

P.S. If you need anything, just ask Thersial. He's family.

Song cleared her eyes and set the letter on the table. She swallowed down some rum to clear the knot swelling her throat shut. Leslie wanted the proof of Dashaelan being his father, and there it was. At least, so long as Leslie's memories aligned with what Dashaelan had detailed in the letter.

Song resisted the idea that formed in her head. Until she couldn't. She cleared her eyes again and made sure she didn't look like she'd been crying. She folded up the letter and set it name side up, then left in search of Leslie. He stood at the helm, a little off to the side, to stand in the shade from the zeppelin.

"Leslie. In my cabin, now, please," she said, trying to sound stern but not angry.

Maps took the helm, and Leslie followed her. She pointed at the seat where the letter sat.

He stopped and scowled down at the paper. "What is this?"

"That is a letter for you. And don't even think about tearing it up. It's my property. And I am ordering you to read it."

"I'm not going to read—"

"Then enjoy my cabin in solitude until you do." Song strode out and locked the door behind her.

Leslie pounded on the door, causing the wood to vibrate against her back. "Song!"

"I will not be negotiated with, Leslie! I gave you an order. Now do it!"

His footsteps retreated on the other side. Ponce stared at her from where he and Lucy—a muscular man with a mean-looking under bite—scrubbed the deck. She motioned for them to resume their own business, then folded her arms and made herself comfortable.

Song waited long enough for Leslie to have read the letter three times as slow as possible before she called, "Do you need more time?"

When no reply came, she unlocked the door and cracked it open a knuckle's width to peek in, as though Leslie would shove through. He wasn't at the door, though, so she entered. Leslie also wasn't sitting at the table.

Back against the bay bench sat his curled figure, knees up and arms wrapped over the top to shield his face. In his left hand he held the unfolded letter, and in the other fist he clutched the neck of a whiskey bottle. She closed the door and locked them inside.

After minutes of staring in which he didn't move, she crossed the room in a cautious manner, as though he might run if she walked too fast. When he didn't move, she sat beside him.

"Leslie—"

He unwrapped his arms from his knees and leaned over to grip her. Leslie clutched to her so tight her ribs ached, but she didn't pry him away. Instead, she wrapped her arms around him and held just as tight. After what felt like an eternity, she urged the whiskey bottle from his fist and surveyed the contents.

"What did I say about you drinking whiskey? Something about you're not allowed, if I remember correctly."

"I only had a little," he said, his words slurring out in his Pishing accent.

"You had half the bottle."

"Oh."

"Are you all right?" she asked.

He released a long sigh and shook his head. "No. Not really."

"I'll listen if you want to talk."

He didn't speak for a long time. Then, so quiet she nearly missed it past the boards of the ship creaking, he said, "Thank you."

She made no reply, just squeezed him a little tighter.

"I didn't want it to be true. This whole time, I didn't want..."

"Why?" she asked when he didn't finish the sentence.

"Because I hated my father my whole life. He sold me. How could I not? But Dash was too kind a man to have done that. I could never bring myself to hate *him*. But this..." He shifted, and the paper rustled behind her. "And now it's too late. I wasted the time I could've had with him."

She wanted to say something to comfort him, but all she could think about was how much time she'd had with Dashaelan, and how much of it could have been his. Song clenched her jaw, wishing she could have granted Leslie some of that time.

"I should've gotten into the cage like you told me to."

She shook her head, though he couldn't see it. "No. You were right. I didn't give you a good reason."

"It was an order from our captain. He always said to follow orders or things could go awry... Proved him right."

"Oh, you heard his little one-line codes, too?"

Leslie released a sad chuckle. "Yes. Who on his ship could avoid them?"

"I'm sorry I took all the time with him that you should've had," she admitted in a whisper.

"You can't blame yourself."

"I can. And I will. He treated me like a son or daughter, while at the same time threatening you. He held a bloody dagger to your throat."

He shook his head. "I never feared he'd harm me." He sat up and rubbed his palm down his face. His reddened eyes settled on the paper. "I wonder if he ever looked at me and suspected."

"Did you ever?"

"When he had that dagger to my throat, actually. There was something about it that made me wonder."

"Perhaps it was the strange irony of your own father with a blade against your neck."

They stayed in a mournful silence for a long time as Leslie's eyes scanned over the letter again.

"I wish he'd just said something instead of telling you to lock me up," he said.

She leaned her temple on his shoulder to look at the words on the page. "Maybe he wasn't sure it was true, either. Or he might have been afraid something would happen to you." Song snorted a laugh. "Daft old man. *You?* You're a step down from invulnerable."

"If we hadn't been arguing, I would've been paying attention to the other ship."

"I would've shot that man the moment I saw his revolver."

Leslie pinched his lips together and held back a sob that knocked through his chest. "You were right, Song. It's all my fault."

She wrapped him in a tight embrace, brow furrowed as she held back her own sorrow pressing into her throat. "The blame doesn't rest on just one person. I know that now. We all should've handled it better, including Dash."

"He told me he was proud of me," he whispered.

"When?"

"His last words…"

"That was to me."

Leslie shook his head. "He said it to both of us. At first I thought it was you. But now… Song, he looked right into *my eyes*."

Fresh tears carved their way down her cheeks. "Oh. I thought he was just staring off at nothing. And accidentally called me son again."

"So did I."

Song gasped in the silence, but didn't let him go. "I wish I could go back and save him."

"Me, too."

They stayed in another sad silence, this one lasting far longer than the others. Both would open their lips to say something, think better of it, and close them. After a while, without a word, Leslie slid down to lie on his side, his head resting on her thigh. She comforted him by rubbing his arm or smoothing his hair away from his face. It didn't take long for the whiskey to pull him into sleep.

Song moved his tied hair away from the mark on his neck and frowned at it. She traced her thumb over it, feeling the scar as though memorizing the mark. A circle with an odd symbol that made her think of a bird.

Leslie's pulse beat against her fingers as she rested her hand on his neck and continued to run her thumb over the symbol.

If I could change the past, I'd start with this.

But she couldn't. All she could do was hate this thing on his neck and hate the men who'd put it there. And all she could do about Dashaelan was mourn.

She stared at the ceiling as though looking at the sky and whispered, "I'll keep him safe for you, Dash."

Twenty-One

Leslie woke Song in the early morning, like he had with Telbhaniich-Zardi, so she could witness the city from overhead. As much as she wanted to yell at him for waking her, it made her happy. These weren't sights she wanted to miss, and it warmed her heart to know he cared that much.

She cursed the confusion Dashaelan had caused in her heart as she clasped on her corset. She could do her best to ignore his words, but any time she thought about how much Leslie cared for her, she couldn't help but remember their conversation. Of course she couldn't love someone she wasn't attracted to in that sense, right?

Daft old man. She flinched. *I miss you.*

Once she'd gotten herself into the short-sleeved tan dress, which swooped low to expose what should have been cleavage—requiring Leslie's help to button the back—they stood out on the bow step. The cool morning wind bit at her cheeks. Then she saw it. It started as a glittering in the distance. As they neared, she realized it was the sun glinting from polished marble buildings lining the riverbank. The river itself widened, creating an oasis. Structures lined the opposite bank as well, though it was not a city.

"Brightsteel mines," Leslie said at her shoulder.

"Oh. I suppose I always thought it was an alloy. I don't know why."

He chuckled. "Because steel is an alloy. The word brightsteel is an inaccurate name created by some merchant in Andalise. The locals call it *Brr'shtyll*, after this river."

"Close enough," she said.

"Aye. Close enough."

As they pulled into the Pajisr port, the smells of the city bombarded Song—spices, livestock, burning sand and incense. A thrill shot through her, coaxing a smile from her lips. People were packed into the streets, and music floated on the air, mingling with the voices of the crowd.

Leslie turned to address the rest of the crew behind them. "Any man caught with a weapon in the city will be thrown into prison until the festival is over."

"So don't get caught," Toothy said.

"Don't carry a weapon," Leslie replied. As he stepped off the skyship just behind Song, he leaned in close. "You may want to find something else to wear."

"What's wrong with this?"

"It's hot out and you've too many layers."

She rolled her eyes, but once she'd made it a ways away from the skyship, she realized the sand underfoot was burning at the soles of her boots and sending its unbearable heat into her feet. She slipped into the first clothing shop she found.

The woman did not speak her language, but she understood Song's need for something cooler to wear in the hot weather. She set her up with a flowing pink silk dress with two straps that tied behind her neck and a skirt that ended mid-calf. It was downright indecent, showing far too much skin and leaving no room for her regular undergarments. Song loved it.

She found a pair of sandals with gold braiding that wrapped around her ankles. She paid for everything by trading the vortex pin Stitch, the seamstress from Tarn, had given her, then returned to the Stars' Bounty to stow her old clothing.

What she hadn't expected to find was Toothy trying to pick the lock to her cabin. She met Ponce's eye, who tapped Toothy's shoulder. When he didn't stop trying, Ponce kicked him in the rear so hard he teetered sideways in his crouch. Upon seeing Song standing over them, he scrambled to his feet.

"Sorry. Weren't supposed to catch us. Lovely dress. Great for this weather. How are you enjoying the—" He pinched his lips together when Ponce elbowed him.

"Tell me what you're doing, before I cut off your hands," Song said.

Ponce stepped forward, a charming smile on his lips. "I was trying to…surprise you. I still could?"

She unlocked the door and leaned away from him. "Surprise me how?"

"Something with the Jewel of Castildi."

Her greed screamed in her chest about trusting him with the gemstone. Her mind, however, reminded her that he didn't have to even give her the Jewel in the first place. "All right, fine. You are well within your rights to reclaim it as your own." She threw open the door and strode in to hang the tan Zardjiian dress in the little closet.

"I don't want to do that," he said behind her.

"It better be a good surprise." Song unlocked her chest and dug into it, withdrawing the silk napkin with the precious cargo inside.

"It is. I promise."

"It's from all three of us," Toothy blurted, as though saying so would eliminate punishment for his involvement.

Song locked her door and replaced the key around her neck. "Of course all three of you are involved. It's never just one."

"You look lovely," Toothy called as she strode away.

She stopped at the ramp and smirked at him. "No need to lie. You're already off the hook."

"Not lying," he said with a laugh.

She made a face, unsure how to take the compliment. "I… Well… Don't lose that." She pointed at Ponce's hands. Then she turned and strode away, flustered.

Several minutes later, Leslie caught up with her as she admired a sword with a blade similar to the ones Dashaelan had been so protective of. "Armalinian flatblades," he said. "They take a certain skill to wield properly, though you already know that."

"Shouldn't you be enjoying yourself rather than following me?"

"I was on my way to a bathhouse I know of. The others may take pride in their own musk, but personally, I could use a refresher."

The anticipation of relief flitted through her. "That sounds like the most wonderful thing in the world right now. Lead the way."

The enormous building had grand architecture depicting ocean creatures and rolling waves. It was the only establishment during the festival which accepted quoine, as it had no use for other items. Song entered first, gripping the towel they'd given her. The room was comprised of two large square pools of water with several smaller circular ones along the outer walls. The only free small one sat next to one with dark purple curtains enshrouding it; at the top, it was sheer to let in some light.

Feeling as though every eye was upon her, she followed the example of others and stripped, then lowered herself into the waiting pool, an arm over her chest, and a hand covering between her legs. The water was warm and seemed to be in constant motion. She began to untwist her hair from the braid when Leslie stood over her. Her arms shot to cover her again, but he kept his eyes trained on hers.

"Do you mind if I join you?"

"And if I do?" she said.

"Then I will find another area to occupy and leave you to fight off any strangers who may try to share." His lips twisted into a wry smile.

"Fine," she sighed. "Keep your eyes above the water."

"I will if you will. Though there's a better solution."

He crouched beside a tray filled with various bottles, which Song had ignored due to her having no idea what any of them were. After a moment of searching, he uncorked one and poured a small amount into the pool. The substance clouded the water and expanded until the whole pool was a soft white, which obscured her body just enough to ease her mind. She averted her gaze as he stripped and lowered himself into the water.

"The openness of Armalinia takes some getting used to, I know. My first time here I was a lot younger, and still held to the more prudish natures of our countries. I couldn't even set foot in this establishment for weeks. It's not mandatory that you bathe here, but the water is lovely." He leaned his head back against the blue-tiled floor and closed his eyes.

"I feel so… exposed," she said.

"Like every eye is on you." He smirked. "Look at them, S—Tsingsei. They don't care about you. They are in their own worlds, as you are in yours. No one is watching you."

Song looked around the room. He was right. No one cared. They had their own things to worry about, and some stranger in a bathhouse was nothing to them.

But she still felt as though there were eyes on her, studying her. She turned to look at the purple tenting behind her. The fabric had been pushed to one side, so a small slit was open enough to look out. She strained to see inside, but the cloth released and fell back into place, shutting her out. She shivered—someone *had* been watching her.

Song let her hair stay free, drying in the hot afternoon sun. She perused the traders' stands with mild interest. She had no use for the trinkets they sold, but she did want something to remember the occasion by. Again, Leslie caught up with her.

"You know, there are more interesting things you could be doing, rather than following me around," she said over her shoulder as she continued on her way.

"I got you something," he said.

"You really shouldn't have."

He took her hand and spun her to face him. Gently, he took her right hand and slipped a ring made of smooth white brightsteel onto her thumb.

"Oh, good, it fits. Are you hungry?" he asked.

"What's this?" She held up her hand as her stomach growled between them. "I suppose I am a little famished."

He took her raised hand and led her through the crowd to an area where square rugs with large pillows in complementing colors were set out in the open on a makeshift floor. The floor stretched beyond the dining area to where locals played music and people danced. The music was a strange sort, with gentle drums, shakers, a strange woodwind instrument and a sort of upright violin with a whining fluidity Song had never heard before.

"I like this music," she told Leslie as he guided her to a setting.

"It was always my favorite part about being in Armalinia," he agreed.

A man approached and set his clenched left fist over his chest, then bent at the waist; Leslie reflected his movements. They spoke in a language Song couldn't understand. The man smiled, bowed again, and walked away. When he returned some time later, he set a large tray on the squat oval table at the center of the carpet. A steaming reptile rested atop some greens and roasted vegetables. The creature's back had been sliced open, and they'd arranged chunks of its meat in a more decorative way with roasted yellow fruit and red peppers.

Song was so taken aback she nearly missed returning the man's courteous bow. Leslie observed her in silence. After a while, he smirked and took a metal skewer stick with two long tines, picked up one of each item, and presented it to Song.

"I can't eat this!" Song hissed, turning her head away.

"The presentation is...shocking, yes. But trust me, you want to eat this."

Song eyed him, then opened her mouth around a frown and allowed him to slide the food inside. The spiced meat was juicy and the sweet pepper mingled perfectly with the sour fruit. Her grimace disappeared, and she accepted the skewer from Leslie to spear herself a roasted tuberous vegetable.

"Why do they leave it like this?" she asked.

"It helps keep the meat hot and moist long after cooking," he replied.

She nodded, then concentrated on eating as much as she could as fast as she could without burning more than two layers from the top of her tongue. When she'd eaten her fill, she accepted a sweet fruit drink from the man who'd brought their food. Song turned to watch the people dancing in the cleared space, their bodies moving in a spur-of-the-moment way, none of the moves predetermined like they would be at high society parties.

Leslie observed her in silence, ideas swimming through his mind, passing visibly across his face before disappearing to make room for the next thought. He stood and held a hand out to her. "Come, let's dance."

"I can't dance like that," she objected.

"Then let's dance the way we know." He gave her a charming smile, but it didn't sway her.

Something else did, though, forcing her to take his hand as though she had no will of her own.

"Just one dance," she said.

"Of course."

At first she felt silly waltzing to the liquid music—surely people were staring. But the way Leslie was looking at her, as though the rest of the world had melted away and only the two of them remained, made the paranoia fade. The feeling from his gaze crept up her spine and raised gooseflesh along her arms in the desert heat. She stared back into his eyes, trying to read his mind. There was only one thought she could see in his ocean-blue irises. Perhaps it was that damned emotion Dashaelan and Sunshine insisted was there.

"Stop looking at me like that," she hissed.

"Like what?"

"You know what like."

He gave her a coy smile. "I'm really not sure I do. Describe it to me."

But she didn't want to. She didn't want to say aloud that he must have cared far deeper for her than anyone knew—a strange enamoration which seemed preposterous. How could Leslie look at her the way he did, knowing entirely too well that his feelings wouldn't be reciprocated? Instead of answering him, she closed her eyes and swayed to the music, realizing it had changed to a new song. Before long, they were no longer waltzing, but moving like the waves tangled together before they crashed upon the beach.

With her eyes closed, intoxicated by the music and the movement, she began to understand it. The way his hands gently pulled her to him. The way he buried his face in her curtain of hair, catching her scent and holding it within his lungs just long enough to form a memory.

She pushed away from him as something strange and frightening knotted within her chest. They stared at each other for a long time; the world had fallen silent around them. Confusion knitted her brow as she frowned at him. He stared back with an expression of sorrowful longing. Leslie reached out his hand to her, and she stared at it, wary as though contemplating gripping a snake by the fangs.

She turned from him and strode to their seating; the food had been cleared and their drinks refreshed. Song swallowed down huge mouthfuls, overcome with an unquenchable thirst. Leslie sat across from her, so deep in thought even she had fallen from his world and he was alone.

The man from earlier set a small dish of berries before Song and bowed. He gave an explanation, but she didn't understand him and so smiled graciously, pressing her left fist over her sternum and bowing. Whatever he'd said had pulled Leslie from his contemplations.

"They are from the *caddarik*," he said, unable to hide his curiosity.

"Who is that?" Song asked as she popped a berry into her mouth. They were sweet and tart all at once, and caused her tongue to tingle.

"They are the veiled ones." He pointed across to the other side of the dining area to a collection of women.

They wore matching ornate veils over the lower half of their faces and long sun-yellow dresses with sheer sleeves that covered their hands when relaxed at their sides. They all had near the same physical build, near the same height, black hair the same length and style, with matching brightsteel chain headdresses that wove through their tresses.

"One of them is the sultan's daughter. I think she's a little older than you now."

"Why do they wear that?" The berries were beginning to taste less bitter, but the dining area also seemed to shift beneath her.

"It is part of their culture. The unwed sultania and her court all wear the same attire and move as one entity. You will never see one of them without the others."

"She has to wed before she can take off the veil?" Song asked, angry with second-hand indignation.

"She would also take it off if she ascended to sultana before marriage."

"Oh. But why all that, though?"

"It's for her protection. Supposedly, the women in their lineage are the most beautiful in the world. I heard rumors in the harbor that this one is the loveliest of all. But I doubt the accuracy of that."

"Does anyone know which one she is?"

"You may want to slow down on those," he said. "Only they know which one she is. That's the point."

"Why do I need to slow down?"

"Because right now the floor underneath you is beginning to wobble, and the world is bleeding together like water spilled on a painting. Your head feels hollow and every breath of wind across your skin is ecstasy."

"What are these?" She slid the dish away from her as though they might jump out and force themselves down her throat.

"They're *agidjo*," he said slowly, calling upon some tentative memory. "Alone they are just bitter berries that are best left on the bush. However, when soaked in liquors, they become not only edible but also slightly hallucinogenic." He stared down at her hands, forcing her to realize she'd been rubbing her palms against the soft carpeting on either side of her thighs. "Especially when you eat too many too fast. The effects shouldn't last too long. You'll be fine in an hour."

"It feels..."

"Indescribably wonderful. I know." He observed her with a steady determination. "Be careful of gifts here, Song. All of them come with a caveat."

Song couldn't stop herself from fulfilling the urge to run her palms across his face. She leaned forward, but the world tipped and she fell. Leslie lurched forward to grab her.

"You caught me," she said as his arms held her close to him.

"I always will."

But she didn't hear that. She only heard the music of his skin, shining bright in the setting sunlight. They sat together, her staring at him in wonder as he cradled her. He let her run her fingertips across his forehead, his cheekbones, his lips. She wove her fingers through his auburn hair, pulling gently to let it slip between each finger, watching as the light shone gold upon it. Then she took his hand, gripping it at the wrist to run his fingertips across her own face, down her neck, over her collarbone and then back up to her lips.

"It's like...the world is made of feathers. Hold me tight, Leslie. I don't want the wind to blow me away."

"It's all right, Song, I've got you."

"Don't call me love," she whispered, stuck somewhere between a dream and a memory.

"I didn't."

She nodded. "Good."

A quarter moon shone down upon the city of Pajisr that night. Darkness had not slowed the festivities, only brought new ones to life. Fire dancers; performances with men and women clothed in black and carrying brightly colored props so the items seemed to move unaided; music continued to play in the dining area.

Song had been lying against Leslie, staring up at the stars for so long she'd lost track of time. She no longer feared being blown away by the wind, but the world was still feathers. She was also vaguely aware that they'd been talking for some time, but could not recall any subjects they'd spoken of.

"I don't like this feeling," she admitted in a near whisper.

"The *agidjo* can be quite overwhelming when you eat too many."

"Not that…this."

"What?"

"I know what I want, and this is not it."

He took a breath, then deflated, seeming to surrender to not knowing what she was talking about. "Perhaps you were wrong."

"I'm not wrong! Don't you ever say I'm wrong."

He set the backs of his cool, curled fingers against her cheek to soothe her. "That's not what I meant."

She stayed quiet for a moment longer, then exhaled all the air in her lungs in one dramatic whoosh. "I don't like this feeling."

"What feeling, Song?"

The one where I don't know what you mean to me, she thought. *The one where I feel like I could love you, but I don't even know what love feels like. And I don't know how to figure it out.* Now that she'd thought out her response, she took a breath to blurt all of it out for him. Instead, what came out was an audible sigh.

As one, the *caddarik* approached the two. The women each spoke a few words at a time with another interrupting to finish the sentence.

"They would like you to dance with them," Leslie whispered in her ear.

"What if I don't want to?"

"Why not?"

"Because I'm afraid I'll float away," she said.

"You can say no."

"But I *do* want to."

"You'll be fine, Song. Your head might be floating, but you are not going to float away."

"What if I do something I don't want to do?"

"You won't. But if you're really that scared, you can stay here with me, hating that feeling."

She stared at him. "I don't hate it. I just don't know what to do with it…"

"Except ignore it," he finished for her. "Go. Dance. Enjoy yourself, Song."

With his help, she stood and took the outstretched hand of one of the *caddarik*; her skin was soft and her hands small and delicate. Another took her free hand, and hers were just the same as the first's. It frightened Song. She feared she was seeing double several times over. They twirled around her, a mass of silk. Then one stepped forward. She held her open palm up, offering Song a single flower petal. She let the *caddarik* woman set the petal on her tongue. Minutes passed before anything happened.

Her eyes widened as the music became louder. Colors shouted at her from all directions. The eyes of the woman in front of her seemed to smile.

Song's mind blurred. She swayed to the music. The world became a swirl of dresses and veils, silks and hair. Incense. Wind. Music. Smooth stone walls. Echoing giggles. Kisses on a veil. She followed the smiling eyes. The promise of something wonderful. Silk sheets. Soft skin. A woman here. Lips at her neck. A woman there. *Yes?* Hands running the length of her body. Night air on bare skin. Long black hair. Smiling eyes. *Yes.* Blindfold. Darkness.

Ecstasy.

Twenty-Two

Silk sheets and a cool breeze on her bare skin welcomed Song in the morning. She opened her eyes, preparing to cringe at the brightness of the sun and expecting the pounding of a hangover to leave her feeling miserable. But her eyes didn't protest, and her head felt fine. An immaculate room greeted her. The sheets on the bed were golden, the bed frame painted creamy white. The upholstery in the room matched the bedding, while the walls were sand-colored stone and the floor polished grey marble.

Swirling memories of the night she'd spent in that room brought a warm blush to her cheeks. It was dizzying and out of order, but she remembered every moment. Song wrapped the soft golden sheet around herself and searched for her clothing. After a few minutes, the door opened, and she jerked upright. The *caddarik* stood in the doorway, their long hair tied up in identical topknots. One strode forward to wrap a silky robe around her, another took her hand, and soon they'd whisked her down the hallway and through a set of slatted double doors into a bathing room just as immaculate as the bedroom.

They removed the robe and urged her into the porcelain pool set into the marble floor. One woman stripped off her robe and kicked off her flat shoes, leaving on her wide legged grey pants and plain tan apodesme. The others followed suit. Three of the women lowered into the pool with her while the remaining two knelt with combs to part her hair. Each of those two worked with half her hair, brushing it with detangling combs and then thick whisker brushes. As those two worked, the three in the pool used cloths to rub sandalwood soaps across her skin. One of them, though—the one with the smiling eyes the color of bright amber—used her bare hands. The other two worked on her limbs or back, but this one rubbed the soap over her abdomen.

Song recognized differences in them like this, so she gave them names in her head. There was Smiling Eyes, who ran her delicate hands along Song's stomach. The washing girl on the right had a mole on the inner part of her left breast, so she called her Mole. The other had freckles across her décolletage, like one might have on the bridge of their nose—she called her Freckles. One woman behind her to the right had a deeper voice than the others, so she called her Deep. The other couldn't have been less delicate with Song's scalp if she'd tried, so she called her Jerk.

When Smiling Eyes trailed her hands upward, Song slapped her arms over her chest. The women laughed, and Smiling Eyes said something.

"I don't speak Armalinian," Song said.

When it became clear to Smiling Eyes that Song would not remove her hands, she spoke to the others. Freckles replied something with an impish tone and Jerk giggled. With a laugh, Smiling Eyes worked the elaborate knot between her breasts free, unwrapped the garment, and set it on the floor beside the pool. She took Song's right hand with gentle insistence and set it on her own breast. She recognized that feeling from the night— something she'd experienced past the blindfold.

Smiling Eyes coaxed Song's left arm away from her chest, then ran her palms over to lather the area with soap. Song had always considered herself tan, but her skin seemed pale against the deep copper of these women.

Song had been so consumed by the beautiful eyes capturing hers that she didn't notice when the two stopped styling her hair, only that it had stopped. In her peripherals, the other women exited the pool now that almost every inch of her had been cleaned. She ran her fingertips along the silky copper skin at Smiling Eyes's collarbone. She became incredibly aware of the hand trailing down her stomach, over her bellybutton. Heat crawled up her neck, but not of embarrassment. A hot desire swelled through her as the touch reminded her of the night before.

The exploring hand slid down, tangling in the hair between Song's legs. The woman paused, her eyes locked on Song's, asking a question without words.

Song hesitated on nerves. "Go on," she whispered, and gave a single nod.

The delicate fingers found the right place to touch that made her gasp. Smiling Eyes moved her fingers expertly, exploring the area. She leaned forward to an angle that let her veil fall to the side so she could kiss the spot just behind Song's ear. She whispered to her, kissed her, and continued her exploration of Song's most intimate parts.

Song's voice rose against her will. A shock of ecstasy rippled through her and she threw her head back, her cries echoing through the bathing room. She gripped the edge of the pool to keep from falling into the water as Smiling Eyes continued. She didn't stop until Song's cries died to desperate moans. The woman laughed and whispered something, kissed behind her ear, and removed her hand.

Song floated through the women returning to dry her and convey her to a dressing area. She stared in a long mirror as they wrapped her in a purple dress made with the softest silk and hemmed and belted with glistening white lace. It secured over one shoulder, leaving the left bare. The skirt flowed around her legs, one long slit at the front teased glimpses of her right knee when she took steps. They stooped to clasp white sandals around her feet. Jerk and Deep had styled her hair, and now she could see it—brushed to shining with three braids over each side, wrapped from front to back, like a cage around her scalp. They had woven brightsteel chains into each braid, which shimmered whenever she turned her head.

Next, they sat her on a cushion to apply some sort of liquid to her eyelids, dragging it out from the corners. When she opened her eyes and saw herself in the mirror, she discovered two black wing-like lines on the outsides of either eye—one from the top lid and one from the bottom. She'd seen countless women and men around the city with this bit of makeup. All had been finely dressed, and she wondered if it was a sign of status.

Smiling Eyes—wrapped in dry clothes, her feet still bare—knelt in front of Song and sat on her heels as Jerk settled the captain's key and Pishing medallion back around Song's neck, and Freckles slid the white ring onto Song's right thumb. Jerk finished by affixing her jeweled North Star hairpin at the back of her head where the braids met.

In Smiling Eye's hands was a little box, which she held with outstretched arms and a bowed head. Song hesitated. The room froze in silent anticipation. She lifted the lid with cautious curiosity. Inside was a brightsteel necklace—the white metal pure and shimmering. The pendant was a strange sort of eye shape with a purple stone at the center, like an iris.

"For me?" Song whispered. She eyed it covetously, trying to remember what Leslie had said about gifts. She reached out to take it from the box. "I love it."

Smiling Eyes set the box down and motioned for the necklace. After Song handed it over, she walked on her knees to lean forward and secure it around Song's neck.

"Thank you."

Smiling Eyes reached up to unhook her veil from her ears and lower it from her face. Song froze in shock. She'd never seen a woman so beautiful. Her face was more square, but her jaw was soft. Her nose thin and her lips thick.

"Bloody hell... Are you the princess?"

Smiling Eyes didn't give any hint that she understood. Instead, she leaned forward to place several kisses to Song's lips. Song remembered these lips from the night before. She remembered them on her own, trailing down her body, and setting kisses to the area between her legs. After Song kissed her back, Smiling Eyes replaced her veil and stood.

Mole took Song by the hand and guided her back to the room she'd woken in. Someone had since made the bed with golden bedding of a different pattern than before. Food sat at a short table in the middle of a carpet with cushions in an enclosed patio. Silk curtains danced in the wind between the pillars of the archway. Mole motioned at it, then left.

Now alone, Song took a moment to exhale and let her body and mind have a minor panic attack over everything that had happened. All of it had been wonderful, and every moment perfect. And yet there was a strange anticipation in her chest and she had the desperate urge to run back to her ship and leave port immediately. However, she'd promised her crew the full two weeks.

She paused in her pacing and stared at her hands—one gripping a plate of flat breads and the other holding one covered in a creamy cheese and onion spread. She hadn't even realized she was eating until that moment. Song shoved more of the food into her mouth, deciding to finish quickly and get out of this place.

The patio had a tall sandstone brick wall around it for absolute privacy. Song dragged the table over and removed the items from it. It was too short. There was a stand with a vase off to the side, so she moved the vase of flowers and put the stand beside the table. She used them as steps to get up and look over the top of the wall. The road was not far down, and she guessed she was on the first floor of the building.

Song boosted herself up, causing the stand to tip and fall. In one movement, she swung her legs over the top and dropped to the sandy street below. Pedestrians stopped to stare.

Song chuckled nervously. "Fine day. Yeah?" She pushed past and strode through the streets until she spotted Toothy at the dining area. "Have you seen Leslie?"

Toothy stared at her in unmasked shock for a full minute. "You look lovely."

"Stop it."

"Smell lovely, too."

"Toothy!"

He laughed. "I have not. Ponce is looking for you, though. There he is." He waved for the man to come over.

"Who's your fri—" Ponce jolted backward as he blinked at her, mouth agape for an uncomfortable minute. "Song."

"What did you get up to last night?" Pinch asked just behind him. He reached forward to slide his hand into the other man's.

"I think I slept with the sultan's daughter, and they dressed me this morning and I just escaped from the palace," Song blurted.

The men took a minute to process.

Toothy narrowed his eyes. "You *ran away* from that?"

"*Yes!*"

"Why?" Pinch asked.

"Because! I don't know! I panicked, all right?"

Ponce chuckled and shook his head. "Here. Finished this morning." He held out a little box, much like the one Smiling Eyes had held out.

She took it and opened the lid with a scowl that shifted into a grin. "Oh, Ponce, thank you!"

Inside was the Jewel of Castildi on a white brightsteel chain with an intricate filigree brightsteel setting holding the gem at the thicker end. She hugged Ponce, but closed the box so none saw it.

"Excuse me," she said, slipping past the others as she spotted the serving man from the night before.

The man smiled and bowed, left hand clenched over his sternum, as she was realizing was custom. When his eyes noticed something about her, they flashed wider. He clenched his right fist over his chest and bowed deeper.

"Do you know where the man I was with last night went?"

He responded in Armalinian and bowed deep again.

She pointed at the place where they'd sat. "Me and my friend. Right there." She motioned at her head. "Red hair." She grabbed a lock of her own hair. "His hair." She pointed at a red cushion.

The man smiled and bowed again, then motioned in a direction farther from the palace and the river. He bowed again. Song huffed in impatience, put her fist over her sternum and bowed, then strode away in the direction he'd pointed.

After a few blocks, she recognized an uneasy feeling crawling up her spine. It was the feeling of being watched. She stopped to look at some fabric a vendor held out, then cast her gaze back the way she'd come.

A man in a red shirt and wide legged black pants stared right at her. She turned and wove into the crowd ambling through the market. At a stall she ducked behind a tall man and slipped into the alley behind the merchant, then took off at a run. She emerged onto a smaller road, turned right, and sped to an alley cast into shadows by canvas canopies strung from one side to the other.

Song raced until she found an archway surrounding a door. She shoved herself into it and gripped the jewelry box to her chest.

Several minutes passed, and nothing happened. She peeked out from behind the corner. Not a single soul tarried within the alley past the bustling street. She turned to continue out the other end. A door to her left opened to a man readying to untie his trousers to use a corner. The door closed on the sound of laughter and music—a tavern if she ever saw one. A place she could get answers.

The man had stopped what he was doing, though. He stared at her, eyes wide and frozen in a stunned silence. She chose to ignore him and head inside, but he grabbed her arm.

"Tsingsei Gould!"

"Bollocks."

She fought against him, shouting to draw attention or scare him off, but he kept his painful grip on her biceps. She spit in his eye, and he backhanded her hard enough to knock her to the ground. The box popped open and the Jewel of Castildi tumbled out into the sand.

Song grabbed the stone in her fist like a dagger. She lurched to her feet and buried the sharp tip into his eye. He wailed, clawing at the socket as he stumbled. He tripped and fell backward to howl in the sand.

A man shouted in Armalinian. Song spun, heart pounding in her ears and throat clenched tight. The man in the red shirt raced toward her, unsheathing a brightsteel kris from the thick red cloth around his middle.

She didn't need to question him. She knew she'd just been caught with something akin to a weapon and had started a fight. Song turned and raced from the alley as he shouted after her.

Twenty-Three

$\mathcal{S}$ong reached a busy common area. No vendors or merchants, just citizens and their laundry, shopping, or children. She stopped at a water barrel to clean the Jewel, then clasped it around her neck. She shoved all four necklaces into her bodice and continued on, her head whipping around at every noise.

"I'm looking for my friend," she said to a passing woman. "Red hair. His name is Leslie." She said this while looking at every person near enough to hear.

Most continued walking, some stopped to blatantly stare. She repeated his description and name over and over, begging any who would even look at her.

One woman stopped, a shallow crate of fresh food in her arms. "Leslie?"

"Yes. Red hair. About this tall." She held her hand over her head.

The woman jerked her head for Song to follow, so she did.

"Mirja," she said after a while. She was a shorter woman with wide hips and a round face. Her eyes were a deep green mistakable for brown in the shadows.

"Song. Do you speak Common?"

"Little."

The woman led her to a two story brick insula and ushered her through one of the many doors on the lower level. Inside was quaint, not cramped but not spacious, either. Mirja set her box on a counter and strode into another room. Song followed without thought, only to witness Mirja slapping Leslie's bare rear. He was asleep on a long mattress on the floor, face down, the dark arm of another person draped across his back. Song flushed and spun out of the room.

"There are kinder ways to wake me, Mirja," Leslie said with a chuckle.

"Not now." She said something in Armalinian.

"Song?"

"Yes. I'm here," she said.

"I'll be right out."

Mirja exited the room, releasing a thick curtain from a hook so it fell to cover the doorway. She motioned toward a square green carpet with brown cushions. "Sit. Tea?"

"Yes, thank you."

Leslie emerged moments later in trousers and nothing else. He gave Mirja a squeezing hug as she passed, then sat adjacent to Song. "How did you find me?"

"I asked everyone I saw until Mirja found me. Since when do you sleep so late?"

He studied her appearance, a crease between his brows. "We were up late. I take it you had fun with the *caddarik?*"

Her cheeks heated. "I did. With one, at least. How did they even know I'd be interested? Do I *look* the sort to—"

Leslie lifted her hand so the white ring was at her eye level. "A ring on the right thumb indicates interest in the same sex or gender as yourself."

She frowned at the little thing, and resisted falling into sappy tears over just how much the gesture of him buying the ring for her meant, now that she knew the reason. He could've never given it to her, and no woman would have known to approach her, and she'd have remained too shy when sober to try her hand at charming a woman who may not have even wanted the advances of a lady. She felt not only seen, but acknowledged and even validated, and for that she wanted to hug him and cry. It was a dramatic reaction, though, so she clenched her jaw and swallowed back all of her emotions, choosing to deflect away from herself.

"And did you have…fun?"

He chuckled. "I did. Mirja is an old friend."

"Saved you life," Mirja said as she set a tea tray on the low table.

"And I will never forget it."

She kissed his cheek and returned to the kitchen area.

"*Friend* from your first visit?" Song asked, a sly smile on her lips.

"Yes. She and her wife were more than happy to let me stay last night."

Mirja laughed and said something in Armalinian.

"And the rest of the festival," he added.

Song accepted a cup of tea and sipped it in the silence following. "I might be in trouble," she said just above a whisper, so only Leslie would hear.

"What sort of trouble?" he asked, leaning closer, as she had.

"A man was following me. I ran. But then someone recognized me. I fought him off, but the other man who'd been following me saw. I ran away before he could take me in or kill me. Whatever they do when you break the peace law."

Leslie ran the fingers of one hand through his tangled hair. "Oh. Well, this is not good."

"Can you help me get to the ship and I can hide there until the festival is over?"

He nodded. "Yes, that might be the best course of action. I'll stay, too—"

"No, stay here. Enjoy your time, and their *hospitality*. I can take care of myself."

The curtain lifted to secure back in the hook, and the person Song believed to be Mirja's wife came out. They wore a plain dress, but had a distinctly male figure. She couldn't help but stare—especially at the strange tattoo in bright sky blue ink on their forehead.

"I thought you said Mirja had a wife," Song hissed.

"Don't stare," he hissed back. "Yes, this is Aevi, Mirja's *wife*," he said, loud enough to make it an introduction. "She doesn't speak any Common."

Song returned the courteous slight bow from Aevi. "You'll explain later?" she asked Leslie.

"I can explain now. Aevi is a woman inside. That tattoo on her forehead tells others that is who she is, since her physical body is the opposite."

Song looked at Aevi, her arms wrapped lovingly around Mirja from behind as that woman prepared food. "And this is common?"

"Not particularly. It's accepted, though. Here in Armalinia, at least. If you see someone who looks like a woman, but has a similar tattoo in green, that is someone who is a man on the inside. It's considered socially reprehensible if you intentionally call someone the wrong thing. Go too far, and you could be fined."

Song sipped the tea—it had a spice to it, and a hint of citrus. "This tea is amazing. I want to load the ship with it. Anyway, why would you be fined?"

"Because you'd be assaulting a person's very identity. Personal identity is a sacred thing for them. Armalinia is a spiritual country. Not in the same way as Aibhànocht. They don't believe in gods, but in the holiness of your spirit and the spirit inside each of us. Even within other creatures. They pray before killing an animal for food, and it's treated more as a ritual sacrifice than a slaughter. Who you are in your heart is more important to them than what you are on the outside."

"And yet they make the most immaculate goods."

Leslie chuckled. "Outward decoration complements inner beauty."

"Is that why the *caddarik* dressed me like this?" She opened her arms to show off the outfit.

"Purple is the color of royalty. Maybe they see you that way. To adorn you in so much Brightsteel is…*hmm*."

"One necklace is from Ponce." She withdrew the enormous stone and patiently waited as the women crowded her to fawn over it.

"Good call keeping that hidden. Lower classes won't know what it is, but nobles, and even some merchants, will."

She tucked it back into her dress top.

"*They* dressed you?" he asked after a moment.

"Yes. After forcing me to let them bathe me."

Leslie froze and blinked at her. "Oh. I see…"

"What?"

"Bathing someone here is a sign of respect. If someone of a higher status bathes you, though, they are seeing you as an equal and acknowledging your spirit. It's an honor for them to have done that. They were, indeed, elevating you to their level as royalty. At least from a social perspective."

She made a face. "Oh, so now I'm a princess."

He chuckled. "Any idea which of the *caddarik*'s eye you caught?"

Song shook her head, not wanting to admit just yet that it could very well have been the sultania. "She was beautiful, though. Her whole body is perfection." She bit her lip at the thought. "And her face—"

"You saw a *caddarik* face?" Mirja gasped as she and Aevi brought in a light lunch.

"Yes?" Song said slowly.

Mirja and Aevi spoke over each other in Armalinian as they sat down and angled closer to Song, as though hanging on every word she might speak. Leslie said something with a chuckle, and they laughed and sat straight.

"What was all that?"

"They were asking you what she looked like, but I had to remind them that the permission for knowing was granted to you, not them."

"We are excite," Mirja said. "Sorry."

Song smiled. "It's all right."

"Everyone is eager for the unveiling of the sultania," Leslie said.

"All *caddarik*," Mirja added.

Even though she'd just eaten at the palace, Song ate some of the food offered here, not wanting to be rude by refusing. It was of lesser quality, but good all the same.

As they ate, she thought about everything, letting her assumptions of the country click into place. Individuality was more celebrated here than anywhere Song had ever been. No one batted an eye over this woman in a man's body, and no one batted an eye at the woman who'd spent the night in another woman's bed. Come to think of it, no one had even given Pinch a second glance when he'd taken Ponce's hand in the middle of the crowd.

If her heart had any desire to stay put, rather than fly around the world forever, she felt like this would be where she'd want to make her permanent home. A place where no one would think twice about a woman in trousers who shared a bed with other women. A place where she could be herself. Where she could be free.

They decided to wait until evening before venturing out of the apartment. In that time, Song met Hanan, Mirja's son, as he returned from the day's schooling. He was a young boy, whom Leslie was all too eager to see. Hanan was polite, but hid behind his mother at the two strangers in their home. Then he left again to play with his friends in the courtyard.

"You're familiar with him?" Song asked Leslie.

He smiled and nodded. "Mirja was carrying him when we met."

"Where is his father?"

Mirja smiled. "You can tell her."

He let out a long breath. "I killed her husband the night we met."

Song blinked at him. "I'm sorry, you what?"

"We'll ignore what I was doing, but I heard him shouting. Hit her so hard I heard that from inside. I went out to help. We were both drunk. I punched him, he fell back and hit his head… never got up."

"Then you fell," Mirja said. "You saved me. I saved you." She wrapped her hand through his to squeeze once.

"I couldn't live with myself if I'd left her to fend for herself after that. Helped raise Hanan for a while. I didn't leave until Mirja said she'd be fine without me."

"Why not just stay forever?" Song asked.

Leslie stared at the tea in his cup. "I couldn't. I've always felt the need to keep moving. Because if I stay anywhere for too long…"

"Roman will find you."

Mirja pursed her lips, and Leslie held out a calming hand.

"Mirja knows my history," he said. "That name is not welcome in her home."

"Get me in the same room as him, and I'll make sure he knows exactly how welcome he is anywhere," Song growled.

"Let's not threaten regicide."

Song made a face and stared out the window. "It's about late enough, don't you think?"

"Yes," he said. "Let's get you back to the Bounty."

Aevi wrapped a large, sheer shawl over Song's head and tucked it over her shoulders. Then she wrapped one over her own long brown hair. Mirja called to Hanan as they left the apartment and the group traveled across the city through back streets. When they reached what Song assumed was the commons center, a vast crowd had gathered. The four looked amongst each other.

"Stick together," Leslie said.

He took Song's hand; she took Mirja's, who took Hanan's, with Aevi at the end. They wove through the crowd like a serpent, though at least other people were kind enough to step aside. Leslie lurched to a stop, causing Song to smash against him. She followed his blank stare to a gruesome scene.

A man knelt, both hands removed and bloody stumps chained to a pole. Someone had nailed his hands through his palms on the pole above him. He was undeniably dead and put out as some sort of display. Song swallowed, barely recognizing the man, but knowing who he was because of his one sunken eyelid.

"That's the man who recognized me," Song hissed.

"Are you sure?"

"He grabbed me and I stabbed his eye out."

Leslie let go of her hand and pushed through the crowd to read the sign hammered into the ground. She released Mirja and followed. Leslie's wide eyes met Song's.

"What?" she demanded.

"Come on." He wrapped an arm around her shoulders and one through her biceps.

"What does it say?"

"That man was executed for a different crime. But we should hurry—" Leslie released her and shoved her away from himself, lurching the other direction as a figure dove at them.

The crowd backed away to make space as the man in the red shirt stared Leslie down. He withdrew his kris; Leslie put up his hands. The two spoke back and forth, the man yelling as Leslie tried to remain calm. The man lunged.

Song jumped between, readying a command to her *kijæm*. But the man's kris stopped short. He brought it back to himself and bowed, right hand over his chest as he lowered his head to look at the ground. He said something.

"What mess did you get yourself into this time?" Leslie hissed behind her.

"I didn't do anything!"

"What did the *caddarik* say to you?"

"I don't know!"

"Did they give you something?"

Song froze. She moved the shawl to the side and pulled the thinner of the two brightsteel chains from inside her top. The eye pendant came free from the purple fabric and dangled in the air.

Like an ocean wave, the entire crowd moved. The front row set their right hands over their sternums and bowed low, eyes on the ground. As the following rows of people noticed, they, too, bowed.

"Leslie? What does this mean?"

Twenty-Four

"All gifts come with a caveat," Leslie murmured under his breath. "I warned you."

Song bit her lips together. The two stood straight-backed in the entryway of the polished marble palace. The crowd which had followed them there had grown as they traveled and now stood cheering behind them.

Arriving there was the first time she'd actually looked at the building. To say it was breathtaking was an understatement. Marble columns lined the front, the bases and roof all decorated with creatures from both reality and myth. Above the huge cream colored wooden double doors sat an enormous brightsteel North Star, a near twin to the one on the Stars' Bounty. Song couldn't drag her eyes away from it.

Leslie followed her gaze. "Did you not know?"

"Know what?"

"The Stars' Bounty is an Armalinian ship. The star is one of their most dearly held mythos. It represents a spirit."

"What spirit?"

Leslie gave her a sheepish smirk. "That's one story I was too drunk to remember. I'm sorry."

"How drunk were you back then?" she asked on a scoff.

"Remember how drunk you were after Dash?"

She snorted. "Most of it's a blur or complete blackout."

"About like that. For almost a whole year."

She furrowed her brow, unable to imagine him that far gone. Before she could continue the conversation, the doors opened. The man in the red shirt came out and stood to the side. Following him was a man about the age of Song's father—somewhere in his forties, maybe older. A draped purple shirt wrapped around him and white wide-legged pants with brown sandals completed the outfit. A brightsteel circlet rested in his short black hair. There was a single North Star attached to the otherwise plain circlet; it gleamed against the copper skin of his forehead. Leslie bowed low, but Song hesitated in her confusion. Then it hit her: this was the sultan. When she finally thought to bow, her body second guessed the action and tried to curtsey at the same time.

The sultan didn't react in any way. He strode closer and pushed up her chin with his fingertips. She wasn't sure why he did this, as he was the same height as her, and could have looked straight into her eyes. Over his shoulder, in the sunset-lit hall, the *caddarik* had collected. They talked amongst themselves, none stepping forward. He said something, and the women floated out as one, wrapped in indigo robes. Without at least their décolletage showing, Song couldn't tell any of them apart, except Smiling Eyes. He asked the question again.

"*Vae. Ja'i harkinon baelimra,*" Deep said.

"*Ja'i sultania,*" Freckles said.

"*Drr* Andalise," Jerk said.

"Gould Tsingsei," Smiling Eyes said.

The man released her chin and looked into her eyes. "Tsingsei Gould of Andalise." He let out a long breath as he scrutinized her.

"Yes."

"You?" he asked Leslie.

"I'm Leslie."

"What are you to this woman?" He motioned at Song. His Common came forced and careful, as though he couldn't quite form the words on his tongue.

"He's my friend," Song blurted.

"Not lover? Betrothed?"

She blushed, eyes wide. "No."

He looked at Leslie for confirmation.

"Just a friend and protector," Leslie said.

The man thought for a moment, looked at the *caddarik* and nodded once, then turned and strode inside. The *caddarik* swarmed the two, forcing them into the hall, and the doors closed behind them, shutting out the cheering crowd.

Something strange happened then, where the women all turned their attention on Leslie and ignored Song. They circled him, running their fingers through his hair and turning his face this way and that as they talked between themselves. Leslie said something, and the women gasped as one, then tittered in excitement. They spoke back and forth to him, each seeming to ask a question between his responses. Song caught him saying something about Tsingsei and they all stared at her. She blushed from her forgotten spot off to the side, out of the way. Smiling Eyes replied.

"What are you saying?" Song asked.

"Figuring out what you got yourself into," Leslie said.

He pursed his lips as Smiling Eyes squeezed his cheeks to make him look into her sparkling amber eyes. They spoke back and forth for another minute before Leslie released a long, exasperated sigh.

"It's worse than I feared," he said.

"What? What is?"

"You…accepted a proposal of marriage from the sultania herself."

Song's voice caught in her throat. Her gaze locked onto Smiling Eyes.

"They executed the man in the commons for assaulting the betrothed of the sultania. The man in red is…your royal bodyguard."

Song snapped out of her daze. "I… Why? Why me?"

Leslie asked a question and Mole replied.

"They call you the Princess of Andalise."

"I'm not a princess!"

"You are to her. Whichever one she is." He glanced at the faces and shifted uncomfortably as one took his hand, running her fingertips along his palm and the pale underside of his forearm.

"This is a disaster. When you said it was bad, I never would have guessed—"

"That isn't even the worst part."

"How could it possibly get worse than that?"

Leslie clenched his jaw, like he was focusing on ignoring the hands all over him. "Armalinians have an...odd fascination with... red hair. It's exciting to them, for some reason."

Song snorted. "And?"

"And now they're propositioning me, too."

An hour passed, slow and uncomfortable, as Song sat in a lavish meeting room, trying to make conversation with Sultan Ky'r Vadji, who was the only person in the room who spoke Common. The *caddarik* had whisked Leslie away, but the five returned a short while later, giggling and without him.

She'd endured awkward introductions to the Sultana Ky'r Kalej—Vadji's wife—and Sultani Ky'r Djinri, their middle child and only son, who wore a less ornate veil over the lower half of his face. Their youngest of three was a girl in her teens, who wore a decorated veil and had her own entourage of matching girls—though these he called *caddria*. Song didn't want to ask why, and risk a long lesson on nuance in the Armalinian language, or politics, given in painfully slow speech by the sultan.

When Leslie entered the room, he'd been bathed and dressed in expensive clothes he was blatantly irked about. He sat beside Song and fidgeted with the fine silk shirt as though it made him uncomfortable.

"When they didn't return with you, I feared the worst," Song said.

"Yes, well, they tried to bathe me themselves. Saved by servants, whom I convinced I am more than capable of bathing myself."

"You refused them bathing you? But you said—"

"Someone in my…previous station does not deserve to be recognized in such a way." He clenched his jaw, as though fighting back the blow he'd caused his own pride.

She nodded in acceptance, choosing to drop it. "Did you also get to dress yourself?"

The corners of his lips tightened. "No."

She giggled into a fist as he pouted.

With Leslie there to translate, the sultan spoke in quick Armalinian. Song sat in stunned silence as Leslie translated for her, or summarized his negotiations refusing his own betrothal.

"It's as I feared," Leslie murmured after a long silence. "She's used to always getting her way."

"Something I used to be intimately familiar with."

"I might be able to talk myself out of all this, but she's set on having you… And you did already accept the proposal."

Song stared at the women, her lips tight as she met Smiling Eyes's gaze. "I'm not a bloody princess! I'm nothing at all! Marry someone else!"

Leslie translated for the *caddarik*. "They say you're not nothing. They knew you were special when they saw your hairpin. Precious few people are even allowed to wear it."

Song scoffed. "It's just a damned hairpin! I think Dash nicked it from a merchant vessel or a passenger ship."

"Perhaps an upperclass woman or merchant-noble. A shaman might be more likely."

Song seethed as Leslie continued negotiating. After several minutes, he gave a sigh of relief, followed by a frown.

"Well, good news and bad news."

"What?" she asked through gritted teeth.

"Good news for me is she's willing to forego me on one condition."

"Let me guess, I have to do something to ensure that *you* are comfortable." She scoffed.

"I'm sorry, but I am trying. Your choices are to accept her caveat, or you and I will sort of—in a roundabout way—be married. Kind of."

Song made a face. "What's the caveat?"

"You have to marry her the day after the festival ends."

She jolted in her seat. "So soon? Not even a letter to my parents?"

Leslie shook his head. "You're almost twenty, and that's not how things work here. Your life choices are not your parents to make, or even approve of."

The room quieted to a heavy silence in which Song seethed and Leslie pleaded with her, using only his eyes. She didn't want to be a sister-wife to Leslie—nor did she want to be a wife at all. She didn't want to be forced to stay in this hot, sunny country, away from her ship and crew, and their adventures. Nor did she want to stand out from the crowd or have a guard following her every step. And she most especially didn't want anyone to know that Tsingsei Gould had been found.

Song lurched to her feet. "I won't marry you! I don't even know your bloody name!"

The room grew quiet and Smiling Eyes stood. She took Song's hands in her own. "Lyella."

Twenty-Five

The quarter moon had carved itself into the night sky. Song stared up at it. Just beyond the wall of the patio were festivities and music and food that she was missing out on. Sure, she could have scaled the wall again, but Ryk'r, her royal bodyguard, would track her down and drag her back again. Just before they'd allowed Leslie to leave the palace, he had made this fact crystal clear to her.

A burning lump hardened in Song's throat as tears rolled down her cheeks. She hadn't felt this trapped and hopeless in years. And back then, right when she'd needed saving, Altain had swooped in to pluck her from all those troubles. She closed her eyes and wished against all hope that the same green eyes she couldn't even remember the shape of would pop up over the wall. That Altain would reach out and she could take his hand again.

"Why are you crying like an idiot?" she growled, mashing the heels of her palms into her eyes. "You're a powerful Touched who can escape anytime you want." She wiped her face and took a deep, calming breath. "Then again, that could be the last thing you ever do."

"It's a good thing you talk to yourself."

Song jumped and looked up to find Ponce staring down at her.

"Been searching for bloody ever."

"What are you doing?" she asked.

"Whispers told us of your predicament. Don't worry, Captain, we'll get you out of it. Preferably without bloodshed—including yours."

Song's brow furrowed. "What are you standing on?"

"Toothy."

"Hello, Song!" Toothy shouted from the other side of the wall.

"Whispers is here, too. Looking fancy."

"Did you really think," Leslie said just loud enough for her to hear, "that I would leave you here alone?"

"You fought so hard for your own freedom, I couldn't be too sure," she said.

"It'll be easier to make a plan from out here. And to smuggle just one person."

"Smuggle me how?"

Ponce waved his hand in the air for her to be quiet. "You'll know when it happens. Sorry, too risky to say anything. Also… don't really have a plan yet."

She nodded. "All right. I trust you lot. Go enjoy the festival without me."

Ponce looked down beside him. "Whispers says he'll come back tomorrow. Seems a shame for you to miss it."

"All right. I—" Song whirled around to look at the opening door as Ponce ducked below the ledge.

"See you later, Song!" Ponce said.

The robed and veiled woman came closer, almost unsure. She didn't seem to have heard Ponce, and for that Song was relieved. It took a moment for it to set in that she'd come alone. She stopped just shy of where the dim moonlight stretched its fingers into the room, as though not wanting it to touch her. She motioned for Song to go to her, so she did, but stopped in the archway to lean on a pillar, arms folded. From there, Song recognized those amber eyes. Sultania Lyella, her betrothed.

"Do you understand anything I say?"

Lyella furrowed her brow. She pointed at herself, then her ear, then at Song.

"You know some Common?"

Lyella nodded.

"But you don't speak Common?" As Song spoke, she gestured to Lyella and then her own mouth.

She shook her head. Neither said anything as they stared at each other.

"You tricked me," Song said, motioning between them. "You *lied*."

Lyella nodded. "Y…yess," she extended the word as though unsure if it was the right one.

"Why?"

"Sultania Gould Tsingsei."

Song scowled past the entertaining way she pronounced her last name more like 'gold'. "I'm not a princess."

Lyella stretched out her hand. After a minute, where neither moved, Song let out a long breath and went forward. She let the sultania guide her to the bed and sat beside her. Lyella raised her hands to her veil, then paused, uncertain. After a moment, she released a nervous laugh, then unhooked the veil from her ears.

"You're not used to taking it off around strangers," Song observed.

Lyella stared, oblivious.

Song pointed at the veil, covered the lower half of her own face, then made a motion of taking it off. She motioned at herself and shook her head. Lyella furrowed her brow, then raised them in realization.

"No." She said it clipped and short, so it felt more like a punctuation mark than a word.

"Am I supposed to have even seen it?" She skipped having to repeat, and instead spoke in a slow, thoughtful cadence, motioning in relevant ways.

Lyella gave her a breathy laugh and stared at the cloth in her hands. "No."

They stayed in suffocating silence for a minute.

"You know you can't make a prisoner fall in love with you, right?" Song snapped.

Lyella chewed on her bottom lip, wide, smiling eyes oblivious to what Song had said.

The sultania stared at her hands, then shoved the veil back over her face. Now behind it, she seemed to relax. She spoke softly in Armalinian, reaching up to Song's hair. After a nod of permission, she began unwinding the braids and set the hairpin and chains on the side table. She retrieved a comb from the vanity across the room, then sat and ran it through Song's tresses, smoothing them with her palm.

Lyella untied the shoulder of the dress and Song crossed an arm over her chest without thinking. The sultania lurched to her feet in shock, her eyes locked beneath Song's chin.

"Oh, you know the Jewel of Castildi, don't you?"

"Castildi," Lyella echoed. "*Akh'tilak Sultana Castildi.*"

Song blinked, recognizing the words separately. They'd introduced Ryk'r as *Akh'tilak* Ryk'r. Sultana she knew to be queen. "Is Castildi a person?"

Lyella fell into an excited story in which Song understood nothing. The woman crossed the room to get the silk robe from a hook by the door and returned to urge Song to her feet. She talked the whole time in such a passionate way that Song felt if only she could understand her, she'd be hanging on every word.

As Lyella scanned over Song's blank expression, she grew quiet; her smile dimmed, though her eyes remained bright. Once Song was in the robe and she'd discarded the dress in an unceremonious pile by the vanity, Lyella crossed her arms to think. Then, as though something mystical jolted inspiration into her, she stood straight.

Lyella removed her robe as she spoke slowly to the cadence of a silent song. She reached up and removed her veil as she said, "Sultana Castildi."

Song realized she was acting out the story, and smiled as the woman tossed the veil onto the bed, then assumed a fighting stance. As though the magic of her movements were enough, Song understood the tale.

Warrior Queen Castildi was a beautiful woman. Everyone coveted her, like jewels and quoine. Men from all nations fought for her, but she wasn't interested. Castildi had slain enormous serpents and battled—Song wasn't sure what it was, as Lyella crouched and pinched her fingers open and closed, then motioned over her head from behind, one finger out to poke at Song. Song giggled and moved away from the jabs.

Castildi had refused the hands of all the most powerful men in the world. Instead, she'd taken one wife and one husband. Neither was anyone important, and the circumstances had seemed random. She told everyone that she didn't choose; it had been destined. For her, those two had been more important than appearances or treaties. And she loved them until the day she died.

Lyella opened her eyes from where she lay on the floor like a corpse, hands clasped together over her chest. She stared at the ceiling for a long minute, then turned her gaze to Song.

"Sultana Ky'r Lyella," she held her right hand out to her side—the hand she'd used whenever referencing the wife. "Sultan Ky'r Antian," she held her left hand to the other side. Then she clasped her hands over her heart. "Akh'tilak Sultana Ky'r Castildi."

Song's lips parted in unsure shock. "Are you named after the wife?" She motioned as best she could to convey this.

"Yes," she said, grinning.

"Castildi was your…"

"*Tri, tri, tri, tri troj-adma.*"

Song chewed on her bottom lip, eyes narrowed. "I'm going to assume you just said great, great, great, great grandmother. Sounded like it could be that."

Lyella pushed to her feet and lowered down to sit so close to Song that her heartbeat thrummed against Song's arm. She set her palm to Song's cheek.

"*Ank'i yr* Sultana Lyella."

"Did you just call me your Sultana Lyella?" Song couldn't help the laugh that snorted from her nose. "If anything, I think I'm Castildi." When Lyella gave her a blank smile, Song made the same motion of wielding weapons that Lyella had. "*Akh'tilak.* Me." She patted her chest.

This caused Lyella's eyes to sparkle with excitement. She pressed forward to kiss Song, long and deep, exploring her mouth with her tongue. After a long time savoring the sultania, she broke free to breathe.

"I want…to slow down," Song said, trying to motion the phrase. "Is that all right?"

"S-s…lo…"

"Slow."

"S-low…"

"Down."

"Dow…n." Still, she gave a curious stare.

Song sighed and crawled between the silky sheets. She motioned for Lyella to join her. The sultania grinned and began untying her apodesme. Song grabbed her hand and shook her head, then again motioned for her to join. Bewildered, Lyella slid in beside her. Song made sure the woman was comfortable, then lay her head down to use her shoulder as a pillow. After a moment of uncertainty, Lyella began stroking Song's hair as she held her. Soon after that, both women fell fast asleep.

Twenty-Six

When Leslie returned to the palace the next day, he'd dressed in his own humble clothing, not a single expensive thread to be seen. Song waited in silence as he spoke with the sultan and the *caddarik*. It came to a point where Sultan Ky'r was visibly ready to be done with the conversation. What brought it to a close was when he spun on the balls of his feet to bark something, a finger pointed to scold Lyella directly. He turned and used the same tone with Leslie, motioned to Ryk'r, then stormed from the room.

Song fidgeted, picking at a fingernail as she waited for something else to happen. Lyella took a deep breath, put her nose in the air, and strode from the room—the *caddarik* sweeping through to keep up. Ryk'r adjusted to stand closer to Song, his posture straight, jaw squared, chin high, and hands folded over the band of cloth which hid his kris.

Leslie took a deep breath and let it out. "So he's that sort of negotiator."

"What?" Song asked.

"He makes concessions and compromises in a way which gives him the upper hand. However, he doesn't think you are important enough to waste this much time on. So he has granted you permission to enjoy the rest of the festival, but only in my company and with your guard in tow."

"What did he say to her?"

"That he wouldn't waste another minute on her rash actions. He's far too busy." Leslie motioned for her to follow him out the front doors.

"Keep prodding him, and perchance I can get out of the engagement entirely."

"No. That one is not going to happen. The slight it would be in the face of the sultania would cause outrage."

Song pursed her lips. "She tricked me into accepting, and there's no way I can escape? Seems unfair."

"There's no precedent. No one has ever backed out of a proposal from a royal. It's a great honor." Leslie glanced at her, his brow furrowed. "Why are you against it?"

"I don't want to be trapped here." She fiddled with the front of her teal dress as they strolled through the markets. "Perhaps you *should* marry her, though. Maybe she'll accept you in place of me."

He scowled ahead. "Why?"

She chewed on her bottom lip. "Because of Roman."

They stopped so he could stare at the sad frown on her lips.

"What does Roman have to do with this?" he asked.

"If you married the sultania, surely they'd protect you from him. They wouldn't allow a member of the royal family to have such a bounty on his head."

"They might force me to stay here. What makes you think I'd want to stay? Do you want me to?"

"Of course I don't. But I'd rather know you're safe and alive, instead of dragging you around the world, risking your life."

"I would rather risk my life than stay here with those women. I don't care what sense it makes and what advantages it gives, I will not marry the sultania."

"Why are *you* so against it?"

"Because I've been owned by someone before, and that's the feeling I got when they swarmed me. I was no longer a person, but a thing they wanted. For the mere reason of the color of my hair."

Song chewed on the inside of her cheek, trying to hold back the thought that crawled into her mind.

"What are you thinking?"

"You don't want to know." Song stopped to eye a silver kris dagger with a serpent's head pommel.

"Maybe I do."

The merchant, now finished negotiating a trade, spotted Song. As he came over, his gaze drifted to the eye pendant. He bowed low, his right fist over his chest, and spoke in quick sentences, then began motioning at every item in front of Song.

"What's he saying?" she asked.

"He's wondering what caught your eye."

"This." She set her fingertips on the handle of the dagger. "What trade would he accept for that?"

The man took the kris, sheathed it in a serpent-body scabbard, and held it out on his palms as he bowed.

"A wedding gift for the sultania's *ghija*—her betrothed."

Song made a face. "As much as I love free items, that puts a stain on it."

After a short negotiation, Leslie said, "He will accept the honor of kissing your hand as a trade."

Song made a face, but kept her covetous gaze on the kris. "All right, fine."

She held out her hand so he could kiss the top, as was customary in most countries. However, the man turned her wrist to kiss her palm, then placed the dagger in it.

"Thank you," she said, gripping the item close to herself as though he might take it back.

"*Ank lighen*," Leslie said, so Song repeated the phrase to the merchant.

He smiled and bowed low. Ryk'r eyed her as she slid the dagger into the bunched cloth belt at her waist.

"Tell him if he has a problem with it, he can fight me for it," Song said.

Leslie translated to the man, but Ryk'r didn't respond and kept his pose of hands over his own cloth wrap belt.

"That's what I thought." She turned to continue walking.

"What was it you were thinking, by the way?" Leslie asked.

"It's absurd. You'll hate it."

"Tell me, anyway."

She chewed at her lip and gave him a wicked smile. "I was just thinking it's a shame you aren't interested in being her play thing. You'd have beautiful children with her complexion and your red hair. They'd be absolutely breathtaking."

Leslie said nothing for a long time as they passed merchant stalls and bowing people. "You're right. It's absurd."

The next two weeks found Song divided. She spent what time she could enjoying the festival—occasionally joined by the *caddarik*. With Leslie there to translate, it was easier communicating. However, it felt less personal. Song liked the times she was alone with the sultania, and they had to do strange dances of gestures and motions to communicate. She enjoyed reading Lyella's body like a book every night.

At the beginning of the second week, Song was not permitted to leave the palace. They forced Leslie to bathe and dress in expensive silks, and tasked him with translating for Song through a day of preparation for the wedding. She had to stand and play mannequin as a tailor pinned fabric around her. After that, she met with an etiquette trainer who went through expectations and behaviors she would have to know to avoid causing insult. Finally, she spent hours learning a dance with Lyella. The instructor explained the movements and the meanings. Song took on what they called the dominant role, given to the taller of any pairings.

After an extravagant dinner in which Song had to put her new lessons to the test—and to her surprise, passed—Leslie left, and she retired to the room that was hers for at least one more week. Lyella joined her after a while. She slid her arms around Song's waist from behind as the latter stared up at the moon.

"Do you ever wonder if the moon feels trapped in the sky?" Song said. "Or maybe it's free, but loves the world too much to leave."

Lyella stared at her with her brow furrowed, a cheek pressed to Song's shoulder.

She sighed. "Never mind."

When she turned, Lyella took her hands and put them in the initial pose of the dance. She hummed the tune as the two slowly went through the motions. By the end, Lyella was grinning. She tucked herself into Song's arms, an ear to her chest. If she'd seen the action done to any other person, she might think they were in love. But she didn't believe they could have loved each other so soon. In fact, Song's heart longed more than anything to return to the skies.

Lyella hadn't lain with her every night, but Song coaxed her to the bed with a kiss. She wanted to run her fingertips over every inch of the sultania. So she did. She caressed that soft skin with her palms, kissed it with her lips. Lyella writhed at certain kisses, like those at her breasts. Song kissed her way down the soft abdominal flesh. She found herself cradled between Lyella's legs. She set a soft kiss on the woman's inner thigh. Their eyes met, and the sultania nodded.

"Yes," she breathed out.

With no idea what she was doing, Song proceeded. There she got the first delicious taste of a woman. Lyella stopped her every so often to guide her wordlessly, showing Song just how she wanted to be touched. Once she knew what she was doing a little better, she let the woman's sounds tell her if she was doing it right. She chased those sounds until Lyella screamed and writhed on the bed. And even then, Song didn't stop. She wanted more. And so she continued until Lyella was hoarse and could barely move.

Song wiped her chin and crawled up to lie beside the sultania. The woman stared at her with half-lidded eyes, mouth open as she panted in the aftermath. Song delivered a self-satisfied grin, which made Lyella giggle. This time, the woman curled up to lay her head on Song's shoulder, and fell asleep soon after.

She stared up at the ceiling, thoughts whirling in her mind. This felt right—not Lyella in particular, but her being with a woman. And yet she didn't feel like she could love Lyella the same as she thought she loved Leslie. Again, she questioned if even that feeling was, in fact, love at all.

Her thoughts ran away with the music playing blocks away. Soon enough, thoughts of the bounty on Leslie's head plagued her mind. She scowled at the ceiling.

Once I'm out of this mess, I have to get him out of that one.

The end of the festival came, and Song feared she'd lost her opportunity. The day of the wedding arrived, and she trudged through preparations in a numb silence. Servants bathed her. They styled her hair with braids and brightsteel.

Some part of her still clung to hope, though, so anything not placed on her for the ceremony, she collected in a pillowcase shoved under the bed. All her gifts and dresses hoarded like a greedy sprite, in one place and ready to go with her at a moment's notice.

She hadn't seen Lyella all day, as was custom. Once they'd finished adorning her, Song stood in front of the tall mirrors, staring at the stranger in the reflection. They'd put her in a burgundy gown with brightsteel, gems, and pearls all sewn along the skirt and the top of the bodice in an intricate pattern. It was made of heavy fabric and weighed her down like the suffocating gowns in Andalise. On her head they'd placed a tiara with a brightsteel north star, and from it flowed a sheer golden yellow veil that covered the back of her head and draped over her shoulders.

The designer had explained everything to her, translated through someone who spoke broken, slow Common. Lyella had chosen the burgundy for her after she'd told her she was a warrior. Red was the color of a warrior in Armalinia. The golden veil was a tradition for women. It represented sunlight and a blessing upon their heads.

Behind her stood a less stuffy gown of white and silver, which she would wear for the matrimonial dance. She rather liked that one, with its soft silk and long train that looped onto her middle finger.

Palace guards had gone to fetch Leslie that morning, but returned empty-handed, saying the man was nowhere to be found. This broke Song's heart. Of all the times he'd been there for her, she needed him now the most. Instead, she would be alone while tying herself to a woman she'd tried so hard to fall in love with in just two weeks, and had failed. Not that she didn't care deeply about Lyella, she just couldn't manage what others described as love. Perhaps it was too fast, or perhaps she would never feel it.

Dusk was threatening sunset. It was time. Any minute, someone would come for her. Without thinking about it, she locked the door, wishing for a chair to stick under the handle. Song paced the room. She had to do something. But what?

The knob turned. A voice shouted from the other side.

"Bugger this. I'm getting myself out of here if it kills me," she said.

"I'd prefer if you didn't."

Song spun around at the voice. Hovering over the floor of the patio was Leslie, one arm reaching out as he gripped a ladder hanging from seemingly nowhere. She nearly cried.

"Don't just stand there—"

A shoulder crashed against the door.

"—come on!"

Song grabbed the white dress from the hanger, unable to bring herself to leave it behind. Then she tore her pillowcase of things out from under the bed.

"Really? You're stopping for treasures?" he asked.

"What kind of pirate would I be if I didn't?"

The door crashed open as Ryk'r and another guard stumbled in. Lyella shoved past them, looking so beautiful it knocked the breath out of Song's lungs. They had adorned her in an orange gown similar to Song's, but with yellow and gold accents. She looked like a wildfire meeting a golden sunset on the horizon. Her face veil matched the gown, but she also had a golden veil on her head.

"Tsingsei!" she cried, and lifted her skirt to rush across the room.

Leslie took the pillowcase of goods from Song, but she paused as Lyella shouted for the two guards to stay back.

"I'm sorry," Song said. "I can't do it, Lyella. I just can't."

Lyella stepped out of the room and looked overhead at the skyship. Her gaze fell to the figurehead, and a sad understanding washed over her. "*Ank'i yr Castildi. Jr ank gal kheshto ji'ir Armalinia, ank'i yrn isagal.*"

Song froze, captured by what sounded like a curse being placed on her very soul. Lyella removed her face veil to smile at her. Tears rimmed her eyes. She leaned forward and locked Song in a deep, desperate goodbye kiss.

"Good...bye, Tsingsei."

A wry smirk twisted her lips. "Call me Song." She chuckled at Lyella's confusion. "Ask about me." She set one last kiss to Lyella's lips, then hopped onto the ladder beside Leslie. "Get me out of here!" she shouted upward.

The rope ladder raised, and the ship took off. Down below, Lyella repeated what she'd said, shouting it after them until Song could no longer hear the sultania of Armalinia.

"She's more beautiful than I imagined," Leslie said.

"Regret turning her down?"

"No. Do you regret leaving her behind?"

"No." Song stared at him as he looked up, checking the distance left until they reached the ship. "Thank you for coming for me."

"Of course. You'd do the same for any of us."

"What did Lyella say to me? It sounded like a curse."

"'You're my Castildi. If you ever set foot on Armalinian sands, you're mine forever.'"

Twenty-Seven

Wind tangled through Song's hair as she closed her eyes. She'd been spending more time on the bowsprit, feeling the wind in her hair and the freedom in her veins. This day she stood out, hair untied and arms spread wide. It had been a week already since they'd stolen her from the Armalinian palace, and the joy of waking up in her smelly hammock on the battered Stars' Bounty never got old.

She hadn't yet given the men a destination or an order. Everyone continued their duties as they knew to. Song had thought over and over about where to go next. A voyage to the northern land required they stop for winter clothing and gear, maybe even a special winter weather zeppelin wrap. A voyage to the great sea required far more provisions than they had, but they wouldn't need extra gear.

Leslie leaned on the railing behind her. "Are we going to keep flying aimlessly so you can pretend you're a bird a little longer?"

She smiled and dropped her arms. "A few more days, perhaps."

He chuckled. "Maps is wondering if you at least have a direction in mind."

"That depends on where we are."

"Somewhere between Armalinia and Pishing."

Song stared out at the sparkling blue ocean. The dream she'd had the night before replayed in her mind. A darkened sky, a blood red sun, and ocean for as far as she could see in front of her. "How would you feel about weeks, or even months, with this sort of view?"

He followed her gaze and sighed with a contentment that mirrored her own. "I think it would be peaceful."

"We'll have to load the cargo hold with provisions. No room for pillaged goods."

"Only thing down there is a bit the men took from Barton, and what we couldn't sell."

Song nodded. "Best place to offload that and resupply is Telbhaniich-Zardi."

"I'll have Maps take us to the other side of the city. Try our luck with different merchants." Leslie turned and left her alone.

A few minutes later, the ship drifted right as they adjusted course.

That night, she sat at the bow with the men as they ate. Ponce and Pinch sat off to a side, serenading the crew with Pinch's concertina, or assaulting their ears when Ponce took the instrument. The sound was vile—even when Pinch wrapped his arms around his partner to hold his hands and move them. Thumbs had been indulging her in her favorite stew, and promised one with fresh mushrooms after they resupplied. She smiled and leaned her head on his shoulder as a sort of hug.

"I didn't properly thank you lot," she said. "I really thought I was going to be trapped there."

"We would've come for you a *lot* sooner," Sunshine said. "But loadin' up took a good while."

"Dragging men out of women's beds," she said with a laugh.

"Dockmaster was a right pill about us taking so long," Knots said. "Hardtack and me had to cool him off."

Beside him, Alton chuckled, but said nothing. It had genuinely shocked and pleased Song when she'd seen him aboard the ship.

"Speaking of Hardtack," she said, "Leslie, go fetch the contract."

The crew cheered and Knots slapped Alton on the back.

"I didn't expect you to come back from the festival," Song admitted. "Welcome to the crew. Officially."

"The men told me stories," Alton said. "Thumbs told me you risked your own life just to make sure he didn't die. Told me what you can do with your *kijæm*. Only a fool would turn down being part of something so great."

"Oh, please, you'll make me blush."

Leslie set the list of names beside her with a pen and ink. She wrote his real name and nickname, then waited as he knelt beside her and signed.

"Drinks for everyone except Leslie!" she shouted.

After they'd had their drinks and they had returned the items to her cabin, she called all the crew members on deck. Song stood at the bow, staring at all the faces. Some she couldn't name but knew them well, others who were more family to her than her parents had ever been.

"I have an announcement. I didn't want it passed around you lot to get bollocksed up. We're heading back to Telbhaniich-Zardi to sell off any cargo we don't need. Then, we're going to load up on water and food that'll keep. Lots of hardtack—sorry, mates. The reason being…we're going to go see if there really is a load of nothing out in the Great Ocean."

She hadn't expected the roar of approval that bursted from the men. But they cheered, and her spirits rose. A laugh forced itself from her throat.

"What if we find something?" Toothy asked.

"Then it's ours for the bloody taking," she said.

The men cheered.

"Let's go find Song's Island!" Pinch shouted.

The rest of the men broke into chants of *Song's Island*. She hadn't even thought about what to do if they found something. She especially hadn't thought about what they would call whatever they found—barring it already having a name. Now that they'd said it, though, she couldn't deny it had a tempting ring to it.

The next day found Song at the bowsprit again, one leg stretched along the length and the other dangling down. Bruce sat just behind the railing, drawing her—she suspected, since there wasn't any scenery. It had been a quiet day on board, though the excitement of their next adventure was like static in the air. The whistle blew over her head. Two pips.

Song turned her head to shout to the helm, "Steady on!"

"Aye, Captain!" Maps shouted from the table behind Leslie.

A minute later, Alton shouted, "That's her! That's the Harpy's Claw!"

Song spun around. "You mean Darian?"

"The very same."

She grabbed the whistle from around her neck and called Toothy out of the crow's nest. "Make ready!" she shouted. "Leslie, turn to intercept!" Song gripped a rope and dragged herself up, then leapt over the railing.

The men rushed to their usual positions, Sunshine having just woken.

"Are you good to fight?" she asked him.

"Aye. Just awake enough."

"Good. Don't get yourself killed."

She raised her voice. "All right, gents, this is different. We're here for one reason above all others. Take prisoners. Especially if they have black hair. Do not kill Darian."

Alton stood beside her. "Permission to join the boarding party."

She looked out at the other vessel as they sped closer. "Granted."

Leslie took her elbow and led her away from the others as Maps steered the ship. "Song, you should stay on the Bounty this time."

"Why?" she demanded.

"Because this is too personal to you."

"But—"

"Let me lead the boarding party. Do you trust me?"

"I do. I just…"

"What?"

"Darian was the first pirate I ever encountered. I'm…afraid."

His expression softened. "Of what?"

"That he'll take someone else away from me this time. Someone I can't live without." Her eyes locked on his.

Leslie wrapped her in a tight hug. "I won't let that happen. Stay on the Bounty, and don't use your *kijæm*."

"Do your job right, and I won't have to."

"Today we'll have your answers, or your friend." He released her and strode to where the others stood ready.

Song lowered her goggles as they neared the ship. The Stars' Bounty ran alongside them. She picked off a few men as they swung from the Harpy's Claw, shooting them out of the air. Her aim was true as ever, sending her shots into their foreheads. Others thought better of swinging over, and her crew made it across without interception.

Her eyes scoured the deck until she saw him. Darian. At least, what she thought was Darian, since his face hadn't burned itself into her memories. What had stuck with her, though, was that verdant coat. The first time she'd ever seen him, he stood out on the streets of whatever city Altain had kissed her in. The same green coat that gave him away when he'd dragged her around the deck of the Dauntless, as though she didn't weigh a thing.

Darian stood at the opposite side of the Harpy's Claw, scowling at her. It took all of Song's willpower to keep herself from flying across and slapping him before killing him. All of it felt like a dream. Her mind half didn't believe she was really here. Finally. Face to face with Darian.

She forced herself to look away, scanning the deck for anyone with black hair and green eyes—though she'd be lucky if she saw anyone's eye color in the mayhem. There were a few, but two were dark-skinned and one was far too old.

"Surrender now, and I'll accept parley!" she shouted.

Darian stared across at her, his scowled deepening. "Ready the claw!" he shouted.

"Ready the what?" Song hissed.

"We have to stop the claw!" Alton shouted, and disappeared below deck.

None of her crew followed him, all too busy with their own fights. Something clicked; metal on metal, a low, booming *thu-thunk, thu-thunk* echoing in the air from its size. Song sent her gaze down over the side of her ship to the belly of his. It was deep, like Alton had said, but at the center was a strange, gigantic cog. It moved a bit with the clicking like clockwork gears.

"Fire when ready!" Darian shouted.

A boom like a cannon fired. A rope connected to something swung from the far side of the Harpy's Claw, propelled by the spinning cog, and disappeared beneath the Stars' Bounty faster than Song registered it was happening. She had mere seconds to wonder about it before the entire ship jolted.

It lurched, sending her forward to nearly tumble over the side, then ripped back again. The only thing saving her was her iron grip on the railing.

Song turned her head and her stomach dropped. There it was, a grappling hook with claws each the size of a man. The sharp ends had embedded in the deck. Below one of them was a man she didn't get a good look at in the chaos, impaled beneath the cruel spike.

"Steady on your feet!" Song shouted to the men scattered about the deck.

The entire ship shuddered violently beneath her. The clockwork clanking echoed through the air as the gear wound slowly back the other way. Song grabbed the railing to keep her footing as the deck tilted. It continued sideways, turning the belly toward the other vessel. The mainmast creaked as the zeppelin refused to tilt off its axis.

Not far from her, Knots lost his footing and tumbled into the opposite railing. He snagged a secured rope dangling beside him as a large crate slid his way. It broke the compromised railing alongside the hook, dragging him over the side with it.

Bells grunted, clinging to the mainmast. Song gripped the railing with one hand and stretched her other out for him. The mainmast groaned, splintered, and snapped like a twig, flinging Bells to the other side of the deck and over the edge. Huge splinters of wood exploded at her. She turned her head as they shot against her leather hood, trying to break through and impale her.

Men shouted and screamed beneath her. Cannons on dollies thundered across the floorboards and slammed against the hull until it splintered and popped open with a deafening *crack*. Song dangled from the railing, then climbed over it to crouch on the side of the ship.

"Song!" Sunshine called from the other vessel.

"Don't do it!" Leslie shouted, knowing the words were already forming on her tongue.

"I have to!"

He gritted his teeth and fought his way to the railing, then jumped over the side.

"Leslie!"

She looked down and found him dangling from the rope that ran between the two vessels. He lifted his sword and swung hard several times to cut through the twisted braids. His eyes locked onto hers, then he brought his blade up to sever the last strand. Leslie fell out of view as the skyship flung itself the other direction like a pendulum.

She wrapped her arms around the railing and held on, her eyes staring over the side at the multiple rippling splashes in the water far below. Then she saw the rope. No man clung to the end. One of those splashes must have been Leslie. She had a split second to wonder how many of those had been her crew before the body of the ship swung back again.

"*Suh edehts!*"

Light exploded around the Stars' Bounty, surrounding it on all sides to grip the hull and stop the motion. Song stood on deck, hissing orders for it to right the mainmast, retrieve her crew from the enemy ship, and pull her men out of the ocean.

Her eyes met Darian's. He smirked, knowing he'd won. Her heart burned with anger. Altain might have been on that ship. She was so close. She was looking right into Darian's eyes. And yet she knew she had to let him go if she was to get out of this with the lives still left aboard her ship. And so she choked out the command for some of her *kijæm* to split off and push the other vessel far away from her crippled one.

Soaked bodies floated onto the deck as someone shouted for help over the side. Song rushed over to find Knots dangling from the rope tied with a bowline around one ankle, his hands wrapped around Bells's as they clung to each other. She brought them up with her *kijæm* as a swirling mist dissipated to display Leslie lying on the deck, head turned to one side.

She ran to him and shook him. He didn't move. She put her ear to his face, but he wasn't breathing. She slapped him as panic crept through her, but he didn't flinch or react in any way.

"I don't know what to do! What do I do?"

Then it came to her. She removed her gloves, ripped his shirt open, and said the words that formed on her tongue. *Kijæm* slithered to her palms, covering them in a sparkling layer. She set her hands to his chest, and something jolted between her skin and his. His chest heaved as the bones in her hands and arms tremored with a pain she'd never dreamed could exist. It wove through her like lightning, sending her to her back, cradling her arms to her chest as she screamed.

Leslie turned over and coughed his entire lungs' worth of water onto the deck.

"Song! Over here!" Knots had torn open Hairy's shirt as he lay soaked and unconscious on deck.

She sped over as a few crewmen came up from below. She set her hands on Hairy's chest; the jolt shocked between them. Song cried out as another man wailed behind her. Hairy didn't move. She tried again and again. On the third heave, he coughed seawater up and turned over, allowing Knots to help him recover.

She ran to another crewman and ripped open his shirt. She tried to make out a face under the brown hair, but her vision was blurring. Her arms felt as though they were breaking every time, but she continued with just her right hand to lessen the pain. This man didn't wake.

"Song!"

She rushed to the man screaming her name in desperation. Song set her hand on a blond man's chest. Her vision doubled from the pain, but she forced herself to remain upright. The first man cried out and snapped backward, taking his hands off the body as her *kijæm* sent the searing agony through her, into the chest of the man under her hand, and up into the arms of the other. The blond remained unmoving; the brunette writhed in pain, and she resisted doing the same.

When she'd gone to every unconscious man, five hadn't woken. *Five of my men drowned today.* She choked out a small sob. Tears rolled from her eyes. She wiped at one and looked down. Her palms were blackened, and where she'd used the back of her hand to wipe away the tear was a streak of blood.

She set her blurry vision on the man who'd dragged himself back up after her *kijæm* had sent him screaming. He set his forehead to the other man's and screamed.

"Nebhàr!" Ponce sobbed, dragging the lifeless body into his arms to grip him tight.

He rocked on his knees, gaze sweeping across the deck as though searching for another solution—one that hadn't failed, like Song had. But when no answers came forward, he pressed his forehead into Pinch's cheek and cried until he could barely catch his breath.

Song wasn't sure what to even do, and so she cried, too, as she leaned back against the broken mainmast to keep herself upright. She sank to her knees and held her hands out to the sides, unable to move her fingers from the searing pain and the sensation of shattering still streaking through her bones. She screamed out all the pain she'd tried to ignore as it built into something too great to not voice. Over and over, she screamed until her throat ached. Even then, she didn't stop.

Leslie crawled to her and held her face as she wept tears of blood. It trickled from her ears, painting the skin along her neck. Her nose released a rivulet of red into her mouth, staining her teeth. He took one of her hands and she jerked it away, tilting her head to scream her agony up at the zeppelin overhead.

"Song, you need to release it," Leslie said, too exhausted to use his fake accent. His eyes trained on the glittering mainmast over them.

"I can't," she sobbed. "I'm the only thing holding the ship together."

He shoved to his feet and stumbled to find men fit enough to fly. Pickings were slim, but he rounded up enough for a skeleton crew and took command of the vessel. As Song cried and concentrated through her pain on staying conscious, the men forced the Stars' Bounty to limp to the nearest port.

In front of her stayed the two blurry figures. One crying over the other. She stared at his brown hair as she finally recognized who knelt before her, and a knot formed in her throat.

"Ponce..."

"Th-the c-cannon..." he sputtered. "Nebhàr s-shoved me out of the way, b-but..."

How many of the men had been crushed by the falling cannons? She didn't even have a casualty report to know how many were dead or injured, and how badly. "I'm sorry."

"It's not your f-fault."

But it was. And she knew it. If not for her blind desire to get Altain back at all costs, they wouldn't have even stopped to attack Darian's ship. And for what? For all she knew, Altain was long dead, and she was chasing a ghost.

After a long time, Leslie came up from below deck and sat beside her with Doctor's bag. He coughed, his lungs still recovering from drowning, and focused on her right hand. He found a salve and gently spread it over the blackened, blistering skin of her palms and fingers. Leslie gripped Song's wrist to keep her from jerking it away as she screamed in pain, all the while suppressing his cough as best he could.

He pushed up her sleeve once he'd finished and scowled at the black and purple bruise covering her skin like a long glove. The dark color continued up her arm, deep into the sleeve he'd pushed up to her elbow. He circled around her and spread the salve on her left palm, then pushed that sleeve up as far up as he could. Her skin was brown and yellow to the elbow. The damage had not been as severe as with her other arm.

"We'll give him a proper burial," he said over his shoulder. "I'm sure Sunshine knows the prayer."

"Piss on the prayer," Ponce spat.

A haunting silence overtook the deck as the survivors stared at each other and at the bodies strewn about. No one had to say anything for them to know they shared the same thoughts and felt the same hopelessness.

Song leaned her head back. "I don't know how much longer I can hold it."

"If we find enough ropes, could you secure them around the ship to keep it from falling apart?" Leslie asked.

"I... Maybe."

Ponce moved to follow Leslie below.

"No. Stay with Nebhàr," Leslie said.

A sob forced its way through his lips. "He's not going anywhere."

Every man who was able brought anything which could substitute as a rope, including sheets and even hammocks. Bruce emerged with a thick coil of rope, favoring his left arm. Without a word, he sat beside her and set his hand on her cheek, then closed his eyes.

The burden on her mind eased, and she felt as though it was draining less of her energy to maintain the hold. With this new vigor, she sent the commands to bind the ship with ropes at the weakest points. The thickest, strongest ropes tied off on the railings up to the top of the mainmast to loop into the hoops. When she finished, she took a deep breath.

"Thank you, Bruce."

He yawned and tipped over right there to sleep.

Leslie crouched beside her. His blue eyes captured hers, and he nodded. "Sleep, now."

"Don't bury them without me," she whispered.

"We'll try."

He lowered her sideways, resting her head on the deck. She whispered one last order to her *kijæm*. Minutes later, the Pishing blade embedded its tip into the deck between them.

Twenty-Eight

To the surprise of both Leslie and herself, Song remained unconscious for just one day. She woke feeling hungover, her eyes rimmed with dark black circles. Her arm felt like hammers had beaten it and looked about that way. Her left arm was blue and purple in patches, but her right arm was black and blue from fingertips to mid-biceps.

Leslie helped her out of the hammock. Song gripped him tight, though it hurt. It was worth the pain, just to be able to hold him. Tears rolled from her eyes and an uncontrollable sobbing overtook her. He held her just as tight, not shushing her or trying to calm her down. His one hand smoothed over her hair, petting her as some form of comfort. A long time passed as she wept in Leslie's arms.

I nearly lost him. I did lose him for a minute.

When she calmed enough to speak, she said, "Don't you ever do that to me again."

"I promise I won't, if you won't."

"I promise."

"You should've been out much longer. I don't understand."

"Perhaps there are answers in…" She stopped cold as she remembered the lifeless body of Pinch sprawled out on the deck. Her need for the answers held within the holy book seemed insignificant now. "Casualty report," she whispered, a phrase she'd never wanted to utter.

"Seven injured, but they should recover fine. Five others...we're not sure. They may recover, or their injuries could claim them."

"How many dead?"

"Ten. And one unaccounted for."

"Who is unaccounted for?"

"Hardtack."

She shook her head, dazed by the numbers. "He went below deck on the Harpy's Claw. He was trying to stop the hook."

"Given the state of our ship, I'd assume they killed him."

She shook her head. "No. I won't say one of my crew is dead until I have proof. I held on this long for Altain, I'll do the same for Alton."

"Fair enough. Would you like to see the damage? I'm sure the men would be more than happy to know you're up. After Telbhaniich-Zardi, a lot of the men feared this would kill you."

She let out a long breath. "The day is still young. I may yet drop dead. Or fall into a sleep I never wake from."

"I'll remain optimistic you don't. We've had enough bleak news to finish out the year." He wrapped his arm around her waist and supported her as she circled her left arm behind his neck. "Tell me if you need to stop."

She nodded, and they made their way to the door, slow and wobbly. The sight on deck was grim and sent Song's stomach into a freefall. Still clinging to the Stars' Bounty was the Harpy's Claw's massive grappling hook. The sharp tips remained embedded into the deck. Someone had covered the man pinned beneath as best they could with a blanket. His face flashed in her mind, and now out of the chaos of battle, she recognized him as Knuckles, the only crew member with a right hook near as vicious as Thumbs's.

Nine bumps beneath long strips of spare canvas and blankets lay out along the bow. One man sat amongst them, staring off into the distance as he cradled the hand of a corpse. Leslie helped Song limp over and lowered her down to sit beside him.

She wrapped Ponce in as tight of a hug as she could. "I'm so sorry, Henry," she whispered.

"I keep thinking I'll wake up," Ponce whispered into her shoulder. "I doze off and snap awake thinking this was all a dream. But he just stays dead. He just... This can't be real. He can't be gone."

"I wish it weren't."

"Can you bring back the dead?"

Song shook her head. "I can't. Otherwise, I would've gotten Dash back."

"But you're more powerful now. Can't you try?" His voice didn't carry even a hint of hope—false or otherwise. He let out an ugly sob.

Song concentrated through the fog of her mind, begging words to form that could somehow bring Pinch back. Her mind responded with hollow silence. Not even a single hint of a command. "I'm sorry, that's still not something I can do."

"I figured," he said. "I bloody figured."

She rubbed his back, then leaned away, wiping her own tears from her eyes. "Leslie, show me the damage to the ship."

Leslie helped her to her feet and supported her descent down. Most things were still scattered about, though the table and benches had been set right so men could sit at it now.

Sunshine shoved to his feet. "You're up. So soon? How are you feeling?"

"About as well as the Bounty looks," she said. "Anyway, as you were. Let's get on with it."

Leslie helped her into the doorway of the crew's quarters. She stared at the half sorted mess. Part of the ceiling and wall had broken, the grappling hook still clinging to the ship like a cork in the hole.

"Why haven't you thrown it into the ocean?" Song growled.

"It's too heavy," Leslie said.

"I can—"

"Don't even think about it," Sunshine snapped behind them. "When you cry blood, that's your hint to bloody stop. I don't care how quick you woke up this time. The immediate effects are gettin' worse."

"Fair enough," she said.

"Oh, I expected more caterwaulin'. Had a whole lecture planned out."

"You were going to invoke Dash's name to make me feel guilty."

"Damn right, I was."

Song stared at Bruce in his usual corner, drawing, his left arm tied up in a sling. Beside him was Thumbs, his right ankle wrapped tight.

"Let's continue," she said.

They descended to the weapons hold, and Song froze at the sight. Cannons had battered the side of the ship open. Only two remained, wedged between support beams and planks still intact.

"Ten cannons lost," she said. Her gaze swept the room. "Powder barrels and cannonballs are all gone, too."

"It's an expensive loss. Almost as much as patching that hole," Leslie said. "The…"

"What?"

"The Stars' Bounty…I fear she's lost, Song."

"No." Tears burned her eyes.

"It would cost less to buy a whole new ship. The damage is—"

"I said *no!* This is Dash's ship. This is my home."

Leslie released a long breath. "As you wish, Captain. One deck left."

The bow cargo hold at the bottom of the ship was in shambles, though hull integrity had not been compromised in there. She stared at a spatter of blood against the wall.

"Doctor," Leslie said.

The knot stuck in her throat from the moment she woke tightened. "He was on this ship as long as Dash."

They turned for the aft cargo hold door, which had been closed. Normally reserved for stolen goods from other vessels, while the other was their supplies, this one had been emptied. Injured men lay sprawled out or propped up. They had opened the portholes to allow fresh air to blow through, but the smell of blood clung to the room.

"Captain," Hairy acknowledged from his position on the floor, a makeshift splint on his left leg and one on his left arm. "Whispers, would you mind getting Bones out of here before he starts to smell?"

"Died an hour ago," another man said.

Song scanned the area for Bones, the man with strange skeletal tattoos across the backs of his hands. He lay unmoving, not far from Hairy, his entire body battered and his clothes and bandages bloody. Leslie left Song using the doorjamb for support and returned with Bells and Sunshine. They wrapped the dead man in a blanket and carried him up to the main deck.

"Eleven dead," Song said, a hollowness spreading through her insides. "Names?"

Leslie released a slow, mournful breath. "Pinch, Doctor, Lucy, Blades, Leftie, Powder, McKay, Knuckles, Paddy, Bishop, and now Bones."

Her chin wrinkled, and she closed her eyes. She didn't want to admit out loud that she only knew half of the faces that went with those names. The other half had been no more than names on a contract, or faces without a name.

Leslie urged her back to her cabin, where she curled into a ball on the bay bench and wept.

"I shouldn't be captain," she said. "I said it over and over. This is our punishment for not having a Krell leading us."

He took her hand in both of his. "Stop. This has nothing to do with you."

"But it does. This never would have happened if Dash was still alive. Or if you were captain."

"Song, you didn't cause this, and neither did me not being captain. This was Darian. He would've done it no matter who was in charge. He's done it to other vessels before us, and if he replaces that hook, he'll continue to do it."

She shook her head as a tear rolled over the bridge of her nose. "I need to sleep again. I'm so sorry."

"I'll stay with you."

Song dragged his hand up to hug to her chest. "Thank you."

Song woke to a spectacular view outside her windows. On either side of a wide swath of water were tall mountains, covered in both evergreen and deciduous trees. She'd never seen anything like it. It took her breath away.

She slid from the cushions, careful not to jostle Leslie where he sat against the bench, his head leaning sideways to use the cushion as a pillow. By the time she reached the door, though, he was at her side, blinking away exhaustion.

"Go back to sleep," she said.

"I'll be fine. Come on." He supported her as he had the day before, keeping her upright when her legs wanted to totter or collapse beneath her.

Out on deck, Song breathed out in wonder. "What is this place? It's beautiful."

Leslie remained silent for a long time, eyes wide. "No," he whispered, as though trying to change reality with a single word.

Song looked at the navigator at the helm. "Maps, where are we?"

"Headed for Skaaldvik Vyaard. It was the nearest port that would be friendly to us," Maps said.

"Pishing," Leslie whispered.

"Was there really no other choice?" Song asked.

"We're moving at a crawl with dead and dying, Captain. All due respects, but I wasn't going to risk lives and more damage to the Bounty just to avoid this damned country."

Leslie swallowed. "It's fine. It'll be all right. I'll just wear a hood."

"Copying my look? I'm flattered." Her eyes drifted to his jaw. "You haven't shaved in days, have you?"

"I should probably do that."

"Drop me at the steps and go scrape that red hair off your chin."

Leslie helped her lower onto the bottom step, then rushed below deck.

Maps released a slow breath. "Sorry. I know it's a risk. I just…"

"I understand," she said, boosting up one step at a time until she sat at the top. "We can hide him. What we can't do is risk more time flying." Song eyed the mainmast, silently willing the ropes to hold on a little longer. "I don't know what to do."

Maps let out a long breath. "We can hire a barge. They'll know how to handle transporting this old girl somewhere for repairs."

"She's an Armalinian ship."

"Then we should take her to Djori Cove."

"If I step foot on Armalinian sand, the sultania will force me to marry her."

Maps chuckled. "The odds of her knowing you're there would be slim."

Song sighed and leaned her head against the railing as her gaze settled on Ponce, who still hadn't moved from beside the blanket covering Pinch's body. "Leslie said it would be cheaper to buy another ship."

"Aye. And faster. These repairs, even if they started immediately, would take months. And that's after waiting weeks for the ship to arrive."

A hopeless knot formed in her throat. "We should've just gone to Telbhaniich-Zardi. We never should've stopped the Harpy's Claw."

"You didn't know…" His voice drifted off, and neither had the mind to say anything more.

Leslie returned after a long time below deck. He retrieved her coat and boots from her cabin and helped her into them. "Sorry it took so long. I couldn't find my razor and got distracted organizing my trunk. Then I had to ask around for a coat with a hood."

"Did you find one?"

He paused, then lowered his head in a solemn nod. "Aye. It was Bones's."

Song's eyes settled on the newest body on deck. "What do we

do with them?"

"We don't have the canvas or cannonballs to bury them at sea. Skaaldvik Vyaard might have a cemetery, like Talegrove, but it's a lot to bury. We'll figure it out."

"When we get there, don't help me."

"Why not?"

"I don't want anyone seeing me weak. Getting ideas."

"Fair enough."

An hour later, as the sun set enough to cast the fjord in dark shadow, the lights of a small city came into view, nestled at the very end of the mountainous scar. Behind it, a waterfall tumbled from cliff after cliff in a tiered spectacle. It was a humble sort of place, with large docks that rimmed much of the beach for both water and sky vessels. The sailers, though, were a special sort—shallow bottomed with single sails.

"What funny ships," she said.

"Fjord waters are too shallow for ocean vessels," Leslie said. He'd tied back his hair, then tucked it into a knit cap pulled down to cover his auburn eyebrows, and now raised his hood to hide his face. "I've never been this far west. I just know of these fjord cities. They speak a strange variation of Common and the old tongue."

"Jin."

"What?"

"The old language. It's called Jin." She laughed at his bewildered expression. "I've just remembered I bought you a book that'll get us all killed for even having it on board near Pishing."

"What book?"

"It's about the Jinjur people."

Leslie's lower lids rose as he squinted at her. "You know that's a slur, right? An insult for having red hair."

Song patted his knee. "It didn't used to be. Remind me to give you the book once we're out of this dump. It cost an absurd amount of quoine, and I'd hate for that forbidden knowledge to go to waste."

He smiled, though it barely touched his eyes. "I can't wait to read it." He lifted her hood over her head in preparation for docking.

The sheer amount of red-haired people that collected on the dock took Song by surprise. Word must have spread as someone spied the broken ship from afar. She dragged herself to her feet and stood near the pull-away railing. A large man waited until the ship came to a stop. A woman and a man slid a wooden plank across as Toothy opened the false railing.

"Always wanted the Stars' Bounty to *hiirbor* here," the man said. "Never thought she'd be in this shape." His accent was deeper than Dashaelan's and Leslie's. Guttural with rolling, curled r's and vowels that seemed to claw desperately to escape his lips.

"No offense, but we're not fond of your country," Song said.

"You must be Song."

"Aye. I'm Captain Song. I'm sure you have threats and promises of skinning me alive if I cause trouble, but…as you can see, my men and I are in no mood to do so." She gestured at the dead.

Song hadn't realized how strong the smell of dead men in hot air had gotten, as it had crept up on her and the crew. The townspeople held cloths over their nose and mouth, and one woman had vomited over the other side of the dock.

"Come. We can *spiikun* what to do with—"

"I would like to figure that out before I leave this ship. There are wounded below, and my men would like a hot meal. I, however, will not leave this ship until every one of my men, living or not, has been taken care of."

The man and several others spoke amongst themselves. Once they came to an agreement, he nodded. "All right, Captain Song. We'll get your wounded off the ship first."

Song paused on the other quirk of the accent, in which the man said every f like a v. Rather than say something about it, she nodded to Leslie. "Whispers, go get them started."

He nodded and went below. People crossed onto the ship and followed to help him, while others brought cloth stretchers onto the deck.

The tall man stood beside her, arms folded. "I'm Byuurn. What did this to your ship, if I might ask?"

She gestured toward the hook stuck in the deck. "A ship called the Harpy's Claw. She swung that at us and pulled until we toppled. Cannons and cargo did the rest."

"You put up a *sraag* front," he said low to her. "But you lean heavy on this railing. Like you'll collapse if you let go. Has a medic looked at you?"

"Our doctor died in the attack. But I'm fine, thank you. There is nothing a doctor could do for me."

"How can you be so sure?"

"I'm Gifted. And these are injuries brought on by keeping this ship in the sky. Trust me when I say I am in good enough condition to massacre a city, should I be provoked."

Byuurn chuckled and raised his hands. "No need to threaten. Besides, I have it on good word you're as honorable a pirate as they come."

"Whose word?" she asked.

"Shadow." He chuckled when she gaped. "We havens keep in touch."

"To be honest, I was under the impression there was only the one."

"That one's the safest. But there's three of us."

As they'd spoken, men had come up carrying other men or helping them walk. Leslie passed, meeting her gaze as he helped Thumbs limp off the ship. Bruce followed close behind, carrying only his sketchbook. After a while of watching the back and forth of the wounded being helped, and the corpses being taken away one by one, Song sat, deflated, on the steps. She wanted to cry all over again, but didn't dare. She couldn't show more weakness than she already had.

"What are you doing with the bodies?" she asked Byuurn.

"We burn our dead, and so we offer the same to you. It would be faster than digging a dozen graves."

"Then what?"

"We spread the ashes in a ritual. Some are taken back to their homes in *skaakraask*. Bones and all."

"I'll ask my crew if they know what the others would've wanted," she said.

He nodded. "You're a good captain, Song. Few care about their men like you seem to."

"A better captain would've kept them alive."

Twenty-Nine

Night had fallen, and a full moon shone down over the land by the time Song made it to an inn for a chilly bath and a hot meal. Sunshine sat across from her, eating his own meal in silence, but otherwise she ate alone. She frowned at the heavy bread and odd big game stew with peas in it. She wanted more than anything to have Leslie nearby, as though him being out of sight risked his existence.

"The first real defeat Dash led, we lost five men," Sunshine said.

Song eyed him, but didn't reply.

"Two on an enemy ship, and three to cannons. Side of the Bounty was pockmarked from the assault. He called a retreat, rather than a surrender. Two more men got left behind. They signed on with that crew." He chewed a bite of food and swallowed, thinking as he stared at the tabletop. "Every captain will have their biggest failure. Some are worse than others. The important part is what you do about it afterward."

"What did Dash do about his?" Song asked.

"Next time he saw the bastards, he gave no quarter and fought to kill. It was a slaughter."

"Only a fool seeks revenge," she said.

"Yes, yes. He didn't seek it, though. It just fell into his lap, so he took it."

Song clenched her teeth and stared at her hands. "Next time, I'll be more ruthless."

"But you ain't gonna seek it."

She pressed her lips together and didn't respond. Perhaps she wanted to be a fool. How could she not go seeking revenge while also trying to find out what happened to Altain?

"I know what you're thinkin'."

"Do you?"

"Why not arrange a parley in Talegrove? Shadow as mediator. Figure out once and for all about your friend while also settlin' this feud between you and Darian. The entire pirate world talks about it, you know. And who do you think they side with?" Sunshine asked.

"Obviously the wronged one."

"Which one was wronged?"

"Me!" she snapped. "How could you possibly—"

"He didn't wrong Caleb Song. He wronged Tsingsei Gould. To him and everyone else, you've got a vendetta against him for no reason. Make your reason known."

"If I say it's to retrieve Altain, then my secret is out."

Sunshine nodded absently and scooped up a spoonful of food. "Then a mediated meetin' might be best. Fewer casualties that way."

She let out a long, deflating sigh. "Now I see why Dash kept you so close. Mind as sharp as a good knife."

"So you'll think about it?"

"I'll think about it."

~

Song stepped out into the cool night air. She wandered the packed dirt streets until she came upon a hut out away from everything else. Lined up in front of it were several bodies of her dead crewmen. On a stool around the side, where the wind kept the stench of the dead from wafting over, she found Ponce. She walked to him and lowered to the ground as the effort of the day caught up with her recovering body.

"Have you eaten?" she asked after a minute.

"No."

"When was the last time you did?"

Ponce let out a long breath. "Before Darian."

"Have you drank anything?"

"Um…"

"Ponce, you need to—"

"Toothy forced me to take water," he mumbled at his hands.

"Have you been here the whole time?"

"Aye."

Song reached up and held his hand. She'd never done something like that with him. It was strange, but he gripped her hand like a rope, holding on for dear life in case he fell.

"Little softer," she said. "Sorry. My hands are bruised."

"Oh. Sorry." He made to let go, but she held on.

"No, it's fine. This is my good arm."

They didn't say anything for a long time. An owl filled the silence with occasional hoots. Crickets chirruped somewhere in the woods. But the two of them remained in a motionless silence, staring out at nothing.

"It's not fair," Ponce said after what felt like an eternity. He let out a dry sob, but couldn't muster tears beyond them stinging his eyes red.

"I'm sorry I didn't get to him in time," she whispered.

He sucked on his teeth and shook his head, eyes on his knees. "I don't think you have enough power to fix what the cannons did to him. But for a moment, I hoped. I just thought, if only he'd wake up, that you could try."

"I would've tried until it killed me."

"I know."

They fell silent again. Song grappled with saying something, anything, to comfort him. But what could she say? Nothing would change what had happened, and nothing could ease his pain.

Hopelessness trapped her in its suffocating grasp. The weight of her failure pressed upon her heart again. She wanted to voice that it was all her fault, to let him know the depth of her own pain. But she feared what he would say. She didn't want him to tell her it wasn't her fault. It was. And she wanted to carry that guilt until it drowned her. But she also didn't want him to agree with her, because that would make the pain of it that much worse. For a split second, she was relieved Dashaelan wasn't able to look at her with abject disappointment.

The relief didn't last long, as her sorrow for him added onto the pile of dead and wounded, onto the broken mast and shattered hull. In less than one year as captain, she'd accomplished one grand scheme, but managed to destroy the ship, kill one third of the crew, and render half of the remaining men unfit to fly.

"What're we doin' out here?" Toothy sauntered closer, a bowl in one hand and a cup in the other. By the time he reached them, neither had answered. He shoved the bowl at Ponce. "Eat."

"I'm not hungry."

"I wasn't asking."

Ponce took the spoon and stirred the food a bit, then took the smallest of nibbles. "Tastes like sand."

"I don't care what you think it tastes like. You're gonna eat every last damned bite, you pisshead."

"Haven't called me that since we were teens."

"Cause you ain't been one 'til now. Shut up and eat." He held up the cup for Ponce to take.

One small bite at a time, Ponce made his way through the food. He'd sip the water and hand it back to Toothy, who kept his hand up for that very purpose.

It wasn't long before another man approached, slow and quiet, a hood over his head. He lowered down on Song's other side and joined them in their silence. Song turned to stare at what little she could see of Leslie's face. She imagined him being one of the bodies waiting to be burned to ash. A stabbing pain ripped through her, and she guessed that's what Ponce must have been feeling. She couldn't hold back the tears as that final thought broke through her struggling dam of dark emotions.

Song curled against Leslie's side and wept. No one said anything. None of them needed to.

The next morning, Song found each member of her crew who was fit enough that they could gather for a memorial for those they'd lost. A few had no homes and no family that anyone knew of, and so she scattered their ashes in the bay. A local man did their funeral rites while a woman sang a lamentation. The entire city had arrived on the docks to pay their own respects, it seemed. They may not have been pirates, but they were still a part of the pirate world.

Song couldn't help but think of the celebrations her father would go through after they'd executed a notorious pirate. She'd joined a time or two. How big of a party would this have been for him? How big of a party would Elroy Gould throw when Caleb Song inevitably died? Would he ever even know that it had been his own daughter under the hood?

They locked the ashes Song intended to have returned to their loved ones in a storehouse, each one labeled so she could go through the wreckage and find records later.

Ponce stood on the shore, staring out at the rippling bay waters as he hugged the decorated wooden box to his chest. Song stood beside him as the gathering dispersed. Toothy stood on the other side, loathe to leave his best friend alone with his grief for even a moment.

"Captain..." Ponce began.

"Yes?"

"Permission to take leave of the crew."

She clenched her jaw and stared at her feet. "Reason?"

"I want to take Nebhàr home. I never got to meet his family. He always said I'd like them."

Song took a deep breath and set her palm on his back. "Permission granted."

After an hour of asking around and paying from her own quoine, they bought Ponce's way onto a skyship heading to Telbhaniich-Zardi, where he could then buy passage to Aibhànocht.

He left at dawn the next morning, a duffel of belongings over his shoulder and ashes in a satchel he gripped to his chest. Song felt the empty spot in her crew like a gaping wound.

"I feel like I'll never see him again," she admitted between Toothy and Leslie as they watched the skyship disappear around a bend.

Toothy let out a long breath. "I should've gone with him."

"He'll take care of himself," Leslie said. "Has to, so he can make it there."

He nodded absently. "Aye. Loves Nebhàr enough to at least get there. After that, though…"

"He'll be fine," Song said, as though saying it aloud would manifest it as truth, but she wasn't so sure.

Toothy nodded and ambled away.

"Walk you to your room?" Song said to Leslie.

"Sure."

"How are you faring in hiding?" she asked as they strolled toward the inns.

He shook his head as he thought. "I don't know how you handle the lack of peripheral vision. And my head is hot."

Song laughed. "Spend long enough under the hood and you learn to function as though it's not even there."

"I'd rather just get away from here, so I don't have to wear it anymore."

She stared around at the people going about their business, ignoring the two of them. "I don't see why you need to hide here. No one cares."

"They care enough, Song. You don't see them, but there are slaves in this city."

She froze. "What?"

"As an outsider, it's understandable. But they're here. They're everywhere in Pishing. It's not some rare thing in only the bigger cities. This is part of life; part of the culture here. So, no, a man being labeled a runaway slave, though he is a free man, is not safe. I've already torn down several posters just for me."

"It's not up because you're a pirate. It's up because of the runaway part."

He nodded. "And the bit about taking the name of a high lord. Anyone else to do that would get a fine, maybe see some prison time. But a slave? That's the 'or dead' part."

"Did you know I can see places I've never been?" she asked.

"What?" He stopped to stare at her.

"Most Touched can't, right?"

"Song...what are you thinking?"

"No one would suspect me at all. It would look like a freak accident."

Leslie released a long, drawn-out breath. "And if anyone figured it out—"

"You think I care? Let them put all the bounties on my head. I'll be the most expensive pirate in the world, and I'll wear it with pride, so long as you're safe," she snapped.

"I wouldn't be safe, though. The bounty would still be on my head. It doesn't go away with his death."

"Then what do we do?" Song growled.

"I don't know." He tilted his head to urge her back to walking.

They continued in silence to Leslie's inn room. She stared at the painted white door, thoughts and plans whirling through her mind. He leaned a shoulder on the frame and studied her in an equally pensive silence.

"Go get some rest, Song. You need it."

She fidgeted, not wanting to walk away, as though she couldn't rest until they had a plan. After a moment, she gave a resigned sigh. "All right. Fine. I'll see you in the morning."

"Sleep well, Song."

She returned to her own room to nurse a bottle of whiskey, stare at the ceiling, and think. Again, the only plan her mind liked involved regicide, which no one could ever trace back to her. One other thought entered her mind. She shoved it away, though. There had to be a better way than buying Leslie as a slave and freeing him for the second time in his life. The very idea sat wrong in her belly. No, she had to come up with a solution that let him keep his dignity as well.

Thirty

*I*mages of the broken bodies of her crew danced behind Song's eyelids. She hadn't drunk enough to quiet her mind, and now she paid the price with nightmares. Leslie lay splayed out before her on the deck. But this time, no matter how much she put her hand to his chest, he didn't wake. Her hand burned to ash. The bones in her arm shattered and fell into a pile of brittle pieces.

She snapped upright, slick with sweat and sucking in heavy gasps as though she hadn't breathed before. Song wrapped her palm around her right forearm and cradled it as it ached. She flung back the thin blanket and strode to the basin to splash cold water over her face. A glance in the mirror at her arm made her frown and turn away. It was still dark, with a vicious grey and purple bruise that began at mid biceps and stretched all the way to her fingertips. The color had lightened in the week since the encounter, and the pain was less constant, but it still bothered her.

With a deep breath, she pulled on her clothes and coat, tucking her loose hair into her collar. She locked the door behind her and left the inn. Song crossed the dirt street to the other inn and strode to the painted door. Her eyes studied the number five nailed to the center. With a breath, she wrapped her hand around the knob.

"*Kawl-nu.*"

The lock clicked open, and she let herself in. She'd gotten two buckles of her coat undone when behind her the muffled scrape of a sword unsheathing sounded in the darkness.

She presented a wry smile to the door. "And what are you planning to do with that?"

Leslie released a long sigh. "Song. What are you doing in here?" He lifted the edge of the mattress to return his sword to the scabbard.

She said nothing, just clenched her jaw and hung her coat on the wall hook by the door. She stepped out of her boots and took off her clothes until only her underthings remained. Then she crossed the room, lifted his blanket, and slid in, forcing him over. Without asking, she curled up and set her temple to his shoulder.

"Song?"

"I had a nightmare," she whispered. "The crew… Pinch… You…"

He said nothing, just wrapped his arms around to comfort her.

"I don't want to lose you the way Ponce lost Pinch."

Leslie took a deep breath and rubbed his palm over her back. "I'm still here. Thanks to you."

"You're welcome."

He chuckled. "Don't worry, I know you did it for yourself, not for me."

"Damn right."

"How selfish of you." He gave her another firm squeeze. "All seriousness…thank you. I owe you my life."

She tilted her head to meet his gaze in the darkness. After a long silence, she shifted closer. The tip of her nose found the tip of his. She paused, as though giving him an opportunity to stop her. Then she set a soft kiss to his lips. She waited again, giving him yet another chance to protest as she thought over and over where she was going with this. When he didn't say anything, she kissed him again. He turned to face her, his arm behind her head pushed her closer to him as the other drifted across her waist. After a moment, she held him just as close.

Leslie pulled away, his fingers cradling her chin as though holding her back. "Song, wait—"

"Shh…" She silenced him with her lips locked firmly to his.

He pressed his fingertips against her chin again to stop her. "Just wait. You said—"

"I'm sober." She took his hand and returned it to her waist, lifting the bottom of her shirt enough for him to feel the soft skin underneath.

She settled her face close to his, urging him to close the distance. After a moment, he returned his lips to hers, accepting the answer to his question. His fingertips traced over the small of her back and partway up her spine. Her fingers tangled into his silky hair; her palms smoothed across his soft skin. The more delicate aspects of his body made her a little less nervous about being intimate with a man. Besides that, it was Leslie. She knew she loved him. It had to be the case, as she feared she couldn't live without him at her side. And so she let his unyielding love for her take the lead. Perhaps all she needed was one night with him and she would crave him in the same desperate way he craved her.

As though testing how far she would let him go, he inched his palm up, pushing her shirt with it. After a while, when her impatience grew too much, she wrapped her fingers around his wrist and guided his palm to her breast. Something firm pressed to her lower abdomen, and she couldn't stop the heat between her thighs, though her mind hesitated over such an unfamiliar thing.

Memories of the sultania flooded her thoughts, as though comparing the two. The delicate pampered woman's skin versus this man whose otherwise soft skin had rough overnight stubble that scraped like sandpaper on her chin. He didn't have the slope of a woman's waist, or the curve of a woman's hips. No breasts cradled her hand at his sternum.

Song hesitated, but Leslie didn't notice as he kissed along her neck, pressing his hips against her. An unfair thought intruded upon her: she wished him to be a woman—that she would enjoy him more that way. But he wasn't a woman.

I love him more than anyone in the world. She bit her bottom lip as Leslie nibbled the side of her neck. *But do I love him like this?*

She wanted to experience what his love would be like. Perhaps she might find her own, then. And so she chased the thought of him being a woman from her mind and focused on enjoying what she could of the man he was.

Her body's desperate heat urged her to continue and ignore the reservations roiling within her mind. She returned her lips to his, let his tongue explore within. Curiosity sent her hand to his waist, but fear sent it to the small of his back, rather than forward to feel the firm organ between them. Her palm traced lower, and she realized with a blush that he was already completely naked.

Her face heated. She turned her head to break the kiss and pressed her lips together. "Were you going to warn me you sleep nude?"

He chuckled, his forehead to her cheek. "Hadn't yet gotten the chance." He tugged at her shirt to return it to its previous state, as though taking her shock as a desire to stop.

Song stopped him, then sat up and pulled her shirt over her head to throw somewhere behind her. She'd gotten this far, and her body had heated so much that it wanted release more than she had wanted to know if somehow this one man was an exception to her own heart's desires.

"Are you sure?" he whispered as she nestled back into his arms.

"I'm sure."

Leslie released a soft *mmm* against her lips as she returned to the desperate kisses.

Already both so hot and desperate for release, they returned to their previous level of passion. Leslie's thumb hooked into the waistband of her underpants and dragged them down her hip. Once he'd banished the article to somewhere on the floor, his palm slid along her thigh. His hand made its way between her thighs to feel the heat nestled there. She raised her knee just enough to encourage him to continue. Leslie tested her desire with a single finger. She gave a soft moan against his lips in reply.

Song shifted with him as he turned to position himself over her, cradled between her legs. The pressure of him pushed at her opening, and she sucked in a breath. She held it, letting it escape her nose in little squeaks of equal parts discomfort and shock as he filled her. Leslie paused at the noise and started to withdraw.

"Keep going," she insisted, gripping his shoulders as though to hold him in place.

After a lingering hesitation, he resumed, finding a gentle rhythm for them to move together to. He held her like she was delicate and breakable, though she gripped him so hard the bruise of her right arm ached. Their skin pressed together; their naked bodies warmed each other past the chill of the night.

Now she could see the truth she'd been refusing to accept. It was apparent in the way he drank in her kisses, meticulous in his drive to savor every drop. She felt it in the way he threaded his fingers through hers and squeezed against her left hand. It was there on his lips as he kissed along the side of her neck, in his breath swirling hot on her skin. There was no more denying his love. No more claiming he couldn't possibly have been foolish enough to fall for such a woman. He had. Now she knew it, without a doubt.

Song kept her mind on each touch; on the climax building within her. She focused on the gentle rhythm they moved to. The pressure at her core as he filled her was both strange and pleasurable. And Leslie knew how to read her sounds, as though they were a map guiding him to her release.

A thought still haunted her through all of it. Her heart hadn't swollen as she'd expected. Her mind didn't bend to fit perfectly with him. He made love to her, giving her everything he was. And yet, as much as she wanted to accept it and reciprocate, nothing came forward to give to him.

He still had a huge part of her heart claimed in some strange form of love, but now she knew this was not it. However, she didn't stop them. She needed the physical release now, despite it not meaning anything more like she hoped it would, and like she knew Leslie must have wanted.

Song tilted her chin up, lips parted as the pressure within her built. She couldn't hold back the sounds that escaped her throat. Her body responded to him, pushing closer, begging him to take her to that sweet release. When she found it, she gripped him tight and held on. Perhaps this would be it. Perhaps now she would love him the same. She tipped her head back as her ecstasy sent all thoughts, wants, and reasoning from her mind.

Thirty-One

Song's eyes snapped wide as she woke in the morning. Leslie was still asleep behind her, his arm draped over her waist, his other beneath the pillow under her head.

Damn it.

She turned to look at him. His face was so serene in the dawn's light. It hit her with a solid punch of guilt. She didn't love him, and she couldn't bring herself to disturb his serenity with that tragic revelation. And so her mind screamed for her to run—run from his bed and run from breaking his heart.

Damn it, damn everything.

She moved his arm, slow and careful so as not to wake him, then slipped from the bed as quietly as possible. She stooped to find her underpants, pulling them up around her waist. Song took a step toward her shirt and a board creaked under her foot. She froze.

Damn me!

After nothing happened, she padded for her undershirt and dragged it on. She feverishly pulled on her britches. As she buttoned them, the bed creaked behind her. She froze again and glanced over her shoulder at the man sitting on the edge, the blanket wrapped around his waist, his elbows on his knees. He said nothing as he stared at her back, not meeting her gaze.

"S-sorry," she stammered. "I've got to, um—" Song grabbed her outer shirt and yanked it over her head. "Sunshine."

"Song..."

"He wanted to talk to me." She shrugged into her coat and shoved on one boot. "Don't want to keep him waiting."

"Song." He let out a long breath.

When she looked at him, his back was to her, trousers on, and he was working to tie them. She tried not to stare at the crisscrossing scars, but her eyes wouldn't look away.

"Lots of things to do," she said, yanking on her other boot. "Have to find us a new ship so we can get back up in the sky."

"I think it's time I stay on the ground for a while."

She stopped midway through a buckle on her coat to stare at him. "What? No."

"Yes."

"Why?"

He dragged his shirt over his head. "Do you really have to ask?"

She swallowed. No, she didn't have to ask. She already knew it was because of last night. He loved her so hopelessly, and as hard as she'd tried to make herself do the same, it hadn't happened. There was *something*, she couldn't deny that. But she had no way of putting it into words.

"You don't have my permission," she said as she twisted her hair around at the nape of her neck and tucked it into her high collar.

"That's the beauty of it," he said, "I don't need your bloody permission."

"Yes, you do."

He strode across the room, jaw tight, as his eyes captured hers. "You were my captain, not my *owner*." With that, he opened the door and shoved her out as she dragged her hood over her head.

Song spun around as the door shut and locked. "I'm not done talking to you! Open this door this instant, Leslie."

No answer came from the other side, not even his footsteps.

"Krell!" she shouted, trying to get him to at least demand through the wood that she not call him that.

A board creaked to her right, and she turned her head to look down the hallway at a man with his thumbs tucked into his belt as he stared in amusement at her.

"Lovers' spat?" he asked.

"Bugger off, strumpet lips."

His already mean eyebrows furrowed into a scowl. "Someone small as you should watch your tongue, lad."

"I'm quaking in my little boots." She spat on the floor between them and spun around to stomp from the inn back to her own. Down in the tavern, she sat at a table and dropped her forehead onto the surface. *He just needs to calm down. I'll give him the day.*

Hours later, after she'd bathed and changed and had returned to her previous spot, head down and hands over the back of it, Sunshine found her. He sat opposite her and stared at the black hood against the tabletop.

"Did you sleep like that?"

"Would've been the better option," she said.

"Compared to?"

She said nothing for several minutes. "I think I did something stupid."

"What's that?"

"Leslie."

"What about him?"

She raised her head to make a face at him.

"You absolute bloody idiot."

"No need to be so rude about it."

"Apparently, there is a need. Why would you go and do a thing like that?" He motioned to the barmaid for a drink.

"Because my stupid heart is complicated and confused and I was trying to figure things out, all right?"

They sat in silence as the woman brought two steins of ale. After that, he drank, his gaze drifting around the room. Song lifted her head and grabbed her mug to drain half in one go.

"So," Sunshine said after a long time, "how was it?"

Song made a face. "It was…"

"Be honest."

"It was bloody awful."

He chuckled into his stein, shaking his head.

"Not like that. Physically it was…well, I didn't hate it? It was… more than satisfying. He is skilled, with adequate stamina—" She blushed as Sunshine cleared his throat and gave her a look which told her precisely how much he didn't want to hear about Leslie's performance in bed. "Sorry. Anyway, I'm sure it would have been lovely to any other woman. But in the morning…I have never been so sure in my life that I'd rather be with a woman."

"And emotionally?"

"Emotionally, it was lovely. Far different from how Lyella treated me. But…"

"You don't love Whispers."

Song sighed into the mouth of her stein. "Not like that, I don't think. But almost? Maybe? I don't know how to explain it. He's more dear to me than any other person in the entire world, and yet… But it feels like…" She struggled to find the words.

"Like you belong together. Two halves of the same whole. Undyin' devotion and pure adoration, but none of the chains of romance between you." Sunshine smiled off into the distance.

"You speak as though you know the feeling."

"Dash was the other half of my whole. Isn't a day goes by that I don't feel the emptiness he left behind."

"I had no idea."

"It's not somethin' I make known, as few would understand it. But here you are now, in the same predicament. Except I didn't have to sleep with Dash to know I didn't love him romantically." Sunshine chuckled at the glare he received.

She lowered her eyes to the wood of the table. "Leslie said he's staying behind. This time for good."

"Can you blame him? Havin' that love between you, and yet his is different."

"Am I selfish to keep him, even through that?"

"Yes. Heartless, even. But perchance it's a life he'd be willin' to suffer. Maybe not. Won't know until you ask."

"How do I tell him that I want—that I *need* him by my side… I just don't want the sort of life a woman has with a man?" she mumbled into her stein.

"You tell him exactly like that."

"You really think that would appease him?"

"If you don't think an admission like that would satisfy Whispers, then perhaps you don't know him as well as you think. The Whispers I know would take any excuse to remain at your side."

"But you didn't see his face."

"Then sit here all day cryin' in your cup and we'll shove off without him. And you'll never see him again. Tell me, have you picked a worthy replacement?" When she said nothing, he continued, "Oh, but then the last time he wasn't on the crew anymore, you chased him down and got him back, anyway."

Song growled under her breath. "Bugger me. Fine. You win, Sunshine."

"See you both at the dockmasters, then."

"Maybe."

"I said what I mean. Now you go do the same."

Song dropped a few quoine on the table to pay for both drinks and left the tavern. She strode with purpose back to the other inn and to Leslie's room. After a deep breath, she rapped her knuckles on the door. She continued to suck in nervous breaths, shaking her hands as she waited. After a while, she knocked again.

"Leslie, I need to speak with you."

No answer came.

"Leslie, please. Don't shut me out. Let me just…explain."

Still, he didn't answer.

Song took a chance and gripped the knob. It turned, and the door cracked an inch.

"Leslie? Answer me, or I'm coming in."

Silence was the sole occupant of the room behind the door.

The hinges creaked as she swung it wide, scanning the room. Nothing was out of place, but Leslie was nowhere to be seen. The scene looked innocent enough—the disheveled blanket and his footlocker as the only sign that he'd even been in the room. Still, something was unsettling about it. The unmade bed alone was strange for him. What bothered her most, though, was the unlocked door with everything he owned sitting in the chest at the foot of the bed for anyone who entered to see.

Following the sinking feeling in her gut, she strode across the room, taking a breath as she thrust her hand beneath the mattress. At first, she felt nothing and began a sigh of relief. But then her fingers tangled through leather lashes and touched on the braided handle of his sword. Her stomach fell as she knew what such a find meant.

Song strode from the room, but stopped and backed in to frown at the key on the little table by the door. She grabbed it and locked the door, then found the innkeeper.

"You. Where is the man in room five?"

"Remind me?" the woman said, not looking up at Song.

"Tall. Wears a brown coat with his hood up."

"Oh, that one. Saw him go with a couple of his friends. Couldn't even take a step on his own, man was so drunk."

"He doesn't drink."

"I don't know what to tell you."

Song clenched her jaw. "What did his friends look like?"

"Tall, handsome. One blond, one brunet."

She deflated. "That's incredibly unhelpful."

The woman shrugged. "I don't know what to tell you, doll."

Song turned away to leave.

"Oh, uh, they did say something about getting him home?"

Her insides turned cold. She took a few deep breaths, then sprinted back into the tavern, where Sunshine was finishing the contents of her stein.

"That was f—"

"We have to go! Now! Get as many of our men as you can. I'll get us a ship."

"What? Why?"

"Someone took Leslie for the bounty on his head."

Sunshine lurched to his feet and ran off to find the rest of the crew as Song retrieved her quoine and ran to the dockmaster.

She cut ahead of the small line and slammed her sack of quoine onto the table. "I need any skyship you have available. Preferably fast. And I need it *now!*"

Song ran around the city, a frantic mess. She'd signed a hasty contract for a rental ship, then forgot the key to the chain on the wheel. She was sure she'd overpaid after having dumped the contents of her purse across the counter. At a supplier, she hadn't even stopped to count, either. Sunshine stepped in and sent her off with Bruce and Toothy to collect Leslie's belongings and her own, then load them into the captain's cabin on the rented clipper.

She set Leslie's chest down and stared around the room. It smelled foreign, and for that she automatically hated it. It had a desk and two chairs, rather than a table. Instead of a bench in the bay window, there was a low counter with cabinets. Toothy entered behind her and set her trunk on the floor in a corner. Bruce looked around for where to put her dresses. She took them and flopped them over the desk, since there didn't seem to be a closet in this small room.

Thumbs limped in with a wooden crutch under one arm. He hobbled to a chair and settled himself into it.

"What are you doing?" she asked as the other two left to continue preparations.

"Sitting," he said.

"Thumbs, your ankle—"

"If you think for even one second I am not going with to rescue

Whispers, then you do not know me well at all. I would go, even if they had cut both my legs off."

She nodded. "He'd do the same, I suppose."

"Song?"

She turned to find Maps in the doorway, an open map in his hands. "Oh, good, Sunshine found you."

"Came to me before anyone else so I could figure the best course." He strode in and smoothed it out over her dresses. "I asked around. The capital of Ebrinar Province is Carliolace. That's where the high lord lives. Whispers would've been taken there. Now, there are no airship docks in or around the city."

"Why?"

"Rumor is, Duchamp thinks it would invite our kind to come and sully his city. So we have to fly here, to a small town called Yorvaald. They have a transport service to get people to Carliolace from there. It'll be an overnight flight, and you can be to Carliolace just before noon."

She set her hand on his shoulder. "Thank you for finding all this out. I don't know what I would do without you lot."

He chuckled. "I think you'd do just fine on your own, but it's nice to feel needed. We've had enough tragedy, so I'd like to aid in a win."

"And it will be a win," she said. "We'll get Leslie back, ship the Bounty to Armalinia, and go spend more time in a friendlier country to finish healing."

"That sounds like a perfect plan," Thumbs said.

By the time they'd set off, it had only been an hour since she'd discovered Leslie's empty room. The crew members who were fit to fly had all signed onto the mission, and some too injured to even walk still tried to join. A slave had had to nearly sit on Hairy to keep him in bed, according to Sunshine. They would be back for all of them, Song assured. None of her men would be left behind in that damned country she wanted nothing to do with, even more so than she had before.

Sunshine turned the skyship around in the bay and flew over the pirate city, angling up to go over the mountains instead of around. Song stood at the bow, glaring over the land. She would get Leslie back, no matter the cost. And then she would share her true feelings with him. After that, she hadn't a clue. But it was a start.

Thirty-Two

Carliolace, the capital of the Ebrinar Province in Pishing, was a smaller city, though large enough to contain more than its fair share of the negative things of a city. Carts filled with goods lined the street, their merchants shouting what they had for sale. The poverty and the crowds all stood on the other side of the closed carriage Song rode in—children ran alongside, hoping to see within. *Keep the lady away from the filth.* But she wasn't concerned with the poor. She was on her way to visit the real filth.

The carriage took her past an area where the cobblestones ended at a packed dirt square. A post with shackles stood as a monolith beside a gallows and stocks. Behind them was a jailhouse with barred holes in the walls at the ground. Arms reached through, their hands grasping as the faceless owners remained locked away.

On the other side of the city, far away from the smell of poverty, sat Duchamp Hall. The brickwork was painted a bright white, the window-shutters a soft tan. Rust orange-colored banners hung on either side of the black double doors, displaying a black bird with unfurled wings, clutching the tail of a banner in its feet which read 'Mercy In Death'.

"Mercy for whom?" Song asked no one. She pulled her white gloves tighter and tugged at the long sleeves of her blue dress to put them back in place over her discolored wrists.

The carriage door opened, and the driver held out his hand to help her down the single step. A man in a fine suit trotted down from the manor. Song let the corners of her mouth turn up the slightest bit and curtsied.

"I was not aware we were to have visitors—" His accent was near identical to Leslie's, rather than the deeper one in the west fjords.

"No, I was unable to write ahead. It is an urgent matter, Lord Duchamp."

He frowned. "Oh, no. No, no. I'm Gentry, the butler. And you are?"

Song curtsied again. "My apologies. Miss Tsingsei Gould, of Garda."

His eyebrows rose with interest, but otherwise, his face remained unmoved. "Right this way, Miss Gould."

A tall, sturdy man who looked somewhere around her father's age, bearing a deep scowl on his brow, waited at the doors for them. He held himself regally with his nose in the air and his shoulders squared. His light brown hair was cropped short and oiled under control. Song curtsied politely as he stopped before her. The man scowled deeper.

"You're that Garda girl, aren't you?" He treated the name of her home as something filthy to be wiped from his pressed clothing.

"Miss Tsingsei Gould," she said.

"Quite," he replied with a sneer. "Roman Duchamp, High Lord of the Ebrinar Province. But you at least know my name, don't you?"

"An honor, your lordship." Song curtsied again.

"To what to we owe the *pleasure*?" he asked, with a note of distaste.

"I've come to negotiate the retraction of the bounty on Leslie's head," she stated.

Roman smirked. "Leslie? I do not know of any Leslie."

Song cleared her throat and tried to keep the ladylike smile on her lips. "Mr. Wesley Krell."

Roman made a face and led Song into a large study just off the entrance hall. He sat in a green wing-back leather chair behind the rich oak desk. The butler set his gloved hands on the back of a round-top oak chair with a green leather seat, indicating where Song should make herself comfortable. They sat in silence as Gentry poured drinks into round-body glasses, like stemless wine goblets. He set one on the small table beside Song and the other on the oak desk, then bowed and took his leave, shutting the door behind him.

"Curious that you should hold interest in Leech," Roman said. His words were passive, and yet his tone remained barbed.

"Why do you call him Leech?"

Roman scoffed and took a sip of his drink. "He is a slave, and yet my father treated him like a son. He was a parasite to my family. And how does he repay us? He ran away before my father's body was cold and parades around the world using a stolen name."

"Your father granted Leslie his freedom—"

"Questionable."

"—and he has not been 'parading around' as Roman Duchamp—"

"High Lord."

"Quite," Song said, her tone bland, the cordial disposition all but abandoned. "He borrowed the name for only one night in order to accompany me to a benefit for orphaned children. I so desperately wanted to go, but they would not let him in! If I had known what trouble it would cause, I'd have burned my invitation." After a long silence in which he scowled at her as though she were a pest, she said, "What do you mean by questionable?"

Roman's mouth twisted into a vicious smile. "He freed a man named Leslie, not a man named Wesley Krell."

Her jaw clenched so tight it hurt. "Surely it's still valid. Leslie is still a free man."

"The contract for his ownership and the contract for his freedom do not contain the same name. So no, Miss Gould, Wesley Krell is, and always was, my property. He was never freed."

Song bit her tongue so hard it stung as she held back angry words and violent retaliation over his claims. Somehow Leslie's name had gotten confused in his past, and that simple mistake now cost him the freedom he'd been granted. She wanted to argue for that freedom, but without knowing the laws of Pishing, she couldn't make a solid case, nor prove him wrong.

Roman studied her in silence for a long time. Song hid her displeasure at the scrutiny, remaining as impassive and seemingly innocent as she could. He took a deep breath and let it out in a whoosh of a sigh.

"What's done is done. You've wasted a trip and my time."

A stone dropped in her stomach, but she forced herself to not panic. "What do you mean 'what's done is done?' Where is Leslie?"

"In the jailhouse."

She released a sigh of relief. "Surely we could come to an agreement over such a silly misunderstanding? Let me take Leslie off your hands and promise to never again utter your name or set foot on Pishing soil."

"Out of the question."

She studied him, all her initial plans for dealing with him coming to mind. She couldn't kill him, not now that she was here. The connection was easy to make. But she'd had one other idea that she hated, and she knew Leslie would hate. But it was something this man understood. "Then perhaps I might…buy him from you?"

"That particular slave is not for sale."

"Everything is for sale for the right price," Song replied. Her smile nudged at him.

"And do you have the right price?"

Without a word, she wrote a large sum of quoine on a paper and slid it across to him. He sneered at the offer.

"This is an insulting amount."

Song forced herself to remain calm. "I started low in the hopes you'd be happy to be rid of him. I suppose I was wrong."

He slid the paper back to her, and she crossed out the first number, then wrote in a new one. She had a vague idea of how much quoine lined the coffers of her crew. She'd spent so much just to get here that now she was scraping into the men's wages.

"Handsome offer," Roman said.

Song's hopes rose. If he refused that sum, she was unsure how much the men would rebel if she took any more from their pockets. Then again, it was Leslie. She would pay anything. She would write to her father and demand more quoine than any slave had ever been worth, if that's what she had to do.

"Is that a more acceptable number?" she prodded when he'd stared at the paper for a silent minute.

"It's...getting warmer..."

Her heart sank. "Do you have an amount in mind?"

"I might." The clock on a cabinet chimed eleven, breaking the tension. "Ah, it's time for lunch. Come, I will have a place set for you."

"Surely this is no time to—"

"I cannot think on an empty stomach, nor would I ever want to interrupt a mealtime with such nonsense as Leech. Come, Miss Gould, surely you could eat something. You're practically skin and bones."

She sighed her annoyance. "I assure you I am well fed, though I suppose I could do with a bite."

Roman extended his elbow, and she took it, gracefully hiding the disdain she harbored deep in her stomach. He led her from the room to a dining hall, where he left her at the doorway so he could greet his wife with a kiss.

"I love your dress," a girl in her mid teens said. "Bold choice with your bare shoulders."

Song noted that the girl was a young replica of Lady Duchamp. Her blonde hair was curled and pinned close to her scalp on one side, a miniature top hat sat crooked on the other side. Her dress was a deep brown, and the front had been gathered to expose from her buckled brown shoes all the way to her knees.

A leather corset wrapped around her waist beneath her bustline and a short-cropped jacket with ruffled shoulders finished the rather unique look.

"It is the latest fashion in Telbhaniich-Zardi," Song said.

"I thought you were from Garda?"

"I am."

"What were you doing in Telbhaniich-Zardi?"

With no answer for the girl, she forced a bright smile and made a show of staring the girl over from head-to-toe. "I love your dress, too!"

"It's my own design, which I intend to make a trend. I'll have a dress adjusted for you so you can take it all the way to Garda." Her eyes lit with excitement. "Birgit!"

A humble woman with her face turned to the floor and clothed in unimpressive robes stepped from another room and bowed low.

"Give one of my dresses to Miss Gould," the girl ordered.

"I couldn't," Song began. "I don't intend to stay long."

"Birgit will have it ready in no time. I insist."

Right there in the hallway, Birgit took quick measurements with a knotted string, muttering to herself as she studied Song's posture and figure. Roman cleared his throat from the dining room.

"Before our meal grows cold, ladies."

The two shuffled into the room, Song accepting the direction of the butler to sit opposite the young girl. A boy of about eight ran in at the last minute and hopped into the seat beside the girl. He gave Song a shy smile.

"Where have you been, Toren?" Mrs. Duchamp asked.

"Smashin' toads!"

His mother tutted low and shook her head.

"That's not very fair to the toads," Song said.

Toren narrowed his eyes at her. "They're just toads. They don't have feelings."

Roman eyed her and so she forced a charming smile onto her lips. "I suppose you are right."

The small talk over the next hour was unbearable as her nerves wound tighter and tighter. Here she was having a delightful meal, while Leslie sat in a jail cell he didn't belong in. She learned the girl's name was Miriad, and she was not Roman's daughter. Mrs. Duchamp had been married before, but an unfortunate death gave her the opportunity to marry Roman, giving her status in society a considerable boost. Roman's previous wife hadn't produced any children before her tragic and untimely death from unnamed circumstances. The whole thing sounded suspicious, but it wasn't Song's place to say anything of her opinion.

After lunch, Roman would not speak with her over the ownership of Leslie. Instead, he invited her to join him on a carriage ride. She agreed, hoping her amicable disposition would soften his own. Toren slipped in at the last second and sat beside his father, smiling like he'd gotten into a bowl of sweets. Roman set a proud hand on his dark blond head.

When the carriage stopped, the boy jumped out and shoved his way through a gathered crowd, which parted at the sight of Roman. They reached the front of the crowd. It stretched around to circle the city square. Roman guided her to the front, where they had the best, unimpeded view of the stocks, gallows, and flogging pole.

Roman nodded to a man standing on the walkway over the barred windows beneath the building, and the man disappeared inside. Minutes passed before he reemerged, leading a familiar redhead in front of him. Leslie's hands were bound at the wrists behind his back. He stood tall and proud, defiant in his wrongful imprisonment. His eyes scanned over the sea of faces until he found Roman to glare at him. But then they shifted to her. He paused, his expression overcome with shock and relief. The constable shoved him back to walking. They stopped in front of the gallows, and the man turned an inquiring gaze on Roman.

Song spun on him. "We're not finished negotiating!"

"If I do not make an example of him, then what message does that send to others who choose to follow in his footsteps?"

"But not the gallows!" she nearly cried. "Leave him in the stocks while we talk, but don't hang him! Please!"

He shook his head, and the man led Leslie to the stocks. Again, he waited for Roman's approval. But Roman didn't move as he stewed in his thoughts.

"Please," Song whispered, begging him to choose the stocks.

He turned his steely gaze on her, trying to read the contents of her mind. He shook his head, and the man moved on to the flogging pole. Song's heart dropped as Roman gave a single curt nod.

The constable slapped the shackles hanging from the pole around Leslie's wrists, forcing him to stand straight with barely any room between himself and the pole. Another man cut his shirt from him and threw it to the ground. Leslie stood vulnerable under the high noon sun. Song pursed her lips, preparing an order for her *kijæm* to free him and stay the whip of the man who now stood directly behind.

Leslie turned his head and observed the determination spread across her face. He shook his head and mouthed, 'Don't.'

The flagellator cracked his bullwhip; Leslie and Song flinched in unison. She pursed her lips in defiance, but again, Leslie warned her against drastic measures with the shake of his head. The next time the whip cracked, it left a red mark across his back. Leslie surged forward and clenched his jaw, but made no sound. Song, however, emitted a strangled cry that coaxed a vicious grin from Roman.

With each crack of the whip, the flagellator seemed to grow more determined, whipping harder until finally, Leslie cried out. He screamed himself hoarse as the whip tore at flesh which had already been struck. His back obtained a glimmering garnet sheen, making it difficult to tell what area had been spared the wrath of the cruel weapon.

"Please stop," Song growled when his cries became too painful for her to stomach.

"Why would I do that?" Roman asked.

"Because if you break him entirely now, then what pleasure can you take later?" she replied, her teeth clenched as she held back both her temper and her *kijæm*.

Roman lifted his hand to signal for an end.

"May I approach him?" she asked Roman.

He thought about it, then huffed his annoyance at the request down his nose. "No."

Toren ran into the clearing carrying a large, slimy toad. He arched his arm back, preparing a rather impressive throw, which would land the amphibian right on Leslie's shredded back. "Eat toad, villain!"

"*Paikseh!*" Song hissed.

A quick flash of blue light sparkled against the creature's skin. The previously pacified toad sprang to life, leaping out of Toren's grip and landing on his face. It gave a long croak, whipped the boy in the eye with its long, gooey tongue, and retreated to safety as fast as it could scamper. The citizens in the square scattered, running with their knees raised as they skittered about, avoiding the toad in a tangible panic.

"Father!" Toren screamed and ran, palm pressed against his eye, to his father, who'd had his back turned to the entire ordeal.

Song stepped between them, so the boy bumped into her skirts and fell to the ground. She picked him up and gave him a wicked smile. "Do you know what happens to cruel little boys?"

"Don't touch me, peasant!" He broke free of her and ran to the carriage, where his father stood waiting.

With a final long look at Leslie, who leaned his weight against the pole and kept his face turned to his feet, Song retreated and joined the Duchamps in the carriage.

Thirty-Three

That night, Song stole from Duchamp Hall. Leslie made no hint of seeing her when she approached. He kept his head down as he shifted his weight from one foot to the other. She took a bucket from the rim of the nearby water pump and filled it. She cradled it and walked to Leslie. In silence, she set to work cleaning the blood from the wounds along his back with her wet handkerchief.

"I know what you're thinking," he said. He'd given up using a false tongue, defaulting to his native Pishing accent. The roughness of his voice made him sound more like Dashaelan than he ever had before.

"No, you don't." Her voice came harsh and cracked with anger.

"Don't free me, Song."

"I wasn't going to free you. I was going to seal your wounds."

"Especially don't do that." He turned his head to meet her gaze. "Besides, they'll just flog me again."

Song pursed her lips and returned to her task. "I *can* free you, though."

"Don't."

She worked in silence for a while, rubbing one layer of dried blood away so she could clean the next. The water grew redder as she wrung the cloth, watching it drip into the bucket.

"We could slip away into the night—"

"Don't."

"—and be on the skyship before anyone grew wise."

"Don't," he insisted.

"Roman's authority holds little weight beyond the borders of Pishing. At least two countries won't even extradite—"

"Song!" He released an impatient breath, his brow knitting together in a silent plea. "Don't."

"Why? Why can't I take you from here and never return?"

"Because they would put a bounty on your head and raise mine."

She scoffed. "You say that as though I don't already have one."

"The bounty would be on Tsingsei Gould, not on a faceless boy. Captain Song's bounty is one thing, because you hide behind anonymity. But everyone knows who Tsingsei Gould is."

"My father would—"

"Your father couldn't buy your way out of it, not with all the quoine in Andalise. Roman would never negotiate after such a slight. He would declare war on your family."

Hopelessness choked Song. She stared into the red water, at the reflection of a girl who looked tired and scared and so far out of her league that at any moment she would drown, with no hope of rescue.

"How are the negotiations going?" Leslie asked. "I assume that is why you're here as a Gould."

"Never thought in my life I'd be haggling to buy a slave," she said, her face pinched as though the words were bitter on her tongue.

"Not really buying a slave, but rather my freedom."

She met his gaze and squeezed the handkerchief. She'd expected his pride to get in the way, and yet he'd surprised her. "That's a cause much easier to stomach."

Song swallowed back the stone in her throat. For a long, silent minute, she contemplated telling him what Roman had said about the technicality over which name was written on what paper. But one quick search in his eyes told her he was far too hopeless already. She bit her tongue against the knowledge, deciding it didn't matter, anyway. Once she'd found the sum which made

Roman willing to part with a slave he didn't even want, then Leslie would once again be a free man.

"I have offered him every last quoine of mine, plus some of the men's. I'm terrified no sum will appease him."

"Offer mine as well."

"But then you'll have nothing left of the debt you've collected."

He eyed her. "You really think I've a mind for quoine now? If I stay here, I'm dead, and the quoine is meaningless to me, anyway."

Her pirate heart burned with impatience and greed. Why lose the quoine when she could spirit him away right this minute? They'd be gone, their treasuries unspent. "Damn the bounties, Leslie. We could run and hide away in Talegrove or the Impasse Mountains."

"You want me to hide in a cave in the Screaming Cliffs with you?" He smirked.

"Why not? I'm sure we'd get used to the noise."

He released a sad chuckle. "I could never live with myself."

"You wouldn't be living with yourself; you'd be living with me."

He shook his head. "I can't—"

She set her mouth in a hard line. "You don't know how to can't."

"I learned how to from the best." He gave her an accusing stare. "And now I can say with certainty that I *can't* run away with you. I can't hide away somewhere with you."

"Then we stay on the Bounty and—"

"No, Song!" He rattled the chains at his wrists as he tugged against them. "Do you see this? This is Roman's mercy. If we run, it won't matter where we are, he will hang us in whatever inn he found us in." He gasped and hung his head, hiding his face behind an arm, but she could see that he was shaking.

"Rather specific example."

He balled his fists tighter, but said nothing.

"Leslie," she whispered, but he didn't look at her. "Wesley…"

He met her gaze, his eyes red and angry, but he was too exhausted for tears. "Buy my freedom and return me to Tarn, where you found me. I'll make back what you paid, then you can return for it."

"I'd rather you return to the skies with me."

"No."

"Why the bloody hell not?"

"Because I *love* you, Song!" he hissed.

He pursed his lips as he waited for a response she was still choking on. Hearing him voice it, finally, had shocked her more than she'd anticipated. All the words she'd practiced in her head flew away as she stared at him in a mute shock.

"I can't stay on that damned skyship, looking at you every day, knowing that I am nothing to you." He clenched his teeth.

"You're not nothing," she gasped, fighting to keep her composure.

"Close enough. Go back to your comfortable bed, princess." He turned his head from her.

Song tossed the bucket to the side. The water bubbled into a muddy stream before disappearing into the dirt.

"What if I love you, too?" She'd lost her battle against the tears, which rolled down her cheeks to land on her bodice.

"We both know you don't. Not the same, at least."

Her heart ached, and she took a desperate breath. "I *do* love you, just not like that. But I tried. I really did. I wanted to give you the same love back, but it didn't happen. And I panicked because I thought you would hate me if I said so."

He eyed her in the flickering dim light from the gas streetlamps.

"I can't live without you. You can't stay here, Leslie. Because I need you."

"You need me to watch your back," he said.

She set her palms on his cheeks and made sure he looked into her eyes. "I need you to be there with me. I need your music. The duets with Sunshine in the night when no one else is awake to hear. I need you to dance with me without stepping on my toes." She let out a soft laugh and sniffed. "I may not love you the way you love me, but I *do* love you. And I *need* you in my life. Please, Leslie."

"Am I not a regret?" he whispered.

She gave him a soft, sad smile. "No. I don't regret our night together…" Song shook her head and stared at his shoulder instead of his eyes. "My only regret is that it didn't make me love you the same way you love me. And I regret hurting you because of that. I should've just talked to you about it instead of running away… This is all my fault."

"I'm sorry, Song. I'm also to blame. You think I didn't know that was the likely outcome? I suppose I just got carried away by the false hope that you would love me."

"I'm sorry. I just don't work that way."

"No one does. I'm sorry I treated you unfairly. I could've stopped at any point, but I just…"

"Didn't want to." She nodded in understanding. "Neither did I."

His eyes bored into hers as he thought. "Can I kiss you one last time?"

"What?"

"No matter what happens, live or die, I'd like to have one last kiss from you."

Song swallowed. "You're not going to die. But yes, you may kiss me."

She leaned to him, careful not to touch the torn skin on his back. Leslie's lips met hers, softly at first and then more urgent, taking as much as he could for the last kiss he would ask of her. He pressed himself closer, clenching his fists and pulling against the shackles keeping him from wrapping his arms around her. Their embrace was cut short as a guard took Song by the arm and ripped her away.

"Get your hands off her," Leslie growled. He remained ignored as he tugged against his bindings.

The guard stuck a finger in Song's face. "Don't touch the prisoner."

She swallowed away the urge to take his sword and cut his hand off, and nodded.

Leslie sneered at the guard as he strode away on his patrol. He took Song in, staring at her tear-streaked face in the lamplight. "I need you, too. I always have. It took me one hour thinking in that jail cell to realize I could love you without having you to myself."

"So, you'll stay with me?"

He nodded, a sad smile touching the corner of his lips. "It's where I belong."

"Agreed. I shall bargain with all the quoine available to me. I'll contact my father for more if I have to. Whatever it takes. I won't lose you. I refuse."

He released a long breath as he studied her. He gave her a soft, sad smile and nodded in agreement. "In the morning, then?"

"In the morning."

Song spun to return to Duchamp Hall, leaving Leslie to stand at the flogging pole for the rest of the night. When she turned to take him in one last time, standing alone and seeming so much smaller than he was, his face was cast in a mournful expression as he stared back at her. She couldn't bring herself to smile or wave; her heart was too heavy for such reassurances. So she turned back to watch the road underfoot and let silent tears fall onto the exposed skin at her bosom.

―

Song snapped awake the next morning in a guest bedroom of Duchamp Hall. Miriad shook her with one hand and gripped a dress with the other. She tugged her out of the bed and dressed her, grinning the whole time. She even nodded in acceptance of the lie Song blurted over her discolored arms. The dress was tan with black embellishments; black crinoline beneath the lifted skirt, which was buckled up with black straps. It had a matching jacket with a collar that flipped up like a fan around her neck. Thankfully, it had long sleeves, and she could pull on her gloves to hide her blue and purple hands. Miriad offered to style her hair and put a hat on one side, but Song found the look to be silly and so twisted her hair into her usual plait.

As she pulled on her boots, Toren came running into the room, happy as could be.

"You little pest!" Miriad shouted at him.

"I have a message for Miss Gould!" He skittered out of reach of her swinging hands as she tried to bat him away.

"What?" Song asked.

He stopped in front of her and smiled like it was his birthday. She noticed his eyeball had swollen within the socket, causing the lid to strain every time he blinked.

"Your slave is set to hang!"

"What?" Song shouted as she batted him out of the way. The staccato crack echoed from the walls as the back of her hand met his cheek and knocked him to the floor.

Song flew from the room, using the banister to steady herself as she skipped down five stairs at a time. Not waiting for the carriage to be brought around, she ran straight from the manor to the center of town.

When she reached the square, the crowd had gathered once more. All eyes turned to the gallows, where Leslie stood on the trapdoor at the center of the platform, his hands bound before him and his face cast downward. She shoved through the crowd to where Roman stood.

"You said you would think on it!" she screamed.

Roman rounded on her, his face darkening with his anger. "That was before you came to him in the night to ease his punishment with your whorish mouth."

"You dare—"

"Do not speak, harlot. I'll hear none of your perverse lies."

"You bastard!" Song spat in his eye.

Quick as a flash, he reached behind her to weave his fingers through her hair and grip the braid along her scalp. He withdrew a handkerchief and wiped at his face. "What did you think I meant when I refused your request to go to him? Did you really think you could disobey me in my own city and get away with it?" He turned her head to face the gallows. "Don't blink," he whispered.

"Leslie!" Song screamed.

As Leslie looked up—his eyes meeting hers and his lips curving into a gentle smile—Roman gave the signal for his execution to be carried out. Song screamed as the man pulled a lever, which opened the trap door beneath Leslie's feet.

"*Por ehth pæns!*" she screamed.

The rope lit up and began to fray under Leslie's weight. A crossbow bolt careened through the air from over the crowd to cut through the final bit of rope. It embedded into the post as Leslie fell. She didn't have time to stop and wonder who fired the bolt, and from where—but she wanted to. However, the two were far from safe. For now, she needed to reach Leslie and protect him, even if it meant exposing her *kijæm* more than she already had.

Leslie fell through the opening in the platform and crashed onto his side, gasping air into his lungs. Song rounded on Roman, bringing the back of her fist to his face. He released her in shock, his hands cupping his nose. She took off at a sprint toward the gallows platform.

"Leslie!" she shouted, reaching her hand out as though she could touch him across the distance.

He reached his bound hands over his head, fingers splaying in a desperate attempt to grip hers. His mouth gasped to say something, but he only coughed.

Guards closed the distance on her, and she shied away from their grasp. "Get up! Run!" she ordered.

A guard wrapped his fingers around her wrist. Her momentum spun her around to face him and she used the opportunity to send the flat of her palm into his nose; it cracked beneath the impact and he released his grip. She yanked his sword from the scabbard and spun to continue running.

Leslie scrambled forward and pushed himself up once clear of the platform. He stole the sword from a guard standing beside one pillar of the gallows, kicked him away, then charged toward the guards converging on Song.

The guard regained his footing and gave chase, catching the rope around Leslie's neck and attempting to pull him to a stop. Leslie spun around and cut the rope shorter before bringing the blade up again to slash at the man.

By the time Leslie reached Song, she'd incapacitated four guards and was wrestling with another. Without hesitation, Leslie ran the blade through the ribs of the guard and kicked him away. Song used her *kijæm* to break the bonds around his wrists. He whipped the noose from his neck and spun to block the blade of another. The guard turned his attention to Song, swinging his sword in an arc toward her neck.

"Don't kill her, you imbecile!" Roman shouted. "We don't need a war with Andalise."

The blade swung up over her head, the whoosh of the breeze splashed cold against her cheek. She spun to face the man. Song put herself between Leslie and two guards. Together, the men swung both blades down at her.

She raised her sword up to block the blow. The weight of it jolted down her arm. The pain crackled and streaked through the bones all the way to her biceps. In that split second, the bones in her hand and arm creaked and shattered.

Song screamed in agony, dropping the sword as she doubled over. She fell to her knees as darkness crept from the corners of her eyes. Her vision fogged and multiplied. She'd never felt a pain even half this terrible before, and so she vomited and collapsed to the ground. Leslie stepped over her and put himself between the guards and her.

"Leslie," she whimpered as she lost consciousness.

Thirty-Four

Night had set and darkness blanketed the world when Song woke. Her head throbbed and her vision swirled. When it settled, she realized she was lying on a stone floor. The walls were a mixture of carved stone and rough bricks. At the front and over the hole for a window were thick steel bars, which had turned brown with rust. The view beyond them was the wall of a nearby building. A smell clung to the air—smokey with a hint of sweet, cooked meat. It made her stomach churn for a reason she wasn't quite aware of just yet.

She sat up, and pain shot through her arm. Her hand was in worse shape than she ever could have imagined. Under the black bruise, her fingers were twisted and bent in unnatural, broken ways. Her forearm was no better. She couldn't move the appendage, and even trying sent a stab through her that forced her stomach to heave. She leaned over and vomited beside herself. Once she'd settled her stomach and her vision stopped swirling, she focused on removing the jacket from her shoulders and wrapping it beneath her arm. She muttered through clenched teeth for her *kijæm* to tie the sleeves behind her neck.

"Fancy tricks, doll." Across from her cell was another without a window, which contained a tanned man with sandy brown hair nearly the same shade as his skin.

She met his gaze for a long, silent minute. "What hour is it?"

He looked out the window above her and shrugged. "Looks like night."

She released an exasperated sigh. Concentrating her sights on the lock of the gate, she whispered, *"Kawl-nu."* The metallic click echoed, catching the attention of every prisoner in the jail. Song shoved to her feet and swung the door open, cringing as it screamed in protest on the rusted hinges.

The man across from her licked his lips, his gaze fixed on the gate in her hand. "Let us out, and we'll lead you out of Carliolace. We know the safest ways."

"What makes you think I need your help?"

"We know the roads better'n any. In here for smuggling, we are. Duchamp's got a sundown curfew. Guards patrol at night. Got a set routine, they do. But we know best ways to not get caught."

Song realized that 'we' was merely this tanned man. "If you know the best way, then why are you in here?"

"Betrayed, we was. Spied by the little lord, out when he should be in. Skulks about in the dark, he does. Little terror in the making."

"Let us all out," a man to her left said. "I'm accused of stealing from my master, but I merely took too long drawing my master a bath. I'm sentenced to die in two days."

Other men and women shouted their crimes, mostly superficial. With a quick whisper, she unlocked all the gates and they crowded around her in hushed excitement.

"Great show in the courtyard!" one said.

Another patted her shoulder. "Three of them never got up!"

Another hung his head. "Sorry about your lover."

"My lover?" Song asked.

"Leslie," the tanned man said. "Was a good man. We knew him when he was young. Honorable."

Was.

And then her mind recognized the smell.

Horror forced denial into her mind. She shoved past the prisoners, finding stairs leading up to the main floor of the jailhouse. Any guard who got in the way she blinded with a quick word until she reached the front door. She threw it open and turned to the square. Song dropped from the raised walkway before falling to her knees. A strangled cry forced its way out of her throat as a furiously shaking hand moved to cover her mouth. She screamed into her palm as her eyes burned and tears blinded her.

Song scrambled to the stake which had been erected beside the gallows, every cell in her body denying the identity of the still smoldering corpse. Her knees shook, and she fell to the ground many times, but still she forced her uncooperating feet to move. By the time she'd reached the edge of the smoking pile of embers, her entire body shook so violently that she fell at the border, unable to rise again. The tears flowed so freely now that nothing could have stemmed the tide. Through her tears, she saw the poster with his face on it nailed to a makeshift sign stuck into the ground.

The armor of the guards clanked in the otherwise quiet night as they surrounded her.

"Too'ah mehth delb," she managed to choke out.

The courtyard lit a bright red. Shadows danced across the walls of the buildings of guards gripping their throats and covering their eyes. The angry mist carved into their flesh, opened their veins, and their blood drained from their bodies. Song never took her eyes from the figure tied to the stake. He was nearly a skeleton now, his flesh and most of his muscle already burned away.

She screamed as agony tore through her. Her lungs burned, and she couldn't catch her breath. For a minute, she thought she might die. For a much longer moment, she hoped she would. She pressed her uninjured hand over her mouth, then reached out as though to touch him. Her hand stopped short at the heat, then returned to her mouth. She repeated this motion over and over, wanting desperately to set her hands on him. Song wanted to grip him to her and sob against him, but she couldn't. She could only stare at this horrific display in the middle of the city for all to look on like a spectacle.

"Miss…" The tanned man stood beside her. "We'll get you out of the city. Quick, before someone sees." He reached out his hand to her.

"I'm not leaving him," she sobbed. "Not now. Not ever." She bent, pressing in on her stomach as a hollowness gnawed at her middle and threatened to expand and consume her.

He pursed his lips into a thin line and retracted his hand. After a brief pause of observance, he turned and disappeared into the darkness beyond the square, leaving Song alone to grieve.

Minutes passed with only the sound of her wails to fill the ebony night. The freed men circled round the pyre, their heads hung as they paid their respects to the burned man. One holding a guard's sword dripping with blood stepped forward.

"We can't take him, but we need to get out of Carliolace, miss."

Song straightened after what felt like an eternity and noted her surroundings. The prison door hung open, propped ajar by a corpse. Fallen guards littered the courtyard, soaking in scarlet pools the ground struggled to swallow up. The prisoners circling her held stolen weapons, some of which glistened in the flickering light from the streetlamps.

"This time be a bit more discreet, yeah? Any minute, this place will be swarming with guards."

She sucked in a ragged breath. "Let them take me."

"No, miss. We owe you our lives. Can't repay the dead."

Song gasped a cry into the back of her throat. *Leslie would've said the same thing.*

A man who was on in his years, though his hair had yet to turn grey, reached out to Song. Hesitation stopped her hand inches from his before she finally took it. He wrapped his warm grasp around her fingers and pulled her to her feet.

The *clack-clack-clack* of a horse's hooves echoed from the buildings' walls as the tanned man entered the square atop a steed, black as night, with a lightning bolt of white hair along its left shoulder. He dismounted in front of the group and brought the animal forward.

"It's the constable's beast," he said. "We figured he wouldn't mind, as he's currently a doorstop." He looked over his shoulder at the corpse in the prison doorway. "We'll get you out of Carliolace, miss. We promise."

The elder helped her onto the steed. The tanned man led the way as the others circled, keeping watch and dispatching any guards in their path, hiding the bodies in dark corners.

"No one will come looking until dawn, when these poor souls would have been relieved of duty and new poor souls took their places," the tanned man said, his eyes trained on one being tucked under a cobbler's cart.

When they reached the edge of the city, fire flowed through her veins. Song took the reins and pulled the horse to a stop. "What is your name, friend?"

"We're called Bootleg J by many. Jerome by our friends."

"Jerome, there is a skyship in the next village. I will be on it. You and all these people are welcome to seek asylum aboard the vessel if you wish to be taken to a new land."

Jerome thought a moment, then smiled like he'd struck gold. "We'll take that offer."

"Make haste, she departs soon." With that, Song kicked the horse's sides and set off at a rapid trot.

She held back the tears filling her heart and choking the breath from her throat. Each beat wracked pain throughout her body as the bruised organ screamed for attention, which she refused to give. When she reached the skyship tethered to a dock just high enough for deeper bellied ships, she released a shrill whistle. Sunshine poked his head over the side and confusion knit his brow together. He descended the long ramp to stand by her side.

"What's this, then?" He helped her down, stopping to wipe tears from her cheeks.

"Is the crew sleeping?" She didn't wait for him as she headed up the ramp and straight to the captain's cabin.

"What happened to the bargaining?" Sunshine asked, closing the door behind them.

Song stripped out of the dress, her back to him. "I nearly had him."

He helped her, being careful with her misshapen arm. "What happened to your arm?"

"Shattered."

He helped her into her trousers and pirate clothes. "And Whispers?"

"Roman changed his mind overnight." She grunted as he helped her into her coat. "It's my fault." The tears pooled once more, spilling out onto her cheeks. "I should never have gone to him."

Sunshine pulled her head to his chest, muffling the sound of her wails. "I'm sure it wasn't you entirely."

Song pulled away from him, gaining control over her sobs. "I tried."

"I don't doubt you did," Sunshine said softly. "What of Whispers, then?"

"He *burned* him!" Song choked on her own sorrow. "I didn't even get to say goodbye! I couldn't even see him one last time. He's just gone. I…"

He swallowed and gritted his teeth, took a handkerchief from his pocket, and used it to wipe the tears from her eyes. "What do you plan to do now?"

"What I wanted to do in the first place, but Leslie convinced me not to."

Sunshine helped her wrap a long scarf into a sling to keep her arm up, then another to bind it close to her chest. "And what's that?"

"There are a dozen prisoners headed this way. I granted them asylum for helping me escape Carliolace." She exited her cabin and locked the door once Sunshine was out. "Wake the men and keep on your guard. Keep the prisoners below deck and quiet. Ready the ship and fly to Carliolace. Wait above until I signal for you to drop the ladder."

"Where are you going with your arm bollocksed like that?"

Sunshine asked as she hurried from the deck and leapt onto the patiently waiting mare.

"Just do as I say."

"Aye, Captain…"

Thirty-Five

Song stood in the stirrups to keep her balance as the animal galloped beneath her. She passed the party of prisoners on the road as they stayed near the tree line. When she reached the gates of Carliolace, she pulled the horse to a stop before the two guards. She swung her leg over and dropped to the ground. One strode forward, and rather than waiting for him to get to her, she took two steps and rammed her dagger into the side of his neck.

"Mi'h nip."

Red mist swirled around the second guard and shoved him against the wall beside the gate. She strode over and held the eilfaas tusk dagger to the man's throat.

"I'm looking for the executioner," she said.

The air grew acrid with the stench of urine, and the man whimpered. "Vyaantr. His house is marked with a Gemesthie statue. Spare me, please!"

She cleaned her blade on the exposed collar of his shirt. She sheathed it and walked away; her *kijæm* trailed after her like a cloak billowing in a tempest. Once free, the man retrieved his sword from the ground at his feet and ran at her back. In one swift movement, Song drew her revolver and spun, pointing it at him. His feet skidded out from under him as he tried to stop. His eyes locked onto the dark opening at the barrel and widened in equal parts shock and terror.

"Snehl-ys."

No one, not even Song, heard the shot that exited the red-glowing barrel of her revolver and rocketed through the air. It bored a hole into his forehead, exploding out the back to coat the ground in a glistening, macabre, abstract painting. She holstered her weapon and spun, striding away from the scene.

She found Vyaantr by a sign with the flower drawn upon it. The vyaantr flower was a beautiful cluster of bell-shaped buds, which hung their heads facing the ground as though to mourn. Fitting that such a funerary blossom should mark the street of a man who made a living from killing.

The only house with any sort of adornment featured a statue of a woman with four arms—two pressed together in prayer and two holding the sun over her head. It looked just like the statue from Dashaelan's belongings. She let herself in and found the executioner sitting at a desk, writing in a journal. She crossed the room, unsheathing her dagger to place it against his throat.

"I suppose it was a matter of time before my profession brought this upon me," he said, remaining calm as he continued to write. "Can I at least ask who I executed to deserve such a fate?"

"Leslie."

His writing hand stopped and his breath caught. "Would regret spare my life?" When Song didn't reply, he elaborated. "I didn't want to execute that man. He was a good man. I knew him as a boy. He was the pride of Lord Duchamp—the good one, not this cruel man who calls himself High Lord."

"Then why did you do it?"

"If it please you, I didn't do it the second time. I couldn't."

"Then who did?"

"Roman Duchamp himself lit the pyre that killed your Leslie, Miss Gould." He smirked when she said nothing. "Of course I knew it was you."

"Where is the man with the whip?" she demanded.

"His home is two streets down, close to the Hall."

"Should I spare him, too?" she scoffed.

"I wouldn't." He wrote a looping word and ended the sentence with three small dots in a triangle pattern. "Then again, I wouldn't spare me, either."

"I like the way you think." She pulled her dagger away, then plunged it deep into the back of his neck.

The silver blade stabbed out of his throat. His eyes widened, as though he'd expected her to be merciful.

"Before you die, choking on your own blood, know that you're right. I am Tsingsei Gould. However, I'm also Captain Song. A shame you didn't know that before your silly bluff." She ripped the dagger from his neck and kicked him out of his chair.

He stared up at her, one hand on his throat as he gagged on the blood.

"I hope there is an afterlife in which you're executed in the most painful manners, over and over. I just wish I could watch." Song lifted his oil lamp from the table and shattered it beside him. Flames erupted across his clothing. She turned from the sight and left.

The flagellator's house was easy enough to find, the door marked with an old bullwhip nailed to it as a knocker. She let herself inside and jolted at the crack of a whip against skin. From the other room came the screams of a woman muffled by a pillow. Song pushed the door open to find the flagellator and a woman in a rather compromising position of fornication. Whip marks streaked along the woman's back and buttocks.

Rather than waiting to see if the punishment the woman had received was consensual or not, Song strode over, grabbing his own sword from the table. She stood behind the man, then rammed the blade forward.

It took him a few moments to realize what had happened as the blade shot through his chest, splattering the woman's back with scarlet. The woman skittered away, curling into the corner at the other side of the room as she screamed.

"*Snehl-ys!*" Song silenced the woman, then leaned in close to whisper in the flagellator's ear. "This is for Leslie."

He dropped the cat-o'-nine-tails to the floor, and she planted her boot against his back, shoving him forward off the blade. Song dropped the sword to the floor and stepped cautiously across the room, keeping her eyes on the woman screaming without a sound in the corner.

"If you stop screaming, I'll return your voice," she assured.

The woman clamped her mouth shut. Tears streamed from the corners of her eyes. Under her breath, Song released the silence on the woman, who whimpered. Song patted her head in comfort.

"Do you live here?"

The woman shook her head.

"Leave," Song said. She tossed the woman's dress onto her naked body. "Now."

The woman nodded, keeping her eyes on the dying man on the bed as she tugged the garment on. She backed out of the room, terrified gaze locked on Song as though afraid the hooded figure would harm her if she turned her back. The front door closed.

Song stared at the man still dying on the bed. She lifted the oil lamp from the bedside table and smashed it against the wall. The oil splatter erupted in flame and rained down upon his bare skin. The bedding caught, and the fire grew. He gargled out a bloody scream to accompany the sizzle of his skin. With a sneer, she left and locked the door behind her.

Song skirted around to approach Duchamp Hall from the side. Four guards stood watch—two at the base of the stairs by the open gate and two at the door. Using the surrounding wall to her advantage was her best bet.

"*Shiugnit-skei,*" she whispered, gesturing at every lamp in the vicinity.

Darkness consumed the Hall, and the guards called out in shock.

"*Too'ah mehth delb.*"

Red slithered into the air over her and split into four winding tendrils. They stretched over the wall and sought the men. A body hit the ground without the man making a sound. One voice cried out, then gagged and sputtered on his blood. Footsteps ran about in a panic; the men shouted warnings into the night. Two screams cut short. Silence enveloped the street, and the mist seeped back to spiral around her like a tornado of violent fury.

She strode around the front of Duchamp Hall and stepped around the bodies emptying their blood across the white stone steps in little garnet waterfalls. Song entered the manor and stopped as a guard stared at her, no weapon in his hand, but a key instead. His armor differed from the rest—blue underclothes, rather than rust orange, and a stag horn ornament pounded into the breastplate, rather than a bird.

"Who are you?" she asked.

"Nobody. Who are you?"

"Captain Song. What's that key for?" She unholstered her revolver and pulled back on the hammer. It broke the tense silence with a threatening *click*.

"This? Oh. Uh…" His eyes flicked to the door of Roman's parlor office, then drifted over her swirling *kijæm*. "What brings you here so late?"

"I'm here to kill Roman Duchamp and anyone who gets in my way. Are you in my way?"

"I, well…"

"You're not one of Roman's guards. You don't wear his crest or colors. Who are you?"

"How about if I give you this key and you ignore who I am?"

She took a threatening step forward. "I have no need of keys."

"Oh. Well, um—"

"Go to whatever lord you serve and deliver a message, and I'll let you live."

"Go on?"

"Tell them Captain Song killed Roman Duchamp and all the city guards. And tell them it's because he murdered a free man. Go ahead and put all the bounties on me that you wish, but you will never have my head."

The man nodded. "All right, then." He unlocked the door and backed away.

She should have stopped to ask him what was happening. Why was a guard from elsewhere there that night? And why had he been hovering outside the parlor office? What's more is, why had he been so willing to leave, even after she'd declared her ill intent? She didn't ask any of this, though, because it felt like political nonsense. Song wasn't there for politics, she was there for revenge.

She opened the door and entered, commanding her *kijæm* to close the curtains and shut the door behind her. The front door opened and closed. A lonely, tense silence settled across the room.

Roman was slumped over his desk, cheek on a fist, gripping a glass of brandy and snoring lightly. She strode across the room and lifted a pen, then dropped it back to the desk. He didn't snap awake as she'd hoped. With an exasperated sigh, she circled around and leaned back against the desk. Then, ever so gently, she set the toe of her boot against the seat cushion beneath him and shoved it backward. The feet of the chair moaned in protest against the marble floor until Roman slipped forward, hitting his forehead on the desktop before lurching to his feet. To her great pleasure, a black bruise arched over the bridge of his nose and darkened the inner corners of his eyes.

"Good morning, Roman." Song sauntered to the other side of the desk, stopping to touch her fingertips to the clock on the mantle, setting the minute hand back to avoid its chime sounding. "Rough day?"

"My day was fine," he growled. "Who are you?"

"Oh, I'm sorry. Where are my manners?" She lowered her hood, and he gasped.

"How did you escape the jail? Guards!"

"No need to shout. You'll wake everyone." She helped herself to a sip from his carafe of brandy. "Besides, all your guards are dead."

"What did you…? How did you…? *Guards!*"

"Shh!" Song cooed like she was shushing a child. "Calm down, Roman."

"It's Lord Duchamp! You disrespectful little harlot!"

She slammed the carafe down and glared at him, then forced her lips into a cordial grin. "I suppose if we're going to be formal about all this, then you may address me as Captain."

"I wasn't aware whorehouses had captains," he spat.

She rolled her eyes at his lack of imaginative insults. "No, but skyships do. Mine is called the Stars' Bounty."

His skin grew pallid, though he maintained his defiant posture. "C-Captain—"

"Song. Yes. Charmed, I'm sure." She took another swig from his brandy. "I suppose I should have just come like this and demanded you remove the bounty on Leslie's head, rather than trying to be civil and negotiate with you for a price."

Roman straightened, but the rapid pulse beating through the veins in his neck betrayed his fear. "They will hail me as a hero for executing your lover."

"Except that he wasn't my lover. But imagine the hell I would have rained down upon Carliolace if he had been."

"So...y-you're here for a share in the reward, I assume?"

"I want none of your quoine," Song growled. She circled the desk and stood before him, studying his every feature—the vein threatening to burst from his forehead, the beads of sweat collecting on his upper lip and the shallow breathing that squeaked from his nostrils.

"Then what do you want?"

"To watch you suffer."

His breath caught. Minutes passed, long and barbed with trepidation. She raised the carafe to take a drink, and Roman flinched.

"You're much too tense, Lord Duchamp. Breathe." She breathed in and out, as though demonstrating to him.

He took a few calculated breaths, his distrustful gaze locked on hers.

"Did you enjoy that?"

He didn't respond.

"I sure hope you did, because you're going to miss that feeling." She smirked as his face twisted in uncertainty. "*Torth sih-h zolk.*"

Red mist converged on him and forced itself into his mouth, then his nostrils when he pinched his lips closed. Roman's breath stopped, and he gulped like a fish as he clawed at his throat. She waited until panic streaked through his eyes before letting him breathe again.

"Ever wonder how it feels to burn alive?"

She said the words to close his throat again, and he gaped at her. Terror flooded his eyes as blood vessels streaked red across them. He pulled his collar loose as though it might make a difference. He collapsed to the floor and stared up at her.

She poured brandy over the top of him, emptying the carafe. "Should've freed Leslie, Roman. I would've happily left this accursed place and never returned. Instead...I'm going to watch you burn." She took the oil lamp from his desk and broke it on the floor beside him.

Oil splashed across him, and the fire erupted into a fierce blaze that enveloped him. She let him breathe again, so he would live longer, suffering in the heat of the flames. It ate through his clothing, and though he wanted to scream, there was no way he could, as she'd silenced that. He shouted muted words, pleading with her, but she wasn't interested in anything he had to say.

He flailed, weak from the suffocation. His hands grasped for something that might save him. As he reached his desk, he grabbed a pen in his fist. He managed two symbols, which looked like a misshapen A and an L, before he collapsed to the floor to writhe in agony.

She stood back and watched him burn long after he stopped moving, until she could bear the stench no longer. Song exited the room and locked the door behind her, then shoved out the front doors into the night.

After a quick check above Carliolace, she found the skyship hovering over the dull glow of the execution bonfire. She made her way down the middle of the street, her red *kijæm* dancing around her like it held the joy she couldn't feel. As she entered the square, a croaking echoed behind her. She spun around to spot

Toren, gripping a toad. He glared at her and threw the creature, but she dodged out of the way and used her *kijæm* to deflect it. She strode to him and grabbed the collar of his shirt, dragging him toward the stocks.

"Murderer!" he screamed, kicking his feet. "You're a bloody villain!"

She shut him in the stocks and clamped his hands in cuffs so he couldn't pull free through the large holes. She stooped to his level, a cruel grin on her face.

"Being the good guy has gotten me nothing but pain. I'm not a villain, I'm just tired of hurting. I could be a villain, though. If you want me to." She tilted her head. "I could kill you right now."

Her *kijæm* stretched around her in a mass of tendrils, slithering around him as though ready to strike. She stared into his inflamed eye. Crimson spread from his lids and the pupil had paled.

"But I have a feeling you'll get what you deserve."

She turned away and strode to where the ladder hovered just over the blood-soaked dirt in a circle of bodies. She gripped a rung in her hand and set her feet on the bottom. With one last look at the smoldering, black corpse, she said, "Let's go."

Thirty-Six

Song stayed in the captain's cabin. She couldn't go out and face the men, though she knew word had spread. Tears rolled ignored down her cheeks. She'd told them they would hold a memorial for Leslie that night, now that they were a day away from Carliolace and had retrieved their crew members from Skaaldvik Vyaard. But now that it was nearly time, she didn't want to. She didn't want to say goodbye to him, because she didn't want him to be gone. And maybe if she never said goodbye, then somehow he wouldn't be gone—at least, that's what her mind told her. She wanted to deny it until it wasn't reality anymore.

Her heart had been shattering inside her all day—the little pieces exploding out and slicing through her like shards of glass. Her throat burned like whiskey set aflame, and her eyes were dry and scratchy from not enough sleep and too many tears. The times she did nod off for a minute or two, she'd snapped awake and gazed around at the unfamiliar cabin. She'd stare at her mangled arm and the streak of blood on her other wrist from the nosebleed. And then she would realize she had not dreamt the whole thing, and would turn to wail into the pillow.

She'd been awake for hours now, directing her blank stare at the swirling propeller blades outside the windows. Sunshine came in to check on her. He said something that reached her in a muffled blur. She blinked her eyes and focused on him.

"How is your arm?" he repeated.

"It's fine," she said on a distant whisper.

"Is it?"

Sweat rolled into Song's eyes as the effort of holding back the pain taxed her. "Yes."

Sunshine studied her. He looked over her disfigured arm, at the black and purple coloration, and her fingers bent at disturbing angles.

He pinched one. "Your fingers," he said.

She looked down. "I don't feel a thing."

"I'll find someone who can—"

"No. We have the memorial—"

"Piss on the memorial, Song. It won't change nothin', and Leslie will still be dead enough to pay our respects later."

She grunted as her first instinct was to reach out with her right hand to slap him, but the small flex of her shoulder sent a sharp pain to her elbow. She lifted her left hand to slap him, but he caught the slow appendage. Song sent her foot forward to ram the toe of her boot into his shin.

"We're holding it. Gather the men. Have Thumbs pass around Leslie's favorite drink."

"And if I find a doctor in your refugees?"

"Then I'll let him look at me. After we pay our bloody respects." A sharp gasp ripped through her chest, and she buried her face in her palm. "I don't want to do this, Sunshine."

"Then—"

"That's not what I mean! I mean, I don't want to be saying goodbye at all. He should be alive. He should be here with us. I would give my entire right arm for him to not be dead."

Sunshine nodded and pulled her into a gentle hug. He patted the back of her head. "I'm sorry, Song. I don't mean to be insensitive. Just…makes more sense to worry about the livin' first."

"Just get everyone on deck, please."

He left the room, and she cried into her palm. After several minutes, he returned. She didn't bother with her coat. They exited to find each person holding a glass, cup, or small bowl.

"You should speak first," Sunshine said.

She nodded and lowered herself to a stool he placed behind her. "I'm sure you're all aware by now that we're gathered on deck to pay respects to our first mate. I've invited you from Pishing as well because he was once one of you. Leslie was a freed slave. He was my…" She stopped, as calling him her best friend didn't feel like enough. "He was a part of me. My better half." She gritted her teeth and tried to spit out all the words she wanted to say, but they refused.

After several minutes in silence, Bruce said, "Leslie…knew me."

They nodded at each other and she knew he had a thousand words gathered on his tongue but unable to breach the gates of his lips. She knew he meant Leslie understood him. Leslie never judged him and knew he wasn't simple; he just couldn't say the words he thought. Song understood Bruce now, but hers was a different understanding, and not near as endearing as with Leslie.

"I am marked as his enemy. But he was always my friend," Thumbs said.

An older slave cleared his throat. "I remember as a young chap, Leslie would come to the market with Miss Ura. Two of the most important slaves in Ebrenar. And yet, when he came alone, he never took his place at the front of the line. Never wanted to be treated better than any of us, even though he was."

"Why was he better?" Maps asked in a murmur.

"His owner," the man said.

"Whispers was great at reading maps," the navigator said. "Couldn't chart a good course, but tried all the same." He gave a halfhearted chuckle.

Jerome smiled on some memory. "We had three best friends growing up. Peyton, Tark, and Leslie. He used to visit the rest of us in the orphanage, and make eyes at his sweetheart. They both disappeared in the night some time ago. We'd always wondered what happened to them." He stared around at the faces of the pirate crew. "Seems he found that family he was always so desperate for. Always thought it'd include Fiyora, though."

Song stared up at the man, in too much pain for the shock to manifest on her face, and too preoccupied with her grief to choke out all the questions she wanted to ask.

Nearly everyone there shared a story of him, if they had one. Then they raised their drinks.

Sunshine frowned out at the stars sparkling overhead. "To Whispers…I liked him."

A sob forced itself so violently from Song's throat that mucus and hints of blood released from her nose. She wiped it away and swallowed back the water in her glass, tinged with a bit of orange. Men coughed in shock, having expected alcohol. For a moment she thought to honor him by drinking water from then on, rather than whiskey and rum. The idea didn't last long, as a desperate desire to numb the pain in her heart crept into her mind.

A man she didn't recognize approached.

"Yes?"

"My name is Cairn. Sunshine asked me to look at your arm," he said.

"Oh. Are you a doctor?" she asked.

"Aye, a certified medic."

"What were you doing in prison?"

He gave her a sad smile. "Murdered a patient."

Sunshine came to stand at her side. "Tell her the real reason."

Cairn chuckled. "He was an old man living in too much pain. Asked me to end his suffering."

"Sounds like a mercy, not a murder," she said.

"The law sees no difference."

Sunshine set his hand on her shoulder. "You told me to find a doctor, and I did. Time for you to hold up your end."

She hung her head and nodded, letting him lead her back into the captain's cabin. She sat in one chair and he brought the other around to sit in front of her. Horror contorted the man's features as he looked over the damage he could see. She bit into a leather belt as he felt along her arm. Then he took Sunshine outside to talk. Minutes passed as she stared at the empty liquor cabinet, wishing for it to be filled so she could swallow down every single bottle before they came back.

"Captain," Sunshine said as he jerked his head for her to join them.

She followed the two below deck into the galley, where several men stood around the table.

"What's this about?" she demanded.

They converged on her and lifted her onto the table. She struggled against them, shouting as they pushed her to lie back. They tied ropes over her torso and legs, binding her left arm to her side. Bruce gripped her ankles in one massive hand; Bells pushed down on her thighs. Someone she didn't recognize pushed on her hips, another on her ribcage, and a final man at her shoulders.

"*What are you doing?*"

Sunshine secured a belt to a board on the table and wrapped it over her forehead. "I'd ask your permission, but we all know you'd fight us."

"Sunshine!"

"I'm sorry, but the arm is dead," Cairn said.

"What do you— *No! Let me up this instant!*"

Another man prepared something in a spoon over the flame of a candle. The medic sucked the liquid into a silver syringe, then stuck it in a vein of her good arm.

"Stop!"

After a minute, the world wobbled and warped. It shifted and turned around her. A leather lash wrapped tight around her upper arm. She mumbled her protests, but couldn't find the words nor the strength to kick at them.

A razor-sharp shaving blade lowered to her skin just under the tie. She screamed in horror at only feeling the pressure and not the pain as her flesh slid open and her blood gushed out to drip onto the floor. They talked above her, shouting over her screams, as her weak struggles to get free resumed.

The knife worked expertly, slicing through her muscles, veins, and tendons. The arm pulled away without protest, revealing a jagged, broken bone jutting from her biceps. She screamed and squeezed her eyes shut, tears cascading across the bridge of her nose. Her arm vibrated as the man sawed at the bone.

"Do it quickly," Thumbs said at the top of her head.

Searing heat strangled a wail of desperate agony from her throat as hot metal hissed against her flesh. The sickly-sweet smell of burning tissue assailed her, dragging her back into the hopeless desolation of the night before. The pain and sorrow ripped through her until she was welcomed by blessed oblivion.